THE
HOUSE
OF
BIRDS

Morgan
McCarthy

TINDER
PRESS

For Cian

ACKNOWLEDGEMENTS

Thanks doesn't quite cover it, but . . . With thanks to Cian, Jo, Leah and Imogen, Amy and the team at Tinder Press. Thanks too to Nessa Eyre, for her invaluable legal advice, and Sadie Shepherd at Feathers and Fur, for introducing me to the birds.

PROLOGUE

NOVEMBER 1915

Darling,

It's been a long time since I heard from you, but I keep writing, in the hope that you are receiving my letters. I do try not to worry, but find I can't help it, and a letter from you would mean so much. I can never tell you how much I love you, and how desperately I miss you. I thought today about the Anglo-Zanzibar war, supposedly the shortest in history, recorded at thirty-eight minutes. That was how long it took for the English to see off a sultan they didn't much like and replace him with one of whom they were fonder. I wish it were that war you had gone to fight.

Have I any news for you, I wonder? Nothing much. I am still volunteering at the hospital. Boll has occupied herself by falling in love, or so she says, with a very handsome man, despite complaining that the house is a gaol and she will die alone here, driven mad by the tiny noise of Mother's needle going in and out of her cloth, endlessly, though the sound of steel against silk could never really be heard over the noise of Boll telling us how deathly bored she is, and in any case – as you might remember – Mother never actually does any sewing. She's been working at the same piece for nearly a decade, and still nobody knows what it will turn out to be.

Boll's guess is a death's head. My money's on something subtle, but no less devastating.

Anyway, I've no idea whether Boll's suitor is suitable, as far as the business of suiting goes. He seems rather . . . raffish? She seems besotted; wants to talk about him every day . . . where he might have been, whether he has thought of her. And so on.

For this I have some sympathy.

Mother is planning to redecorate the house. I find the idea of this unutterably dreadful. Father wouldn't have had it, and though I don't approve of men putting their feet down, I do wish he were here and he would. I can't bear to think of the house being prodded and pried at and all its beauty peeled away. I suppose you think me melodramatic. Perhaps I am, a little, but I can't help but feel the house is rather like a lovely face with a slightly broken nose and a gap in its teeth, and if those things were fixed it wouldn't be so beautiful, or at least not so queerly bewitching. The tiles might be worn, but they're worn in the shape of our feet; of our ancestors' feet. Not to mention the dented dining table (clumsy Victorians) and the crooked chiffonier (slapdash Edwardians) and the frayed fauteuil from who knows when. And what will become, too, of the blameless birds of paradise – my childhood companions – and Comanche, my confidant; none of them committing any crime other than that of being over a hundred years old, and I never heard of centenarians being bumped off, to make way for fresh, modern humans. And you understand, I know you do, the feeling the house has; of all the years collected in it, like a treasure house. I'm convinced that's the source of the peculiar atmosphere you remarked upon, the luxuriating ease of it, like a lion lolling in the sun, the quietness in the mid-afternoon, when it is filled with light even in winter, and nothing but the sound of the grandfather clock ticking and my mother's mouse-like rustles. (In this picture, Boll has not yet come back from luncheon.)

I was ill, quite recently. I don't mean to concern you, simply to explain the gap in my letters, if you have been receiving them. Anyway, it's all over now. I shall explain when you're home, by which time I expect it will seem like something very small, and not even worth mentioning.

It is cold and dark here; the night dropping down each evening like a great black bear. (I know I told you I would never talk about the weather, but it seems I can't help myself.) Everybody seems to have forgotten the imminence of Christmas. I have already crossed it out in my mind. We must celebrate it when you're home, even if that turns out to be February, or June. Do you know, when I think of you, my memories are always of sunny days – despite our having had our share of sleeting walks, and hats blown off, and wet wool socks – rather as if the past has begun to seem haloed by eternal summer, when really it was probably only a few weeks of sunshine, and the rest rain.

Do you remember the day we sat in the garden here, drinking wine and making plans? I can picture it so well: the house hung with flowers; the sun moving at half its usual pace across the flawless blue sky. We were sitting under the apple tree, and the light edging through the leaves spotted us both. I remember there being apples – though that tree seldom produced anything until autumn, at least, and this might be another quirk of my memory, a mis-stitch in its embroidery. But never mind; there are apples here, round and glossy and incontrovertible, and I am inclined to let them stay.

We were talking about our children and what their names should be, and we gave ourselves the oddest feeling, imagining the same tree in not so many years' time, belaboured by small boots, its apples carried off in grass-stained pullovers and skirts. Do you remember? We talked, too, about the places we should like to see: grand tours to Palmyra, Athens, Thebes. Yet these days I find myself fixing on smaller things: longing simply to sit with you at a coffee house, to eat chocolate cake together, to listen to Fauré, or to argue the merits of 'Catherine' over 'Virginia' – without a thought going beyond to little Catherine or Virginia's arrival.

Darling, it will be over; perhaps not in thirty-eight minutes, but while we are still young, and able to go back to what we were meant to be doing before this inconvenient war came along. They say it will be over by Christmas, but they do talk a lot of rot, don't they, and I never believed it. But spring, perhaps . . .? We here in England have been told a few things, none very comforting, about the Ottomans (whisper it) winning, and the possibility of evacuation. But I suppose you can't write about that.

Dearest love, I wish you would answer me, if only to tell me if my letters bother you. I don't know if my reminiscing consoles you or makes you sadder, if my talk of the future restores you or pains you. I don't even know if my jokes are amusing. Darling, is it too painful to tell me how you are, to set it down? Write to me and tell me to shut up. God knows I'd welcome it. Anything but this silence.

I shall probably have to start this letter again, and write something more cheerful, so I may as well be honest.

I can't guess how you are: I have no idea what it must be like to be you. For the first time, I cannot even imagine it. Your life is a closed door, at which my outstretched hand fails, and drops back.

You used not to write much, I know, but I haven't heard from you in months. What I know of you comes from Hugh's letters to Harriet; I am told you are in good health, whatever that means.

I should like to know what you are doing, what you see. One glimpse through the darkness between us, just a keyhole's worth. You don't have to tell me anything that wouldn't make it past the censors. Just tell me what you are thinking, or something of what you feel. Tell me what you hope for. Just a word, darling, please.

PART ONE

OLIVER

Oliver Mittell, adrift in Friday afternoon, had let his mind wander. It was the first Friday afternoon he'd seen from the outside (which meant: not in his office – the place he had begun to think of as *inside*) in a long time. He thought maybe longer than a year. The date escaped him, lying just out of reach of calculation. It was a strange feeling, moving around the high, empty apartment on a day when everyone else had something to do. He went to the window and looked down at the grey shimmer of the city, trying to guess at how many of its tiny occupants were heading home to their families; how many were going out for drinks; how many were leaving London altogether, getting a head start on the weekday crowds making for the dreamlike green blur beyond its spiked and studded horizon.

It surprised and annoyed him that the place his own mind kept returning to – like a dog chasing a ball that had not been thrown, running to and fro with a look of expectancy, then confusion – was work. He wondered if he had got used to the weight of it; the pressure that he had felt almost as soon as he was inside the glass doors. He'd watched a TV show once in which some retired battery hens were rehoused in a famous cottage garden. Their bearded rescuer had explained that the hens needed to get used to the light and space, gesturing towards the shed in which they were huddling, point-blank refusing to explore their new freedom.

Oliver wondered if the hens had been experiencing the same existential panic as himself, albeit in a more primitive form. He had the sense of a newly wide-open space, and yet one that he was afraid to cross. He didn't quite know what to do with himself; not yet. And so he took shelter in the apartment, trying not to think about what was behind or before him, waiting for Kate to get home.

Kate was in Oxford that morning, something he'd only found out an hour ago, as she had left before he'd got up. He had assumed she was at work until she texted to explain that she'd taken the morning off to meet Mr Hunt, the family solicitor, and would be home early. Oliver was disappointed that he hadn't been able to go with her. He didn't want to interfere with the complicated mechanisms of her family feud, clanking mysteriously along like a sealed production line, turning out new grievances on the hour, but he had wanted to see Oxford again. He hadn't been back to the city since he'd left it, aged eleven, squinting out of the window of his parents' Volvo estate. He always used to insist on sitting in the backwards-facing rear seats: a decision he had regretted that day, as he watched the sandy turrets of the city fade to a pointillist haze in the window, acutely aware that any tears would be witnessed by all the drivers behind.

*

Oliver's brightest memory of Oxford, glowing like Sirius in the distant firmament of childhood, was of the last day of school; a strange afternoon when several things fell into place, though at the time it seemed not lucky at all, but unfair, and it was only years later that he could look back on that day as anything more than poignantly ironic. It wasn't long after his birthday, when he had been given a new bicycle; a gift that had, in the tradition of a fairy-tale reward, unfolded to reveal many other treasures. It turned out that he had been given a whole city. Afternoon after afternoon he cycled its streets – wide or winding, crowded or coolly deserted – as comprehensively as a cartographer, looking for anything vaguely exciting.

He ought to have kept a diary, he thought now. At the time he believed a memory was something you kept for ever. Now all he remembered of those weekday afternoons and their endless doglike rambles – nose down, snuffing along – were a few colourful fragments. An antique bookshop, its furthest reaches swamped in perpetual evening; a bricked-up doorway at the end of an alley; a pound in the gutter; a madwoman in crushed velvet who offered him a ham sandwich; a stone with a mysterious inscription in medieval English that he took home, only to find out it was part of a breeze block, and its carvings unsuitable for translation.

After the summer-holiday hysteria that had collected around the school gate had been shooed off the premises by the teachers, or rounded up and driven off by the waiting parents, and the whoops and cartwheels had died away, Oliver cycled home alone. He was taking a new route today, touring some of the more venerable roads, lined with trees as stately as the Georgian houses set back behind box hedges and twizzling wrought-iron gates. As he turned off one and into another, he saw a girl on a bicycle ahead of him, moving in and out of the late-afternoon sun striping the pavements, silent as a white bird.

He recognised Kate Castle immediately. He was as familiar with the back of her head as the back of his own hand. Two seats in front of him in assembly, three on sports day, but absent in his own classes; being watched elsewhere, by other small boys. He had never spoken to her. Partly because of the different classes, partly because Kate Castle terrified him. She had a surprising amount of presence for an eleven-year-old girl. She caught the eye like a unicorn, her shirt seeming whiter than the other girls', her long blond hair (which she legendarily refused to have cut) pouring down her starchy-bright back. Even her bicycle was white, and she rode it with her hair streaming around her like a miniature Lady Godiva. Oliver, in contrast, was a largely unnoticeable child; a quiet boy camouflaged in the same clothes and hair as his much louder friends. He would have bet his new-found pound that Kate Castle would not have been able to pick him out of a line-up as her classmate, let alone remember his name.

He was watching Kate's back so intently that he felt not just horror but guilt – as if he had gazed too hard, and the force of it had somehow pushed her – when her bicycle wobbled one way, wobbled another, faltered for a third and fatal time, and crashed down on to the pavement. The clatter rang along the empty street. He sped up, wanting to call out but not sure what to say, and by the time he came to a rushed and scraping halt alongside the girl sitting on the ground, he still hadn't had time to think of anything clever or funny or comforting.

Kate looked up at him as if automatically registering the presence of another human, but no more. She looked shocked from her fall: having a sealed placidity undisturbed by his arrival; a lack of interest in her grey eyes.

'Are you okay?' Oliver asked. (Unoriginal, yes, but to the point. He thought he could have done worse.)

Kate held up her grazed hands, the raw skin of her palms studded with small pieces of gravel. They both looked at her bloodied knee.

'Ow,' she said. Then, 'God, what a stupid idiot.'

Oliver thought she meant him for a second, and was ready to accept this judgement. Then he realised she was shaking her head at herself. She didn't get up, occupying herself instead with picking the stones out of her hands. 'I thought a squirrel was going to run in front of me,' she explained. 'But it ran back into a garden instead.'

'Do you think you can walk?' he said.

She looked at him properly now. Her eyes seemed very large. He thought they were the same colour as the moon must be, not high-in-the-sky white, as seen from the earth, but its mysterious grey surface. The Sea of Nectar, the Sea of Crises. Then she blinked, and he realised that she was trying not to cry. Tears collected in her eyes, trembling in a glittering meniscus above her lower lids, but didn't spill. He was deeply impressed.

'Yeah,' she said. 'It's just a couple of grazes.'

Her voice was quieter and less distinct than he had thought it would be. Another surprise of the day: Kate Castle, a mumbler. His confidence grew and he cast an authoritative eye over her bicycle before pronouncing: 'It looks okay. No damage.'

'I don't care, I'm not getting back on it. I'll walk it home. It's not too far.'

'I'll walk with you,' he said, realising he sounded hasty; eager, but that couldn't be helped. If she didn't look delighted at the suggestion, at least she didn't look disgusted, and when he picked up her bike for her, she took the handlebars with a wincing smile.

'You sure you're okay? I could go and get your parents or something.'

'I'm fine,' she said firmly, then, inspecting him, 'We go to the same school?'

'Yes, but I'm not in your class.'

'Well, *obviously.*' She giggled. 'I'd know you if you were in my class. I'm Kate.'

'Oliver.'

'Tell me about yourself, Oliver,' she said, in a self-consciously adult voice. 'What are your plans for the future?'

He was thrown. 'I don't know much about myself. What do people normally say to that?'

'I don't know. You're the first person I've tried it on. I thought it was a pretty good question. I saw a woman say it on TV.'

'Maybe it's better when you're older.'

'I suppose we'll know what we're like then, won't we? Okay, just do the second bit. What are your plans for the future?'

'I think I'd like to be in the pirate business.'

'A pirate?'

'No. I'd be a pirate investigator. I'd go around and find out where the dead pirates' treasure was buried: I mean, like, I'd follow old maps, and disguise myself and question the pirates, or their grandchildren, or whatever, and decipher their secret codes. I'd have a metal detector and other stuff like that, obviously.'

'So you'll have a load of gold.'

'Er, right,' Oliver said, not having thought much about this part of the plan. 'I guess so. What do you want to do?'

'I don't know what I want to *do*,' Kate said. 'I just have things

I want. Like a Persian cat and a pair of high heels. And a cupboard of chocolate and a butler in charge of making sure it never runs out of chocolate.'

'Yeah, me too,' Oliver agreed. 'Except the high heels.'

She sent him a sly look. The Sea of Love. Was that a sea?

'So that's settled,' she said. 'We'd better get married.'

Oliver, hoping to change the subject before the full-body flush rising up to his face hit his cheeks, said hurriedly, 'Do you live around here?'

'No, actually. But that' – she pointed – 'is my aunt's house.'

They stopped outside a house recessed back from its neighbours, allowing it a small, half-enclosed lawn. It was three storeys tall, faced in butter-coloured Headington stone, with pillars supporting a modest pediment. Most of this was covered by a wisteria lavishly laden with hazy purple flowers, like layered smoke rising from the hookah of a caterpillar.

'Cool,' Oliver said.

'I go past some days to spy on my evil aunt. But it looks like she's not home. Her car's not here.'

'Evil?'

'My dad doesn't speak to her. He says she's a mad old bat. I don't really know why. But she does look like a witch. She's got hands like a witch, anyway.' She put her own small white hands up in claws.

Oliver felt the lure of the forbidden like a howl from a Germanic forest; a hair-raising summons from the Romantic. He stared into the wavering glass of the lower windows, reflecting their slightly distorted figures. A path led below the wisteria and around the side of the house, taking his attention with it. Kate noticed the direction of his gaze.

'Want to go and look around?' she offered, in a sticky half-whisper. Their eyes met; something arced between them.

'One million per cent yes.'

e~

The path along the side of the house was half barred by a heap of black bin bags, a couple scratched open by cats or foxes; their contents spilling out. The smell of decay, ripe and sickly, wove through the currents of air like oil in water. Kate's nose wrinkled. She hadn't noticed the rat moving businesslike from one bag to another, its nose twitching brusquely, thorough as a police detective. There was a moment in which Oliver met its intelligent black eye; in the next moment it was as if the rat had never been there at all.

The two of them pressed themselves against the windowless wall of the house, edged past the bags and turned the corner to find themselves in a dense, blazing greenness. It took a second for Oliver to make sense of all the different greens, fighting and coiling like Medusa's snakes, confusing the eye by clambering both horizontally and vertically, in hundreds of rustling layers, before the scene resolved itself like a magic eye picture into a large, overgrown garden. Identities and territories emerged. The darkly varnished ivy was tussling with the white bindweed over ownership of a sagging fence, while not far away, a honeysuckle, unchallenged, had claimed a garden table and swallowed a small tree. The lawn was an army massing under high spears, its regiments filing into the cracks between the paving stones to do battle with the dandelions. Above them the wisteria maintained a lordly rule over the house itself, loaded with its spectacular purple flowers, hundreds of fluttering confetti showers clamouring for the friskings of the bees.

Kate and Oliver walked into the grass, which dusted their socks and navy uniforms with pollen and sticky burrs. His mum was going to have a fit, he thought briefly, a thought that disappeared just as quickly, submerged in the particular euphoria of *somebody else's garden*. Hoverflies scattered as they went. Human artefacts rose from the green tide like shipwrecks: a broken plant pot encrusted with snails, a forgotten pair of secateurs, a water butt brimming with a greenish moon, quivering beneath a dizzy party of tiny flies. A once-trained rose had toppled in one corner, its heavy flowers collapsed on the ground like swooning olden-days women. The smell of the bruised petals mingled in the hot air with the faint scent of the rubbish, which had sneaked around the corner after them.

They looked up at the house, which did not seem to him as repressive as it might have under the circumstances, despite its imposing height. It was much taller than Oliver's own, modern house in the unremarkable outer suburbs of the city. He tipped his head back as far as he could and admired all the little details whose names he didn't know – pediments; eaves; decorative brickwork half hidden beneath the thick twists of the wisteria.

Kate, becoming bolder, had gone to the kitchen window and put her face against it. 'It's not that messy,' she reported, disappointed.

Oliver joined her, and they looked up at the other windows.

'I could climb up and see what's in the bedrooms,' he offered, before being totally sure that such a thing was possible. Love and the wild garden had made him reckless. But as it turned out, the wisteria was unexpectedly sturdy, and finding footholds in it was not difficult. Up he went, crashing through the flowers, bumblebees droning around his ears, until he was at eye level with the nearest window.

'Oliver! Be careful!' Kate's voice sounded further away than he would have expected. He decided not to look back down at her. Adrenalin had carried him up, and if he quailed, he'd have to rely on luck to see him safely to the ground again. Last week he'd read the story of the Monkey's Paw: it had warned him that luck was a tricky customer. Luck had knocked Kate off her bicycle to bring them together, and he didn't entirely trust it not to drop him a storey just so their friendship could be cemented by her weekly visits to his hospital bed.

He looked through the window of the back bedroom.

'What?' he said.

'What?' Kate asked. 'What's in there?'

'Er, birds. Birds?' Then, putting up a hand to block the sun, and squinting against the glass, 'Oh – not real birds. Painted ones.'

'What?'

'I don't know. But . . . it's beautiful.'

The room was a frozen forest, filled with birds; some flying, wings spread in their turquoise sky, others come to rest on its delicately rendered branches. It was at least as bright as the garden outside, and more colourful. The room pulsed with the prismatic light of artistry; an overabundance of it, each leaf or feather different to the last. He gazed inside with the absorption of a much younger Oliver, pressing his wide eye against a View-Master, mesmerised by the oddly lit worlds within.

'Um, Oliver,' Kate said, as quietly as she could. 'Don't rush, but I think I heard a car pull up. And our bikes are out the front.'

THE HOUSE OF BIRDS

The idea of Kate's aunt's clawed hands pursued Oliver in his stupid rush back down. He scraped his leg in his haste, dropped painfully on to one ankle, and hurried after Kate back around the side of the house, where they stopped for a moment flat against the wall. They inched their heads out until they could see around the corner. No car in sight, no dark aunt standing over their fallen bicycles, as Oliver had feared. Still, the two of them crept out into the front garden of the house as if trying not to trip invisible sensors, until the noise of a door closing in the house next door propelled them out into the open; a dash over to their bicycles; a hobbled, awkward take-off down the street, with no time to look back and see the old woman standing behind them, mouthing the beginnings of a curse.

Once they had turned the corner and left the road, they started laughing, euphoric with relief and lack of breath.

'I don't think that was her, you know,' Kate said. 'She'd definitely have stolen our bikes if it had been . . . Oh no! Oh, Oliver . . . *look* at us.'

They were covered in pollen, grass stains, dried blood and leaves. Oliver's ankle, while not swollen, was throbbing steadily. They compared knee grazes and it was established that Kate's was the worst. She acknowledged victory gracefully, with a modest shrug.

'I better get back,' she said. 'I'm already late. And when Mum and Dad see me, they're going to go mental.'

'Oh, right. Yeah. Same here.'

There was a moment of hesitation.

'Are you away over the summer?' she asked.

'We're going to France in August.'

'Are you going to eat snails?'

21

'Probably.'

'Gross.'

'How about you? Not snails. Holidays.'

'We're going to Jamaica tomorrow. I'm supposed to be at home helping with the packing. But whatever I pack will be wrong, so I don't feel bad. I'll see you when we're back, I guess. Unless you're already a pirate investigator by then.'

'Then you could look out for me when you're near the sea.'

'I would,' she said, and for a moment a delicately strung silence stretched between them, vibrating like a spider's line.

Then she said, 'Hey, thanks for today,' and smiled, and they both took up their bicycles again, and limped in opposite directions home.

ℰ

That smile lingered with Oliver, the afterburn not even fading by the next morning, as he mulled his spoon through his cereal and smiled mysteriously at the memory of its faintly awkward gratitude, the pink girlness of her lips, the light gathering in her small white teeth, one chipped.

His mother cast a look into the bowl and warned, 'They'll go soggy.' They already had, but Oliver hardly cared.

The smile was only driven from its number one spot in his thoughts by the news, later that week, that his dad – a chippy – had injured himself at work and couldn't be a chippy any more, and so the whole family was going to leave Oxford and move to Milton Keynes.

'I'm sorry, sweetheart,' his mum said. Her eyes were sparkling with held-in indignation: a rare phenomenon; sighted only briefly, being usually followed by an outburst.

'At least we'll get to see more of Hugh,' said his dad. Oliver's uncle Hugh lived in Milton Keynes and managed a small office supplies company. He was going to take Oliver's dad on, at a job he described ruefully as entry level. ('But if we expand, Bernard, you're my second in command. As soon as we have something to command.')

His mother was not to be consoled. 'It's all very well putting a brave face on it. But it's . . . oh, it's just *disgusting* what they did to your dad.'

'Tina.'

'No, it is. Ten years with that bunch of . . . swine, and no compensation, no sick pay, nothing. It's their fault. They're wriggling out of everything. It's criminal. His back won't ever be right. Everything we've worked for . . .'

'*Tina*,' his father said, with more meaning. 'No point worrying Oliver.'

Oliver's mum accepted this and became thoughtfully industrious at the sink, only one further remark escaping her: something about the rich people hoarding all the money, and screwing over everyone else, until they didn't even know if they'd survive the next year or be out on the street with their house repossessed.

'Tina,' said his dad again, but he sounded tired, and Oliver could see that he was inclined to agree.

'Are we still going to France?' he asked them. He could hear the answer in his own voice; the shaming tremor.

'I'm sorry, sweetheart.'

Oliver nodded, and tried not to cry; but perhaps that was an art that required practice, or some secret kung fu technique, and in the end he found he wasn't as good at it as Kate, not by a long way.

After the family moved, and much later – as Oliver himself left Milton Keynes for shared university lets in London, then to various flats around the city, circling closer and closer to the financial district like a fly travelling towards a plughole – that half-hour with Kate at her aunt's house became something that did not fade but crystallised, a memory he cherished, with the uncomfortable awareness that it was ridiculous to do so. A couple of kids in an overgrown garden, an enclosed room of colour somehow more vivid and more alive than the rest of life; the moment itself as still as the birds that populated the room, unfaded and unchanging, while Oliver's face, pressed against the window, got older and older, though no less wistful.

е⌐

It was fifteen years before Oliver saw Kate again, at a friend of a friend's birthday party. He had looked across the room at her without realising who she was, though her blond hair was the same, long and loose and sliding around her shoulders as she raised her hands, turned her head, laughed; the hair and the woman in perpetual animation. He only caught a glimpse of her in the middle of a small crowd, and didn't think anything more of it until someone at the bar said to someone next to him, 'Kate Castle? Yeah, she's single.' Oliver couldn't help whipping around, as if they had spoken to *him*, creating an awkward moment in which he, the informative girl and her hopeful male friend all looked at each other in surprise. He left the bar empty-handed, in something of a daze, and went over to join the group surrounding Kate.

It took a little while for him to find a moment in which to introduce himself, during which time he took note of her as an adult: the light reflecting off her green-grey dress like the surface of the sea, the grey eyes, now with a soft, clever black around the edges and even more vivid than before, her thin wrist seeming hardly able to hold the weight of her Long Island Iced Tea. Just as before, he was so preoccupied by the sight of her that he forgot to prepare anything to say, so that when a brief silence fell, as silences do, and she turned, almost magically, towards him – to see what this new shape in her peripheral vision would resolve into – he could only say, 'Kate. It's Oliver Mittell. I knew you – sort of – in school,' and hope, wincing, that she didn't draw a humiliating blank.

Unexpectedly, Kate's eyebrows went up and her mouth actually dropped slightly open. He hadn't thought that this was a real-life thing. Then she said, '*Oliver?* No way! I don't believe this! I thought you went to France and never came back. I wondered if you'd really become a pirate.'

'A pirate investigator . . .' he murmured. 'You remember that?'

'Of course. It's one of my weirdest memories.'

They smiled at each other – Kate with affection, Oliver half in disbelief – until they were interrupted by another man asking, impatiently, 'Hey, Kate, did you want another?'

'What? Oh, no thank you,' she said. 'Come on, Oliver, let's sit down somewhere. We need to catch up.'

She looked around, then pointed into a dark corner where two seats faced each other across a small table with a candle. Oliver had the disconcerting sense that the evening had slipped beyond plausibility, but he followed her anyway, wondering at which point his brain (Drugged? Knocked? Insane?) had embarked on this exquisite fever dream.

They sat down and the warm shadows slipped over them.

Kate drank her drink and stared at him with open delight. 'What happened to you really?' she asked.

'My parents moved away before the new term started. My dad had to change jobs and I ended up in Milton Keynes. Not sailing the high seas, unfortunately.'

'Bad luck.'

'Yeah.' He omitted the rest of the story: the year his father spent watching detective shows and avoiding conversation; the oceanic rise and crash of his mother's anxiety about money. Whenever a door was closed behind the two of them, Oliver had the sense of a dark cloud growing behind it, so dense that it was almost a surprise when his parents emerged again, unhappy, silent, but physically unscathed.

'*You* went to Jamaica,' he remembered.

'I went to a hotel,' she corrected. 'It could have been anywhere. That was the sort of holiday my parents used to go on.'

'They don't now? Have they taken to backpacking or something?'

'Uh, they're actually dead,' she said. His smile quailed and scarpered, leaving his face in disarray.

'God, I'm sorry . . . I . . .'

'It's fine. They died when I was at university. A while ago now. They were on holiday, as it happens. A high floor of a hotel in Dubai. There was a fire.'

'God,' Oliver said again.

Perhaps Kate was practised at recovering conversations by now; she was the one to deliver them from the thickening silence. She asked about his work, and seemed impressed by the explanation.

'You must work pretty hard.'

'Pretty hard,' Oliver agreed. It was winter, and he hadn't seen street-level daylight for a fortnight or two. 'Let's not talk about that. Tell me about your aunt's house. I remember it so clearly. You know I've always thought of it as the house of birds. Because of the wallpaper. Which, er, sounds pretty stupid now I say it.'

She was frowning, and he regretted having said so much, sounding so eager. Then she said, 'The wallpaper?'

'Oh – you don't remember it? It was in the bedroom I looked into. It had this spectacular painted wallpaper with birds and trees. It must have been over a hundred years old.'

'Um . . .' She was squinting off over his head, as if to see into the past. 'No, I don't remember. But then I didn't go back after that day. My parents were pretty pissed off that I'd been nosing around there. And they never made up with Auntie Delia. She's still alive, you know, which seems strange as she was so much older than my dad. She could be in a care home now, though.'

'What was the rift about?' Oliver asked. He had returned from abashed to eager as quickly as he had made the outgoing journey, and asked the question without thinking. He was too captivated by his memory of that afternoon, the jewelled room of still birds above the neglected garden, the sunlight of his last week in Oxford, and by Kate herself, as she was then and as she was now, still unicorn-pale, still slender, not especially different in person or manner from the other beautiful girls at the party, but seeming, unlike them, to have an almost mythical substance, mixed from contrasting spirits, invisible flames; the secret of death as well as life. She seemed more *necessary*, somehow. Then her eyebrows raised fractionally, his reverie broke, and he was abruptly embarrassed, asking about something that was absolutely none of his business.

'Er . . . I'm sorry,' he said. 'That's personal.'

She hadn't taken offence, musing only, 'Is it? I suppose it is. It doesn't feel like that, though. I hardly knew Auntie Delia. I heard she was pretty strange. It was the house that caused the falling-out, actually. She and my dad both inherited it, but she wanted it so my dad sold her his half, at a cheap price, and then she started claiming afterwards that he ripped her off. Fairly standard stuff, I think.'

She lifted her hand in a gesture of dismissal, as if to physically smooth over the subject, pressing out awkwardness. Oliver watched her hand; watched her quick smile, her perfect mouth lowered again to meet the straw of her drink, silenced by the overpowering arrival of his own emotion, a tall wave of – not desire, surprisingly, but a piercing, ringing sense of tenderness that felt just as urgent.

Just then the front door gave its familiar dimmed click, softened as all the sounds were up here; absorbed by the mysterious trickery of the flat, the mechanisms that swallowed up the clunk of the loo seat dropping, the cupboard doors swinging to, even the sound of their feet crossing the floor that looked like wood but was tougher than wood, people having done a better job than the lackadaisical trees. He could die noisily in the en suite without Kate hearing a thing in the bedroom.

'Hello?' she called now, and he got up hurriedly, as if to hide the fact that he had been daydreaming rather than dressing, though the pyjamas were something of a giveaway.

'You're back earlier than I thought,' he said, going into the hall. She was dressed soberly today; her hair pressed into a glossy ball, her head and slender neck flowering between the stiff shoulders of her interview suit like a snowdrop. 'You look smart. Is this how people dress for solicitors?'

'I don't know. I don't think anyone knows. I probably could have worn jeans and flip-flops. God knows why I try to impress Mr Hunt. *I'm* the one employing *him*. And he's getting a pretty hefty cut of the inheritance too.'

She kissed him on the cheek; he wondered if she had been going for the lips, before losing heart at the last minute.

'I see *you've* dressed up,' she observed, then, as if worried that she'd sounded too critical, said quickly, 'I'm only joking. You can wear what you want, of course. Uh . . . not that you need me to tell you that.' This last addition made her self-conscious, and she bent to tidy her shoes.

'I didn't know today was the appointment,' Oliver said. 'I could have gone with you. For moral support, or something.'

'Oh, it was all fine.' She took off her jacket. Underneath it her shirt had fallen into thousands of tiny creases. 'I think it's going to be fine anyway. I think greed has blinded the Calverts to the fact that they don't have any sort of case.'

'I'd sort of have liked to go . . . for selfish reasons. To see Oxford again . . .'

'Really? Sorry, I didn't realise you'd want to. I thought you might have been busy researching job stuff . . . ' There was a pause. *Please*, Oliver thought, *don't add anything.* 'Not that, er, you know, there's any pressure to do that.'

And there it was again, the awkwardness. It was almost a week since it had gathered in the flat, and it showed no signs of dispersing. It occupied the space between them like a giant dead jellyfish: translucent, quivering, obstinately glutinous. Over their conversation hung the unspoken truth that most truths in the last few days had gone unspoken. The truth in this instance was that Kate hadn't told him she was going to Oxford because she had been sliding carefully out of bed each morning without waking him, as if trying to avoid early morning intimacy – and the previous night he hadn't seen her at all. She had been out for drinks with a girlfriend and had texted him at midnight saying *Don't wait up*. He wondered what advice her friend had given her. Some rom-com bon mots, no doubt, about deserving the best; not settling; kicking the dead weight that was Oliver to the kerb.

The awkwardness had come about because Oliver had impulsively quit his job, after a month of working later and later and starting earlier and earlier, until the realisation that he'd had only two hours' sleep gave a Kafkaesque flavour to the morning's commute, a sense that deepened during the day: a grey-lit period of strange and surreal absurdity, a hallucinogenic fog through which the familiar forms of his desk and his colleagues, his own hands on the keyboard, writhed and shifted shape – and when his boss finally arrived at his desk, eyes lit with the terrible fires of cocaine and ulcerous pain, and called Oliver a whiny, demanding, unreasonable cunt for requesting a day off on Saturday, Oliver wasn't at first sure if he had imagined it. He blinked once; twice; three times. Then he got up, tried to decide whether to sweep his computer off his desk or make a rousing speech, left it too long to do either, and settled on a wordless exit that turned out to be an unexpected success, if the angriness of one's boss was a measure of success.

The worst part of that day wasn't the shouted threats behind him, reverberating all the way to the lift, or the blank hung screen that was his mind trying to think of his future, or the admin afterwards (because, despite its apparent simplicity, the act of getting up and leaving resulted in more paperwork than if he had given notice), but the two hours of waiting in the apartment for Kate to get in from work so he could tell her what he had done. During those two hours Oliver gave a lot of thought to the theory of the best time to announce bad news. Was it, ideally, the week before the recipient of said news was due to fly to New York for a fortnight; the day after the funeral of the recipient's aunt (even an estranged aunt like Delia); a few days after the recipient had finally sold her own flat, having moved in with the bearer of the bad news only three months before?

Probably not.

By the time Kate arrived home, tired and creased from the heavy air of the Underground tunnels, Oliver had already decided not to tell her. But then she asked, 'Are you okay?' with mild curiosity and one eye on the letters she had picked up and begun sifting – without really expecting him *not* to be okay – and he abandoned any idea of lying or even sugarcoating and dropped the bad news with all the care and ceremony of a digger driver finishing up for lunch. If he had planned it, it might have gone better. But he had opened his mouth to lie and the horrid truth barged through instead, surprising them both.

Films were to blame, he thought later. Not only films, but every book or cartoon or television programme he had ever watched. The line *Tell her the truth!* had been drummed into his unconscious so rigorously over the years that his own free will had been fatally compromised. Then when it came to the aftermath – Kate's open mouth, the various things crossing and recrossing the grey seas of her eyes – all his cultural reference points fell unhelpfully silent. Nothing he had watched had prepared him for dealing with the delicate horrors that followed his revelation: of Kate trying to be understanding – to be cool – with only the odd flash of bafflement ('You *really* didn't plan it?') or even anger ('You couldn't wait a month to find another job?'); both feelings completely justifiable; both of which she would try to deny.

They hadn't talked about it much. Once Oliver had explained that he was under no financial pressure to get a new job, which was handy because he had no idea what he wanted to do, there hadn't been much else to discuss. He guessed that Kate's carefully gentle silences hid sharper concerns: not only her dismay at how he had surprised her, but a reasonable fear that he might surprise her again. He knew that she wanted to work hard, get married, leave work, have children, go back to work – and also that she would never, ever pressure him to hurry this sequence along. That same delicacy or pride was probably what prevented her from accusing him of messing up this barely discussed future, or voicing her fears about embarking on it with someone who might have further acts of cataclysmic flakiness up his sleeve. Still, he knew his advertising had been misleading: he was no longer the Oliver that Kate had signed up for. He was left to wonder how much this bothered her.

'*Anyway,*' she said now, rushing to change the subject, 'you didn't miss much. It wasn't a fun outing. This house thing is a nightmare . . . a really boring nightmare. You know, aside from all the legal complications, the place is almost a ruin. It needs to be totally renovated if I want to make any decent money from the sale. Which means it'll be ages before it's off my hands for good.'

'Hey . . . that's our history,' Oliver said. 'You can't talk about it like that. It's where we met. The house of birds.'

'The house of what?'

'The room with the birds painted on the walls? You know? I guess you didn't see it for yourself. Probably makes it harder to remember.'

'I do remember,' she said, but there was no movement in her eyes, no 'aha' shift, and he thought she was just being polite.

'Well, it was pretty cool.'

'Oh, Oliver, I'm sorry. You sound so wistful! I honestly had no idea you'd be nostalgic about it. I guess I've always seen that house as, I don't know, not *cursed*, exactly, but a bad karma place. It's never caused my family anything but trouble. I never thought I'd end up with it. I mean, I'm surprised Aunt Delia didn't leave it to some cat charity or something. Anything to exclude me from inheriting it.'

'I understand,' Oliver said. 'Not the legal stuff, obviously, but the sentiment.'

'I don't understand the legal stuff myself. I'm worried it's going to take ages, and I was thinking that if those bloody Calverts don't give up quickly – the way they did the last time – I could get the house sorted in the meantime so it's ready to sell when they do.'

'Who *are* the Calverts anyway? Who is it that's started a claim?'

'Their solicitor said he was representing a Mrs Godwin. She's a distant relative of some sort but I have no idea how.'

'Godwin? Not Calvert?'

'Oh, she is a Calvert. Sort of. That's what we Castles call them – it's the side of the family they all come from. Really they're Lennoxes and Montgomerys and God knows what else' – here she managed to make it sound as if patrilineal name changes were a result of the Calverts' basic failure to organise themselves – 'and now Godwins.'

'Bloody Godwins,' said Oliver.

'I think their whole argument rests on some long-lost relative's will. They said it left the house to the Calverts and not the Castles. But they don't have the will, because it doesn't exist. And as far as I'm aware, it *still* doesn't exist.'

'That's the extent of their claim on it?'

'I think so. It's insane, really. They'd have got the house long ago if they had any serious right to it. They tried this before – not in my lifetime; back when my dad and Auntie Delia inherited it. I remember my parents talking about it when I was young and saying that that house was more trouble than it was worth. But I never paid attention, and they obviously can't explain it to me now.'

'No,' said Oliver. He touched her cheek gently and she gave him a look of tolerance, at his habit of sympathy, lingering long after the tragedy had passed. He took his hand back and tried not to look sympathetic. Even after a year, he found the impulse hard to suppress.

As he'd got to know Kate, he had felt more able to offer his support for her early bereavement, but she made it clear early on that she hated it. She was uncomfortable when other people brought it up; almost self-conscious, as if it were an illness, something intimate and shaming. She didn't catch his eye (ready and waiting) when parents were mentioned; when they were moving in together and deciding whether to let out his apartment or hers and he asked her – delicately, euphemistically – if she was quite sure she wanted to live at the same height at which her parents had died, she said, 'What are the chances of it happening twice? I'm safer up here.' And so he gave it up and joined her in the present day, apparently unmarked by bad memories, if not bad dreams.

'Anyway, the good news is that it's sunny outside,' she said now, looking out of the window. 'You haven't forgotten lunch, have you?'

'No,' lied Oliver. There was a short silence, in which he became aware of the effort she was making not to nag him to get dressed; her eyes dropping only once – almost pained, as if they didn't want to but couldn't help themselves – to his pyjamas.

'Right! I'd better get dressed,' he announced, his tone a shade too jolly, almost *avuncular*; and with a tiny shudder at himself he beat a hasty retreat to the bedroom. The door to the wardrobe opened smoothly to reveal rows of pressed clothes, delivered invisibly each week by the team of foreign staff who also cleaned the flat. Next week they would be surprised to see its owner in residence; a mess beyond even their capacity to clean.

Kate followed him in and began undressing, something that – even now – she was endearingly awkward about, wriggling inside a top to remove her bra; holding her shirt in front of herself until its replacement was *in situ*. He felt an uplift of affection that he didn't know how to explain to her – or not without it coming out wrong – and hid his smile by delving further into the wardrobe. He chose a shirt and slid the door soundlessly back to its resting place. Sometimes, he thought, he would have liked to make some noise. The flat was like a padded cell; the only clatterable things the china and saucepans, but they had to be lowered as carefully onto the stone worktops as a baby into a bath. He wondered if this life lived on mute was calming or stress-inducing in its denial of a reasonable outlet for frustration.

As he dressed Oliver wondered what he was going to say to Kate's friends when the subject of his job came up for discussion, which – Kate's friends being what they were – it absolutely would. As if she had read his mind, Kate said, 'You know, we don't have to tell the others about you leaving your job.'

Oliver was surprised by his own thought; so warm and familiar in his head, now turned inside out and strange to him.

'Why wouldn't we tell them?' he asked.

'Oh, I don't know, I just thought maybe you wouldn't want to have to talk about it before you know what your plans are. Or if you decided to go back, or whatever, you might not want the whole world knowing that you left.'

'Kate, I'm not going to go back.'

'Right. Sorry.'

'Please don't say sorry,' he said. 'You can say whatever you want. You can say I'm an idiot. You can say you're upset.'

'But I don't think either of those things,' she said, looking away.

Oliver went to the window, where he watched the progress of a solitary cloud across the sky, heading towards the sun. He willed it to hold fast, but it drifted on, breaking up, dissolving in the burning blue bowl. Disappointed, he looked down to the street below. Londoners from this viewpoint had the look of a flock of birds, or a shoal of fish: a collective, though of course it was only the height that gave them the appearance of a common goal, all flowing in the same direction, towards the steps to the Underground. Beyond them lay the great flat Thames, so bright in the sun that its heavy lead was turned for once to silver. A lie, yes, but a seductive one nonetheless.

THE HOUSE OF BIRDS

His mind went along the river, following it west out of the city, winding it back like a ball of string, tracing each loop and twist of it, until it reached Oxford. He wasn't sure if he could really remember the sound of the small rowboats on the water – the sky seen from under a willow, shifting blue and gold stars caught in a dark net; a bicycle lying in the luminous grass beside him – or if he had partly created this scene, a diorama constructed of fragments of photos and TV shows, glitter and glue and an irresistible nostalgia. But an unexpected fact came back to him: this river was the Isis. He savoured the memory; pleased to reclaim something forgotten.

'You know, Kate . . .'

She looked up, half in and out of a dress, curious at his tone.

'You know . . .' he said again, not sure whether the idea was a sound one, but forging on anyway, 'I could spend the next couple of weeks helping you fix up the Oxford house. I could make a good start on it, anyway. Get things moving while you're away.'

'What?' Kate said. 'Really?'

She looked startled, but not hostile, as if the idea had flapped in as noisy and sudden as a bird – an exotically jewelled bird, maybe – and perched in their flat. They both looked at it warily, wondering if it was going to shit down the back of the sofa. Nothing happened.

'Hmm,' Kate said.

The idea was sound. Who would have thought it? Oliver allowed himself a secret moment of self-congratulation. Then he asked, 'What kind of condition is it in?'

'Ha. It's going to take more than a lick of paint, put it that way. Covered in creepers, and that's just the inside. It's going to be like *Raiders of the Lost Ark*. Oh God. Is *that* why you want to work on it?'

Kate found Oliver's interest in historical documentaries – along with hidden city alleyways, gravestones, and films about lost cities or arcane secret societies – baffling, particularly when she wanted to watch her favourite reality show about trophy wives in America. ('That show is trash,' Oliver once observed. 'So's that thing about the Bermuda triangle,' Kate retorted. 'At least my trash is real.' To which Oliver had to concede she had a point.)

'Well, you know I like that kind of thing. But I'd also like to help you. And to do something with myself. I can't sit around here in my pyjamas much longer. This was the slowest day of my life.'

'So you'd, like, project-manage it?'

'Yeah. I mean, I'd offer to do the plumbing and stuff myself, but I'm not sure that's a good idea.' He laughed. She hardly seemed to hear him: she was wearing the thinking frown she so often bemoaned, worrying that it would give her a vertical line between her eyebrows. Then the frown cleared, and she said, 'You know what, that *could* actually work. And you really want to do it?'

'Absolutely,' said Oliver, and Kate, touched, came over to kiss him. He put his arms around her and her head settled on his shoulder like a small, sleek cat returning to its usual spot. He caught the botanical, ferny scent of her new perfume. In the corner of his eye he could see a corner of her face, wearing its first real smile in days.

'Are you really *sure*?' Kate asked him again before she left. 'It's so lovely of you to want to help me. But it might not be as much fun as you think.'

'You've already warned me about that,' he said. 'Maybe it'll be unexpectedly fun. Maybe you'll even decide you want to keep it.'

She gave a delicate snort. 'Yeah, right.'

They were lying in bed, eking out the time before her flight. From where Oliver's head rested he could see the sky from the window and nothing else. The late summer sun continued its swansong, heroically and tragically dazzling, sending golden bolts of light over the floor, the bed, the pillows with their two upturned faces, one half smiling, one a little disappointed and trying not to show it. He said only, 'It's a lovely house. I wouldn't mind living somewhere like that.'

She moved her hand up to his shoulder; put her head back to look at him, her eyes a pale platinum grey, clouded around with the ghost of her mascara from the night before. She looked concerned. 'But . . . New York?'

Too late he remembered their big move to America; a plan that never really stuck in his memory however many times he pressed it in place; a Post-it note without enough glue, drifting down again and again to the ground. Living in New York was Kate's great ambition. Oliver didn't particularly care where he lived. He imagined their apartment in the cloudy skies of New York would be similar to their apartment in the cloudy skies of London, with the same aimless pigeons flying past. The coffee might be stronger, perhaps. Cabs would flatten and turn yellow. Roads would widen; pretzel carts pop up on the pavements, now sidewalks. Minor alterations. Their friends would be the same kind of people they knew now, their conversation pursuing the same interests: holidays and promotions and affairs and divorce, sounding only a little foreign, requiring – like all the rest of it – only a slight adjustment of perception to forget they had ever moved.

'Of course, New York,' he said reassuringly, but he could still feel the tension in her arm against his chest; the tightness of her neck. He wished they hadn't spoken its name, called it up like Beetlejuice. Because it wasn't a matter of 'Of course, New York' any more. Less than a fortnight ago it would have been; his company had a division there, and he could have transferred out with relative ease if this two-week assignment of Kate's went as she hoped, ending with her promotion, a Manhattan apartment, and a social media profile picture of herself posing ironically with the Statue of Liberty.

As the silence cooled, the way they lay – arms and legs intimately threaded – began to feel uncomfortable, and Oliver was half disappointed and half relieved when Kate picked up her phone and exclaimed, 'Shit! I can't believe how fast the time's gone! My taxi's going to be here in an hour.'

Galvanised, she swung herself up out of the bed in one clean movement, like a swimmer diving into cold water. Oliver had always admired this ability in her. His own getting-up process was more hesitant; gingerly dipping a toe, wincing at the hostility of the morning, looking back sadly at the mussed intimacy of the pillows.

Kate went to the mirror, where she paused for a moment with the expression that always accompanied this routine: head drawn imperceptibly back, a look of quickly descending disappointment, as if she were in a restaurant and just beginning to realise that the meal put before her was meant for someone else. She worried over her body like she might over a car,

speaking about it in the same terms: the importance of invest-
ment and maintenance. She was carefully sleek all over, from
the top of her shiny blonde head to the varnished tips of her
toenails, every one of her surfaces waxed, oiled, buffed.
Standing naked in their similarly white and blonde bedroom,
with its gleaming oak floor and opalescent satined walls, she
looked like a pearl in the nacreous mouth of an oyster. On
cue, there arrived in Oliver's heart the twinge of awe he always
felt at her beauty, just as he was still pained by her bereavement, even though both things were old news now, at least in
Kate's eyes.

Half visible in the mirror, Oliver could not help but be
aware of his own raw and unfinished state. He contemplated
his hair, pressed into wild shapes in the night, his dark body
pelt, the general dishevelment of his limbs against the snowy
bedlinen. He got out of bed; stood up consciously straight. A
new worry struck him: the realisation that Kate would be
thousands of miles away, in a different time zone, with plenty
of time to think. He was frightened of what she might
conclude.

℮

The Oxford house was within walking distance of the train
station, but Oliver's memory of the city failed him and he had
to navigate his way there on his phone, unable to give his
attention fully to his surroundings. What he absorbed of the
spires and bridges came in brief glances, none of it bringing
any particular memory back to him. He couldn't have said for
sure whether his old impressions of the city – the glimpse of
a dome, the sand-coloured stone below the blue sky – had

come from childhood or from popular culture, and as he passed
them he had the feeling that the present day was not recalling
the past so much as overwriting it, pushing it endlessly out of
reach.

His was the only disappointed face in the streets, which
were busy with ice creams, tourists, boats for hire. The
September heatwave had created a general holiday atmosphere. The late-afternoon passers-by had the look of people
unable to believe their luck. Outside wine bars and cafés
they watched the ice dissolve in their drinks; stretched their
arms out to the sun; pointed incredulously at the solid blue
sky.

Oliver left the gaiety behind as he passed from crowded
roads into quieter ones, finally reaching the quietest of them
all, the tree-punctuated approach to Kate's house. Here the
heat seemed to have stilled rather than energised the town.
A haze hung over the roofs and streets; the air felt thicker,
golden and lazy. As he walked along in near silence, the leaves
that had fallen already crumpling gently under his feet, he
caught the scent of that afternoon years ago, when he'd met
Kate; the mingled longing and panic of it. He felt a sudden
urge to look behind him to see if anyone was there. He wasn't
sure whether this was the ghost of his childhood mood – the
spectre of her angry aunt Delia – or the result of Kate's more
recent warning, delivered with one hand already holding open
the door to leave.

'Watch out for Calverts,' she said.

'What? What do you mean?'

'Half of them still live in the area. I already told you that.'

'No, I meant, what would they *do*?'

'God knows,' Kate said ominously. 'I haven't run into them

myself. My parents just said they're a bad lot. They're probably capable of anything . . . Oh, shit, the taxi's calling.'

'You'd better go.'

They looked at each other for a moment, in which the cooled unfamiliarity of the past week collided with the immediacy of their parting. Kate's mouth opened but she didn't say anything. Tears came into her eyes.

'Good luck out there,' he said. 'I'm going to miss you.'

'I love you,' she said, with an odd inflection, as if she were answering something else; a question: *You don't love me, do you?*

She kissed him goodbye – he felt the brief softness of her mouth, her hair dropping heavily against his face, where it absorbed the noise of his 'I love you too' – and whisked herself and her two gleaming cases out of the door in another of her single fluid motions. Before the door closed, she cried, 'Goodbye,' again; last-minute, sounding suddenly childlike, but before he could answer, the heavy fireproof door had swung itself shut.

Oliver did turn around now, giving in to the impulse he already knew was irrational, and looked behind him. The street was empty, streaked with sunlight. Cars passed at the end of the road without turning in, their noises muted. A bird hopped in a tree in the distance. His stupidity was confirmed. Striding abruptly onwards, as if to reassert his authority, he almost overshot the house and had to stop again just as suddenly, right in front of it.

He was struck by the simple fact of its existence; all three of its dimensions, its occupying of the same space as himself. He was reminded of times when he had been shown a picture of a person before meeting them; the picture itself failing to prepare him for the person in the flesh, or in fact doing the reverse, so that the eventual meeting was distinctly strange, as if the more he had looked at the picture, focusing and narrowing his perception to that single image, the less able he was to absorb the real thing. Too much reality, too suddenly. And so he looked at the house for a while, not only in a spirit of assessment but in one of comprehension, because it was so much more itself now that he was standing in front of it.

He had looked it up online a couple of years ago, with the arrival of the technology that allowed him to hover above the street like a bird, or a plane, or Superman, before abruptly descending to stand on the virtual pavement outside. Once again, he found it hard to separate his own memory from the image on the screen, the low resolution house that had become more blurry the closer he got. He wasn't sure whether the cumbersome purple wisteria or the blue front door had been recorded by his childhood or his adult self. He knew that the curtains drawn in an upstairs window and the half-open gate had been something he had noticed later on, because he had looked the house up again on the train down and these details were the same. Back then the house had been occupied by Kate's aunt Delia; now a ghost of the internet, her limbo ending only with the next update, a new camera driving by.

He saw now that a few months on, the house was no longer quite like his composite picture. Its recessed position still gave it the same appearance of having drawn back, as if in deliberate retreat. But the retirement that was once stately now looked vaguely abashed, and the front garden that must have been the last thing to succumb to neglect, having been kept up out of the pride particular to Delia's generation, was as overgrown as the rear of the house had been. Striped spiders had stretched twinkling webs across the elfin, prismatic green. The wisteria was not in flower, while other, formerly obedient flowers had begun a very slow bacchanal: dandelions and roses entwined in the rising grass, bindweed curling around ornamental Japanese acers. The brass number 3 on the door was missing, or stolen, leaving behind a lighter-coloured negative on the blue paint. He tried not to find the absence unsettling. The drawn curtains of the upstairs window had been pulled back, or perhaps taken down; none of the other rooms, in fact, had curtains; a matter of fact removal of intimacies that had left the house looking awkwardly unclothed.

The gate gave a trumpet like a pained elephant as he pushed it open, the noise echoing down the empty street. Oliver looked around, as if people might be drawn out of their homes by it, gathering to stare at his intrusion. Of course, nobody appeared, and he was free to make all the noise he wanted with the key in the stiff lock (which, as it turned out, was quite a lot of noise; scraping, rattling, the hiss and puff of his own exasperation). When he finally got the door open and stumbled into the drift of junk mail that had accumulated against it, his triumph faded as quickly as it had appeared, subdued by the persistent sense of oddness he had been feeling all afternoon, rising up stronger than ever now that he was actually inside the house of Kate's dead relatives, without Kate.

The feeling was intensified by the unusual quiet that closed over him once he shut the front door. The noises of the outside world drew suddenly back. Aside from the absence of human sound, he heard no clanking pipes or radiators, no electric hum from lights or appliances, no gentle groans from the old joists. The silence seemed deeper than in more recently vacated houses, as if it had matured and condensed, distilling over the months into a purer soundlessness. The broken noise of his own feet moving hesitantly over the thinly carpeted hall below the empty light fittings, echoed back from much deeper places within the house, as if it had been scraped out, hollowed like an egg. He felt a weird pleasure at the strangeness of it all, a sense of the out-of-the-ordinary that he rarely tasted (perhaps unsurprisingly) in his ordinary life.

The first thing he did was to go upstairs and look for the birds, but they were nowhere to be seen. He went to each room in turn, even those at the front of the house, increasingly puzzled. When he worked out which of the windows he had climbed up to that day, he stood inside the empty room for a while, feeling almost aggrieved. The mural, or whatever it had been, was gone, and the room was painted a dusty blue. The presumably leaky roof had wept on to two of the walls, leaving a dark continent in the blistering sea. If there *had* ever been birds here – if he hadn't come up with them that day, a surreal finishing touch on a sun-maddened afternoon – they had been washed away by the rain years ago.

This early disappointment dropped back at the prospect of exploring the rest of the house, only to be replaced, room by room, with a comprehensive bafflement. One of the bedrooms was filled with what even his eye, alert to treasure and mystery, must acknowledge as crap. Clothes airers, an old iron, Christmas wrapping paper, a box of men's shoes. Another housed a bed and a majestic burr-walnut wardrobe, which he opened eagerly, half expecting a row of fur coats and a smell of snow, finding only some wire coat hangers. Yet another bedroom contained nothing but a soot-covered dead bird; the rest held nothing at all.

Going back downstairs confirmed that the house was far

from bare, but its contents had apparently been re-distributed under some unknown master plan prioritising neither value nor logic. Some rooms did have curtains, ranging from great dusty showpieces of velvet and rope to simple and ugly floral cotton. A few pictures still hung on the walls, while others were stacked against them. The sitting room was without sofas or chairs, containing instead a few piles of books, a mirror propped against an emptied bookcase, and a teacup sitting in the middle of the floor, lit up by the sun from the large window, as if in a strange solo performance. He noticed the beauty of the large marble fireplace; its frieze with a rearing horse and a few nymphs standing about idly, the whole thing furred already with dust.

He ran his fingers over the ironing board that leant against the wall of what must have once been the dining room, as if it might provide him with answers. Everywhere it seemed that things had been randomly taken down, removed, or stacked to await removal, then left in *Mary Celeste*-esque abandonment. This seemed, suddenly, sadder to him than if someone had systematically stripped the place. An uninterested hand had shuffled and discarded the house's contents, leaving them here and there in a stark demonstration that nobody cared any more about this place, its occupants, or any of its memories; and the desolation of these formerly useful belongings raised an answering pang of sympathy in Oliver himself.

Making an effort at objectivity, he decided that the old place wasn't in bad shape. The electricity and plumbing worked and the light fittings were almost modern. It needed replastering, obviously; several of the floors were covered with patterned carpet from the seventies or eighties, and the kitchen was a mildewed brown and cream horror that he quickly shut the door on. But it wasn't *bad*. Encouraged by the marble fire-places, the delicate ceiling roses and cornicing, he wondered what else might lie untouched. He prised back the plywood that had been nailed over an old oak door; tugged at the corners of the carpets and inspected the blackened wood underneath, without knowing what he was looking for, or whether this was it.

After getting a splinter, he sat down on one of the few remaining chairs and felt abruptly miserable. His own life, chased off temporarily by novelty, swept grandly back in. Why was he here, really? Did he think he would trick Kate into forgetting how unreliable he had turned out to be? Or was he trying to trick himself? He knew he was refusing to confront his future; he had turned away like a stubborn small boy, picking at his nails, trying not to make eye contact. If he planned to stay in the City, he needed to act quickly to repair the damage the sudden break in his CV could cause; if he intended to retrain as something else, as he had suggested to Kate, he needed to think about what the hell that might be. Neither the known nor the unknown seemed appealing. His stomach gave a little slop of fellow feeling; of worry and – not regret, exactly, but a queasiness that might well have been regret, in its liquid form.

In the world outside Oliver's thoughts the daylight vanished, the sun slinking below the rooflines, the rose-coloured light scaling the walls, leaving the rest of the room in shade. He was somewhat startled when he resurfaced in the dim sitting room. The sense of trespassing in somebody else's house returned, along with the persistent undertow of strangeness that he strained to catch and identify, like a reverberating off note, a faint scent of decay, an unfamiliar shadow. A car passed by outside, an unexpectedly comforting noise. Evidence of normal life continuing as it always did; that he was, after all, in a fairly unexceptional house on an ordinary road in a pleasant city. And Oliver himself, daydreaming again. Nothing unusual in that.

Reassured, he picked up a book from the top of one of the piles. Bryce's *Holy Roman Empire*: a dulled sapphire-blue cover with a handsome gold design, slightly battered at the corners. It was apparently published in 1912. He hadn't given the age of books much thought before, and was impressed at the years this one had clocked up. He began going through the rest of the pile, marvelling at their venerability. *The Life of Lady Hamilton*, 1905; *Law and Crime in Ancient Mesopotamia*, 1861; *Markham's England*, 1845 (he sniffed the latter, to find out what 1845 smelled like. The answer: old tree stumps, dust, long-dead mushrooms). He was moving steadily down the stack in a pleasant state of wonderment when *The House of Hanover* (1894) – as if impatient with his stupor – made him jump by falling abruptly to pieces in his hands.

Oliver let out a startled bark that echoed foolishly around the half-empty room. He gathered the pieces of the book back up, the red spine attached only to the covers and frontispiece, the innards all over the floor. It took him a moment to make sense of what he was holding. Somebody had carefully cut out almost all of the book's interior to make room for a folded sheaf of paper, slightly less yellow than the pages. The modification would have gone unnoticed until the book was opened. The thrill of finding out a secret was immediate: a misplaced swell of adrenalin, unable to differentiate between the present and the presumably long-past. He unfolded the papers carefully: a thickly promising hoard of handwritten pages entitled *A*

Revised History of the House of Hanover. Beyond this he found the inked blue filigree – a beautiful calligraphic style he had never seen outside a greetings card – too closely written for his Times New Roman-accustomed eye to make out easily in the low light. He squinted at the first words (*So, here you are!*), then got up to turn the lights on. At this the house finally refused him, with a white flash, a glassy little noise; a fuse blown somewhere he would never find it.

He looked around the room, which was darker now than the street outside, where the lamp posts had begun their night-long watch over the people arriving home, the birds settling in the trees to roost, the perambulating cats. A car door slammed not far away; voices moved away up the road. He hadn't made a plan beyond getting to the house, looking at it, and going back to London. Now the house had cooled and sunk into a darkness that made indistinct and not altogether friendly shapes of its heaps of junk and treasure; he was hungry; and his phone was nearly out of power. He had naturally forgotten to bring warmer clothes, food or a charger. He let himself out and set off in the direction of the station, picturing himself briefly as a participant in a survival reality TV show: failing to forage, build a fire or construct a shelter; earning the hatred of the other contestants; ultimately having to be rescued by the producers as his fellow islanders, hunger-maddened, attempted to roast him on a spit.

The intriguing history was folded into his pocket; he would read it on the train.

A Revised History of the House of Hanover
S. L.

So, here you are!

Rather a strange way to start a history, you must be thinking. What the devil is going on? Perhaps you are beginning to suspect – only one sentence in – that I am not a properly qualified historian at all. There must be men who go around pretending to be historians just as they pretend to be doctors or lawyers or clergymen. Perhaps I am one of these.

You are of course right: I salute your perspicacity. Except for the bit about my being a man, which isn't true. Awfully sorry about that. I am a woman, my name is Sophia, and as you might have guessed, I haven't a degree in history; though I can't really be blamed for that, what with Oxford being manned by men who kept its degrees so miserly close for so long that by the time they decided to allow women a few, it was already too late for me.

I can tell your curiosity is not quite satisfied. You are wondering, perhaps, why I am addressing *you*. A proper historian, you might say, would never do such a thing.

51

And you are perfectly right once again: proper historians take it for granted that there will be a *you* reading – lots of you, in fact – and so they don't feel the need to acknowledge your presence. They are the kings and you are the courtiers. You don't speak unless you are spoken to, and you will never be spoken to. But I! I have no such guarantee. I have no idea whether or not there will be any *you* at all, and so it seems awfully ungrateful of me not to acknowledge you, now that you have appeared.

We will have to politely ignore the awkward truth that neither of us may know for sure who the other is. Rather like being introduced to somebody at a party whose face one knows, but to which cannot be attached any biographical detail. 'We've already met!' cries the old acquaintance. Yet one has not the faintest clue as to when, or how, and – in truth – they don't either. And so small talk is made, in the hope that the other will in some way reveal themselves, emerge from the mist and end the puzzlement. But I suggest to you that there is a kind of equality in this position. You and I don't know one another yet. We don't know whether to trust one another yet. And so we must hold maddeningly aloof, until at last the moment may come when we are face to face and the light of recognition blazes between us; when we can cry with true comprehension: 'Here you are!'

So, while I know you have more questions, I am afraid you shall have to wait. There are vegetables to be eaten, you know, before you may have your pudding. This is not caprice on my part; it is simply that the only way I can answer you is to start at the beginning. Not the beginning of history, nor even the beginning of my life, but the moment for me when everything began to change.

e~

If you want to picture that moment yourself, you must conjure up the quadrangle outside the Bodleian Library, on an early spring morning in 1923. Picture a quiet day; the people crossing the flagstones passing in fits and starts, moving briskly. Few dawdle; only a couple of students in Fair Isle pullovers linger by a doorway, laughing in a confidential way. The low clatter of their voices travels distinctly across the square. It goes unnoticed by the woman standing alone in the centre of the quad, looking up at the Tower of Five Orders, her head tipped back to see from under the brim of her cloche. She is dressed well: not entirely unstylish, but no flapper, either. No brooch winks against the Prussian-blue cloth of her hat; her dark hair is pinned rather than bobbed; her seal-coloured dress is not so short as the ones other women at this time are getting away with. (Yet it would be a mistake to assume, dear reader, that there is nothing she wants to get away with.)

That day there was a distinct snap in the air. The sky was a cold blue above the roofs. The sunlight was stingingly acerbic, like sucking on a lemon. It felt to me (for you must have guessed by now – perceptive as you are – the identity of the woman standing by herself) that there was something not entirely *kind* about the day, which was in the sort of mood one would be wary of if, say, one passed it in the school yard; a bright little creature giving one a look of sudden, canny sharpness. Shortly to be followed by a pinch.

Later, of course, if somebody had suggested to me that it was simply an ordinary, slightly chilly spring day, and that I was in a vile mood, I might have conceded the point. But just then, standing outside the Bodleian feeling its rejection as something almost physical – a large flat palm, moving me firmly away – I felt that the world sneered at me, and I sneered back. I didn't care that I was making myself the subject of public assessment; that I was standing and staring at the building with a ferocity that would only convince those inside that they were right not to have let me in a few minutes before. I was too infuriated even to feel shamed by the unquestionably shaming circumstances of my ejection; of the thought of myself in the recent past, hoping, cajoling – even peering over the gatekeeper's shoulder, at the mysterious dark towers of the interior.

In case you don't already know: to gain entry to the Bodleian, a woman needs either a man – a Fellow, to be exact – or a letter from such a man. I was pretending that my letter of introduction had gone astray, and was being terribly distressed and charming about it. Margot, one of my sister Boll's acquaintances, had claimed to have tricked her way into the Bodleian in just this way, on a dare. Having thus breached the walls, she had wandered around purposelessly with what must have been an uncomfortable sensation of anticlimax, rather like the French mob that stormed the hated Bastille to find only seven prisoners living in relative comfort. 'It wasn't her best prank, admittedly,' Boll acknowledged later. 'Not like the time she joined a suffragette rally and stole a policeman's hat. Or when she got tight and crashed Hugh Lancaster's motor car into a tree.'

'I'm not sure the last one really counts as a *prank*,' I said.

'Oh, my darling, you should have been there! It was a scream. Hugh was frightfully cross: we still razz him about it.'

Thinking back on it, I couldn't see anything wrong with my own performance at the Bodleian: a delicately mixed cocktail of flusterment and big-eyed optimism. Unfortunately, a good forty years separated me from the man I needed to convince, and he was not the avuncular sort. 'I am terribly sorry,' he said, but he looked at me not with regret so much as unconcealed distaste. I gave up. What else could I do? And so – very slowly, and with at least six feet between our male and female bodies, as if we were two repelling magnets – he hustled me off the premises.

I surveyed all of it now – the lopsided tower, the impassive golden stone, the fat pillars, the windows cut into slices by their stone arches, the battlements with their crocketed pinnacles dotted rather needlessly about like a row of fir trees, the hallowed cove of the doorway – and I cursed the lot. Then I turned to leave.

'I say,' somebody said behind me. 'That was a splendid performance in there.'

'I beg your pardon?' I turned as coldly and slowly as my curiosity would allow. The speaker was a student, I thought, though I couldn't identify him with any certainty, with his indeterminate dust-coloured tweeds, gently crumpled; the faint foreign scent of his cigarette, leaving white curls in the air above him. He was young, good-looking; with hair the same colour as the ashlar library behind him, engaging blue eyes, wide shoulders and a firm, rather snub-ended nose; all of which might have explained his feeling able to saunter up this way, with a broad smile that said: you can trust me.

I most certainly do not trust you, said my own tight little smile.

'Awfully sorry,' said the stranger, as if he had heard. 'Please forgive my intrusion. I certainly shouldn't like to interrupt the fine job you're doing incinerating the Bodleian.' Out came his hand. 'I'm Christopher Konig.'

I looked at him for a long moment, keeping his hand waiting in mid-air, as if to demonstrate that I had charge of the conversation. I didn't, of course, and we both knew it, but he waited politely, playing along.

'Sophia Louis,' I said, eventually, as if introducing the hand that extended grudgingly towards him.

'So, what were you looking for? In the library, I should say. I assume there was something you wanted to read.'

'History,' I said.

'What, all of it?' Now he was smiling.

'Exactly. I planned to begin with ancient history, before working around to the rest.'

There was a moment in which he appeared to be trying to work out whether or not I was serious, while I withheld any sort of expression. Then he laughed and said, 'So, not a case of Tutankhamun fever?'

'No,' I replied, rather loftily. Just then Oxford (and, I supposed, the world) was in a state of high excitement over the discovery of the boy king's tomb, and while I shared the curiosity – listening out for the latest news like anybody else – I did not want to be mistaken for a silly girl in the grip of a crush on a pharaoh. His question was a fair one, but I was alert to condescension. 'Actually, at the moment I'm rather more interested in Ephesus and the cult of Artemis. There is so much more to be uncovered there.'

'They're certainly taking their time about it,' Christopher said.

'Oh, but I don't mind that. I like it when one can't find out absolutely *everything*. The Princes in the Tower . . . or the Man in the Iron Mask. Or Zenobia.'

'I know very little about Zenobia,' Christopher said. 'Would you mind enlightening me?'

I inspected him narrowly then, to see whether he was mocking me, but he seemed in earnest.

'She was the Queen of the Palmyrene Empire in the third century. She conquered Egypt and several other lands, before she was defeated by Aurelian. They brought her to Rome, in golden chains, to parade her through the city. But after that nobody knows for sure what happened to her. Some say she died; others that she was given clemency and lived a good life in Rome, surrounded by the sort of educated society she prized.'

'And . . . you'd rather not know what happened to her?'

'If the answer were in a box in front of me I shouldn't open it. I'd rather imagine Zenobia alive than risk finding out that she died.'

'Really?' he cried. 'No: you're making fun of me.'

'Actually, I don't know if I'd open it or not. But I like

the story as it stands. I almost love history more the more mysterious and incomplete it is; the more room it leaves for interpretation. There is something beautiful about *not* being able to know everything, don't you think?'

'You're a rum sort of historian,' he observed, amused. 'Really, you're an anti-historian.'

I watched his face, as I had all the time we had been talking, with a Holmesian attention to detail. If Sherlock himself had been a suffragette he could not have done a better job than I of finding out male mockery or contempt. Yet I came up with nothing, except perhaps a check to my own prejudices. I realised Christopher was older than I had first thought, and not at all what I took him for: an undergraduate in love with his own luck, a sportsman strolling about the quads, stopping on a whim to bait or flirt with a lone female. What I thought was arrogance was simply cheerfulness; where I had suspected flirtation there was only curiosity.

Reassured, I said, 'But surely it's more fun that way. Even if one doesn't know the whole story, one takes something more personal from it; something of meaning. It's almost easier to imagine oneself there if the imagination has a little more freedom. And it's more fascinating the more there is to speculate about . . . But perhaps that sounds awfully flimsy and female.'

'Not at all. It's true that historians love mystery, but only insomuch as they can find out the answers. By which I mean: find out the answers themselves and publish a book on the subject before anybody else does.'

'How depressing that seems. I suppose I *am* a rum sort of historian, then.'

'By rum I meant, er, interesting and imaginative. And I see now I was quite wrong to have suspected you of Egyptomania. You should be standing guard at the entrance to the tomb, warding off the men with spades.'

'Wait, wait, there are limits. I don't at all disagree with digging things up. I dare say we'll never know the truth no matter how much we exhume. Let them dig, that's my philosophy.'

'Well now, if you like a fascinating but potentially fruit-less dig into history, you'd enjoy studying Knossos.'

'How very odd that you bring up Knossos,' I exclaimed.

'Oh, I work it into all my conversations. I find there's always a way.'

'I meant, because I was reading about it recently. But I don't know a great deal about it. Why fruitless?'

'The whole thing reminds me of an unfinished novel, as if H. Rider Haggard got distracted halfway through. It starts with Arthur Evans . . .' Here he broke off and looked at me with concern. 'I say, do stop me if I am patronising you.'

I was startled: usually it was taken for granted that I would be patronised.

'Not in the least.'

'Right-oh. So, Arthur Evans was working on seal stones – here at the Ashmolean, in fact – and became curious about the undeciphered, apparently Mycenaean script on some stones from Crete. Then later, after he found other similar stones for sale in Athens, he went to Crete itself to investigate. He recognised the signifi-cance of the Knossos site, and rather cannily bought

the land. When he unearthed the palace ruins he realised
that he had found the home of his mysterious script.
You can imagine how terribly exciting it would have
been. And the labyrinthine structure of the palace, the
labrys symbol on its columns, and the coins depicting
the Minotaur and Ariadne convinced Evans and pretty
much everybody else that this was the lost palace of
Minos.'

'Are you going to tell me it isn't?'

'Well . . . none of us knows how myth and reality lie
down together – what they got up to before we started
keeping a sterner eye on them. I don't, and neither does
Evans. I haven't said as much to him, you understand.
But that's not exactly my point. What I meant to say was
in support of your argument: that though Knossos has
been dug up – rebuilt, even – nobody actually knows what
the palace was *for*, or who lived there, or why it was
abandoned. Furthermore, the mysterious script has never
been deciphered. I should think you'd be positively ecstatic
about that outcome.'

I could feel myself smiling by then, and resumed my
neutral expression a moment too late.

'You *are*,' he said, triumphant.

'Perhaps . . . a little. Not only because I like mystery,
but because Evans was so presumptuous in what he did.
He had the throne room repainted! When I said just now
that I liked to find a personal element in history, I didn't
mean *redecorating*. And now I hear he's rebuilding the
palace. Quite frankly, it serves him right that the truth
still eludes him.'

Christopher looked at me with dismay. 'But – you know

all about it already. I told you to stop me if I was lecturing you.'

'Oh, well, I don't know all *that* much about it. Bits here and there, like most of my knowledge. I don't get the opportunity to read deeply, so I read widely. I didn't know it all . . . not the part about the seal stones, anyway.'

'I'm not even sure that's right, that part,' he said. 'The details could be wrong.'

'No, you were quite right,' I said, without thinking. He started to laugh. 'All right, so I did know about them.'

'What a liar you are!' he said, and I laughed too. Then there was a moment of silence, swiftly filled with the awareness that we had been standing in the centre of the courtyard for some time; that our voices were rebounding lightly off the stately face of the library, provoking curious glances from passers-by. I realised how quiet it had got now that we had stopped talking.

'I say, I really ought to explain why I introduced myself in the first place,' Christopher said now, somewhat hastily. It was the first time since he hailed me that he had looked anything less than perfectly at ease. 'I followed you out because I overheard your . . . chat, with that ass Beresford. In fact, if you'd come yesterday you would have met Davies, though you'd have had a devil of a time getting rid of him afterwards. You'd have probably considered the pass more trouble than it was worth, in those circumstances.'

I flushed, ashamed of my tactics – the prettily lifted eyes, the soft hand toying with the scarf, the ghastly sidling and wheedling of it. As if he understood, he said quickly:

'You oughtn't to think I disapprove, by the way. God knows, there's no point playing fair if no other chap is.'

'I'm not even a chap,' I said. 'Which seems to be the problem.'

'Well, quite. That's why I should like to offer my services. You need, for reasons that are undoubtedly unfair, a letter of introduction. Have you one? If not, I can get it for you.'

At that, I stared at him. He looked back with a poker face the equal of my own. I noticed that a fleck of brownish gold floated in one of his blue irises, like a leaf on the still face of a pool, or a kite hanging for a moment in the sky. A freckle; a fault, I supposed. Yet without it his eyes would have been an almost featureless blue, regular and dense as oil paint.

Slightly embarrassed, I murmured, 'You guessed right: I've no letter. It seems I'm rather a poor liar after all.'

He gave me a queer look: something almost solemn – sad, perhaps – though I had no idea what had provoked it. Then he said lightly, 'Do try to study the art of it,' which made me think I might have imagined it. He continued in the same tone, 'Now see here, I might be able to get a letter for a sister, or even a cousin, but I'm not going to be able to rustle one up for a stranger in a jam. You understand me?'

'Perfectly, dear cousin,' I said.

He smiled. His teeth were so even and snowily perfect that they were almost sinister. I thought of them biting down on somebody's skin; a shoulder or a neck. I didn't shiver: I was long used to the wildness – the sly silliness – of my own imagination. My head had always been the scene of a great many unspeakable acts: murder mysteries, mistaken identities, moonlight flits. They came and went so frequently – as fast as a turned page – that I barely paid attention to them.

'All right, shall I meet you here tomorrow? At the same time?'

'So soon?' I was almost taken aback by the success of my plan, which had done rather well considering it had started life as a flapper's hare-brained prank.

'Only if it suits you.'

'Yes,' I said. 'Yes please. And thank you so much, Mr Konig. Do you know, I almost forgot to say thank you, and you've been quite utterly divine. I don't know why you should—'

He shook his head, apparently serious again. 'Don't thank me yet. Let's wait and see how it goes tomorrow. Good afternoon, Miss Louis.'

'Mrs,' I said. He nodded, making no comment. We shook hands formally, yet somehow with an air of repressed hilarity, and then he left, and I stood for a moment in the square, slightly dazed by my good fortune, arriving out of nowhere and disappearing almost as quickly, crossing the quad with a light, almost animal gait beneath its tweed, turning the corner without even a glance back over its shoulder, and making me wonder if it had ever happened at all.

As I approached the house – a brusque wind starting up as I turned the corner, as if my own street were shoving me unceremoniously back – it occurred to me to check my watch. When away from home, I would usually glance at it every ten minutes or so, like a solicitous hen minding its chick. Today was the first time in a while that I had entirely forgotten to do so, and I realised that a whole hour had crept by since the last time I looked.

George had bought me this wristwatch – a modish silver Rolex – at a time when watches were new and expensive and George young and poor. Back then I had never seen the point of owning one, as everything I did tended to be organised for me, and I reasoned that as everyone else had a watch, I could always ask them the time. The enthusiasm of my friends' responses when I showed them George's present was the first indication I had that people might have found this rather exasperating.

'Oh no, George!' I said, horrified and delighted, when he gave it to me. We were in the garden, absorbing the last of the autumn sunlight, the air full to bursting with the rustle of the fiery leaves, the drone of the last, devoted bees; the housemaid Sarah singing, somewhat tunelessly, in the kitchen. The scent of fallen apples rose from the grass, cidery sweet, faintly rotten. 'What does it say on the back? "For giving me your time." Oh George!' I tried to conceal my smile. 'It's . . .'

'Ridiculous. I know. As soon as I saw it engraved there, I hadn't the faintest idea why I'd thought it so witty.'

I laughed. 'It's very sweet. And the watch is beautiful. You really oughtn't to have . . . but I *do* love it.'

'I love *you*,' he said, then looked surprised. 'There! I said it. I wondered if I'd ever get up the courage to tell you.'

'What a shame you missed the deadline for the engraving.'

He smiled, puzzling over the clasp. 'But when you look at it, you'll know that's what those words mean.'

'Words are slippery devils, aren't they,' I said, content-edly. The watch fastened, I left my hand in his and laid my head on his shoulder, feeling the wool of his blazer scratch gently at my ear; smelling the sweet, meadowy scent of his neck, and thinking I'd never again be so happy as I was then.

Pained, I sent the memory packing, and hurried my pace, though whatever time I arrived home, I knew how I should find George. Sitting with a newspaper propped in his hands, as if he were still reading it and not simply gazing out on the cold sunlight of the empty street outside. He favoured a chair in the drawing room, placed in between the window and the sombre grandfather clock, from which strategic vantage point he was able to keep an eye on the movements of both time and his wife, with only a slight turning to and fro of his eyes.

I gave my hat and coat to Margaret and dawdled for a while in the hall, asking her about her mother – who had had a nasty cold not long ago – and debating the merits of the new vacuum cleaner.

'Oh, it's wonderful, I'm sure, ma'am,' Margaret said dubiously. 'Very noisy. I suppose that means it's working.'

Her eyes slid imperceptibly in the direction of the drawing room, in which George was surrounded by his usual silence. He resented the inroads the vacuum cleaner had made on the layers of quiet he had worked at care-fully over the years, built up and up like a French polish; a thick, glassy lacquer laid over every surface. Yet he tolerated the new arrival, confining himself to the observation, in Margaret's hearing, that the ghastly thing sounded like a banshee and was in all likelihood possessed by the devil. Since then Margaret had been eyeing it warily, not knowing whether or not George was serious. I was unable to reassure her: I wasn't entirely certain myself.

After a short while, Margaret began to fidget, turning on her hip, one foot inching stealthily in the direction of the stairs. When she murmured something about the silver still wanting polishing, I gave up and released her, watching her hurry away over the black-and-white tiles of the hall in her black-and-white uniform, as stark as a Tenniel etching. Sometimes I thought about taking up the chequered tiles to uncover the comforting, slightly worn geometric patterns of the Georgian floor I remembered from my early childhood, before my mother had allowed one of her friends, a red-haired she-wolf by the name of Mrs Simmonds, to 'update' the place, an unpleasant process that began and ended in the hall, my mother having died before it could go any further.

I stood there a moment longer, delaying, before I said to myself, *Do pull yourself together, Sophia, you silly ass*, and went into the drawing room to greet George.

The drawing room was large and papered in a cool, glaucous blue; my mother, who professed herself intimidated by its formality and seldom spent much time there, always said it ought to have been in some great Italian villa overlooking the Adriatic. Elegantly airy at the height of summer, it was distinctly chilly at this time of year, with no fire lit. The afternoon sun was still here, only moments away from taking its leave, but no heat had collected here during the day, and the light that bore in was stark. Its precision had the effect of softening the other forms of the room – the stiff ivory curtains, the white stone – so that they appeared coldly distant, lost under arctic water, like dimly glimpsed icebergs. The light had caught George squarely where he sat, turning his face and pale grey-brown hair quite white. Today I had thought the sun sharp, or cruel; now I realised its absolute indifference. If anything should make me imagine a God, it would be this light: this long, dispassionate stare.

I crossed the room and kissed George, who did not get up. He had an old leg injury that always started to ache around this time, as if the flesh remembered the moment of its grievance and began to mourn again. It would subside before summer. He tilted his face with his customary grimace of apology. His cheek was soft and chilled against mine.

'It's awfully cold in here, George. Why don't you have a fire lit?'

'It's quite all right.'

I sat down opposite him, trying to work out his mood. It seemed lighter than usual, though this could sometimes be deceiving; a stray reflection off the surface of dark water.

'How was your . . . little jaunt?' he asked, but without true rancour, as if the library were an inconvenient relative of whom he disapproved but felt bound to enquire after. I supposed that he believed my little jaunt had failed, and was ready now to be sympathetic.

'You wouldn't believe it, darling,' I said airily, 'but I met the most delightful old fellow – a Beddington, I think, though I was in too much of a fluster to catch his name . . .

Beringford? Bendicks? – and he was positively charming about it. I'm terribly excited. I've longed to look inside for so long. And to read the books at last! It all seems rather a dream.' I eyed him as I spoke, wondering if I had overdone the airiness. I thought of Christopher telling me I ought to learn to lie. You don't know the half of it, I might have said to him. I lied daily, sometimes hourly. I was always feeling 'fine, darling'; I always slept soundly, and had a heavenly morning. Margaret never broke anything, a half-asleep Mrs Boxall never burnt the toast at breakfast, the draper never overcharged and the neighbour's Siamese cat never dropped torn and bloodied mouse carcasses on the front step. My afternoons with Boll were always jolly good fun, and Boll always sent her love.

George didn't appear too disconcerted by either my success or my little pantomime, so I continued. 'I thought I'd go back tomorrow.'

'Tomorrow?'

'Why not? I might as well make the most of it, before they chuck me out.'

'But . . . can't your pet don prevent that? What was his—'

I interrupted him. 'Why, yes, but I don't know how long for.' Aware that I was committing myself to a lie I knew I should have to pay devoted service to, guard and protect, honour and obey, until death did us part, I added, 'He's rather old, you know. I'm worried he mightn't be around for much longer. At the university, I mean.'

He frowned, struck by a new suspicion. 'I've no wish to cast doubt on the man, Sophia, but are you sure you know his motivations? Age is no guarantee of good behaviour.'

'Oh George! He was perfectly paternal. I thought him a delightful old chap. He said I reminded him of his daughter.'

One minute into the lie, I thought sorrowfully, and already a daughter to remember. To turn the conversation away from my dubious don, I asked George how his day had been.

In answer he held up the newspaper.

'Two pickpocketings yesterday on the Broad,' he announced, as if I had asked, 'So what new crimes did you find to worry about today, darling?'

'I don't see that that's anything to get worked up over,' I said. 'Must you . . .'

But I let the question go, for there was no conviction in it. We both knew that he must; that he was compelled to do it, like a dog barking at a noise outside. I should have called it atavistic had it not been painfully evident that it was not innate but schooled, a product of his years under the tutelage of the Great War. Not that I knew very much about that time; his life then may as well have been a history book to me. He signed up shortly after war was declared and trained with the Bedfordshire Regiment. Within a year he was a second lieutenant on his way to Gallipoli, and – having survived that – went on to Gaza. After his leg was injured in early 1917, he came home. I knew nothing else. His letters from overseas were so brief and elusive that the censors found nothing in them to strike out. And then when he got back: silence.

'Need I remind you that these are dangerous times?' he said now. 'First people steal humbly, modestly, and then they grow bold. They are poor, they are dispossessed; what have they to lose? Unemployment breeds resentment, as if there weren't resentment enough already. The Bolsheviks and Jews are encouraging strikes and unions. The war has left people without livelihoods, without . . . their health. Former soldiers, turning to violence. A crime wave is beginning, just as predicted. It isn't simply about money any more. There is real hatred out there, Sophia, damn it . . .'

I had heard this speech too often to listen for long. But I waited patiently as he connected riots, rapes, murders, declining church attendance, increasing divorce rates and the failing economy, by calculations I suspected were as mysterious to him as they were to me. It was as if he stood at the newsstand and saw the papers laid out before him – one howling about Bolshevik attacks, another warning of national debt, and another – a prim little gasp behind raised hands, peeping through the fingers – whispering of rape and dismemberment, and perceived them all as symptoms of the same evil. He looked out of the window onto the dignified chestnut trees, the little dogs trotting amiably on their leashes, the people passing and wishing each other good day, and saw through them to a black and smoking chaos.

'You know, darling, I read that crime hasn't risen much in the last decade,' I said mildly. 'Someone wrote the other day that it's actually dropped, compared to Victorian Britain.'

'You *read* . . .' George began, before he stopped; frowned – found he couldn't say anything more, so long as we were both pretending that the discussion was academic:

simply a matter of his reading materials versus my own. He used to like reading history, when he was at Cambridge. It was what we talked about when we first met, against the hazy green background of a croquet party in Berkshire, when I was a friend of a daughter and he a friend of a son. The daughter and son themselves I barely remember; already faded and indistinct by the time George and I started arguing shyly yet vividly over Empress Theodora, as if it were they who resided in the history books. I believe the daughter married, and emigrated to India. Her brother was killed at the Battle of Megiddo.

George and I were eighteen and twenty when we met; not much older when we married. My parents thought the union hasty; I expect we thought it awfully romantic. We had only met a few times, our conversation riven with the bashful silences and misunderstandings of a much earlier era, but there was something there that glowed through regardless, making everything else seem less alive, less meaningful. That time felt so long ago now it may as well have been Mayan, or Roman; it seemed almost as exotic. The conversations under potted palms while somebody poured tea; the tiny untouched cakes: oh, we were not at all hungry. Harp music, late afternoons; the drowsy, dust-mote-laden air of my old dreams. When George left Cambridge, he said he would finish his degree after the war. Now he said that history was all very well but it wouldn't save our lives: that the newspapers were the only sort of reading that might do any good; and just in case the newspapers didn't protect us, there were always the two shotguns, one in the outhouse and one beside his bed.

He stared at me gravely now, as if I were an imbecile, and said, 'Do try to understand, Sophia.'

'I'm not sure I do.'

'You know I can't walk with you to the library.' He gestured at the injured leg, declining, as always, to dignify it with an acknowledgement.

'I only use the main roads,' I said. 'In daylight. Really, George. There's no need to worry about me walking alone.'

There followed a short time in which both of us were quite still and silent, the conversation continuing only in a mutual gaze. His hovered between hawkish and uncertain; stubborn and suborned. I kept my own steady and gentle, waiting placidly for the moment of realisation, which came at last, a quick duck of his head, a murmur: 'Forgive me, Sophia. I do know the roads are not dangerous. Sitting indoors for so long, I forget.'

That these moments of realisation were coming later and later, and less and less frequently, was something I did not care to examine. What good was examination anyway? Being a woman is like being a schoolchild: you may do well at examinations, but you'll have a devil of a time convincing anybody to give you a job.

'I'll keep my wits about me,' I said, with a carefully judged smile, not wanting him to feel laughed at.

'Thank you for humouring me. My God . . . if anything were to happen to you . . .'

He reached out, and I put out my hand. His fingers closed gently on my wrist, turning it over as if to marvel at my palm, the strange flower of my upturned fingers. I thought then that if some horror really did remove me

violently from the serene stone streets of Oxford, dropping me on to the front page of a newspaper, all black
and white and smudged from my sudden transition, it
might not be George's ruin but his manumission. To be
suddenly relieved of the burden of worry, to no longer
be tormented by the fear that he would lose his wife; to
see at last, perhaps, that life without her was almost exactly
the same as it was before.

I looked at him now – not trying to draw out anything
of our old intimacy, exactly, but almost as a reconnais-
sance, to work out where in that territory it might be
hiding. I refused to believe in its death. His skin was brown
now, not white, and his hard jaw was strange to me, but
there was something – even now – of the old George
about him; his mouth still soft and fragile, almost like a
girl's, his eyes still a colour that wandered gipsy-like
between brown and green, refusing to commit to either.
I saw the vestiges of it in his translucent eyelids; his rare
smile – but the last sighting of that was so long ago, I
wondered if it might be extinct. The lines that drew down
from his nose to the corners of his lips were as deep as
if they had never lifted. It was impossible not to see that
I had known him best as a boy: that during the war he
grew up, in a way mysterious to me, and that there was
nothing boyish about him any more.

Guilt, like a sleeping animal I was attempting to step
over, woke and snapped at me. While I had been laughing
with Christopher, George had been alone at home. Like
a dog he sat up silently at the window waiting for me to
come back, never understanding that I would; each
absence as terrifying as the last. His devotion might have

been hard to bear at times, but it *was* devotion, inarguable, dark and heavy. I wondered if it might be made light again. It had been so long since I tried to revive our old happiness that for all I knew he might be ready now, lacking only the means to escape his confinement.

With this thought, I sat down opposite him and ventured, gently, 'I say, I wonder if we might host a little dinner. We could invite the Salviatis.'

George looked up, as if startled. Francesco Salviati was one of his old school friends: the closest, now, of these friends, though this was largely owing to the fact that he was our family solicitor. I had never liked Francesco: he was unrelentingly bloody to his reticent wife, reserving his corvine, rather heavily done charm for the war widows and spinsters among his clientele. He never appeared to notice that George had changed in the years since they'd played cricket together, back in the endless afternoon of their schooldays. I found both his inexorable nostalgia (George had told me something of the misery of boarding) and the obliviousness to George as he was now rather suspect; as if Francesco had something missing within his self that prevented him from identifying what was missing now in George.

'You needn't go to any trouble on my account,' George said. 'And you needn't pretend you're fond of Francesco, either.'

'Pretend?' I murmured, half heartedly.

'On our wedding day you called him a cad. As I recall, you thought him a "shifty, polished-up black beetle", and you said he ought to sidle back under—'

'Oh! Do stop. I forget sometimes how accurate your

THE HOUSE OF BIRDS

memory is. As you know, I'd had a little champagne, and really it's too beastly of you to repeat things said after champagne.'

I said it affectionately, and for a moment George almost smiled. His eyes became vague, as if hunting for our wedding day in the distance, trying to make out the two of us, tiny and almost unrecognisable.

'You *were* tight,' he remembered.

'So your mother told me,' I said, laughing. 'She confiscated my coupe.'

George's smile slipped away, then. I hadn't been sure whether the mention of his mother would amuse him or not. She had died before George came back from the war and so had never known him as anything but her darling boy, her pale-haired prince, bright and sweet as the family's blond Labrador puppy. There was a photograph of the two of them, taken one summer the day before the dog slipped its collar and was never seen again. That same day, ten years later, Britain declared a state of war between itself and Germany. George's mother was never persuaded to see the two things as unconnected.

'We might visit your father, now I think of it,' I said, wondering if this would cheer him up, and if not . . . well, the smile was gone now anyway, and was unlikely to reappear. George's father haunted a parsonage in Bedfordshire, white-haired and wraithly and seeming only half present – not one of the table-clattering, crockery-hurling types of ghost, but the abstracted sort, drifting in and out of rooms with his eyes fixed on some other time. As such, he was regarded fondly by the living. I didn't mention George's older brother, who was perfectly pleasant but had not been his mother's darling boy, and – rather like a party guest delicately sparing his hostess awkwardness – had taken himself off to America long before I met George.

'I can't think,' George said. He turned his face away. 'Not today. Must we discuss it now?'

'Of course not, darling. But don't let's leave it too long,' I said; almost saying *too late*, but stopping myself in time. He seemed to hear my meaning anyway, and the absence of a smile deepened in his face. That was exactly what it was, I thought, looking at him: an absence. His expression was certainly not happy, but nor was it sad, or stirred: an utter lack of active feeling that was somehow more desolate than the real thing.

I reflected that, for all the talk of a generation of youth snatched up in the greedy hands of war, the generation *I* had somehow mislaid was the one above. My mother and father and George's mother were dead. George's father was with us, but in name only, and whenever I got a telegram I felt my stomach plunge, certain every time that it would be the announcement that he had made his departure official.

'I could do with having you here now, damn it,' I told the spirits of my parents, as if I might tempt them into reappearing and saying, 'Mind your language, Sophia!' I even wished sometimes for George's mother, who had never much approved of me. A month after the wedding she saw me with a book and said, 'About time you put those aside and started getting on with something important,' before casting a meaningful look in the direction of my stomach – or very possibly my reproductive organs – as if she hadn't been quite clear enough already.

'Ignore her,' George had said later, laughing. His face had been nothing but a different texture in the soft, purplish black. The nights were always darker in that Bedfordshire village, as if they knew what we got up to. His mother's advice had been so hilariously redundant back then, ladled out pompously at a time when the two of us were convinced we had invented sex – or at least were doing a rather better job of it than anybody else. Though George and I had married young and untouched, though we were both shy by nature, and our knowledge of the mysteries of the unlit world beneath the bedsheets (an utterly foreign land, of which few explorers would say what they had seen) was desperately poor, we had somehow worked it out.

I supposed it was love that had been the secret; the codeword. God knows it hadn't been the book of Indian illustrations read in haste in the bedroom of a friend's older brother: the serene-faced lovers lying at odd angles, birds flying stiffly above. Nor had it been the cautionary story about the friend of a cousin of a friend, who, it was said, had enjoyed sex so much that she did it too often, and one day she stood up and all her *innards* (an unwritten rule that this word had to be hissed by the teller of the story) fell out. Even the glimpses I had picked up from books – Ovid, *The Decameron*, the garbled account of *Fanny Hill* whispered to me in the dorm – were confusing rather than instructional. No: George and I had found it out together, eyes closed and hands put forward, like swimmers in dark water, walkers lost in caves, and the revelation of it had been so gorgeous and unlikely that thinking of it now brought tears to my eyes.

If George's mother were around now, she wouldn't have stood for this, I thought. The days of laughing about her advice were over, and now – six stone-cold years later, with the prospect of my own children hovering always in the possible future, never drawing any closer – I might have welcomed her interference. I wondered if George had noticed, in private moments, how unnaturally quiet the house was; how different it would be if the sounds of our family were to rebound from wall to wall, up the stairs and along the hall; if he imagined their faces, both new and familiar, their raucous beauty. But he didn't even appear to notice that I had stopped speaking; he was sunk again in his silence, as if grateful to be released from the conversation.

e-

I left the room feeling sombre, though nobody would have known it from the pleasantly vacant face I wore until I got into my bedroom and closed the door. Once inside, I set about talking myself into a better mood; reminding myself how well the day had gone. I had expected that George would be more concerned by my walking alone than the time I spent away – or even the rather fishy account of how I had sailed so effortlessly into the Bodleian's closely guarded interior – but I could never be quite sure. His admiration of my mania for history was the first thing I loved him for; I hoped it would be the last bastion to fall. He had been one of the only people who *did* admire it, in fact: even my mother (otherwise a perfect mother, good and wise and loving) looked at me with consternation when I said I longed to read history at university. She was worried about my being exposed to ridicule and contempt, though her thoughts never quite hardened into those words. Boll put it more plainly. 'Dear God,' she said. 'You just have to try to shame us, don't you?'

I suppose at this point I shall have to introduce Boll into the history. The time seems right, though ironically Boll herself never could appear on cue, slipping in half an hour after the last latecomer ('You darlings! I didn't think you'd all have waited for *me!*'). But promptly now, without further ado, allow me to present my younger sister. Boll: the bee's knees, the cat's pyjamas; Zuleika Dobson reborn as a narrow-hipped flapper, shaking the dreaming spires awake with her contentious hemlines and knife-edge bob. Her name floated along the Isis like the secret breath of Aphrodite, casting unwary punters on to the rocks. You'd never have guessed she didn't like sex – was terrified of it, in fact – but more of that later. I expect you're dying to meet her. You're in luck; she has arrived just this moment into not only my history but my house.

'Your sister, ma'am,' said Margaret, managing to hide the better part of her disapproval and envy, but not quite all. A teeny, tiny narrowing of the eyes gave her away. I didn't let on that I'd noticed. 'Wasn't she expected . . .'

'An hour ago. I know. Still, would you please bring tea to the morning room, and ask Mrs Boxall to dust off some cakes or something. Thank you.'

I went downstairs. George, with the second sight that

seemed particular to my sister's visitations, had removed himself to a prudently unsociable location; the drawing room as I passed it was empty, fallen into shade.

'Darling,' cried Boll. 'You look *too* divine.'

I glanced down at myself, startled, before realising that this was merely an invitation for me to reciprocally admire Boll herself, resplendent in a mink-collared dress, moving with a faint and mysterious jingle that turned out to be the clash of a new charm bracelet.

'You look rather lovely yourself,' I said, obliging.

We sat in the parlour at the back of the house, the last place to capture the sun, reeling it in to spill over the eau de Nil walls, the satinwood escritoire and the low, elegant sofas. This room had been furnished to my mother's own taste and had not changed since she used to sit here, beginning but never finishing a piece of needlework, her hands dawdling and falling still as she lapsed into one of her reveries. When I was small, I asked her what she was thinking about. 'Thoughts are secret, my dear,' she said. 'If they weren't, I'd have told you them already.'

'So,' I said to Boll, maliciously, 'how's golf?'

Under the Cupid's bow, the rouged cheeks, the curled eyelashes lavish with mascara, I caught sight of a quick, shifty look, before Boll became immediately absorbed in lighting our cigarettes. I sat back, unhurried, as the smoke circled in the air, waiting for her to answer.

'Shut up,' said Boll.

'I expect you'll have forgotten the bet we made?'

'What bet?'

'Indeed. I bet you five pounds that you'd have given the whole thing up within six months. But it's only been a fortnight. I assume something disastrous has happened.'

'If it had, I certainly shouldn't tell you,' Boll said, eyeing me. 'You'd only be beastly about it.'

'Oh, do tell, Boll,' I pleaded. 'I get so little news.'

'I suppose you'll hear about it from Piers anyway. My swing was a little off' – here she lifted her chin; some of her usual swagger having reasserted itself – 'but my stance was beautiful; everybody told me so. It was simply the swing. Anyway, I gave Lottie Cassell a bloody nose. It was too, too shaming.'

'You hit her with the ball?'

'Not exactly.' Boll fiddled with her cigarette case.

'How did you hit her?'

'The wretched club sort of . . . flew out of my hands. I have very small hands, you know. Really they had no business giving me such large clubs. Oh, it was too ghastly. But she ought not to have stood so close behind me. And you can stop smiling, Sophia! Don't be a swine.'

'Oh no, don't be cross, Boll. You're all ruffled and lofty. You look like a cat that has fallen off a sofa.'

'I might have guessed you wouldn't be sympathetic.'

'I am sorry. Really. Tell me, have I seen that brooch before? It's delightful.'

This was a shameless piece of flattery, but Boll was conciliated, and fingered the spray of seed pearls with almost childlike pleasure. I had learned over time how to placate her, because I could never please her: frustrating her either with my mockery, or boring her with what she called my 'bluestocking routine'.

My mother liked to maintain that Boll and I used not to

be so dissimilar; that our characters only diverged on the day of our father's death, a day spoken of so often that it had taken on the weighty, slippery quality of myth. Our father – by turns a frightening barrister, a sentimental husband and a foolishly devoted parent – died of a cancer when I was six. In the flurry of his final days, Boll and I were largely forgotten, hanging uncertainly around the sickroom door as doctors went past; some carrying black bags, some with nurses following on behind like a Greek chorus. At first there was only one doctor, the familiar, sportive Dr Wycombe, who usually attended our family. Then came a specialist, Dr Belleville, who resembled a sea lion, with a silken moustache and irises that floated darkly in his mournful eyes. Then the last doctor, whose name even my mother couldn't remember because he was only there for a few hours. It took Boll and me a long time to stop thinking of this hurried fat man, by association, as the killer of our father.

Nobody knew, in those final days, when exactly my father might leave us. He faded; he rallied, he faded again. Inevitably, our vigilance slipped. It was only by chance that I was in his room at the exact moment of his death. I had wandered in to stand at the foot of the bed – it was likely that I was only there to complain about Boll, or ask for some chocolate. My mother was sitting by my dozing father with her needlework lying untouched in her hands, her eyes dry, the same abstracted blue as always. There seemed nothing out of the ordinary. People often say that they can sense death or disaster coming: some preternatural aware-ness steals over one; there is a sudden change in atmosphere, a shiver up the spine. But I felt none of that. I just happened to be looking at my father as his face gentled, relaxed, and his mouth dropped slightly open. I thought he had fallen asleep until the nurse glanced at him, took his wrist, and said, 'Oh!' Then my mother sprang up, and started to cry.

Poor Boll, who was jumping up and down outside, trying to reach an apple from the tree in the garden, missed the whole thing. According to my mother, this was the moment the two of us took different paths. I, with my glimpse of death, turned serious: took to my books, became prone to thinking too much, stared too long at people's faces – in a way that disconcerted them – while Boll remained exactly the same, blithe and careless as ever, except perhaps with an unconscious note of defiance, a queer sort of childish understanding that the world wanted to catch and sober her if it could, and that she must harden herself to its efforts.

'You didn't bring Daphne,' I said now, disappointed.

'I say! I did mean to bring her along. I quite forgot. She likes seeing you, you know. She isn't quite so maddeningly shy when she's with you. Yes . . . I wish I had brought her.'

Between Boll and her little daughter, Daphne, there was a deep and irreconcilable gulf of understanding. 'I just don't understand it,' Boll said once, mystified. 'Piers and I are so terribly sociable. And it's not as if she's mistreated. Remember our old nurse – what a termagant she was? I can't remember a day going by that I didn't get spanked with the hairbrush . . . how I hated that damned brush. Do you remember when I hid it? But Mrs White is a perfect darling with Daphne. And Piers and I certainly aren't cruel to her. Though God knows she can be trying.' She had glanced at the corner where Daphne was playing, silently, with some old toy soldiers of George's (long since renounced by their original owner), then turned back and confided, 'I tell you, I get the queerest feeling that she *disapproves* of me. Sometimes I just want to take her by the shoulders and demand she tell me what she's thinking.'

'Thoughts are secret,' was what I said then, smiling at the memory. 'Remember that?'

'I haven't the faintest idea what you're talking about,' Boll said.

She looked at me now and said musingly, 'Do you know, I shouldn't be surprised if she ended up like you.'

'Is that such a bad thing?'

Boll didn't answer. She blew a thin stream of smoke into the air between us and watched it rise and collapse, misty in the sunlight. Then she said, 'I hope she doesn't waste all *her* beauty,' and sounded so unexpectedly sad that I couldn't bring myself to tease her.

Daphne was truly a beautiful child, her features hovering strangely between Boll's and my own, nothing at all like our mother's, which were regular and bluntly serviceable, pleasant rather than striking. She had my eye shape and mouth, Boll's dainty brow, and shared the same jaw with us both. It was as if a family argument had been fought over her face, a sibling rivalry: points conceded, ground lost. It seemed remarkable that, having been so much battled over, her little face could look so serene, so calmly adult. I delighted in its occasional lapses into childishness; coaxing a rare cry of excitement from her, or a surprised smile. Afterwards she would return to her usual state of quiet observation, as if she were a miniature fisherman, or a sniper, endlessly patient. When she was very young, she would watch Boll dress in her silks and feathers and apply her make-up; a small face hovering in the corner of the looking glass, unmoving and pale. She never tried to touch anything or ask questions, and indeed Boll often forgot she was there. She shut Daphne in her dressing room several times by mistake, before she was old enough to reach the door handle on her own.

'So, tell me again how Margot got into the Bodleian,' I said, casually.

'Oh no.' Boll put down her tea and stared at me with frank horror. 'Did you try? Sophia, this is just too, too . . .'

'You know, darling, if *you* read more books you mightn't be lost for words so frequently.'

'Too shaming,' finished Boll. 'Why do you want to, that's what I should like to know. It can't simply be the books. It's as if you want to be a *teacher*.' Suspicion disturbed the smoothly powdered surface of her forehead. 'You don't, do you?'

'Actually, I should rather like to be a teacher,' I said.

'What a beast you are,' Boll said, exhaling smoke violently, like a discomposed dragon. 'But I'm not even going to get angry with you. You can't teach once you're married. You're razzing me.'

I quirked my mouth, deliberately equivocal, and Boll took this as confirmation.

'You have a sadistic streak,' she informed me. 'For a moment I truly thought you wanted to be like one of those awful women refusing to give up the jobs they had in the war. I read about it actually – yes, you'll be delighted to hear I do read – a very worry-making piece about what's going to happen to all the poor men without work. God knows why those women are clinging on so. They must be positively unmarriageable. In fact, they probably need the jobs.'

Having thus talked herself into a corner, she stopped abruptly.

'Please do carry on, Boll,' I said. 'I'm longing to hear your conclusions.'

'I suppose you're not being serious. But I can't tell you how depressing it is watching those factory girls trailing home each night, in their artificial silk stockings, making a frightful racket.'

'They have hard lives,' I said. 'Why begrudge them a little pleasure?'

Boll was unimpressed. 'You sound just like a Bolshevik. You know, Piers says your problem is sometimes you don't understand that society is better just as it is. There's a natural order of things, and when you upset the balance, all sorts of ghastly things can happen. Just like' – a note of triumph here, as she managed to reconcile her earlier confusion – 'just like all this equal pay and jobs for women. I must say, one would think you were a plain girl from the way you talk. When you said the other day that you'd have been a suffragette! It wasn't even remotely amusing. And it's not as if you're *poor*, either.'

This last remark glittered in the air for a moment, its sharpness not entirely concealed by the perfumed smoke.

'You're right in one respect,' I said. 'There aren't enough

jobs, and it wouldn't be fair for someone like me to take a teaching position.'

'Well, quite,' said Boll.

'But I like to think that when Daphne's older, it will be unthinkable for girls not to have the same education as boys.'

Boll pulled a face, and said, 'Darling, I *do* hope not. Imagine all the women getting as insufferable and pompous as men,' and at this I couldn't help but laugh.

'Speaking of men, how is Piers?'

I knew Boll wouldn't ask about George. The two of them were such fantastical opposites that the existence of one almost cast that of the other into doubt, and so it suited them both to pretend they had never met. On my side, I rather liked Piers, Boll's husband. A good deal of charm and a passing resemblance to that blond, blue-eyed darling of chocolate-box manufacturers everywhere, the Prince of Wales, accounted for much of Piers' success in life, not least with Boll. Our own parents had hovered equably at the fringes of society: little minnows chasing in the sun-patched shallows, quite content and hardly even aware of the bigger fish striking powerfully upriver, the pikes and fat trout. But Piers' family were very much of the pike variety, something that made a tremendous impact upon a young girl whose acquisitive dreams had hence far been modest: a monogrammed silver cigarette case, a gramophone perhaps, a little sip of champagne here and there.

Piers bought her the lot, and more. He took her to Paris, and to parties where they danced to jazz played by the newest Negro bands (here, I confess, I was silently and terribly envious). When we found out later that Piers' family – rather less enchanted with his prodigious spending – had cut him off, and that he was in fact stony broke, it seemed to us that he and Boll had enjoyed such a great deal of fun that it would be rather mean-spirited to complain. And while he was *persona non grata* with various society hostesses, he retained enough connections to guarantee the two of them a hangover every Sunday morning. Exactly how they afforded it all on Boll's inheritance, which was as modest as her dreams used to be, I didn't like to ask.

'God knows,' said Boll. 'He's off motoring around with some new chum of his. Robert? Robin? I haven't seen him in days.'

When Boll went home, leaving the characteristic scent of gardenias and her Gitanes (an oft-mentioned reminder of her time in Paris) to drift invisibly in the hall, I went to find George. He was in his room, sunk in one of the blank, desolate moods that seemed at times to swallow him, leaving only a glimpse of a man's shape, seen ripplingly as if through fathoms of water, a night drowning. When I came in, he raised his hand; a slight movement, hovering for a few brief moments above the flannel of his knee, but one I understood. I wished him goodnight and went to my own room.

These dark moods of George's usually ended in nightmares; I would hear him sometimes crying out in the night, a muffled noise passing through layers of plaster and brick, softened like the crackling of bombs falling on distant houses. Then, if I stayed awake longer, I would hear him get out of bed to walk around the house. He always followed the same pattern; going downstairs at first, into the drawing room, then the dining room, the back parlour, even the kitchen and pantry. Having completed this round – I had begun to think of it as a patrol – he would return upstairs to check each empty bedroom one by one, finishing at my door, where he would break stride for a moment, as if faltering, before going back into his own room, and shutting the door.

Some nights I would hear him walk around more than once before dawn. I wasn't certain whether these night walks of his were connected to his nightmares, or if I only heard them after his nightmares had disturbed my sleep. I didn't feel able to ask him about it. The first night I heard him making his rounds I thought him a burglar, and cast about, half asleep, for something to use as a weapon. Then I identified the unevenness of his walk: one footstep dotting down lightly, the other over-emphasised, and lay back first in relief, then in growing bafflement. In the morning I asked, 'Couldn't you sleep last night, darling?'

He blinked, then looked away and said, 'No, I slept very soundly,' his unnecessary firmness making obvious both the lie and the impossibility of questioning it.

But that night it was I who slept badly; dreaming of my mother, who had lost her needlework and was wandering from room to room, crying out for something she had never paid attention to.

'Why do you want it so badly?' I asked her, but her

blue eyes were soft and far-off, and I knew she couldn't hear me.

My mother died of the Spanish flu in 1919, one day a solid, familiar middle-aged woman, the next a quarantined outline – shockingly small – in a bed that was later burnt, giving off a strange scent of the cinnamon she thought would cure her. So soon after the war her death seemed to me a nasty, stupid joke; like emerging from a lengthy recuperation in hospital and being hit by a motor car. Accordingly, I was both baffled and angered by it. At her funeral we stood in a drizzling fine summer rain; not so much mournful as irritating. My hair, pressed close to my head by my hat, felt hot and scratchy; like somebody else's hair. I had expected that in my grief, small things would be dwarfed by the tragedy at hand, and it was an unpleasant surprise to realise that they had become intolerable. The dolorous music and speeches washed over me, murky as the water swirling into the gutters. People got up as black beetles stroked my cheek and my arms until my skin felt quite worn down with sympathy. It took a long time before I stopped feeling angry about my mother's death, at which point a sadness settled over me instead, quiet and deep, like an overnight snow.

When I finally fell back into sleep, I dreamt that I was standing outside the Bodleian at night, the moon staring at me, wide and white with fright. I was waiting for Christopher. At some point I knew that he would never come.

The sense of this clung to me even when the arrival of Margaret in the morning restored the real world, with a clink of china and the rising steam of the tea, jolting the curtains open and remarking, 'It's a fine day today, ma'am. Out again, are you?'

'Yes, I shall be out for most of the morning, I expect,' I said, doubtfully. Already I struggled to recall what Christopher looked like; already he was improbable, an impression of his face arriving and leaving intermittently, as if he were one of the shifting, vaporous people one encountered only in a dream, and eventually forgot.

George was sleeping late, and I left the house without seeing him. When I was a not-so-small child, sometimes when my mother was looking for me, calling from room to room, some hitherto-hidden beastliness would prevent me from answering immediately. The longer it went on, the more the urge to hide would grow, until I would feel a quite unreasonable panic grip me at the thought of being discovered. This morning I felt as if I were playing that asinine game again, and the closer I got to leaving without encountering George, the more desperately I needed to do it, until finally I stepped out of the front door with a crash of relief, a giddy light-heartedness that made me want to cry out, or run down the street in triumph.

As if I still had one foot in the world of dreams and one in the everyday, the streets of Oxford seemed unfamiliar to me that morning. It was another bright day, with hefty white clouds passing over the sun; the sheets of light and shade dropping down abruptly, feeling almost solid. The many spires of the city looked to me like something elves might have built, or goblins: ornate stone palaces with towers like upturned stalactites, an intricate inverted city on the roof of a cave, reflected in a subterranean pool. The students in their black gowns massed like over-sized crows; even the bicycles lining the railings looked unaccountably foreign. The small child asking persistently next to me, 'Mummy, may I have an ice? Mummy? *When* may I have an ice?' might as well have been speaking Siamese.

As I approached the Bodleian, I saw Christopher standing by the door. He was facing half away from me, in the direction of the sun, wearing a pale fawn suit and soft homburg, smoking a cigarette and watching a magpie bounce insolently along the flags. The fat clouds had all but cleared out, and his face was almost unknowable in the bright light, yet I recognised him immediately. He had not seen me, and the unexpected freedom of not being spotted stopped me in my tracks.

My dear and sharp-eyed reader, you might now recall the picture with which I opened this history: a woman standing defiantly in the centre of the quad, as if she had a perfect right to be there, glaring up at the formidable towers before her. Consider now this rather sorry image: the same woman hovering at the very edge of the picture, almost unnoticeable, paralysed with some mysterious fright. What the devil was wrong with her? I didn't know, myself. (Or: I didn't know myself. Both were true, then.)

I will tell you a secret: what galvanised me finally was not the prospect of the library itself – for that had become a thing too much hoped for to feel real, somehow – but the memory of my own laughter the last time Christopher and I spoke. It was not my usual social laugh, a practised, restrained jingle, like the clashing of Boll's charm bracelet. It was a true laugh, and I felt its unfamiliarity;

the disruption of it bright and almost painful, like ice floes breaking up. I made jokes – yes – but without real humour. I had become sardonic without amusement, flippant but not light-hearted. The last time I had laughed was with Daphne, and that was a queer feeling too: a small jolt of happiness, reminding me how strange happiness had become.

Later, I thought about that moment of hesitation. It was moments like this, I supposed, that constituted history – albeit on a grander scale – sending it one way or another, tumbling irrevocably into the future. In my own case, I raised my hand and smiled, and walked over to where he stood, on the neat line dividing the shadow from the sun, his own hand lifted to shade his eyes from the light, as if in a salute.

PART TWO

OLIVER

The arrival of Oliver's train at Paddington was a jolt, shunting him rudely back into his own life an hour after he had left it. His eyes – having got used to following each curl and twizzle of Sophia's elegant hand, tracking its path as diligently as a pair of bloodhounds – blinked and teared up when he raised them back to the modern world: the fluorescent lights overhead, the people filing along the aisle to disembark, bundling past in a bulky cascade of coats and bags, a rapid hammering of voices. This sense of complete and utter alienation only lasted a moment, however, and he was able to insinuate himself into the press of bodies as it tailed off, tucking the *Revised History of the House of Hanover* back into his pocket as he left the train and moved off under the great glass arches of the station, making for the hotly breathing mouth of the Underground.

Even the damply overfamiliar return of the everyday – the usual stops of his line, the eviscerated newspaper blanketing the red and blue seats, the presence of a large man to his right emitting a disturbing low rumbling noise (Oliver had no idea where from) – could not destroy the enchantment. Was enchantment the right word? He felt like *this* was the enchantment: the train, the man, Oliver himself. Real life was Sophia, hesitating in her lucid Oxford morning, wondering if she should cross the square. He often felt at odds with the present day after watching too much television, but it didn't usually persist as long as this feeling, which lingered with him as he walked home, ate a sandwich bought from the supermarket and drank a glass of wine, slightly perturbed by the uncharacteristic emptiness of the flat; the absence of another human to remind him what Oliver himself was.

He texted Kate: *Found old diary in the house. Was it once owned by a couple called Sophia and George?* Then he saw this wouldn't do and sent another: *I love you. Hope all's well. No Calverts today.* She didn't reply, and he realised that in New York, Kate was still at work. The last thing he had seen of her was an update across her social media accounts, showing herself with a glass of wine in the airport's business-class lounge. Oliver privately wished she wouldn't do stuff like that. But then all their friends did it, and Kate said that if she didn't, it was like letting everybody else down, because they had shared and she ought to share back: carefully edited pictures of infinity pools, hotel bedrooms, sunlight reflecting stingingly from the bonnets of brand-new cars. No clinked champagne flute escaped the winking eye of her smartphone, and once this was done, she became impatient to finish up and move on to the next thing. In a near-argument (as close as they ever got) in the Piazza San Marco, he once accused her of seeing things not personally but from the perspective of her online audience.

'But what's wrong with that?' she said. 'I see something and I want to share it.'

'But *why* do you want to share it?'

'Why do you want to keep things to yourself? You're like

a hoarder – of moments. If you think about it, *you're* being selfish.'

Oliver, derailed, had abandoned his attempts to articulate what he meant. It had been a long afternoon of Bellinis, and it didn't seem worth it. He wondered now what would happen to their history if the internet were switched off, but he was too tired to pursue the thought. He lay on the empty double bed among the varying shades and textures of whiteness, took out Sophia's manuscript, and promptly fell asleep.

He found Kate's reply in the morning: *Having a blast. Wish you were here though. No idea who Sophia and George are. Old diary . . . WTF?*

He was sharply disappointed that Sophia wasn't anything to do with them; slightly peeved, even, as if she had misled him. His feeling of immersion in her world had cleared with the arrival of the morning, and standing inhaling the bracing black steam of his coffee, he felt a little like he had woken up from a one-night stand, remembering his drunken declarations of undying love with vague embarrassment. The diary, or history – whatever it was – lay where it had been left in the bedsheets. He texted Kate back (*Don't worry, it's not that interesting*) and went to have a shower.

e~

On his first day back at the house, Oliver's existence slowly folded into a welter of *stuff*, as he roamed the abandoned rooms like a Blitz survivor, picking over the heaped and meaningless possessions of Kate's distant relatives.

'Just strip the place and sell everything, or chuck it out,' Kate said on the phone, when they got a chance to speak.

Oliver had found out why the house was in such a surreal condition when he had arrived: Kate had already begun to clear it. 'Don't you remember? It was when I first heard about it. I went down there and hired a skip.' He did remember, vaguely: one day a couple of months ago, when he was barely aware of the sudden bequest, submerged as he was at work, walking at five in the morning out into the clammy grey dawn, moving through the Underground like a dead man, getting home at nine with his head scratchy and dim, his last bit of energy sighed out somewhere between Farringdon and Whitechapel. 'It was too much for me, though. And too much for the skip. I filled it up and the house was still full of rubbish.'

'How did you decide what to put in the skip and what to sell?' Oliver asked.

'I saved the good stuff and threw out the junk,' Kate said, sounding mystified. 'It's pretty obvious, isn't it?'

Oliver conceded this, trying not to think of how much good stuff, quietly modest about its provenance, might have been taken for junk, and how much junk might have flashily passed itself off as good stuff. Though it was true that almost everything was junk. The set of plastic tumblers decorated with sunflowers, the dusty tinsel, the defunct microwave. He had taken everything out of the bedrooms, leaving the echoing rooms with only the mysterious dark silhouettes bleached into their wallpaper, ready to be stripped off and begun again. He put anything that seemed significant in the drawing room: a delicate fringed lamp, a set of gold-embellished saucers without teacups, a 1960s chair, stacks of mirrors and paintings, more piles of old books. He wasn't sure how much of his collection was practical and how much sentimental. As he worked his feelings towards the house had changed; the initial sense of not spookiness exactly, but *oddness*, having subsided, making way for a kind of affection that he liked to think was mutual.

'So, what was all that about a diary?' Kate asked.

'Well, I'm not sure it's even a diary. It calls itself a history of a family called Hanover, but their surname is Louis.'

'There haven't ever been any Hanovers or Louis at the house,' Kate informed him. 'And I've now been emailed all the family crap from the solicitor, so I ought to know.'

'No Sophia? No George? Boll and Piers?'

'Nope.'

'Oh. Well, anyway, I'm not sure if it's fictional or if it's really the story of her – Sophia's – life.'

'Is it interesting?'

'Well, she's just managed to get into the library . . .' Oliver began.

Kate started to laugh. 'Sounds *wild*.'

'It's more interesting than I've made it seem,' Oliver said, defensively.

'I'll take your word for it. Anyway, I'd better go. I'll call when I can. I'm not sure when I'll get opportunities to talk . . . they've really booked me up in the evenings. I'm going to be knackered.' But below this exaggerated ruefulness, there was excitement: Kate thrived on the rush and the exhaustion, shrugging off jet lag like a winter coat and readying her work smile, going gladly into the noise and the light, nailing Mai Tais with the head of accounts.

Oliver contemplated the quieted phone in his hand; the return of the silence in the house. He looked at Sophia's history, lying on a little inlaid table in the crowded drawing room. He felt guilty at having represented her so poorly – an irrational desire for her not to be misjudged, or dismissed – but at the same time there was relief at it still being just the two of them: Oliver and Sophia, reader and writer. More than that, he didn't want Sophia's pages to be exposed to the sceptical skim of Kate's descending eye; her gaze narrowing with bafflement, turning away with a shrug.

By the time evening came, he felt himself and the house to be on such good terms that it seemed natural for him to stay the night. He had got the water and electricity switched back on, and something about the underlying trickle and buzz of its arteries – the gentle pops of the floorboards, like cracking knuckles, flexing underfoot – made the place feel like a living home again. He liked, too, the quality of the light in its interior, an illumination that felt soft and sheer, perhaps owing to the age of the windows that filtered it: glass of true refinement, refusing to allow the light to shoulder brashly in; forcing it to be patient, to be subtle.

He dragged the newest-looking mattress into the only bedroom with a curtain rail, a room at the back of the house, the window of which had captured something of the overgrown garden beyond, a bright scene netted in grey ropes of wisteria. When the sun went down, he realised from the volume of its hooting that an owl had set up home somewhere near the window; possibly in the room itself. He gave up and went downstairs instead, towing his mattress into the sitting room and taking the curtains with him, draping the dirt-spotted velvet somewhat haphazardly over the window, where it did the job of smothering the light with a heavy finality. He reflected with some satisfaction on this den he had created; his sleeping on a strange nest of his collected treasure, like an unambitious dragon. He thought about uploading a picture online – *New pad!* – just to baffle their friends.

He was too tired to read the history again that night, and over the rest of the week work on the house prevented him from finishing it. He had always been a diligent worker. When he was young, his parents were fond of telling a story (from which nobody was safe; not at the school gate, not at dinner parties, and certainly not at parents' evenings) about how they once left a six-year-old Oliver sitting in the garden near a pile of bricks taller than him, ready to be turned into a wall, and when they came back he had built the wall himself. Of course it was structurally unsound and had to be taken down, but his parents' audience always marvelled, dutiful and on cue, at Oliver's industriousness. Over twenty years on, he thought, and he was still living up to the legend of that bloody wall.

It had been a long time since he had taken true pleasure in his work. At his firm, labour was an urgent and miserable thing, and sometimes he felt like it was being physically compressed out of him, his body shrinking as he sat at his desk. Here at the house he felt something of the satisfaction he might have felt as a child, sitting in the garden, stacking up his bricks. It hadn't left him with much time to read, however. He had woken up the last few mornings lying awkwardly on the mattress, the pages of Sophia's history in his hand, his eyes having refused to reacquaint themselves with its handwriting. But despite this, and despite his disappointment at the lack of family ties with Sophia, some kind of connection persisted. He found that scraps of her writing often floated back to him at odd moments; randomly evoked images or phrases. He understood what she meant when she said that thinking too much about something could make it seem almost unreal; actually, he felt the same as she did about a lot of things. Her sense of dream and reality within her everyday life was like his own: both of them seemed often unsettled, not quite at home with their surroundings. Past and present, dream and reality; these things slid and shivered in the corner of the eye, never quite sharpening into focus.

Kate called him later that week, in the small window of time in which they were both awake and she was at leisure; the phone balanced between her shoulder and ear as she dried herself from the shower and got into her evening clothes.

'How's it all going?' she asked. 'The house, I mean. And . . . anything else. Stuff in general?'

Oliver started to tell her about the work he had done, embarking on a lengthy justification of the interesting things he had found and preserved. By the time he realised he had gone on too long, Kate had already picked out an answer from his ramblings – like a squirrel neatly extracting a seed from its casing – and was on to the next topic.

'So it's going well. I booked the garden man, by the way, he's coming tomorrow. He didn't mind it being a Saturday. Oh, and there's good news. I've looked at the solicitor's stuff and it seems – he's pretty sure – the Calverts don't have much of a case about the will. But I got a ridiculous voicemail from one of them asking to meet up and discuss it, and then another, angrier one saying that we can't work on the house in the meantime. They sounded pretty furious.'

'What?' Oliver said, alarmed. 'What do you think they might do?'

'Well I don't think they're going to murder you, if that's what you're worried about,' Kate said, clearly amused. 'What *can* they do? Maybe stay out of dark alleyways for a while, though, just in case.'

'Ha,' said Oliver, glancing out of the window at the unyielding night of the street. 'What is it exactly their argument is based on?'

'Oh, that the house should have gone to some great-aunt or something, on the Calvert side of the family, but that there wasn't a will, and so it went by default to someone's husband instead – Tom Castle – on *our* side of the family. It's complicated. I'll meet up with Mr Hunt and deal with it all properly when I'm back. He says there's plenty of time.'

'You're sure you want me to carry on? With the house, I mean.'

'Why not? You aren't really frightened of a few little Calverts, are you?'

Oliver laughed. 'Absolutely not.'

But despite his claim, he found himself peering out of the sitting-room window again before he went to bed. One of the plastic curtain rails had fallen down under the dusty weight of the velvet drapes he had rigged up, so he had been sleeping without them, waking when the sun rose. At night he couldn't help but feel exposed, the lamp glowing behind him and the road beyond invisible, lit only by passing cars like white will-o'-the-wisps. Any Calvert could walk up and look in if he or she wanted – take in every detail of his odd nest, the mattress on the floor, the piled valuables – and Oliver wouldn't even know. Squinting out into the road, he felt like a mouse: Calverts circling above like owls in the darkness, seeing him – *knowing* him – though he knew nothing about them.

The next morning Oliver got up, looked out of the window to reassure himself once more of the emptiness of the sunlit street, and was startled to see a woman standing on the path to the front door. ('Startled' was how he would later put it; in fact he jumped violently, then fell still, his heart squeaking and flailing as if he really were a mouse in the grip of an owl.) It took a few moments to establish that the woman had not seen him standing transfixed; that with the balance of light and dark no longer on her side, she might not even have been able to see through the window. Moreover, she was looking at the front door without anger or discernible intent. If anything, she appeared uncertain. Possibly she had got the wrong house. Oliver looked more closely at her, but she had turned away, gazing down the road, and all he got was a brief impression – a small body in a large jumper, a lot of hair – before she appeared to come to a sudden decision, marched up the steps to the front door and rang the bell.

The noise released Oliver; whatever enchantment had rooted him to the spot fell away, but he still didn't know what to do with himself. He backed away from the window and stood against the wall, as far out of her possible line of sight as he could get, and wondered whether to answer the door, now that there was a possibility of *not* answering it. He considered the arguments against. Firstly, he was wearing a pair of track-suit bottoms and an old T-shirt, a joke gift worn exclusively for decorating (and, more recently, sleeping), with the word *Gangsta* above a picture of a cat with a gun, and which he felt put him at something of a disadvantage. Secondly, she could be a Calvert. The real thing, live and kicking and only metres away. She rang again, the bell that had always sounded rather portentous, and never more so than now, reverberating through the empty house like a terrible gong.

The second ring made up Oliver's mind. He had already left it too long to answer. He would just wait it out. He pressed himself mulishly against the wall (reminded, briefly, of the day he and Kate hid in the garden from an imagined Aunt Delia), making sure all his extremities were out of sight of the window – which, it now occurred to him, he had left open.

He craned his neck to establish that the window was defi-nitely open. It was. If the woman came back down to the steps and looked at the house, she would notice it, if indeed she hadn't already. Evidence that somebody was home – or worse, that nobody was home, leaving her free to put her head inside to take a look.

With a baffled groan at both the general malice of the universe and his own blundering efforts within it, Oliver went to answer the door, flinching as he collided with the heavy brass wave of the third clang of the bell. He swung it open to let in a sudden amount of light and the irritated stare of the woman on the step, who moved back slightly and said, 'Oh!'

'Hello,' Oliver said.

'I thought you weren't going to answer,' the woman said, by way of explanation. She seemed put out that he had.

'Well,' Oliver said, unsure of the correct response. 'Here I am.'

'Right.' She looked at him with no apparent lessening of her hostility. 'I'm Lena. You've probably heard from my parents – Mr and Mrs Godwin.'

Alarms shrieked. Lights flashed. The Godwins. The worst of the Calverts. Oliver's composure dissolved into a collection of squabbling impulses. His middle-class politeness answered, 'I'm Oliver Mittell,' as his eyes widened with what must have been unconcealed dismay. His hand half rose to shake hers before he realised what it was up to, and put it firmly into his pocket.

'So can I come in?' she asked.

There was a moment of silence, in which she took him in, the three-day stubble, the T-shirt, his vacillating in the doorway like a damp towel hung in the wind. Then, with a dismissive 'Ffh!' noise, she stepped inside, and he found himself moving back to let her past.

'You're Kate's . . .?' she asked, and he looked at her blankly. 'Husband?' she supplied. 'Fiancé, boyfriend, relative? Or just a really dedicated builder?'

Oliver didn't answer immediately, struck with guilt at the thought that whatever hopes he might have had about becoming the first or even second of these were now on very shaky ground. Even the third was in some doubt.

Lena was looking at him with suspicion, as if wondering whether he had anything to do with the house at all – was perhaps in the midst of a burglary, or simply squatting. He couldn't say, either, that there wasn't some truth in this.

'Boyfriend,' he said, conscious of the silliness of the word. Lena received this information with due contempt, only raising her eyebrows, then turned away to look with interest at the interior of the house. She walked out of the hall towards the sitting room, Oliver following behind, with no real idea of how to stop her. As she stood in the doorway, apparently silenced by the oddness of the Aladdin's cave before her, his initial flusterment died down somewhat and without her dark, displeased eyes on him – holding him blackly while giving nothing of their own away – he took the opportunity to look at her properly. She was a little shorter than him; apparently thin, though it was hard to tell under her heavy-knit pullover, which looked like it had belonged to a man, its collar and cuffs large, and starting to unravel and fray at the edges, as if the heat of her annoyance had fried them. He felt slightly scorched himself. Yet even in the midst of his horror at her being here in the house – his worry over what she might do – he found a moment to wonder what she would be like when she was at rest. Because, without apparently taking much care to be so, she was an unusually good-looking woman: black curly hair, lowered dark eyebrows, a simmering crème de cacao glow to her skin.

She swung back to face him and he tried not to flinch. 'What *are* you doing here?' she asked. 'Are you living here?'

'Ah, yes. Sort of.' Thinking of how to explain it now, to a hostile stranger, he realised how strange it was, to have intended to go back to London each night, and then to just . . . *not*. At his and Kate's apartment his clothes would still be lying on the floor, a half-finished cup of coffee turning opaque in the kitchen. Probably a light or two left on, knowing him. He had abandoned his home for this new life on a floor in a dilapidated house in Oxford, where he knew nobody, lived on takeaways and wine he drank from a lone brandy snifter, and felt obscurely, defiantly content. In the end he said, simply, 'It seemed easier to stay here at night.'

He might have imagined it, but for the first time Lena's air of disapproval appeared to give way to something a little gentler, an almost imperceptible softening of her mouth, a hint of the possibility of amusement, even if it was not quite the real thing.

Then he added, without thinking, 'Only until it's finished,' and the look – if it had ever existed – was gone.

'*Finished*,' she said, in a slow, meaningful voice that did not seem to bode well for Oliver. 'So what is it exactly you're doing? What will the house look like when it's *finished*? Talk me through it.'

If Oliver had been more prepared for this conversation – better informed, or at least better dressed – he might have been able to evade her; to slip and sidle out of danger. But he was caught for the moment between two panicky impulses, the first being to beg her to stop saying *finished* like that, the second being an obedient impulse to tell her everything. So he did the latter, and there was a painful while in which he recited Kate's plans – to turn the box room into an en suite, install a downstairs loo, knock down the pantry wall to create a kitchen/breakfast room, combine the sitting and dining rooms into one large open-plan living space – just like an estate agent, if ever an estate agent had to enumerate the many desirable features of their spacious five-bedroom family home while their client stared at them furiously, curling up her hands as if she were about to hit them.

'Those rooms are big enough already,' Lena snapped. 'What did you have in mind, a basketball court?'

'Haha,' Oliver said, warily.

'Haha? That's not laughing. That's just saying haha. Why did you say that?'

'Because I'm uncomfortable, and I have no idea what else to say.'

Lena seemed to respect this. She shrugged. 'Fair enough.'

But if Oliver had any hopes for a reprieve, he was to be disappointed. Lena had already turned to the large marble fireplace. 'Look at this!' she said, loud with new outrage. 'You're going to pull this wall down and take all the fireplaces with it? It's ridiculous. It's . . . it's disrespectful to the spirit of the place.

Why can't you just buy a brand-new glass cube or something? This will never be what you two want it to be.'

As soon as the words were spoken Oliver felt their basic truth, chiming with something embryonic in his own mind; but these were new thoughts, untried and unexplored, and the need to defend himself from harm required more immediate attention. 'We're not going to live here,' he said hastily, but this only seemed to make her angrier.

'Of course you're fucking not. You're going to "develop" it. Fucking yuppies. Did you watch a programme on it and thought you'd give it a try? No, stop, it was a rhetorical question. Jesus! Not only are you profiting from a crime – and you know that you are, whatever anyone says, because people don't just vanish – you're going to ruin a beautiful house! Listen, you can't go ahead with your plans, whatever they are. It doesn't matter if they're good plans or insane plans – and they're insane, by the way, just in case you're in any doubt about that – you can't work on it. Not until the dispute is legally resolved. If you do anything else besides making weird piles of fucking bric-a-brac, we'll be *on* you. You'll be in serious trouble.'

'Okay,' Oliver said. He sensed that the right thing to do was to say as little as possible, in the hope that her anger would exhaust itself. Miraculously, it seemed to work. Lena stepped back and sighed, as if acknowledging that he was not a worthy opponent. Her black gaze moved off him and on to the nearest stack of possessions, which happened to be the books he had investigated on his first day.

'Why *have* you piled all this stuff up anyway?' she asked.

'I didn't think it was junk,' he said, then added, 'That's not an expert opinion.'

'So you're not chucking it all in another skip, then.'

'Of course not.'

'You sound shocked,' she observed. 'Yet a while ago, you two managed to fill a skip with all sorts of valuables. I saw it. You're fucking right it's not an expert opinion' – here she mimicked not only his accent but his voice with a surprising degree of accuracy – 'throwing out deco lamps and Ercol tables. You smashed half that tea set over there and saved the rest. You people are actually mad.'

Oliver felt it disloyal to admit to Lena that he and Kate had not exactly been operating as a team, but was unable to resist a hopeful 'Did you manage to salvage anything?'

She looked surprised, then suspicious. 'What I could, yes. What do you want – the money? Because I can tell you—'

'No! I just wanted to know.'

She looked at him with confusion, and then, with a final, heartfelt 'Mad!', she turned and walked back towards the hall, like an offended party guest.

Oliver went after her, his fright having had time to make room for some curiosity. But she didn't allow him any questions of his own. Instead she turned at the door and gave him one last angry look – landing hard, so that he stopped and blinked – and warned, 'Don't forget. You tap just one brick with a hammer, and you'll be in *deep shit.*'

⌒

After Lena left, Oliver, somewhat spooked, was reluctant to take up arms against the house, and ignored the calls from the contractors he had so minutely researched days earlier. It was too early to call Kate and see what she thought; and in any case he wasn't sure what he would tell her. There was nothing more to clear, and the skip had been hoisted away. He was left in a silence made deeper by its echoing bareness, all the empty rooms seeming to wait for him, as if left similarly at a loss. He and the house looked at each other and mouthed, *So what do we do now?*

The doorbell, with impeccable comedic timing, answered them both with another of its great sonorous bongs. Oliver wondered if Lena had got halfway down the street, realised she had forgotten one of her threats, and was waiting now on the doorstep with a raised finger and an 'And furthermore . . .' ready on her lips. He went reluctantly to answer it, and found not Lena but a genial-looking young man in a grey suit.

'You must be Oliver,' the man said, putting out his hand. 'I'm Mark. Mark O'Reilly? From Luxter and Sons?' Failing to provoke the look of comprehension he was hoping for, he added, 'I've come about the garden?'

'Oh, right. Sorry. Kate did tell me about that. It's been a strange morning.' Oliver wondered why the gardener had come in a suit. Perhaps that was what all gardeners wore these days, between jobs. God knows he'd never hired one before. The man was carrying nothing but a folder, which was also confusing. 'Ah, do you need to get changed somewhere?' he asked. 'Get your things ready?'

Now Mark looked confused, as if Oliver's bafflement – an airborne virus – had made its way over to him. 'Get changed?' he asked.

'I just . . . Never mind. Er . . . you did bring your own tools, didn't you? Only I don't think we have any here. I think I saw a pair of shears in the garden the other day, but they looked pretty rusty.'

Mark's chin went up and his mouth opened in an 'ah' shape of dawning comprehension. 'Oliver, I think there's been a mix-up. I'm here to look at the garden and advise you on how much of it you can sell, as a plot of land. To maximise the value of the property you've got here.'

'A plot . . . for what?'

'For one, maybe two new residential units. Houses.'

'Oh,' Oliver said. 'Okay.'

'So, shall we go and have a look?' Mark said, gesturing at the side of the house as if he were the homeowner, escorting the slow and stupid land agent into the garden. Oliver accepted his role and followed him.

Aside from an initial glance from the kitchen window at the vast and tangled wilderness of the back garden – less vast and more tangled than his childhood memory – he hadn't explored it further. Now the two of them stood at the edge of a thigh-high expanse of grass, quivering under a breeze dusted with pollen and tiny butterflies, lapping at the trees that bordered the garden. A large oak was identifiable in the distance; another tree stood bowed and alone in what must once have been the centre of the lawn. The ivy he remembered, and the water butt with its spinning constellation of flies. A bird he couldn't identify struck a single metallic note from a mass of honey-suckle that had spilled from the neighbour's garden over the fence and onto an old trestle table.

They both put their hands up to their eyes to survey the scene, though it seemed unnecessary; the light feeling so soft, the garden steeped in it, a gold haze gathered over the green. Mark talked, and Oliver hardly heard, tipping his face up to the sun without exactly realising that was what he was doing. The warmth infused his closed eyelids. It seemed miraculous how long the September heatwave, the grace period, had held. He remembered Sophia's hard spring sunlight with its sting of hostility; the heavy, thick heat that had surrounded him and Kate as they stood in this spot. This sun, years older and wiser, felt more mellow; more benevolent. It lingered with its grateful public like a movie star bestowing smiles and autographs, leaving its waiting limousine to dawdle at the kerb.

Oliver opened his eyes. Mark was still talking.

'It should net you quite a tidy sum,' he was saying. 'These old houses are great in that sense; all that garden space going to waste. So much potential.'

'I'm sorry,' Oliver interrupted him. 'But we don't want to sell any of the garden.'

'You . . .? But your wife . . .'

'Our circumstances have changed since you spoke to her. I'm afraid we aren't able to sell any of the land. It's a complicated legal situation.' He started walking back around to the front of the house, Mark having no choice but to follow. Oliver carried on talking – 'I'm very sorry to have wasted your time. If I'd realised the appointment was today, I'd have phoned the office, but – as you know – I thought you were a gardener. It's miscommunication all round, I'm afraid. Hope you haven't come too far. Sorry. Thank you for taking the time to visit' – until he had walked Mark back to his car, interposing his body between the agent and the house like a security guard, or a sheepdog, manoeuvring the man into the vehicle, and finally thumping twice on the roof for good measure, something he had only previously seen on television but which struck him now as a suitably authoritative gesture.

Even after Mark was gone Oliver felt inexplicably angry. He walked back around to the garden and into the grass, brushing his palms over its flowering heads. Money, money. It seemed he couldn't escape it. He felt it hard in his throat and stomach, as if he had swallowed it, tasting like poison, the bloody tang of copper on his tongue. He thought about his substantial savings – though not substantial enough for Manhattan, or, for that matter, Canary Wharf. He thought about his work, beginning and ending in the dark; the cocaine, the cheerfully brutal meetings, his boss saying, 'Tired? I don't give two shits about tired. The only thing I care about is fifty million pounds, which is the value of this deal. If you're worth over fifty million pounds, feel free to go ahead and fuck it up. Are you worth fifty million pounds, Oliver? What do you think?'

Oliver picked up the shears that lay near the kitchen wall. Then he began, methodically and furiously, to cut the grass. The shears were aged and stiff; his hands blistered almost immediately. Green piled at his feet. His arms started to ache. Little blue butterflies got prudently out of the way. An investigative robin came and went. Gradually, about a quarter of the way across the lawn, his fury subsided. He was standing underneath the tree in the centre, and he realised that the grass around him was full of fallen apples. A few were left in the branches above, green and rose-coloured and untouched by wasps. He picked one and ate it ruminatively. It was sharp but good. Standing in the tree's shade, he was reminded of something; not a part of his day with Kate, but something else, some other stirring of childhood perhaps; a memory he couldn't quite get hold of. The more he focused on it, the more it receded, until he had to admit defeat.

Recognising that the rest of the lawn was beyond his abilities, Oliver found a pair of gloves and went to tackle the smaller garden at the front of the house, where better results could be had in a shorter space of time. As he worked, he tried to move the watchful spiders that lived here out of the way of the devastation. Impressed by the intricacy of their leopard-like amber markings, he tried, unsuccessfully, to capture one on his phone; then, getting fed up with the phone's persistent buzz and trill, dropped it back into the house through the open window. Finally he addressed the delicate work; gently detangling the clematis from the wisteria, the honeysuckle from the laurel, repinning them in place. He realised he was almost surreally happy.

A neighbour – an older man in a Barbour – went by, glancing at him with interest and a tinge of scepticism. An hour later he returned with a shopping bag and, seeing that Oliver was still there, hailed him cheerfully. Oliver – feeling he had passed some sort of test, of actual-personhood – chatted to him for several minutes, in which it became apparent that the neighbour believed Oliver was moving in and Oliver did not exactly correct him. He found he was enjoying the place the house must have in communal memory; the solidity of its history, layered deeper and deeper over the years. It went with the growing protectiveness he felt about it: his reluctance to portion it up and sell off the pieces. At the same time, he knew that this was an entirely imaginary custodianship, and an inappropriate one. He was bedding himself in like a bit of grit in an oyster, hoping to be changed into a pearl purely by association. If Kate could see him now, she would be baffled. If Lena could hear him, she would be disgusted. He had the feeling that Lena was watching him scornfully, as he nodded in agreement with the neighbour – including himself in the story of the house, in local tradition, without having done anything to earn it, while planning secretly to betray and mutilate it.

The neighbour, oblivious to Oliver's internal wranglings, spoke warmly of Aunt Delia, touching briefly on the house's much-disputed ownership – 'Nothing causes trouble like a will, eh?' – before skimming off the subject, dragonfly-like, and remarking gratifyingly that the garden hadn't looked so good in years. 'Poor Delia wasn't able to look after it, at her age,' he said, and Oliver nodded sympathetically, as if he were completely familiar with Delia's declining years.

When he went back inside to fish for his phone behind a crockery-covered stool, he found a text from Hugh, a colleague of his – a good friend – which was both polite and deeply uncomfortable. It seemed strange that less than a month ago they had been doing coke together at a friend's birthday strip-club jaunt, watched by two tolerant girls in nipple tassels. It wasn't his exclusion from that life that Oliver minded: in fact, he preferred crouching in the long grass, the still sunlight, relocating spiders. But the speed at which their easiness had disappeared bothered him. He got the impression Hugh wished Oliver himself would disappear, to save on awkwardness. The text finished with a stiffly phrased enquiry: what did Oliver plan to do next?

'That, dear Hugh,' Oliver said aloud, 'is the fifty-million-pound question.'

He called Kate that evening, after he had showered the mud off his arms and the leaves out of his hair in the pink-tiled bathroom, and eaten his third takeaway of the week from the excellent Indian restaurant a few roads away.

'I've been gardening,' he told her. 'Only one spider fatality. I don't think it was my fault, though.'

'What? How come?'

'I'm pretty sure it was dead when I found it.'

'I meant, why are you gardening? I thought you were project-managing?'

'Ah. Yes. I can explain that,' Oliver said, though he wasn't sure how, now that his earlier anger had subsided and his intense feeling of protectiveness over the garden was beginning to seem somewhat irrational.

'Didn't the garden man come?'

'Yes. There was a misunderstanding there. I thought he was a gardener. Anyway, we talked, and it was becoming apparent – that is to say, it was *established* – that your idea of selling a garden plot might not, in practice, work very well.'

'How so?'

'Well, I thought you wanted to sell the house soon. Selling a plot of land will slow everything up. It's not a quick process, and it just adds a huge amount of complication. Plus I was talking to a neighbour earlier, and, you know, these backyard developments are often the subject of objections and appeals. People resist them. I just think it could be a giant headache, and delay you.'

'I guess that makes sense,' Kate said.

'Oh,' Oliver said. 'Good.' He felt slightly guilty at the success – the watertight rationality – of his own hurried improvisation.

'And I definitely don't want any more stress,' she continued. 'Thanks for thinking of me.'

'Er, speaking of stress.' He was so tired that he had almost forgotten Lena's visit; it seemed, in fact, like it had happened days ago. 'Your distant relative Lena Godwin came over. She looked around and saw what we were planning and warned me about carrying on working. She sounded pretty serious about it. I wasn't sure what to do.'

'What?' cried Kate. 'How bloody dare she! How the hell did she manage to get in? Did she sneak in, or barge past you, or what? Actually' – she became thoughtful – 'if she pushed you or something, we might actually be able to use this.'

'I . . . sort of let her in,' Oliver said. 'Sorry.'

'Oh, okay. Still, bloody cheeky of her. Tell me again what she said. All the details.'

Oliver went over the whole incident again, omitting the aspersions Lena had cast on their eye for antiques, their credentials as property developers, and their mental health, on the grounds that it would probably make Kate angrier than she needed to be. He had judged the situation correctly; Kate's anger did not require any external energy source, being as it was a model of perpetual motion, refuelled by her own marvelling at Lena's total rudeness and general awfulness as a person. Running out of things to say about the morning's visit, she widened her range, remembering how Lena, who apparently had been a few years above another of their cousins at the local school, had once been suspended for slapping another girl, and furthermore, that she had slept with 'mostly everybody' in Oxford.

'Really?' Oliver asked, intrigued but disbelieving. He couldn't imagine it. Then he reproved himself for trying.

'Yes, she's officially an utter slut,' Kate said firmly.

'I thought you didn't approve of that word,' Oliver said. 'The other week you were telling Joanna that it was disgraceful that promiscuity was okay for men and not women and it ought to be okay for everyone.'

'Of course I was,' Kate said patiently, 'because Jo's – well, she's been around. I had to say that to make her feel better. Anyway, that's different. She's my friend. Lena, on the other hand, is the bad kind of slut.'

'Right.'

'She probably wanted to sleep with you!' Kate exclaimed. 'That's why she was so reasonable. I don't think she's usually a very civilised person at all.'

'No,' Oliver said, thinking of the black, black contempt of Lena's stare, of *fucking yuppies*. 'No, I'm fairly sure she didn't want to sleep with me.'

Kate accepted this, apparently having too much fun musing over various explanations for Lena's strange behaviour to become attached to any one theory. She came up with a few more ideas, none of them charitable, before realising what the time was and crying out, a high note of pained indignation, as if someone had pinched her.

'Oliver! I have to go! Can we talk again tomorrow? You're right, let's be safe and not do anything else to the house in the meantime. I'll try to find a moment to call Mr Hunt and check the situation. God, I'm so sorry your time's being wasted like this.'

'It's not a waste of my time,' Oliver said, surprised, before remembering he was technically meant to be looking for another job.

'You know this house isn't a priority, right?' Kate said, having presumably had the same thought. 'I mean, don't let it take over. You've got more important stuff to think about. Not that there's any pressure to, obviously. I mean, it's your life.'

'I am thinking about the important stuff,' lied Oliver. 'I'm just taking a little time over it. Retraining, finding another career . . . I don't want to make any more mistakes.'

'Sure,' she said. 'Except . . . maybe don't leave it too long? I know you've got savings, but you don't want a huge gap on your CV.'

'Maybe I'll discover how good I am at doing up houses. I really *could* be a property developer.'

She laughed, but it was a thin sound, and when she rang off, her *goodbye, miss you, love you* was threadbare, as if starved down to skin and bone.

Once she had gone, Oliver sat still for a moment, worry flooding up, carrying him on its wave like a cork; a feeling usually confined to the quiet thinking time before he fell asleep. He suspected that when Kate got back, she was going to end their relationship. A few months of dating and a few months of living together did not add up to the kind of mileage that could mitigate one partner's erratic swerve off road. He thought of all the other things about him that Kate had formerly smiled at, or tolerated, because they were such a charming mismatch: things that might now take on a more sinister cast. His daydreaming in retrospect a warning sign; his enthusiasm for the past and not the future a red flag; his lack of passion the writing on the wall.

Actually, the current whereabouts of his passion was something that Oliver himself would have been curious to discover. As a child, he had been passionate about so many things – sticks, pirates, jumping on bubble wrap – and would hurl gale-force, King Learish tantrums at the prospect of their loss. As an adult he was more . . . what? *Chilled*, Kate would have said, sweetly. *Apathetic*, he thought in private. As he got older, he had lost the sense of urgency that went with liking something. He suspected sometimes that he allowed himself to be carried along by Kate's vitality. She kept him talking when he might otherwise fall silent; her nights were fun, her dreams were exciting: and even if it was somehow not quite the kind of talk or fun or excitement he might have chosen himself, he didn't actually know now what he would say or do or choose in her absence.

He thought that if he really cared for something he would chase it – fight for it – but he was twenty-seven now and he hadn't found much he cared about yet. He tried not to suspect that he never would. His friends talked about having 'drive', but Oliver never felt it. They all said, 'Live for the weekend,' but Oliver was the only one who meant it. He had worked hard at his job, but there was a lack of will in his activity that made it feel closer to inertia. It had been the good job his parents had wanted for him, nothing more, though at one time it seemed like that was enough; back when he announced that he had been accepted to study finance and had been rewarded with a misfiring clap on the back (his father) and a waterlogged hug (his mother), and thought that he could finally feel less anxious about the two of them: their pitiful pension pot, their small house in Milton Keynes, the promotion his dad was still waiting for, eight years on.

He wondered if his quitting was really an escape to freedom, or just something else that had been determined for him; a mechanism wound by his parents more than fifteen years ago, as he sat in the back of the Volvo and watched Oxford slide down the rear window like a melting snowman. Was it nothing more than a meaningless rebellion – or, worse – an act of sabotage? He had been indifferent to his university course, hated his job – but now he felt ambivalent about his independence. The thought of his financial security gone, his prospects for the future suffering irreparable damage – of everything blown out like birthday candles, with no wish – fermented into a swelling panic when he dwelt on it, which he tried not to do. It hadn't worked like it did in films, he thought. He should be opening his own juice bar right now, writing an acoustic guitar song, hiking across the Andes and discovering the secret of life, or himself, or something.

Unable to sleep, Oliver sat up with one lamp on and looked at the marble fireplace. Lena was right; it did seem a shame to take it out. And the room was pretty big already. The nymphs gazed back at him with something of her depthless reproof. Even the horse appeared to be giving him a dirty look. The house had got colder, having failed to capture any of the heat of the day, and he wished he had kept something to burn on the fire. But then he didn't know when the flue was last cleaned, and he didn't want to risk a chimney fire, whatever that was. Also, he had never successfully started a fire in his life. He and some friends had attempted it once when they were staying in what was, for them, unusually rustic lodgings in France. 'Fucking hell,' their friend Max had marvelled, after they had exhausted all their ideas and resorted to splashing brandy liberally over the firewood, 'it makes you wonder how fires ever get started by accident, doesn't it?'

Fucking yuppies, came Lena's voice now, and Oliver wondered if he was destined to hear this every time he failed at the practicalities of life; the words burning him afresh with every discarded hammer, unmended plug socket, unhewn log.

The heating, of course, was not working, and he had no idea how to fix that either.

Instead he put on another jumper, propped a pillow against

the wall and sat with a glass of wine to watch the empty fire-place. Daydreaming: now this was something he could do. Sophia came into his mind: her claim that history was more interesting – more personal – the less complete it was. It was another of the things she wrote that he felt he might have said himself, if only he'd given it some thought. He remembered one of his favourite books as a child, about civilisations lost under the sea; its illustrations of shoals of fish dawdling around pillars and pyramids. Even now he would watch any history or pseudo-history documentary in which underwater cameras tracked over the jutting ribs of battleships, or the giant heads of statues were lifted streaming out of the waves. One had tempted him with a link between Atlantis and the ancient volcanic eruption at Santorini. Though the touted connection was tenuous, the documentary was fascinating: the evidence that the eruption had not only devastated the island of Santorini, which collapsed into the sea like a soufflé, but caused a tsunami that wiped out the Minoans on neighbouring Crete.

Trying to recall the details, he looked it up on his phone and realised that Sophia and Christopher might never have known about the burial of Santorini's capital, Akrotiri, it having not been excavated until the late sixties. They certainly wouldn't have known what happened to the Minoans. This thought caused him a dull pang, a strum of melancholy, because Sophia would have loved the story of Akrotiri, a whole town evacu-ated before the ash fell. No bodies were found, no valuables save one gold ibex, hidden under some floorboards. The even-tual fate of the evacuees was unknown; whether they were caught in the tsunami, or made it to the mainland.

Would Oliver himself have wanted to know why the Minoan civilisation vanished? Would he enjoy documentaries as much if they were able to answer the questions they so teasingly posited: *Sodom and Gomorrah: Truth or Fiction?*, *Stonehenge: The Final Piece of the Puzzle?*. He wasn't sure if the lure of the past was a search for meaning or a deferral of it; he couldn't have said where the true pleasure lay. But it was another question that could never be answered, because the past would never be fully known, and so no comparison could ever be made between the relative virtues of knowing and not knowing. Even if all the biographical information on a person could be accessed – as he supposed was possible now, in the age of the internet – knowing them would still always be one step beyond the capabilities of someone who came later. It would be like trying to guess at the feel of someone by handling their old clothes; extrapolating their thoughts from the emptied concavities of their skull.

He picked up his jacket and took Sophia's history out of the inside pocket. Was *this* the closest thing to understanding a stranger? He wasn't sure if it was possible, even if the stranger were able to represent themselves fully and accurately. And that was another thing. He had read so far with the sense that he was getting close to her somehow – being allowed in, welcomed with a wink and a near-promise of some sort of relationship – but he had no way of knowing where she was leading him, or even if she was telling him the truth. This realisation was unsettling; at the same time it did not lessen his interest.

It was late, midnight, but Oliver wasn't tired, and he had no reason to get up early the next day. So he poured himself another glass of wine, found the page that ended with Sophia crossing the quad to meet Christopher, and leaned back against the wall to continue where he had left off.

A Revised History of the House of Hanover
S. L.

When I was a girl of about seven or eight, I had a German fairy-tale book, each page of which folded out into a scene: a wolf tucked up in bed, a wintry wood, and – my favourite – a beautiful, ornate gingerbread house. I used not to care much for the paper figure of the witch, with her horrid clawed fingers and her sad eyes, or the rather commonplace little characters of Hansel and Gretel themselves, in serviceable smocks. It was the house that entranced me: the inlaid arches and lattices, the tiny coloured sweets winking like rubies and emeralds and sapphires, the dark, scrollworked cocoa tracery of the arching wood beams. I used to lie on my stomach and gaze in, imagining myself shrinking, or the house expanding, so that I might live inside. And now, as if the book propped in front of the furiously wishing child had really begun to billow, rising like a giant cake, I found myself magically inside Duke Humfrey's Library at the Bodleian, which looked like nothing so much as my old dream come true.

This is not to say, dear reader, that I was having an *entirely* delightful time thumbing my nose at the laws of both society and physics. The other side of my miraculous transportation was the feeling that despite the solidity of the library – the sternness of oak and stone; the reek of thousands of leathery, tobacco-ochred pages; the dim, collected substance of the light, as if it were weighted by old words, by layers and layers of learning – it too was collapsible. I felt that the beams that ribbed the ceiling and the lines of domino bookshelves might at any moment fold suddenly inwards, like a compressed concertina; a book snapped closed and put away.

I was sitting alone at a desk with a history of the Stuarts open in front of me, my head supported for who knows how long by one hand, so that a telltale red palm mark would by now have blazed itself on my cheek: the bluestocking's shame. With the instincts of a mouse – or a snake – I had chosen a spot for myself cradled below the pillars of the shelving, just beneath a great window which I imagined would turn me into a silhouette, barely even female, to the casual eye. Moreover, I had come to rest so far out of the main human currents of the library, which was almost empty, that the chances of even a casual eye falling on me were low. It had actually occurred to me that if I were to die in this spot, sitting upright, chin on chest, I might go unnoticed until summer came to penetrate the library's stonily refrigerated dim. If Christopher should not come back . . . but here I stopped myself. Of course Christopher was coming back. The scene that played out in my imagination of his murmuring something about looking for a book, retreating out of sight, then turning and fleeing the library was quite absurd. Yet it lingered; a sly, slinking fright.

At first I had taken Christopher for a swaggering post-graduate, a little lord of the quads. Then I gave him the halo of the Good Samaritan, radiating a diffuse goodwill that had simply happened to focus, in that single lucky moment, on myself. Once through the door of the Bodleian, however, he had confused me again. He had told me that this afternoon I should be playing the role of his sister, but he said it seriously, and rather awkwardly, so that my own urge to laugh withered on my lips. Then, after establishing just as awkwardly where I should sit, he left to find some texts from Mexico and told me he'd be back shortly. He had now been gone for almost an hour.

What I had expected to be carried out in the spirit of a caper – pulled off with a knowing smile, a conspiratorial wink – seemed to have become something uncomfortable, an obligation I thought he must regret. I imagined his experiencing the sensation of embarking on an anecdote that is not as amusing as one hopes; having to doggedly continue until the end, at which nobody would laugh. And I myself hadn't the nerve to brazen it out. I wasn't so confident as Boll's friend Margot, that pretty, iron-clad vacuity, marching in like an empty suit of armour, with no purpose beyond the march itself.

I couldn't concentrate. My hands had sweated as I swore Bodley's oath, as if they knew my truest and darkest intentions: that I really *did* intend to mark and damage the books, to set about incinerating the lot with a book of matches and some alcohol, smuggled perhaps in the secret recesses of my bosom. Perhaps that was the reason women were forbidden. Suspicious anatomical design: too many hiding places. And so I had mumbled under the eyes of the men like a schoolgirl groping for her declensions.

You've made it, Sophia, I reproved myself. The least you can do is read the damned books. Start with the one in front of you, there's a dear. But it didn't do any good. When Christopher did return, a hazy patch of light in his fawn suit, I was quite shamefully relieved.

'Frightfully sorry to have left you so long,' he murmured. Though he was standing quite close, the dim light of the library had defocused his face; erased the lone freckle of his iris. 'I was bearded by a colleague at the other end of the library. He wanted to bitch about another colleague's paper, which I hadn't read, though I did a decent job of pretending I had, and said some deeply cutting things about it. Anyway, I didn't want to draw him over in this direction so I had to wait until he got bored and left before me. But you can imagine how long it takes for academics to tire of the sound of their own voices . . .'

'It's quite all right,' I said, without being entirely sure if it was. Though he spoke lightly, it was without amusement; something I knew well enough to identify in others. When he sat down near me (after checking politely, with a Victorian formality, whether it might not be offensive for him to do so) I found myself still less able to concentrate and began sneaking glances at his profile, now bent down in apparently intense withdrawal. I still felt the queasiness of only being here by a whisker: I needed – and how maddening that was! – something more reassuring from Christopher, whose former friendliness was harder and harder to remember. I'd crossed the quad on a memory of a laugh; now I felt I couldn't do without another. I considered myself well trained in the art of enduring long, painful silences, but now, abruptly sick to death of restraint, I surprised myself by leaning over and asking (in a low voice, reader, I am not a total savage) what he was reading.

'Actually, I was trying to find something I read the other day,' he said. 'I thought you'd have rather enjoyed it.'

'Really?' I tried not to let on how pleased I felt, and possibly succeeded only in looking prim.

'It was about the alleged madness of Caligula: that visit to the English Channel that nobody can quite explain, his order that his soldiers collect seashells. Of course none of the sources are reliable . . . I thought it rather interesting, anyway. The mystery of the whole thing. He might have been up to anything. It may have been that he really did believe he was taking on Neptune and winning. Or it might have been grimly apparent to both himself and the soldiers that he had failed in some way, but he stood with his jaw clenched and ordered them to grovel in the sand, to humiliate them too. Or it might have been a joke.'

'Or it might not have happened at all.'

'That too, yes,' Christopher said, and smiled. It seemed my credit had not been entirely used up. 'Tell me, what are you reading? Or are you simply going over all the pages with black paint?'

'I've been bad,' I admitted. 'I quite forgot my plans to read about the ancient Britons and ended up with the Stuarts. I'd got off to such a good start, too, with Stonehenge.'

'Making sure nobody has found out what it was yet?'

'Naturally.'

'And what's the latest?'

'Still no clue.'

'Good-oh.'

We looked at each other for a moment, and the humour seemed to quiver in the air, as if demanding some explanation, something to qualify it; heightening the awareness that we were simply two strangers, and had no right to be smirking at each other in a library. I said, somewhat hurriedly, 'I was reading about Charles II's flight from England. It's fascinating. Over six weeks he pretended to be all sorts of different people – a servant, a labourer – and he had to learn to speak and act differently. He had a few near misses but he was always able to talk his way out of them.'

Christopher looked sceptical. 'I suppose a natural ability to dissemble never does a leader any harm.'

Without having any real attachment to Charles II, I felt nonetheless that I ought to defend him from this charge. 'I actually don't think it was like that. To do it he had to abandon any ideas of divine right, or his own legend. I don't believe he would have survived had he been as stubborn or arrogant as his father. He always said that having to put himself in the place of the common man was an insight he valued. How many other kings could have said that?'

'So he was the best of a bad bunch,' Christopher allowed.

'If you like. But really, ought we to judge someone harshly for lying, or hiding, when they face death?'

'Good God, far be it from me to judge. I myself should

dress up as Mata Hari if I thought it might get me out of trouble. And not even that much trouble. An unpaid grocer's bill.'

'An overdue library book,' I suggested.

'A stern look from the Dean.'

We both laughed – and there it was again, the glimmer of camaraderie, shaken out of thin air. Emboldened, I asked, 'So, do you really have a sister? Are we doing her a disservice? Is she out at this minute at a tea dance, unaware that her very femininity, the purity of her indifference to books of any kind beyond romance, has been besmirched? Perhaps she felt a shiver when I walked into the library under her name.'

At that he looked at me in a way I wasn't sure how to interpret, and I worried that I had sounded too mocking: hard or sarcastic, when I only meant to be whimsical.

'You have a way with words,' he said, and smiled. 'I haven't a sister, so you can sleep easy at night.'

'Delighted to hear it.'

'So am I: she sounds intolerable. And I already have two intolerable brothers.'

'I'm sorry . . .' I began, but he shook his head.

'Oh, they aren't villains; only asses. They're both older than me – they managed to sidle around the edges of the war without ever seeing direct combat, though to talk to them you'd think they won it between the two of them. Oh yes, they taught the Germans a lesson they won't forget. And in all their conversations with me there's a tinge of pity – because I couldn't prove myself like they did. And under *that*, an even quieter whisper, of contempt, as if I'd somehow wriggled out of it, by being born too late.'

'Christmas must be jolly.'

'Ah, it's not so bad as I make it seem. We just . . . look at life differently.'

Our talk had got louder without us realising, and a man inspecting the shelves some distance away glanced over at us, then looked away quickly, as if he had come upon something scandalous. We both noticed it, yet we were not to be so easily derailed now, only lowering our voices again, leaning in closer to be heard. There was something enjoyably taboo about the whole thing, and I was enlivened by it, even as I realised that we had moved into dangerous conversational waters: that of family, a subject on which I had to choose my words carefully, or risk being either untruthful or disloyal.

I fell almost at the first hurdle, when he asked if I had brothers or sisters. 'A sister. We're different too. Really I was thinking of her when I described your imaginary sister.'

'Then I do apologise for calling her intolerable.'

'Good heavens, don't. I should think she'd be far more upset if she heard a rumour was going around that she'd been seen in a library.'

He laughed, and to keep the moment alight I cheerfully sacrificed Boll to the flames, telling him about her golf phase, her equally brief tennis phase (sporting a bandanna in which she fancied she looked like Suzanne Lenglen), her seasonal longings for a lapdog, her cigarettes from Paree. He looked amused, but became thoughtful, quieter, and said, 'It's a queer thing, don't you think, having the same blood as someone so alien to you.'

'Queer, and at times maddening.'

'Perhaps that's why so many families secretly – or openly – loathe each other. One wouldn't care how bloody they were if they were strangers, but because they are made from the same material as oneself, there is a sense of outrage, that they *aren't* the same. It can't be got over; it can't be borne.'

'Well, quite, but I shouldn't say I *loathed* Boll,' I said mildly, slightly startled by his vehemence. For a moment, too, I was aware of my own mildness, saw it objectively: an awful, genteel restraint; a decorous smothering of feeling, smoothing its rough edges, hushing its wild cries. Wherever had I got that from? I wondered, but I knew immediately. Where does anybody get anything? I thought of my mother, lips clamped together, sewing away madly whenever my father drank too much port after dinner.

In any case, I wasn't even sure if my claim was strictly true. I didn't feel a hatred of Boll, exactly, but I considered the attitude of cool mockery I had always adopted towards her, my determinedly amused detachment, and wondered if that was worse. Guiltily, I recalled Boll as a child, crying over something or other, as the teenaged Sophia sat with her face turned into her book, pretending not to hear.

I wanted to ask more about Christopher's family, to atone for my repressive reply, but I was worried he might ask more about my own, so I changed the subject.

'I say, when you spoke about kings earlier, you seemed awfully unimpressed by the lot of them. Does that mean you're a republican? Or even . . . a Bolshevik? *Do* say you are. I've never met a real one.'

'I'm not sure what I am,' he said. 'There are a lot of things I'm unimpressed by. Christ, that sounds an awful pose, doesn't it? But I'm not a nihilist. Not quite. I suppose present-day things don't interest me as much as the past. People attach so much weight to the moment, but in another moment it will be over and something will have taken its place. The past, at least, has the decency to stay still.'

'Though it may be hidden,' I observed. 'Or pretending to be something it's not.'

'Yes, thank you, Sophia,' he said drily. We sat back and smiled at each other, with all the stifling stiffness of earlier quite vanished, and when he asked, 'So, when would you like to come again? I'm at liberty tomorrow, and Friday,' I felt suddenly close to tears with the relief of it; of not only having the opportunity to read, but to do so away from my own home, where I felt myself little more than a barometer, endlessly trying to gauge the atmospheric fluctuations, the clouds collecting above me.

He misinterpreted my expression and added, 'Of course, you might not be planning another trip at all, or not so soon, anyway . . .'

'Tomorrow,' I said.

'Then tomorrow it is.'

As he was taking his leave, he turned, a thought occurring to him. 'Hold on. You never told me what you thought Caligula was up to that day.'

'I didn't? No, I suppose I didn't. Well, since you ask, I like to think it was a joke. They were tired, and they had reached the end of their journey, and when he said it, they all laughed.'

I walked home that afternoon wondering why I had been so friendly to Christopher; not just allowing the conversation to stray beyond the purely academic, but steering it there myself. Being so long out of the habit, I had forgotten what friendship was like. I had got by for so many years with only books and my own thoughts that I'd almost begun to think of myself as a solitary character, a lone wolf – or perhaps an odd fish. It was with faint surprise that I recalled that this had not always been so; that I used to have a life of dances, dinner parties, punting, long, heat-dazed afternoons of croquet or tennis. But the friendships that had held fast all through the dreary, unhappy war years took hardly any time at all to devolve into acquaintances, then near-strangers, once George returned. I had collaborated in the process myself; the careful unpicking of tightly sewn bonds. Not simply because I suspected it was either that or be the martyr of my empty hall table, a chimneypiece starkly bereft of invitations, but because I felt sorry for the hostesses who might feel a frisson of dread at the thought of George and Sophia Louis. Even if nothing too ghastly happened – George's irrational arguments, his sudden black moods, his mute stare at his plate, as if its arrangement of pastry and chocolate were a complex and sinister puzzle set to entrap him – the expectation of it would hang over us all. Like refined Pavlovian dogs we would sit in glassily tense anticipation, trying not to watch George.

I remember one of the last dances we attended. I knew it was to be the last even before I accepted the invitation. Yet I felt that I *would* accept, and I wheeled around the floor in a fever of nervous defiance and impending disaster, knowing that Rome was blazing behind me. I never forgot the collected sweetness of the flowers, the smoke weaving itself sensuously into my hair, the desolate scent of it the next morning. That night someone asked George how he was and George, gripping his glass whitely, said, 'When I see people laughing and capering like this, as if they were amnesiacs, or idiots, quite frankly I wish them all dead.'

'I suppose we shan't be invited back,' was all he said, once we'd got outside into the night, and rather than sounding bleak, or regretful, I was surprised to hear a queer sort of triumph in his voice; not only over the startled party guests – dizzy and stupid with the future – but over me, for asking him to come. After that night I began refusing the invitations still sent out of duty, or pity. I could tell my friends (who were good sorts, after all) were sorry, but relieved, and George himself said nothing about it.

Sometimes these days I encounter my former confidantes on the Broad or shopping at Cape's; meetings that have ceased to be difficult. So much time has passed that we can have no expectations of each other. Safe from the prospect of rekindled intimacies, we talk without awkwardness – become quite affectionate, even. My present circle comprises only Boll, Piers and George. Though it must be acknowledged that with Boll and George not exactly *simpatico*, and Piers appearing only from time to time, flitting in and out depending on how jolly the company is, it isn't quite a circle so much as two sides; the territories of rival powers. And yet again I find myself standing alone, right in the middle, in no-man's-land.

Before my walk home took me too far out of view, I cast a last look back at the Bodleian, the absurd pinnacles rising above the rooftops like a stone forest, a circle of frozen firs. To me it was no longer a goblin fortress but an enchanted faerie glade, beyond which the snow swirled and animals howled, having no power to cross its border. Within those bounds a friendship might spring up: a queer sort of friendship, owing its existence to a random set of very specific conditions, a collision of coincidences. Delicate and improbable as a rare flower, it could not survive the chill of the world beyond its glasshouse: context would be the death of it. This was what I told myself as I hurried home, until a soft, clinging rain set in, chilling my hands and face until I shivered and drew my arms up; until – as if I could not protect it – my happiness too quietened and huddled into itself, like a wary creature, taking shelter under a leaky roof.

When I got home, I found George sitting as expected in his usual place, angled only slightly to face the speckled window. The rain outside had dimmed the interior, turning an already watery palette into a grey wash, and George himself into a statue sunk in a lake, his features made vague by the quivering light, the tiny reverberations of the droplets on its surface. I had to look twice before I realised he was even there, the drawing room having the stiff dignity of abandonment, of long stillness, as if it did not contain a living man.

I went in and gave him a light, vague and entirely

dishonest account of my day. He listened without much comment, until I told him that I planned to go back again the next day. At this he visibly paled, as if I had put a newspaper down in front of him with the headline: Young Wife Found Dead in Gutter.

'Tomorrow? I . . . I thought you would only be spending a day there?'

'Only a day?' I replied, affecting surprise, then added, piously, 'I hope I should never give up learning. And the library is much the best place for it.'

'I don't doubt it,' he murmured, looking preoccupied. I could almost see the panicked movements of his thoughts, as he wondered how to keep me in the house, short of outright forbidding me to leave it.

'It's just a terribly dangerous time, Sophia, you must understand that. The streets still so dark. There was a murder in Bicester last week. They haven't caught the culprit.'

I had anticipated this. In fact, I had read all the morning's papers in preparation.

'Yes, darling, I saw that. The police believe it was an inheritance case. The son paid somebody to bump off his father. I shouldn't worry about that . . . he's certainly not in *my* will.'

There then followed a peculiar exchange in which George played his macabre cards and I countered with my own:

'. . . a motor car crash on the High . . .'

'But that was late at night, and the driver was a well-known drunk.'

'. . . a spate of burglaries . . .'

'I am not a house, George.'

'. . . several pickpocketings . . .'

'I've heard about those, and shall be sure to be on my guard.'

It might have been funny if he weren't so white, and his voice so strained. In the end he said, 'You've no idea how much I . . . You think me overprotective. But nobody ever believes anything bad will happen to them.'

'But darling, it usually doesn't. You needn't worry about me. Really.'

'Needn't worry,' he repeated, turning the words over like something he had found washed up on the shore, a never-before-seen creature from the deep. He poked at it with his stick, not understanding.

Eventually he looked up, and, with a gesture of apparent surrender, a pained look that I couldn't meet, said: 'God knows I can't stop you doing what you want to do, Sophia. Perhaps I'm wrong to try. It's simply that you're the one good thing I have in this wretched world. I couldn't bear to lose you, even if I don't deserve you.'

I was taken aback by this sudden declaration; the passion with which it was delivered. He stared so hard, as if he might overpower me with the force of his unhappiness. I hadn't seen him so agitated – so intent – since the days immediately after the war. That was the time in which things were silently settled between us: that I would give up my work, and he would give up his fear and sink instead into the strange, solemn sleep in which he had been submerged ever since. But now it was as if he had suddenly woken up, not into lucidity but a drugged panic, and I was at a loss as to how to talk him round. I tried to speak kindly and cheerfully. 'Perhaps if you didn't think me so good, and yourself so terrible, you'd be happier, George.'

He gave a humourless cry of a laugh, a startled, bleak sound, like a door slamming. 'I don't choose what I know. And I *know* you to be good. Why, if you weren't, then . . .'

He left this unfinished, and I didn't say anything, not wanting him to imagine any other possibility.

'We can both be good,' I said, but this didn't sound convincing to either of us, and George didn't answer.

After a little while – or a long while, it was hard to tell which – I understood that he was not going to say anything more; that he had, in fact, fallen utterly back into his own thoughts. I wasn't sure whether he had forgotten even speaking to me at all. I never could get used to these passing lapses of attention, blotting out his former sharpness – his once-perfect recall – like dun-coloured clouds pasting themselves thickly over the sun.

'I shall just speak to Mrs Boxall about supper,' I said softly, on the way out of the room.

'I'll eat later,' George said, with a vague wave of his hand, by which he meant, 'This will be another night in which I take supper in my room, and you must decide whether to do the same, or sit alone at the dining table, monitored by the uncomfortable Margaret.'

I left the room and headed gladly towards the kitchen, crackling like a fire at the centre of the house. As I went down the passageway, the warm yellow light of it stretched its fingers down the wall; a welcoming clamour of pans arose. I could smell dough, and brandy, and cinnamon. I arrived in the doorway with what must have been a rather foolish smile, making Mrs Boxall send me a quick, curious look. She, of course, didn't view the kitchen quite so romantically; I thought it might be rather tactless of me to try to explain the pleasure I took in visiting it.

'Good day, ma'am?'

'I suppose it has been. How are you? Is that cake?'

'Sooner or later it will be. Plum cake.'

'How very lovely. Mr Louis adores plum cake.'

Mrs Boxall nodded, unsmiling. There was a moment of silence, in which the understanding that Mr Louis didn't give two hoots what cake was put down in front of him hung in the air, mingling with the rich perfume of the baking.

'Anyway, Mr Louis and I will eat separately tonight. Just another nursery supper, I'm sorry to say.'

'No call to apologise, I'm sure. Will you be wanting beef tomorrow? I've some in the meat safe. A nice fillet.'

'That sounds divine. I say, did you think about the refrigerator at all? I should've thought it'd make things a little easier for you.'

'Well, ma'am, it's not that we're not appreciative, and you're very kind, but Margaret and I were talking, and Margaret's brother said as how someone he knows heard of one that exploded. The gas in it, you see. And I was thinking that I'd just as soon *not* have a refrigerator, if you don't mind.' She delivered this hurriedly, as if it had been long-rehearsed, and gave me an apologetic look once she had finished.

'Good Lord, you mustn't worry about offending me,' I cried. 'I simply thought you might like it.'

Now (for I might as well be honest with *you*, dear reader), this wasn't the entire truth, and my kindness was not all it seemed. I paid far more than factory wages and plied Margaret and Mrs Boxall with electrical goods because I lived in constant fear that the two women, oppressed by the atmosphere in the house – which was both dull and electrically charged, like the oily billow of a pending storm – might at any moment find it all too much and give notice, taking everything friendly and normal away with them.

'In honesty, ma'am, we're only just getting adjusted to the vacuum cleaner. Not that it isn't a very handsome thing, and I'm sure Margaret is most grateful for it. But I don't see any need for a refrigerator, as things stand.' Mrs Boxall was firmer now. 'I'm not sure they'll catch on, if I'm honest.'

'Then I give in. But let me know if you change your mind, do,' I said.

'Ma'am . . . Lord knows why I'm telling you this, but there's not enough for us to do as it is. Margaret cleaned the step twice yesterday.'

'Hm. Well, tell her she needn't do that. She could have a break. She could read a book! There are plenty here she might borrow.'

'Very thoughtful of you, I'm sure,' Mrs Boxall said, managing to sound exactly the opposite of sure.

Alarmed at this abrupt discarding of pretence – the fiction that our household needed a maid and a cook, which so far had been delicately maintained by both myself and Mrs Boxall and ignored by George, who never noticed what was being done or how much money was spent – I said hastily, 'Good, good! I say, I ought to let you get on,' before adding, 'I shall *so* look forward to the cake,' and fleeing the kitchen, by which I hoped to prevent her giving notice, at least for another day.

℮

The following day was so strikingly sunny – almost flamboyant in its brightness, all the birds singing feverishly, the trees twinkling like emeralds (and, best of all, no notice from Mrs Boxall) – that I decided to drink up its gaiety for as long as I could, and told George that I'd lunch with Boll before going to the library.

'I expect I shall be out for most of the day,' I said, eyeing him, but – as I had expected – the mention of Boll had distracted him, sending him into his own hasty manoeuvrings, glancing around for cover like a trapped fox, his answers brief and evasive, so determined was he to avoid the prospect of an invitation.

I walked past the overwrought Victorian eaves and verandas of Boll's road with a rather childish smirk; an irrepressible glee that travelled down my arms (swinging mannishly) and my legs (on the verge of a trot). Small things delighted me unexpectedly: an outburst of blossom on a single cherry tree, a white cat staring down from a high wall, a late droplet from the night's rain clinging tremblingly to its leaf, before landing on the end of my nose.

'I must say, you look nice,' Boll said, with surprise, when she came to kiss me. 'Are you wearing rouge?'

'Just a brisk walk,' I said.

'I suppose rouge was too much to hope for. Anyway, I'm frightfully glad you came today . . . I should like you to see the new dining room, now it's finished.'

She led me through into the sudden emptiness of the dining room, formerly stately, now scooped out like a duck egg, pale blue and echoing. I exclaimed over the pearlescent uplighters; the light new drapes at the window. I forbore to ask where she had got the money for it. Or, for that matter, the new dress she was wearing: a bluish grey like an evening sky, dropping in a deep V to reveal a white silk underlayer, its pleats tumbling around her calves as she walked; the whole thing set off triumphantly by the fiery blue stones of the earrings swinging below her dark bob.

Once luncheon was over and we had slipped into a companionable silence – Boll having successfully concluded a lengthy character assassination of one of her best friends in the Oxford smart set – I pleaded, 'Do send for Daphne.'

Boll raised her eyebrows, but was tolerant, and Daphne was duly delivered by the nanny. She evidently hadn't been told that her aunt Sophia was visiting, and when she came in she looked wary at first, as if wanting to hang back, propelled forward by a drilled politeness. She reminded me of a spaniel called off the scent, silky head lowered obediently, with perhaps just one, barely notice-able, flicker of rebellion in its eyes; one final glance towards the trees. Then, realising who I was, she rushed gratifyingly forward, and put her face up to be kissed.

'Darling,' I murmured into her soft hair. 'Let's see you.'

She stood back so I could tell her, tediously, how much she had grown over the last month. I noticed how her once-blond hair had darkened, like a ripening nut, a neat little acorn of a bob; admired the fine, milky skin she had inherited from my mother.

'From me,' corrected Boll. 'Mother was terribly lined.'

'Not always,' I said. 'Daphne, I heard a story I thought you might like the other day. About King Charles the Second, and his flight to France.'

'Dear God,' Boll said. 'Do make it a short one. I'm in danger of dozing off as it is.' She began searching ostentatiously for a Gitane, but by the time I'd got to the end of the story she was leaning forward just the same as Daphne, the cigarette gently smouldering between her fingers. The resemblance between them, in this quiet moment, was at its strongest. Daphne's pale light usually dimmed beside her mother's darkly glittering bob, the much-vaunted white skin in which her gentian eyes and bloody lips flashed like jewels on satin. Together and stilled, I could see the bone lines they shared; the profiles struck from the same die.

When I had finished, Boll remarked, 'I say, you make it sound almost interesting. So, what happened?'

'What do you mean?'

'Charles! Did they behead him or not?'

'*Mummy*,' Daphne said: one weary little word.

'Actually he lived as a farmer in France for several years,' I said. 'Then he got caught out.'

'How?'

'It was the geese. What people don't know about animals is that they have a sixth sense. They can tell when people are frightened.'

'Like Cynthia's ghastly Pekinese!'

'Yes, or when they're lying. The story goes that they can even sniff out royalty.'

'Good Lord. So what then? What did they do?'

'Oh, heavens, I don't know. I hadn't expected to get so far with the lie, to be quite honest. I hadn't thought up anything beyond the geese.'

'What a beast you are,' Boll said, put out. She sat back in her chair and readdressed herself to the cigarette, turning it between her restless fingers.

Daphne giggled, but kept one eye on her mother, as if wary of perceived complicity. She was more perceptive than I, for it was only a few questions later (in which I established that Daphne's new favourite animal was a chameleon; that she had thought of a 'much better' version of 'Little Red Riding Hood', before getting stuck on the ending; that she hated her new neighbour Louisa, while at the same time yearning for Louisa's curling blond hair) that Boll, growing bored, abruptly decided that we'd had enough bosh for one afternoon and sent Daphne back off to the nanny.

'Next time, I'll tell you about Crete,' I said, and she turned in the door and gave me a smile – quick and enchantingly sly – that struck a high, almost painful chord in me.

'You're a bad influence on her,' Boll observed. 'I'm glad to see her *talk* for once, but she's intolerably pert after you visit. Must you take things so far?'

'Sorry,' I said, but the word clinked like a counterfeit coin, and Boll's eyebrows drew down.

'When you have a child, I shall take great pleasure in spoiling it, and turning it into a perfect little monster,' she informed me.

This struck more of a blow than she could have intended, but I answered lightly, 'If it's a girl, you can take her for cocktails and teach her poker,' then asked, to turn the subject, 'Tell me, who was that? What happened to Miss Fanshawe?'

'What? Who?'

'The new nanny. You have a newer one.'

'Oh! I wondered what the devil you were talking about. I thought perhaps some old school friend, or something . . . I never can remember the names of the nannies, you know. It's their fault for being such lifeless creatures. Thoroughly forgettable. But Miss Fanshawe was much the worst of them. Dull *and* unobliging.'

'Did she give notice?'

'Yes, over nothing at all. She was taking a day off one Sunday, to visit her mother in hospital or something dreary, but I was at a dance on Saturday with the Trevelyans – remember them? – and having far too much fun to come home immediately, and then time ran on, and we decided I had better stay overnight. Then I obviously had to eat breakfast, which never happens as quickly as one would like – don't you find? – and by the time I got home at four or so, Miss Fanshawe was in a snit about the whole thing. But what could she do? She couldn't just *abandon* Daphne' – here Boll smiled at the memory of having outwitted the dutiful Miss Fanshawe – 'but oh, she was an awful prig about it. I told her she ought to be more grateful, for we really do treat her well – why, I gave her an old frock of mine the other week, with only a small tear – and that was when she gave notice. Daphne was the only one sorry to see her go. She cried for about a week. But I dare say she'll get over it and become just as attached to Miss Whatever-her-name-is.'

'That seems rather hard on Daphne,' I said. 'And, Boll, *I* could have taken Daphne for the day. I should love to spend more time with her.'

At this Boll's mouth kinked out of its Cupid's bow. She never liked to be reproached, and she drew herself up now like a grande dame and said, 'Perhaps if you hadn't decided to live like a sad old spinster you wouldn't be so concerned with *my* family. She's not your daughter, and you know, darling, it's really none of your business.'

There was a short silence after this. Boll – in all likelihood regretting her spite but too proud to say so – busied herself with lighting another cigarette, by which means she was able to avoid my gaze. 'You're quite right,' I said humbly. 'Though I hope you'll permit me to ask a little about your family, now and then.'

'Of course,' Boll said, looking uncomfortable. 'Don't be an ass. You know what I meant.'

'In which case, I'm curious to know when we might be welcoming a little brother or sister for Daphne.'

I had long suspected that Boll hadn't wanted her first baby, though this was something I could never ask about. I had a partial answer now in her rapid blink, her hands making for her long string of beads, which she began counting through her fingers like a rosary (a reaction identical to that last observed in a conversation about the outbreak of war babies in 1915).

Boll had married Piers on a spectacularly rainy day in April 1917, after several months of excitable courtship and a few weeks of mysterious edginess and haste, during which she held whispered conferences with our mother and cried a lot in her room. Back then Piers was a war correspondent for *The Times*, and was seldom seen in London, preferring to drink in overseas hotel bars with a strange collection of local dignitaries, attachés, spies and journalists from rival newspapers. Boll seemed to spend rather more time talking about Piers, her misty, dazzling hero, than she actually spent with the real thing (somewhat puffier beneath the eyes and grubbier around the edges), for when Piers *was* in England, he was usually marooned in a turbulent whisky sea with his louche editor, Hugh. Unfortunately for Piers' career, though fortunately perhaps for my sister, the two men had a falling-out, rumoured to be over expenses, and not long after his and Boll's wedding – at which Hugh's place was an accusing patch of empty air at an otherwise high-spirited table – Piers left his job.

The resignation caused a good deal of fuss. It wasn't that Boll was particularly concerned by the loss of the work. No – Piers had had many such fallings-out, his past a dangerous landscape of chasms and icy tundras, left behind while he moved ever forward, the path before him smoothed by his family, until even their influence or patience ran out. It was that with the war still in full swing, he faced the unspeakable possibility of actually joining in. And so we waved him off as he left for Sandhurst (his habitual charm barely concealing his gloom, as Boll's uncontrolled sobs ululated in the smoky air), worried over him when he was about to be shipped out to France, and then raised our eyebrows when, perfectly on time, the Allies won the war and he didn't have to go after all. ('That's *too* like Piers!' Boll said, delighted.)

Daphne had appeared rather quickly after the nuptials, in November 1917 (her first birthday destined to be lost in the hullabaloo of Armistice Day), which went some way towards explaining the hurried wedding preparations. 'She's frightfully *big*, isn't she?' Boll's friends liked to say mischievously, appearing like bad fairies over the cradle. 'Considering how early she was.'

Now I should like to interrupt briefly to point out to you, my dear reader, that were it not for this document, you would quite possibly never hear anything other than the official account of Piers and Boll's wedding, an epic of champagne and orange blossom and quite unrelenting bliss, Boll being quite as effective at rewriting history as any emperor or pharaoh. To see her blink now and reach for her necklace, as if her memory itself had twitched, flinching to the touch, was the only evidence of past anxiety: red eyes, voices behind closed doors. But that is enough of that. Back to the present day we shall go, to Boll's parlour, in which the woman in question had dropped her beads, was lighting another cigarette and saying, almost snappishly:

'I most certainly do not want another child.'

I raised my eyebrows at the tone.

'Oh, Piers was just haranguing me about this the other week. It's all very well for him! I damn nearly died. And the nausea, for weeks afterwards, from the chloroform. Too, too ghastly. I should like to know if *he'd* do it in my place.'

'I do understand, Boll,' I said gently. I lowered my voice. 'But . . . how does one go about not having one?'

Boll spoke more airily now, as she always did when

THE HOUSE OF BIRDS

she knew something I didn't. 'Oh, there are ways. Obviously I avoid the whole business if at all possible. But if things do . . . you know . . . well, there are things one can buy. Just look at the advertisements in the back of magazines and you'll see. It's absolutely no use asking the doctor, obviously.'

'Well, quite,' I said, still mystified.

Boll looked at me sharply, as if examining me for signs of disapproval. As if not entirely satisfied, she added, 'Piers claims to adore Daphne, but really he barely sees her. *I'm* the one raising her.'

I found I hadn't the energy to make fun of this claim, and she continued, 'In any case, we can't afford any more children. We're stony broke,' and now there was a tightness in her voice not only of grievance, but of satisfaction in having aired it.

I watched her curiously, wondering whether she was about to loose her resentment at last, let it out of the kennel where it had crouched, chained and softly growling, chewing over its bone, since our mother's death. But she did not say, 'You should not have been given the house.' She drew back from the brink, delicately, and contented herself with adding, 'I might have to become a teacher. Or go to Australia and become a farmer.'

'I say, you're surprisingly well acquainted with current affairs,' I congratulated her. 'You know, I don't think the Group Settlement Scheme is such a terrible idea. I can almost see you in gumboots, with a lamb tucked under each arm.'

'Beast.' Boll said this so often it might as well have been

my nickname – Beauty and the Beast – but this time the word emerged with genuine anger; the minutest baring of teeth, gripped together behind the coy rosebud curve of her lips. There was a distinct chill in the air.

I tried a different approach. 'But nobody has any money, Boll. Everyone's hard up.' At this she looked almost immediately bored, so I added, pontifically, 'Why, we're only just out of depression, and when one considers income tax and the rising national debt—'

'*Must you?* You'll give me a headache. I think I feel one coming on already.'

With Boll shooed off the subject, and danger averted, we returned to our small talk, while I wondered exactly how badly off she and Piers were. The magnificent hoard Boll seemed to believe George and I were sitting on consisted of the house and a modest, quietly decent amount of money from various bequests and the sum George received from the government after the war. Meanwhile, Boll and Piers's fortunes seemed to mysteriously ebb and flow; there would be dark references to debts and sprees, closely followed by uninhibited excess: Havana cigars and hothouse flowers, a silver shaker for cocktails drunk at the picnics where they danced to the wispy music of the new portable gramophone. There seemed no use in reminding her that though I had the house, she had got most of the money, because it was spent and forgotten long ago, and of no account now in her weighings-up. The house was something Boll always dwelt on when she was in the midst of money troubles, but lately these troubles seemed to come harder on the heels of each other, and were less easily fixed, while her flashes of anger in my direction had become more frequent, and harder to distract her from once they had sparked into life.

Though I had not been aware of the way our inheritance had been divided until after my mother's death, I could guess at my parents' motivations. Anybody could. It wasn't favouritism but simple logic. I put it to *you*, dear reader: if you wished to see a house kept for all the generations of your descendants, which sister would you will it to: the one with the love of pleasure, or the one with the passion for history? Of course, for all our reasoning, none of us knows how things will turn out, and my sagacious mother and father couldn't have foreseen that the naughty daughter would be the one with a clever and wonderful child; that it would be the good daughter who found herself unable to pass perambulators in the street without a pang, an inaudible note of despair; the one to go like a ghost each night to her blank white bed, knowing that nothing – no heat, no kindling – would ever begin there.

From Boll's house I walked to the Bodleian, quickly becoming flustered by the unusual heat of the afternoon. From a delicate, rain-spotted beginning the sun had gathered force, and I was unprepared for it. I crossed to the shaded side of the street, taking off a glove discreetly so that I might run a finger around the back of my neck and under my collar, checking for dampness. I could feel my hair flattening itself against my forehead. It didn't help my rapidly blooming anxiety that I was late to meet Christopher, Boll having embarked on a lengthy anecdote just as I had said I ought to leave. I tried and failed to find any design beyond simple self-absorption in the delay; but as I walked hurriedly along the street, I couldn't help but feel the world was plotting darkly against me, and I glared back at it, just as ready for a fight. In my mind, which had run down the street ahead of me, Christopher was giving up and walking away. I saw his tawny back pass under the arched entrance to the quad, too far ahead to call to.

When it came to it, all the unfortunate futures I had spun out of the air evaporated as I arrived at the Bodleian, saw Christopher waiting in his usual spot, already waving, and was immediately confounded anew by the impossibility of finding some sheltered place to tidy myself. At this point I felt it important to give myself a quick talking-to ('Don't let's be a silly woman about it, Sophia. You're at a library, not a damned debutantes' ball') as I crossed the quad, waving cheerily. And by the time I had reached his side, I felt almost equable about my appearance, until he smiled and I couldn't help but dip my head a little under the brilliance of it, struck by the perfection – the ferocious youth! – of his clean white teeth and rather sensuous mouth. I turned my head away as if I might duck his gaze, feeling not only discomposed but, at twenty-eight, quite unforgivably *old*.

Once we got inside, I excused myself to powder my face and arrange my hair, and felt immediately, shamefully happier for having done so. I stood in the small shower of light let in by a high window and looked at myself in my hand mirror, rather sharply. I seldom saw my own face for long in the mirror; studying myself was almost like drifting into sleep: a surfacing of images, unconnected and uncertain. Other faces rose up into my own, other features suggested themselves. Boll's bright blue eyes, my mother's nose, Daphne's sensitive, childish mouth. I saw my own face as it was when I was young, or would look when I was old, or even – lapsed as it was into stillness – as it might look in death. At this last thought I'd usually have to blink or twitch my mouth, to shake the impression off. But now when I looked at myself all I saw was *myself*, peering at my own face rather narrowly, cannily, as if wondering how much I might get for it at auction.

Back in the central caverns of the Bodleian – enclosed in the dim graduations of wood and paper that I hoped in time would become as comforting to me as they must be to a returning man – Christopher and I found our books and passed an hour or so reading at adjoining tables. Yet, after an interesting interval with the Aztecs and Incas, my eyes grew fatigued: dawdling over words, forced back to reread, rebelling once again. My mind, too, had become skittish. It wandered over to Christopher like a friendly dog, ignoring my sharp whistles. I had noticed that since we last met, our familiarity had rusted up a little, as if it had been years since we saw each other and not hours. I suspected that part of this was my fault, for only half returning his smile. Now I began wondering at ever-decreasing intervals if he might speak to me, or if he thought me absorbed in my reading and not to be disturbed. Then I wondered if he was doing the same thing, and if we both of us should be forced to remain in our places, shy and stubborn, until darkness fell and a librarian came to throw us out.

At this point he turned to me and asked, unexpectedly, 'What did you do during the war?'

I looked up, startled, as if I had been caught out.

'Apologies,' he said, misreading my expression, 'I ought to have asked if you minded my disturbing you. I've a bad habit of getting to the end of my thoughts, forgetting that nobody else has been privy to them, then speaking to people as if they ought to understand.'

'I don't mind one bit. In fact, I was doing the same thing. Daydreaming, I mean. But you must tell me how you began at' – I glanced at his book – 'Demosthenes and ended up at the war.'

'I was thinking about war in the abstract. Nothing particularly coherent. I wondered whether my lack of experience of it would make me a better or a worse historian. I thought you might reassure me by arguing for the former. Then I wondered what sort of war you had.'

'I don't know, yet, how I feel about the war,' I said, hesitating. 'I think that perhaps it will be something that makes sense only once it's long past; when it can be viewed historically, not personally. It isn't as if I saw combat – my experience was quite second hand. But even that experience was difficult . . . to make sense of.'

He waited, and there was a forbearance in that I admired; his being prepared to watch me struggle to form my own words, as if he trusted that I would do so and was in no hurry to step in with some of his own. I told him briefly about the time I had spent as a VAD nurse at a hospital that the late Lady Rothwell (a family friend, through the vaguest of connections) had opened at her house near Kennington.

'She was a remarkable character. I can scarcely describe her. One of those formidable women who ought always to have been in charge of something more than servants and balls. A pity it took a war to allow her abilities to be utilised. She was . . .'

I hesitated again, unwilling to seem gossiping, yet wanting to capture something of the enchantment of Lady Rothwell for him. She had been a slender, white-haired woman, small yet forceful, affectionate, peremptory, unshockable – and quite insane, with a perfect mania for ordering and cleanliness. None of this was to the detriment of the hospital she opened, which had one of the lowest rates of death from infection in the country, and once the nurses got used to lining up bottles and boxes in order of size, and not mixing linens of different colours, they spoke of her with possessive fondness: their beloved tyrant, their iron-hearted mother.

'She was magnificent,' I said. 'Anyway, I chose nursing instead of fund-raising or joining a sewing guild. I'm still not sure why; I was always rather squeamish. Boll certainly thought me mad. She began a muffler for the men at the front, though the war beat the muffler to the finish line.'

We laughed, keeping the sound low, but I was already contemplating the impossibility of the rest of the story, which could not be made light or presentable.

'I'm not sure I could have borne it,' he said.

'There was never that choice: whether or not to bear it.

It's a matter of not knowing what one is signing up for, and then finding out, but not being able to walk away.'

It was true: none of us VADs left, though I saw several swaying greenly in the corridors, and once a girl fainting, clutching at a tray of scalpels and forceps, bringing it clattering to the ground. The trained nurses were sceptical of our ability to deal with the arriving men, who were not only wounded but louse-ridden, frostbitten – still muddy, even, as if they had limped straight from their trenches to our door. But we did deal with them; we were pinned there as if by some great weight, our physical comprehension of war. I could understand no more of it than that pressure, and even sitting at my table now in the civilised gloom of the library I could not think of it reasonably. All I had was that feeling, itself an accumulation of other feelings: an Impressionist painting composed of many small and terrible moments. The unexpected arc of blood from a man's mouth, red and violent; the dying summer light in the tall windows on a night without electricity; the Sisyphean struggle of a gassed man for every breath, rolling endlessly away from him. What happened at the hospital was, in essence, unspeakable. It was the daily transfiguration of bodies: moving from life to death noisily, or slowly, or all of a sudden, so that one might turn around with a bedpan and an observation about the weather to find that the patient who might have replied or defecated was dead. That this all happened under the eyes of the portraits of Lady Rothwell's ancestors, below the towering ornamented arches of the Wren ceilings, somehow made it worse: the contrast between human aspiration and human reality.

I said, 'I wonder if it was there that I decided history was about feeling more than fact; that it would always be beyond us. Because the facts are beyond imagining, and the feelings are beyond words. In my first months at the hospital I kept a diary of the men who died when I was with them. I suppose I thought it might help me remember them. But there were too many of them, and I realised that in a few years I *shouldn't* remember them; that all I would have would be that list of names and dates. So I stopped.'

'Ah,' he said, and there was a silence. Compelled to ease it, I gave a thin little laugh.

'I'm not sure if that quite answers your question.'

'Too well. To put it into general terms: somebody who had been part of a war might have more connection to the wars of history, because to imagine the feelings of those people requires some experience of what they might have felt.'

'But the study of history is only that list of names and dates. There's no requirement to demonstrate connection when one writes a paper.'

'But that's not how *you* think,' he said.

I said lightly, 'What does it matter what I think?' and then there was a queer moment: he looked up and our eyes met, but the contact was jarring, somehow, and I looked away.

'But you are right,' I said, quickly, to spare him the polite reply he might feel obliged to make. 'I do think any story of the past contains the truth of the present. Not the detail, I mean, but the human truth.'

Of course, part of the human truth of my time as a

VAD was my marriage to George, who arrived home with his leg injury in the second year of my volunteering. He was grey and silent and thin then, as if all the substance had been drained from him. He came to the house to be cared for by the three of us: my mother (capable), Boll (erratic) and me (unsure). He used not to talk much, in those early days, except to thank us with the politeness of a stranger for looking after him, and to ask – again with that strained formality, as if working to keep to social rules he struggled to recall – to be left alone. Yet he simmered, too; with the turning-over of griefs and rages I could only guess at. Once it became apparent that he preferred to be left in silence to examine the newspapers or listen to the wireless, as if he were waiting for some news that might have meaning only to him – a signal, a message in code – I went back to the hospital. His physical recovery had progressed quickly, and in any case my mother had managed to install herself as head nurse in a coup I didn't even notice until it was over, simply by being rather more efficient than I at anticipating his needs.

I hadn't expected George to notice my continuing volunteering, let alone to mind it, but as it turned out (the first of many misapprehensions and wrong-footings to come), in this I was mistaken. He was preoccupied with the fear that one of the patients, gripped by fever or simple insanity, might attack me, and though I argued gently with him, he remained utterly obdurate.

'I tell you, the only lunatic *I've* seen is George himself,' Boll said pertly, before she was hushed by my mother. Though I knew the remark issued more from her own frustration at that time – her social life sadly straitened, no word from Piers for weeks on end, and her efforts to draw George out in the evenings (a measure that revealed her desperation) continually rebuffed – I nevertheless thought she might have had a point. He had brought the war back like a foreign virus inside him, its invisible chemistry working in his blood. Finally one night I came back late, driven home by Lady Rothwell's daughter, and found him weeping in his room. It was the first time I had seen him do so. With his hair clenched in one hand, the other raised as if to ward me off, he said, 'I wish I had died with the others,' and wouldn't let me hold him. I stood and watched him cry, my own hands locked together, hard with fright.

After that day I told Lady Rothwell I would have to give up my work. She held my hand, an unusual gesture for her, and I felt the pulse in her fingers thrumming under the cool, dry skin.

'Look after yourself,' she said, which again I thought odd, but I simply nodded, not knowing what else to say.

Christopher hadn't answered me; he too appeared carried away by some unexpected contemplation, and I thought he looked sad.

'What was it like for *you* during the war?' I asked.

He blinked and looked back up. 'Forgive me. I was thinking about what you said. During the war? Well, I was a self-absorbed, conceited schoolboy when it started – a little Latin-reciting beast indistinguishable from all the other little beasts of the playing field. Then my brothers left, and I was consumed with a single terror, which at times seemed a premonition: that neither of them would come home. I did some rather predictable things: prayed at chapel, berated myself for sneering at them with my school friends, for calling them clodhoppers and philistines, promising I should think of them more kindly if only they might be returned to me. I swore I'd be grateful for ever.'

'But – that doesn't sound at all conceited.'

'Not yet. The thing was, the fear I felt was not so much for them as for myself. I needed them to be who they were, so I might be who I was. Do you see?'

'Yes, though I think you're being awfully rough on yourself. You were only a boy.'

'Well, then they did come back, which I wasn't at all prepared for either.'

'Were you not grateful for ever?'

'Not for long. I believe I had new nicknames for them within the year.'

I started to laugh, remembered almost too late where we were, and closed my mouth hurriedly on the sound. A student at the other end of the room, nothing but a black-robed shape, looked around, then away. Christopher was smiling too, but as I looked at him I thought I saw something more complicated in his expression: the workings of memory, ghosts passing, the unconscious seriousness in his mouth. I felt certain, suddenly, that he was playing the same game as I: making a joke to distract from the truth; like a queer sort of hide-and-seek.

I said, impulsively, 'If I may ask . . . did you lose anyone?'

'Yes. My best friend, in a Zeppelin raid. I was in his

THE HOUSE OF BIRDS

parents' cellar, filching wine for the two of us. When I went back up the stairs, there was nothing left.'

I understood my foolishness then. I had rushed to confirm my suspicion when I did not know him well enough to hear his answer, or know what to say. I found myself gazing at his hands on the table, which lay so still and calm – looking so peculiarly wise – that tears came, stupidly, to my eyes.

'I'm terribly sorry,' I said. He nodded and changed the subject, and I took up the new conversation gratefully, as if we were two tourists in a formal garden who had glimpsed, beyond the gravelled paths and box roses, a wild and frightening terrain, and had hurriedly turned away. But in the civilised itself I saw something suddenly grotesque; I was repulsed by the terms allowed to me: that of the conventional, the conversational, the rules that limit what can and cannot be said by two people two days into an acquaintance. In that moment I felt a flare of hatred; not only for myself, but for Christopher – who was returning to his book, explaining that he had to finish his notes for a seminar the next day – though I couldn't for the life of me have explained why.

Dear reader: a new scene. A woman hurrying alone over the dim cobbles of the High, hampered by the heels that catch between the stones, forcing her to move awkwardly. She is panting slightly, though only you are close enough to hear it. Her face is white, her nose red, her eyes are bright and fevered. She has forgotten to put on her gloves.

The streets of the city have emptied as the light slipped from them, the only other people moving quickly, as she does. Nobody seems inclined to stroll or saunter: not the students bicycling past with their scarves stretched out behind them like streamers; the men in bowler hats and suits threading along from the station; the older woman in furs who alights from a taxi and goes quickly up the steps to her hotel, her head tucked low under her hat.

It was only from these hunched and hurried passers-by that I realised it had grown cold, as if some invisible wave had passed, carrying away all the warmth of the day. I could scarcely feel it: I was hot with haste. Christopher and I had stopped in the quad outside the Bodleian to finish whatever conversation we had been having (trivial talk that I could not even remember now), and in that time the sky had cooled from a pale fiery blue to its present near-navy, blotted by inky clouds. Shadows had vanished into the general darkness; lights flamed in the windows I passed.

I had no idea exactly how late it was. I thought we had left the Bodleian at around three, and I couldn't remember hearing church bells, though they must have rung. My watch, formerly so reliable, had stopped; its face a hole from which the time had drained out. Not that I had checked it. I thought it funny – in an utterly humourless way – that the inscription *For giving me your time* had turned out to mean that after all, and not *I love you*; almost as if George had sealed our fate the day he fastened it around my wrist. The words now seemed almost a command, or a threat. I hurried my pace until I caught up with the lamplighter ahead of me, silhouetted against the dusk at the top of his ladder, like an Indian rope climber. I wanted and yet didn't want to pass him; to swim out beyond the circumferences of light cast by the glass bowls, below which I had passed safely, moving from pool to flickering pool.

My own street when I reached it was entirely dark: thick impasto textures of black and grey, stirred overhead by a faint wind through the trees. I didn't see George approaching until I had almost reached him, and then I started rather violently.

'My God! George,' I said, putting my hand to my heart like a Victorian.

He stopped, but said nothing, and for a moment I peered at his shadowed face, struck by the thought that it might not be George after all. It was certainly unlike him to have left the house; the strangeness of it was jarring, like seeing an unfamiliar hat on one's bed. A harmless hat, an empty bed, yet an absolute wrongness in the juxtaposition. As I looked, I saw that the man in front of me was indeed George, that he was looking at me strangely, almost as if he were trying to work out if I were indeed his wife, and that his thick wool coat was distorted around the shape of a shotgun, held upright, close to his body.

I don't know whether it was fright or prudence that compelled me to act as if there were nothing unusual in any of this, and to say, 'What in heaven's name are you doing out here?' though the words fluttered faintly once they were out, as if unable to cope with the sturdier air, dissolving into a tremolo.

'You were late. I was worried,' he said. His tone was

one of impatience, as if he might have added, 'And naturally I took to the streets with my gun.' His expression had not changed: I realised it was one of intense scrutiny. Having established who I was, he was now trying to work out what I was up to.

I pretended that all was perfectly ordinary. I did not glance at his coat. I told him I had run into a school friend. I apologised. I held up the stopped watch, like a hypnotist, as if trying to draw his eyes away from my own. I said it would not happen again. I essayed a joke but it sounded toadying, and my little laugh emerged as a thin bleat, so I gave up the jovial approach. I remembered the last time I came home late, the night I found him sitting up in bed with his head in his hands, looking as if he wished the head gone, for causing so much pain. I couldn't tell if this cool, watchful irrationality was better or worse; whether some more critical damage had been done; something internal broken, sprung loose like the mechanism of my watch.

After what seemed like an age, he turned and I had no choice but to walk with him back to the house. Neither of us spoke. I looked straight ahead, hearing but not seeing the limping irregularity of his gait, the laboured breathing. Once home, he went wordlessly to bed, and I lay alone, feeling the pressure of his silence like something physical; felt myself weighted by it, pressed into the bed and eventually into a restless, unhappy sleep, chased from one dream to another by careening motor cars, by witches and murderers, at last reaching the locked door of the Bodleian and realising that nobody was inside; there was nobody at all to help me.

PART THREE

OLIVER

Oliver stared at this, the last page of Sophia's history. He turned it over, once, twice, and then (stupidly) a third time. Her handwriting ended halfway down the page, as if she had been interrupted. But then at the bottom there was a scribble, in different ink but unmistakably her, as if she had run out of paper and – with nothing else to hand – picked up the page again to write a little reminder to herself, which was nothing more than a reading recommendation: 'Must read: *Labyrinths of the Ancient World.*'

Oliver was both baffled and outraged. He felt keenly that Sophia – so aware of her reader – had treated him unfairly. At her own invitation, he had started to get to know her. He had stayed up until 2 a.m., stiff-backed and dry-mouthed, because he liked her, and he wanted to know the rest of the story. But she had left everything – George's anger, her undiagnosed attraction to Christopher, her playful conversation with her imagined reader – suspended halfway down a page. She just hadn't bothered to finish it, and, apparently having lost interest, had laid the history down, only returning to jot down an item on her to-do list.

'*Really?*' he asked the surrounding towers of antiques/junk, made mysterious by the night. They maintained their mysterious silence. Even the owl outside had shut up.

'Oh, fuck the lot of you,' Oliver said, and went to bed.

He began the next day with a faint hangover and a sense of disillusionment. Sophia had been right: the past was gone, and his attempts to recapture the life of it could only end in defeat and inauthenticity. He went into the bathroom to shower and scrub the lingering black wine stain off his teeth. Through the window above the sink he noticed that the strangely sunny weather had turned, and the sky was a chalky grey. He doused his face forcefully in cold water, with a grim satisfaction, as if punishing himself for getting carried away, and went out of the bathroom with every intention of not thinking about Sophia's history again.

It was unfortunate, then, that Oliver's mid-morning walk to the chemist, in search of painkillers, took him past the Bodleian, or at least within a few roads of it: so close that it would have been ridiculous not to have a look, seeing as he was in the area. He stood in the quad and looked up at the Tower of Five Orders. A stray memory wandered into view and, after only a short struggle, allowed itself to be captured: Oliver as a child, stopping with a half-eaten chocolate bar to gaze up at the tower until the chocolate melted over his hand. Strange to think that Sophia might have stood in the same spot, aiming her glare at the same place.

It occurred to him that he didn't even know what the Five Orders were – they sounded arcane, hermetic, reminding him of alchemy and secret societies – and he was consequently disappointed to discover, when he looked it up on his phone, that they represented types of architecture. Examining them again, he was less impressed. Sophia was right: the ashlar crenellations and pinnacles did look a bit silly; pompous in their lopsidedness against the flat, colourless face of the sky.

Around him groups of tourists came and went, streaming across the square in haphazard lines, collecting together in clumps before unrolling and streaming away again. Others stopped to take pictures, the general flow diverting around them. Students and a few others crossed in straight lines without stopping. Male students, female students, wearing the same wool hats and scarves. He overheard one of the passing tour guides tell a group of Japanese people that Bodley's Librarian was now a woman. Could this news have made it to Sophia's ears, wherever she was now? He carried out a brief calculation, and was shocked to realise that it was almost ninety years since she had stood here.

Oliver stood for a quiet moment in that private sort of embarrassment that begins and ends only with the self; no less uncomfortable for not having been witnessed by others. Without realising it, he had begun to feel more and more that his reading could end in a real meeting between the two of them. But she was dead – of course she was. He thought of how miffed he had felt over her sudden, unexplained signing-off, and could have winced. He had been too enchanted by the immediacy of her voice to spend much time adding up dates and facts. He had read with lazy absorption, a suspension of any sort of critical analysis. This was not unusual. He was a man who could happily give his mind an hour's holiday, waving it off as it rambled away over the hills. It happened when he watched television, or simply slipped into a daydream: he would lapse into his thoughts and not even notice himself exiting the room, until Kate's voice broke in: 'Hey, Buddha, wake up.' At these times she could make him jump just by touching his arm. Sophia's writing had the quality of one of his own reveries; a daydream in which – for the first time – someone capable had taken the reins.

He returned to the quad, in which, by not having moved, he had been assimilated into a group of Spanish teens.

'And visitors to the library still have to swear Bodley's Oath, even today,' their tour guide said. 'Does anybody know what Bodley's Oath is?'

I do! Oliver wanted to say. But he kept silent and eventually the group (having failed to guess) moved on towards the library entrance. It occurred to him that he was probably lonely. Being around so many other people reminded him of how unfamiliar he was here; how far from a person who would welcome his talking to them. In fact, the only person he had had a face-to-face conversation with in the last week was Lena, and she was emphatically not the welcoming sort.

A thin drift of grey rain had, unnoticed, begun to collect on his forehead and nose. He wiped it with his dewed sleeve (succeeding only in spreading water evenly over his face) and walked off in the direction of the chemist, before realising that his headache, left unattended, had quietly slipped away.

Oliver found a small café and took a table by the window, looking out at the city he had just been wandering; feeling far fonder, now that he was warm, of its rain-speckled cobbles, the shimmering facades, the quivering surface of the Isis. He watched the umbrellas bobbing by like stately black birds. He had bought a coffee in order to log into the Wi-Fi at the café (his phone signal at the house being intermittent at best; a slyly beckoning will-o'-the-wisp) and look Sophia up. Like a parent waiting for their teen to get home at night, he had gone from anger at her lateness to worry. He was concerned that there might be a more sinister reason for her abrupt silence. The last glimpse he had been permitted of her was after her bedroom door had been closed and her light turned off: a woman lying alone in her bed, her unpinned hair around her white face, her eyes open. Finally, and late in the day, he had caught something of her alarm.

Once the phone indicated with an insouciant flash and wink that it was connected, a message from Kate loaded. *Mr Hunt says all should be fine. Calvert case is nonsense. Okay to go ahead with work!* Oliver looked at the screen for a little while, trying to work out how he felt about this. Having failed to come up with an answer – or at least one that made any sense – he closed the screen without replying. Then he took out Sophia's history and began reading through it, looking for search terms. After a while, he considered the three or four notes he had made and reflected on how unsatisfactory the manuscript actually was when it came to hard facts. Sophia had apparently meant what she said about not valuing detail. Verifiable references were scant; he had several names, a couple of vague dates, and no addresses at all. What was it she had said? He leafed back, and found it: *I decided history was about feeling more than fact; that it would always be beyond us.*

Oliver could understand this. He remembered his own life in terms of significant moments; of atmospheres and feelings; of layered associations. The chart music of one summer soundtracking its euphoria; the discovery of a former girlfriend's infidelity, confessed on a climbing holiday, forever accompanied by the fog that came down from the mountains that week, rolling thick and clingy and cold over everything, like wet wool. How could this ever be preserved or recorded? He wondered if his internet search for Sophia was somehow missing the point.

He typed her name anyway: *Sophia Louis*. A predictable mass of results came back, too much to pick through. Typing *George Louis* brought down an avalanche of news items about the present-day royal baby. He tried *Christopher Konig, Oxford University*, without success. A protracted ramble through the history of the Bedfordshire Regiment failed to unearth George's name, which he thought was odd. His coffee went cold and he ordered another from the sympathetic waitress, who evidently had taken his intense phone activity and accidental face-making for the coping mechanisms of a man who had been stood up. He thought he might be on a winner with *Piers, war correspondent, The Times*, but was left, mystifyingly, with nothing. He knew *Boll, Piers, Daphne* would be a failure from the beginning, and Francesco Salviati was apparently an archbishop in Renaissance Pisa.

His second coffee cold beside him, Oliver put his phone down and stared out of the window, aggravated. It had stopped raining. Sharp slices of light showed between the grey clouds, which had previously seemed so impenetrable. As a metaphor he considered it inappropriate timing. He picked up his phone and left the café, catching as he did so the eye of the waitress, who gave him a rueful smile, a minute shake of her head at the infinite unfairness of the world.

As if the Bodleian had woken Oliver's memory of Oxford from its long, senile doze, he found himself recognising more and more of the city. He loitered on bridges he had once dropped stones from; peered through barred gates at familiar quads. Already pleased at this recovery of his history, he was delighted when he turned down a side street and found the second-hand bookshop whose gloomy depths his child self had once plumbed, both wary and seduced. The window displayed the kind of books that made up the stacks of his own temporary bedroom: handsome leather slabs with embossed gold lettering; substantial, authoritative books, from a time when information was not easy come, easy go; giving itself up only after proof of true commitment.

And then only if you were a man! Sophia said, sharply. *And a wealthy man at that.*

Oliver acknowledged this – quite liking the way her voice would arrive at odd moments, like an echo in his own interior – and went into the shop. As he opened the door, a bell rang jarringly above him, presumably startling the absent proprietor into activity. Footsteps sounded overhead. Bits and pieces of the owner came back to him: an older man, grey hair, a bow tie that may or may not have been a later embellishment.

Just as before, there was nobody else in the shop, which was long and narrow and hard to move around without bumping into overloaded display tables or mismatched shelving. He knocked a rack of bookmarks standing by the window and looked at them curiously, wondering who ever bought them. Moving further into the shop, he had the sense that he could be in any era between 1870 and 1970: anything but the present day. Despite its large window, the place was dim; the light becoming heavier, yellowing like aged wine. In the amber depths of the furthest corners dust motes rose gently as he passed. When the owner appeared from some stairs in the corner, Oliver was satisfied to see that he was indeed an old man with a pair of glasses on a chain, and a bow tie, looking exactly the way the owner of a second-hand bookshop ought to look. He had evidently nipped off for a sandwich, the crumbs of which still decorated his shirt.

'Sorry to keep you waiting,' he said.

'That's all right.' Oliver was amused at the idea that his time was precious. 'I was just passing by. I came in here once when I was young.'

'Is that so,' the man said, seating himself on a stool behind an inappropriately new laptop, giving every appearance of not giving a shit. Oliver felt obscurely disappointed.

He tried to increase his relevance. 'Um, I actually have some old books and I was thinking maybe I ought to bring them in. I don't really know anything about them.'

'Bring them in, by all means,' the man said, without glancing up from the screen. 'We don't have enough books here. The shop's half empty, as you can see.'

'Haha,' Oliver said, uncertainly.

At this the owner finally looked up, an unsmiling gaze over his spectacles. 'Is there anything else I can help you with? If not, feel free to roam. *Peruse*. I'll be here, catching up on my Facebook messages.'

In the absence of any indication as to whether he ought to take this statement seriously or not, Oliver moved off to look at the antique books, and was almost immediately captivated by *The Ancient History of the Babylonians*, a large forest-green volume with the venerably scarred hide of a bull elephant.

'That'll be thirty-five pounds. I thought you were selling books, not buying more,' the proprietor observed when Oliver took it to the counter. Oliver opened his hands helplessly. He would present it to Kate later as a humorous Jack and the Beanstalk moment: Oliver heading into a bookshop in the hope of making a killing, emerging with an overpriced, out-of-date tome and a bookmark. Typical. Left to himself, his instinct was not to cut but to accumulate: he expected that the returning Kate would find him suffocated in a collapsed heap of his own collected finds, like a tragic Womble.

'Well . . . I'm not sure I do want to sell. I think I'd rather find out a bit more about some of the books I've got.'

'You're the boss,' the proprietor said. His lips, gesturing towards a smile, revealed a glimpse of teeth as yellow as the pages of his books. Oliver would have put money on the existence of a pipe somewhere in the vicinity.

'I was wondering – is there a way of tracing old books? I mean, are there records of when they're bought and sold, and by whom?'

The man's teeth appeared again. 'Like, say, a central database? Tracking the whereabouts of every second-hand book? I suppose we book dealers would log on with a secret code. We'd have to, really, because we'd be accessing the private information of the general public.'

'I didn't mean every book. Just the rare ones. Or the valuable ones.'

'Are your books rare and valuable, then?'

'I don't know.'

There was a long silence in which Oliver struggled to maintain eye contact with the older man; his grey eyes floating behind his glasses like sharks in an aquarium, possibly hostile towards the viewer, possibly not in the least interested.

The man, abruptly, appeared to relent. The yellow teeth appeared once more. 'Do you think your books might have come from *here*?'

'Well, there's a good chance,' Oliver said. He felt the tiny yet distinct fibrillation of excitement; caught the far-off sound of the hunt. He leaned in. 'I found them at a house. I'm really interested in finding out who owned them. I thought perhaps if just one of them happened to be an important book, I could find out where the rest had come from.'

'I've been here fifty years,' the man said. 'And furthermore, I have a photographic memory. Name a book and I can tell you if it's come through this shop.'

'*The House of Hanover*?' Oliver said eagerly. There was a short pause. 'You're being sarcastic again, aren't you?'

'Yes.'

'Okay.' He saw the pipe then, sitting behind the computer, but it was of no comfort. There ought be a law, he thought, banning the use of pipes and bow ties by anybody but benevolent old gents, so that people like Oliver would not be misled.

'You don't know much about books, do you?' the man observed. 'Well, I tell you what, come back here tomorrow with these potentially rare and valuable books of yours, and I guarantee I'll give you a very fair price for them.'

'Thank you,' Oliver snapped, making for the door.

Behind him the man started laughing, a sound like a disused garage door being forced open. 'Bring them in,' he called. 'Textbooks, fiction, non-fiction, I'll buy them all, and put them on the international database.'

Oliver shut the door hurriedly and moved away down the street, not wanting the other man to enjoy the sight of his consternation for any longer than he had to. Only when he was out of view did he glance back, almost suspiciously, because it was exactly the sort of place from which a wandering shopper purchases something that turns out to have an ancient curse on it, attempts to go back to rid themselves of the item, then finds that the shop itself is not there, and furthermore, nobody in the area has ever heard of it.

The owner, clearly, was slightly mad. Probably lonely. (Another unwelcome vision of his own trajectory.) Then the man's parting words came into focus.

Fiction.

What if Sophia were a character in someone else's novel?

At first he was dismayed at the thought. She had seemed so real; to the extent of almost hearing her voice as he read. The idea that this intimacy could be fraudulent made him feel suddenly embarrassed. Had he fallen for a kind of literary Turing test?

He walked quickly, almost slipping on the cobbles with their découpage of fallen leaves, slick with rain. His perturbation was fading as he went. New thoughts arrived: Sophia's, not his own. He wondered if Sophia herself would consider her reality or fictionality an important distinction. Probably not. Whether she was a writer herself or only a writer's idea, there was still human truth at some level of her character. That was what she valued. Should Oliver mind if the personality he considered himself on familiar terms with was not strictly real? If she *had* been real once, she was dead now. But if she were a character written by a present-day writer – the heroine of a period piece – she might still have a strange kind of life.

The prospect was an immediately exciting one. If he

couldn't meet Sophia, he might be able to meet the person who had created her. And even if she were only a half-finished idea, there was the possibility that he could speak to that person and find out (over coffee, not in a remote house with cable and a sledgehammer) what they believed had happened to her, and *that* – he thought – might be enough to satisfy him.

He smiled as he walked, amused by his own capacity for philosophical manoeuvring; his ideas of what was important and what was truth sliding and blurring simply to allow his relationship with Sophia to retain its meaning. But he was confident, finally, that this was one of his efforts she would approve.

e~

'Do you know if anyone who lived here wanted to write?' Oliver asked Kate when they next spoke. 'Maybe talked about starting a novel? That book I found . . .'

'I thought that was a diary?'

'Well I don't know now. It might be fiction, which is why the names aren't right. It could have been written by someone who lived here. It *is* set in Oxford.'

'Oliver. You remember the situation with my relatives, right? I didn't even know my aunt, let alone whoever owned the house before her. Let alone the bloody Calverts.'

'Yeah,' Oliver said, disappointed. 'I don't know why I thought you would.'

'I'm sorry. I know you like secret mysteries and all that. But I have no idea what belonged to who. Those books could have come from anywhere. Aunt Delia was a total hoarder. She picked up loads of rubbish at car boot sales and who knows where else. You must have noticed.'

'Yes. Never mind . . . It was a long shot. I wanted to ask you something else, too.'

'Oh?'

'About the house.'

'Oh.'

'I've been doing a bit of research – Google stuff mainly – and I was thinking about the fireplaces. Did you notice the one in the sitting room, by the way? With the horse? I started to think of it as Incitatus.'

'Inci-what?'

'I was reading about Caligula the other day. You know, the Roman emperor. He did a lot of insane stuff like ordering his soldiers to collect seashells.'

There was a silence on the other end of the line. He wasn't sure of the tone of this silence. It sounded heavy. He carried on under its prickly weight.

'Anyway, one of the other things he supposedly did was to make his horse, Incitatus, a consul. The horse would even invite people to dinner, and I suppose they'd have to go. But it's like a lot of stories people told about Caligula apparently being mad. It could just have been him taking the piss. Like making his soldiers pick up seashells because they'd been useless. Or implying a horse could do the senators' jobs.'

'Are you seriously telling me a story about a horse that may or may not have been a senator?'

'Sorry. It was meant to be a story about the fireplace.'

'Old fireplaces, secret manuscripts . . . What are you, Harry Potter?' Concern entered her voice. 'Oliver, are you okay?'

'Yes. Yes. Everything's fine.' Oliver, unused to having his

say, was struggling. He abandoned the indirect approach.
'Look, what I meant to tell you was that I was looking into
old houses on the market, and basically, buyers these days
value original features – like fireplaces and cornicing – more
than they do modernised properties. And, you know, the sitting
room *is* pretty big already. I just don't think it's a good idea
to knock everything into one open-plan space. I think that the
best – the *wisest* – thing would be to renovate what's already
there.'

'Sure, sounds good,' Kate said.

Oliver, ready with his next argument – his hand already
raising the notes from the afternoon's googling – found himself
abruptly derailed.

She continued, 'I mean, I don't mind one way or the other.
If it's quicker this way, great. I'm sure you know your stuff.
God knows *I* haven't researched any of it. The only thing I
want is to get this house off my hands so that I – *we* – never
have to think about it again.'

'Oh. Right,' Oliver said. 'Great.'

Kate, misunderstanding his tone, rushed now to conciliate
him. 'I didn't mean to sound ungrateful. Or dismissive. What
you're doing is really important, and I appreciate it.'

Oliver looked around the room, contemplating his
surroundings in the light of the usual world, in which this
was simply an old house they needed to offload, where he
had found a few abandoned diary pages – or an attempted
novel – that had nothing to do with anything. He took in the
reading lamps standing on an old steamer trunk, the ornate
stacks of books, the worn-down velvet of the arms of his
chair. The mismatched porcelain tea set, the ship in a bottle,
the single silver candlestick, the old radio he had tried and

failed to fix. His own bed in the centre of the floor, under the old embroidered eiderdown with its faint smell of camphor. Above it, the peeling paper of the ceiling; the cornicing; the familiar landscape of the night.

Beyond the room, his mind went out into the mildewed kitchen, still untouched; the emptied-out bedrooms; the stripped walls and ceilings, echoing floorboards. Had someone lain in one of those rooms above and thought about what Sophia, their heroine, might do next? Or rather, what might happen to her? She was perhaps closer to the latter than the former; her power all in evasion and lying low. Her Herculean task was simply to navigate the choppy waters of her life, squinting into the night, steering between the rocks. There was something of her history here, he was sure of it; he couldn't believe she had nothing at all to do with this house. But then he couldn't believe *he* had nothing to do with the house, beyond tarting it up and selling it on.

Perhaps, he thought, he might have got too involved.

'I'd better go,' Kate was saying. 'My food's going to be here any minute. I love you. Maybe . . . try to get some sleep, okay?'

After he hung up, the small sense of desolation he had felt returned, larger and darker, as if it had run off to fetch its big brother. It was a sadness he knew he had brought on himself. It wasn't as if he had been carried here like an unconscious sailor drifting into a lagoon, the dim blue waters below the mangroves, a place where history pooled and collected. No: he had insisted on coming; he had been looking for refuge and here he found it – or created it, threading together the house and Sophia and his own fantasies, spinning it around himself as delicately and carefully as a spider web. It would never have taken more than a motion or two – from someone who had no idea the web was even there – to bring the whole thing down.

He felt disappointed in himself. Was this what happened in the absence of Kate? Was the expiry date on his ability to self-regulate really so short? He should be able to control his own slide towards the past – God knows he was familiar enough with it by now. He could sit for hours watching old cartoons, reminded irresistibly of being seven on a Saturday morning, the long, idle hours before lunch. He would revisit anything he had done before – the beach trips and music and chocolate bars of his youth – in the hope of capturing the same sense from it, never quite succeeding. And it was apparent that he could hoard, if he were given the space, filling it with anything that took him back. It was depressing to wonder if he'd have done anything new at all without Kate; as if she, rushing enthusiastically into the future, had hold of his hand, Oliver allowing himself to be towed along, sometimes willingly, sometimes trailing behind, dragging his feet like a child, looking back hopelessly over his shoulder.

Kate was right, he was wrong. Whether it felt true or not, the truth was that within a few months at most he would never see the house again, and he was never going to find out who or what Sophia was. Sophia was right, too. She had told him all along that history wouldn't give him any answers, and it had been stupid of him to think that her own would be an exception. He would have to accept not knowing, even if the not knowing wasn't quite as much fun as she had promised.

One thing comforted him. He went to the fireplace and felt a moment of pleasure. He ran a finger over the bas-relief nymphs, the arrested flutter of their draperies; the muscled flank of the horse, almost slippery in its perfect smoothness. The stone was honey-coloured in the lamplight, but cool to the touch, carrying the charge of the frosting night outside. He had done something, at least, that he could be proud of, even if it was only saving a fireplace.

It was eleven o'clock, and though that week he had been staying up much later, his schedule slipping further and further into the nocturnal, he felt suddenly exhausted. He went to bed with an unhappy feeling of relief, grateful not to have to be Oliver, at least for a few hours; to be instead the Oliver-like person of his dreams, like him moving without real volition, like him getting into trouble, but saved at the last moment by fantastical or absurd interventions: a giant, a talking book, a mobile phone with a blinking chat message window in which words from Sophia appeared in her own blue handwriting:

Oliver?
Oliver, are you there?

The next day, a Monday, was cold and sharp, the late heat-wave apparently having gone for good. Oliver, crossing the gravel-dotted mud of what passed for a car park in the countryside, pulled his blazer around himself, thinking – too late – that he ought to have brought more clothes from London. He was wearing a sweatshirt he used for painting, a wool blazer, and an old purple scarf he had found in the house. He had left his rubber boots lying outside overnight and a toad had moved in; he didn't have the heart to relocate it, and so he had gone back to the leather loafers he last wore when he stepped off the train. They, and the hems of his jeans, were clogged already with mud. But whatever he looked like – madman, itinerant, Alzheimer's patient – it wasn't a yuppie, at least. That seemed important.

He stood at the edge of the enclosures and squinted out over the fields at the figures in the distance. The wind was harrying the clouds, driving them across the sky like sheep; the blue inbetween was the more intense for its infrequency. The bareness of the light out here stung his eyes. The wind picked up the hair of the people in the field, pulling their coats out. They were watching a large bird of prey – Oliver didn't know enough to name it – bank and ascend above them. He could better identify the types of human he was watching: a mother, father and young son, and, standing a little apart from them, Lena.

The hawk disappeared into the branches of a large oak, before Lena whistled and the bird came down, a dark shape diving straight through the wind, a clean line to her raised arm. She handed it to the boy.

Oliver wandered towards the enclosures, not knowing how much longer the demonstration was going to take. Lena's website (the snappily named Oxfordshire Falconry and Owl Conservation Centre) had informed him that she was fully booked for the day, and so he had taken the bus here, to the outskirts of a village on the outskirts of Oxford, in the hope of catching her when she had finished.

He was relieved to be out of the house, which had suddenly filled with contractors, performing their surgery on its stuttering arteries and nerves. Not only did the head electrician and the head plumber seem to be embroiled in an obscure feud originating three years ago in a flooded mansion in

Henley, he found it oddly unsettling to watch as people filled the silent rooms, treading heavily above him, and more so once they started sawing floorboards and chasing pipes. There was no question of him making himself useful to them. Still, he wanted to be useful, and it had occurred to him that the fraught relationship between the Calverts and the Castles might be an opportunity for him to make a difference. And so here he was, milling about under the sharp eyes of the birds, wondering if this was a good idea. Now that he was here and his bus had left, not to return for another hour, his visions of peacemaking had begun to seem slightly preposterous, if not outright hazardous. He wondered if birds of prey could pick up on the general vibe in the same way as dogs, and attack him on Lena's behalf. He wished he had worn a hat.

Not even his unease could override his nosiness, however, and it wasn't long before he was peering over a hedge at a cottage he guessed to be Lena's. It was the only house on the property, and was far too close to the birds for anyone else to reasonably live there. He wondered if the owls kept her awake at night, as his own did. The cottage and garden were extremely pretty – almost parodically pastoral; the house with its soft yellow stone and lavish clematis, the garden with its planters of lavender, sinuous willows, an old green Land Rover under a pear tree, a ginger cat asleep on its bonnet. The sun made another of its brief appearances, lighting up the trees, the crooked slate roof and the mushroom-dotted lawn, warming his face for a moment before being overrun once again by the hurrying clouds.

He realised it had been a few minutes since he had heard a whistle, and he went back towards the birds' cages, where he loitered next to a tabby owl the size of a watermelon. There was a moment in which the two of them made eye contact (owl: severe. Oliver: alarmed) before it rotated its head away and closed its great orange eyes, as if he wasn't worth bothering with.

'Hello,' he said, hoping it would look at him again. It ignored him.

On the bus – where he'd been the only passenger apart from an old woman with a wicker basket who looked at him suspiciously but stopped short of saying something to the effect of 'You're not from round these parts' – he had planned what he was going to say to Lena. He thought brevity would be best; getting out what he had to say before she was able to find something to throw at him. *I'm not going to do anything structural to the house. You were right about that. We'll just do a sympathetic renovation . . .*

Here he stopped, picturing Lena's expression.

Sympathetic, she would say, mockingly. *You bloody yuppie.*

He noticed a small brown mouse weaving unconcernedly in and out of a hedge, only a few feet from the perch of a large red kite, which was watching Oliver with a fixed enmity and hadn't registered the presence of smaller prey. He marvelled at the madness of this mouse, straying into the land of owls and pussycats. He wanted to hiss at it: *Get out of here!* He wondered how much of his own unease he was projecting on to the rodent, which, with a twitch of its tail, disappeared once more into the hedge, and didn't come back.

'Oliver, right?' said Lena. She was standing by the gate to the field, looking more curious than angry. Having only seen her anger in full force, he wasn't sure how long it took her to achieve boiling point. He was counting on having at least a few minutes. 'What are you doing here?'

'Hi, Lena. I just wanted to tell you I'm not going to do anything structural . . .'

She apparently wasn't listening; her head was cocked, taking in his clothes. She herself was wearing one leather glove, scarred and bloodstained, and a torn Barbour. 'You look like a hipster. Is this your idea of country dressing?'

'Er . . . no.'

'This isn't even the countryside. This is the Cotswolds. Very different.'

He ventured a joke. 'Does that mean people don't have shotguns?'

'No.' She looked at him for a long moment, in which it became apparent where the kite had learned its stare. 'We still have shotguns.'

He heard the voices of the family crossing the gravel to their car: the only car he had seen as he entered. It wasn't that he thought Lena would actually *shoot* him. All the same, he wouldn't have minded some paying customers around, their presence enforcing the usual rules of civilisation. She leaned on the gate, unhurried and not apparently in any mood beyond that of fostering unease, and gave an unreassuring smile.

'So, you were telling me what you were doing here.'

'Yes. Right.' Unwillingly, he approached to within striking distance. 'I just wanted to explain that after some . . . thought, we decided we wouldn't do anything structural to the house. No knocking down walls or taking anything out.'

'Why are you telling me this?' she asked. 'Apparently we can't stop you anyway. I'm sure you already knew that.'

'I thought you might want to know. It would make me feel

better, if I were you. And anyway' – he ignored her snort and hurried on – 'no matter who ends up with the house, it will only be improved. It will be a sympathetic renovation. I mean, true to what the house already is.'

'Sympathetic,' she murmured, but didn't add anything else. He took this as a good sign.

'I just thought you'd appreciate knowing what was going on.'

'So you've said. And this is why you're here – just to make me feel better?' Her eyebrows were high. He couldn't tell if she found this funny or offensive. He wondered if the man in the bookshop was a distant Calvert. Or perhaps it was an Oxonian thing. It seemed he was destined to always be on the back foot, one crucial step behind the locals; never to be let in on their joke.

'Look, I don't really understand the situation with your families. I don't think even Kate does. It's unfortunate that circumstances have put you on different sides. But it doesn't have to be hostile. I mean, it's always better to be amicable . . . right?' he said, sounding more hesitant than he would have liked.

'That's debatable,' she said, but without real force.

The kite behind them, as if bored with their conversation, let out a sudden high cry, like a whistling firework. It was a noise he had previously only heard in the distance above him, not right behind his back, and he jumped.

'It's his feeding time,' Lena said. She had noticed him flinch, but she didn't seem contemptuous. 'When I saw you, I thought you were here by accident. That you wanted to see the birds and didn't realise I would be here. That would have been pretty awkward.'

'I like the birds,' Oliver said. 'I've never seen them so close. I didn't know kites were so large. Or so formidable-looking. I thought it was a bald eagle at first.'

He had said it almost experimentally, to provoke her scorn – the same impulse as the one that compels people to touch a plate once they've been warned that it's hot – but she just nodded, and said, 'Lots of people think that.'

'I was actually reading about falconry the other day. It was in a book about the Babylonians. Apparently this guy Layard found a bas-relief of a man with a bird on his wrist in the ruins of the palace of Sargon II. That would mean that falconry was around in 700-and-something BC. Apparently that would have been the first evidence of it. But then I googled it and couldn't find a picture of the bas-relief, which was a shame. Er, anyway, you probably know all that.'

Lena tipped her head and narrowed her eyes, as if she might bring him into focus and in that way make sense of him. Then she laughed.

'What's so funny?'

'You aren't actually quite like I thought,' she said.

'How do you mean?'

'Well, I thought you were this, I don't know . . . Rolex-wearing, gym-visiting, BMW 4x4-driving *consumer*. The kind of person who thinks Dubai is the ultimate holiday destination. Who says things like "put a pin in it". Or "sympathetic renovation". Who types LOL. Who *says* LOL. Someone who buys men's fashion magazines. Who'd post a picture of two fucking glasses of champagne and a hot tub on Instagram. With multiple hashtags.'

Oliver looked at her in dismay, assuming she had spoken to people who knew him, or somehow accessed his and Kate's social media accounts, before realising that she was picking failings out of thin air, and it was only by inspired guesswork that most of them had happened to hit home.

He laughed half-heartedly, feeling stung, and more than a little fraudulent. 'I think you can tell I don't read fashion magazines.'

'Fair point.'

'What got you into this?' he asked, not only to turn the focus away from his own lifestyle, but out of genuine curiosity. 'Falconry, I mean?'

'I saw a flying demonstration when I was ten, and I didn't want to do anything else after that. I always liked animals, but birds are special. The relationship you have with them is different to other animals. You can't have that sort of equality with a dog or a horse, and you can't work with a cat. Though I've heard people used to hunt with cheetahs in ancient Egypt. I guess you'd know all about that.'

'I had no idea.' he said. 'I've never been friends with a bird. There's an owl living near my window who keeps me awake. I don't know if that counts.'

'In central London?' Lena asked.

'Ah . . . I'm still living at the house, actually.'

'So you really are sleeping there.' She raised her eyebrows again, and he thought that he had never seen such an expressive and yet unreadable face. She frowned and twisted her mouth, and her eyebrows shot up and down, her features in perpetual motion, like a storm at sea, but he couldn't tell whether she was entertained or angry, surprised or dismissive, approving or disapproving.

'I really would like to see the birds flying,' he said. 'Not for free, I mean. I'd just be a customer.'

'Well that's a given,' she said tartly. 'I'm actually fully booked over the next few weeks.'

'Oh. That's good for you.'

'It's been a good couple of years,' she said, then frowned, and tapped on the gate. This little moment of superstition made him feel more relaxed, somehow. He tried not to show it.

'Look,' she said, 'if you want to come around with me now while I finish up, you can meet the birds.'

'I'd love to.'

He followed her quietly while she 'finished up': an activity seeming mostly to involve the tossing of limp yellow chicks, like bedraggled dandelions, into the waiting beaks of the birds. Oliver looked away delicately as they ate. He heard crunching.

She spent longest with a kestrel with a damaged wing, talking to it softly. It was the first time he'd heard her sound affectionate.

'What happened?' he asked.

'He got beaten up by the local kites. He looks a bit of a state now, but actually he'll be fine once the feathers grow back.'

'Why did they attack him?'

'He just got too close. They don't like it. They think they're in competition, when they're not really. But you can't tell them that.'

'Animals are cruel,' he murmured.

'Everything's cruel,' she said, sweetly.

He felt vaguely, stupidly piqued at this. 'I'd like to think I'm not.'

She laughed at him. 'You just don't know what you're capable of.'

When the finishing up was finished, she sighed, took her gloves off and faced him, giving him her full consideration. He stood awkwardly, waiting for her conclusions.

'How did you get over here – the bus?'

'Yes.'

'It's going to be another half-hour before it comes back – do you want a coffee or something? I'm having one.'

'That would be great,' he said, surprised. 'Thank you. That's really kind.'

'Don't let's get carried away,' she said, but as she turned away in the direction of the cottage, he thought she sounded amused. 'We may as well stay out in the sun. Wait here, I'll bring them out.'

Oliver looked up and saw that she was right: the sun had been out for a while, as if it too had relented and decided to play nice. The clouds had all discreetly withdrawn and the wind had dipped, allowing some of the warmth of the past week to return; the embers of the Indian summer. He unwound his scarf and sat down on a grassy slope, facing the sun. Over the hills, the domes and spires of Oxford were visible in the distance, glinting in the light like Eldorado. Out here was silence. Noises came to him gradually, each one arriving distinct and unhurried. Wood pigeons cooing fatly in the trees in the distance, a lone lingering bee droning over the purple drifts of Michaelmas daisies. The sound of the kettle boiling, from the open window of the cottage. A quiet rose from the aviaries, a hush that seemed nothing so much as lordly, as if their inhabitants considered themselves above pointless chatter.

He was wondering what sort of bird he'd be – not a hawk, or any sort of raptor (too haughty), or a raven (too canny), but something odd and hapless, like a dodo – when Lena came back out with two mugs. He couldn't think of *her* as a bird, though she did have a good line in cold stares. He found it difficult to assess her in any kind of objective way. Something about her was too close up, too immediate, to take stock of. She had taken off the old coat and put on a loose shirt; her face looked rinsed and bright, without the smudge of dirt – or blood – he had noticed on her cheek as she worked.

She sat down next to him on the grass and handed him his coffee. The sun intensified the rum colour of her skin, like fired ceramic. He wondered what her heritage was; trying to place the thick dark hair, her black eyes. 'God, this is nice,' she said, not noticing his gaze. She was rolling up her sleeves, to turn her forearms up to the sun; a funny, almost trusting gesture, like a cat showing its belly. The skin there was slightly paler, he saw. Not having previously been able to look at her properly – being more concerned with coping with *her* alarming scrutiny – he took the opportunity now that her attention had slipped away; noticing her small hands with their short, chipped nails, her legs, stretched out, neat and lean in their narrow jeans. Her hair was in a ponytail but the wind had pulled curls out here and there, which clustered around her face, spiralling down her neck. He remembered, unwillingly, what Kate had said: *she's fucked mostly everybody.*

'I'd have offered you a ride back to town,' Lena said. 'But the Land Rover's broken down. Jim – my husband – has the car, and he won't be back until later.'

The news that she had a husband was jarring; though it shouldn't have been, Oliver thought guiltily, and perhaps *wouldn't* have been if he had been acting like a decent human being and not checking out her legs. He had never been given to assessing other women, making the private calculations that his friends claimed livened up their day; added 'spice', as if women were an array of condiments. Oliver could identify beauty when he saw it, but beyond that his imagination failed. Perhaps it was only his awe of Kate – an ever-present, often dizzying disbelief that she was his girlfriend – that had kept him on the straight and narrow. It seemed that nearly every hour without her he had discovered a new bad habit; another tumble downhill. In dismay he had watched himself slip into aimlessness, hoarding, chronic pottering, daydreaming, drinking too much, eating badly, carrying out hopeless investigations. And just when he might have thought that was the end of it, he was proved wrong again – because only a week into Kate's New York trip and here he was, staring at the sultry hollows of her distant relative's neck. It wasn't looking good for Oliver, as a person.

Realising he had left a pause hang for a beat too long, he hurriedly asked, 'Do your parents live around here too?'

'Yeah.' She pointed. 'Back towards Oxford. How come?'

'I was wondering why it was you I . . . met. And not them.'

'They're calmer than me,' she said, and laughed, and after a tiny hesitation, Oliver joined in.

'So you're a Godwin?' he asked.

'I was once. That's my dad's family surname. I'm a Lennox now.'

'Lena Lennox?'

She narrowed her eyes at him. 'Yeah. I know.'

'So . . . you must have grown up around here. That must be nice. For your family to be so much a part of a place – part of the history of it.'

'Well my father grew up in Grenada. Grenadan mother, English father. He's polite about it, but you can tell he thinks it's cold and shit here. You've got my mother down, though. She's Mrs Community. She's a Calvert by birth.'

'Calvert . . .' he said.

She was looking at him more sharply now. Slow to pick up on the change in atmosphere, Oliver asked, 'So do you know much about the Calverts who lived in the house years ago?'

'Look, let's not discuss that. It's a sore point, okay?'

'Oh God, yeah, sure,' he said hurriedly. 'I wasn't trying to . . .'

'I know. You're just a nosy fucker,' she said, more gently.

'That's about it.'

'So, I'm going to guess that your family are fairly normal. Hence the fascination with ours.'

'They're pretty boring, yes. If they've got any secrets they've hidden them well.'

There was a moment of equable silence, both of them contemplating the sunlit hills, as if their families lay just beyond them – which in Lena's case he supposed they did. The faint scent of the coffee spiralled up to him; he felt suddenly, unreasonably peaceful.

'How did you know I worked here?' Lena asked.

'I just googled Lena and Oxfordshire. Your website was the first result, and your photo was on it . . . Don't you think it's strange how easy it is to find people now?'

'Well, I do pay Google to make sure I'm easy to find. But I know what you mean.'

'We take it for granted that we can usually look people's contact details up somehow. And half the time you can see way more than that: people put everything online. But it's going to make a lot of work for future historians, isn't it? If the internet is still going hundreds of years from now, it's going to be a mammoth task to research the past. There'll be an impossible mass of personal information to sift through.'

'And we'll never be properly *gone*,' Lena said. 'You know, there usually comes a time after someone dies when there isn't a trace of them left. Their bones are mulch, any record of them has disintegrated, anything they made is gone; they're so far back in their own family history that their descendants wouldn't remember them. But we won't ever have that time. It's sort of disturbing.'

'Unless there's nuclear war, or an asteroid, or something.'

'There is that,' she agreed, apparently comforted.

'You just don't think about it until you try to look up someone from the past – from only a few generations ago – and you realise how hard it is.'

'Who were you looking up?' she asked, and this time he picked up on her tone.

'Oh, just a writer. Not a famous one. I was enjoying their book . . . I wanted to find out more about them.'

She nodded, then lifted her head suddenly, as if she scented something on the wind.

'That's your bus coming.'

He heard it too, then, the ponderous bulk manoeuvring around the hedgerows.

'Don't worry, you won't miss it. It waits here for a while. Last stop.'

They got to their feet and she led him back through the aviaries towards the road.

'Thanks for the coffee,' Oliver said. 'And showing me the birds.'

'If you're still around in a few weeks, you could come by on a clear day and see them fly. It's quieter the closer winter gets.'

'I will.'

She looked at him sideways. 'Thanks for coming out here. I appreciate the effort. I know I gave you a hard time, before.'

'Well, thanks for reconsidering your opinion of me.'

'I've reconsidered, have I?' she said, eyebrows up.

'Er . . . I'd hoped so.'

'Okay. I'll give you this. You're not a total cunt.'

'I'll take it. Thanks.'

They stood for a moment by the road, Lena holding the two coffee cups. Further down the hill the empty bus had pulled in and switched its engine off. The driver appeared to be reading a newspaper.

'And by the way, I don't hate Kate,' Lena said. 'I don't even know her. She seems to be behaving reasonably under the circumstances. You can tell her I'm not her enemy. Or my parents, either. This isn't really to do with her.'

Oliver hesitated, embarrassed, when he tried to think how to answer this. Kate hadn't been quite so magnanimous about Lena. The bus driver, restarting his engine, came to his rescue.

'Go on!' Lena said, giving him a little push. 'Take care,' she called, unexpectedly, as he ran waving down the road, holding on to his loose scarf to prevent it escaping over his shoulder. By the time he had boarded – to the evident amusement of the driver ('Rush hour, eh?') – and looked back, she had gone.

As the bus carried him back to Oxford through the darkening green lanes, the sun fading as quickly as it had appeared, Oliver sat feeling uneasy. He had ostensibly succeeded in his aim to, if not make peace between the two families, at least ease the hostilities. Yet he couldn't help but feel a sense of betrayal – his own betrayal of Kate, though what form exactly this had taken he wasn't sure, and when he broke the conversation into its constituent parts he couldn't pick out a defining moment, a point at which he passed from innocence to guilt.

℮

Oliver still hadn't managed to shake off his sense of wrong-doing by the time Kate called that evening. When she asked him what he'd been up to, he was almost tempted to confine himself to an update on the contractors' progress and not mention his visit to Lena's house. As soon as he told her about it, he realised his instincts had been correct.

'You went over to her *house?*'

'I didn't actually know it was her house. I knew she ran that bird of prey place out of town. But why does it matter if it was her house or not?'

'It doesn't matter,' Kate agreed. 'What matters is that you . . . you went behind my back and fraternised with the Godwins!'

'She's not a Godwin,' Oliver clarified, needlessly.

'Not a . . . For God's sake, I don't bloody care whether she's a Godwin, or a Calvert, or a horse that's been made a senator. Why didn't you tell me you were planning to do this?'

'I sort of went on the spur of the moment. You would have been at work. I didn't have much else to do. I thought they had no chance of getting the house, so it couldn't have done any harm. I really didn't know you'd be angry about it.'

'I wouldn't be angry about you spending a romantic after-noon with a woman who hates my guts?'

'She said she didn't hate you.'

'How very generous of her,' Kate cried. 'She's a modern-day saint.'

He waited as Kate riffed sarcastically on the subject of Lena's extraordinary beneficence, comparing her favourably with Mother Teresa, suggesting that shrines be erected in her name so that pilgrims could visit, and so on.

'Look,' Oliver said, when she had finished, 'I'm really sorry. I thought I was being helpful. It did seem to make things more friendly. Surely that's a good thing?'

'*How* friendly?'

He felt stung, though whether the sense of injustice was enhanced or dampened by the fraction of truth in Kate's suspicions, he could not have said. He was taken aback by her anger – which was unusual – and even more surprised at the indignation he felt rise up to meet hers. 'Kate, come on. She's married. And I would hope that you'd trust me.'

She lowered her voice almost immediately, sounding abashed. 'I *do* trust you. But married doesn't mean anything. Look at Otto. Look at Lauren and Seb. Or Francesca, finding out about that girl two months after the wedding. Two months! I heard Lena's husband spends half the year in Silicon Valley. He paid for her to start up her business, and just lets her get on with it. He doesn't care that she's having affairs.'

'I don't see what's in it for him,' Oliver said. 'And how do you know this anyway?'

'Family talk.'

'Family gossip.'

'Now you're defending her?'

'No. I don't care about her, or her marriage. I'm sorry, okay? I should have run it by you first.'

'Okay,' Kate sounded comforted by this. 'So . . . what was her house like?'

'An old cottage, from what I saw.'

'Damp and poky,' Kate said with satisfaction. 'And what did she say – that she didn't hate us?'

'She said she didn't know you, and you weren't her enemy, and it wasn't anything personal.'

'Hmm.'

'And she said I wasn't a cunt, which seemed like a compliment.'

'Ugh,' Kate said with distaste. 'I hate that word. It's so bloody crude. But then she's not particularly feminine, is she?'

Oliver hesitated, unable to think of an honest answer that wouldn't endanger their new and fragile accord. He didn't think Kate would want to hear that Lena, without evidently bothering much with products and styling, still possessed a stray, clean sort of beauty; that even when she was striding around waving the carcasses of dead chicks as she talked, she had something about her – a low, ember heat. It was in the way her body collected itself, her eyes, the precise voice that dropped, occasionally, to a ductile murmur. Sex appeal: perhaps it could never really be ignored. Though Lena wasn't thinking about it, the evidence of her sensuality must surface from time to time, and though he wasn't looking for it, he couldn't help but catch it, like a scent on the wind.

'If feminine means not having a bloodstain on your cheek,' he said, carefully, and Kate laughed with delighted scorn.

They talked for a little longer, Kate cheering up enough to update him on the lives of their friends, about whom she had heard more news than he, despite her being in New York and Oliver only in Oxford. As he listened, he felt a kind of fatigue settling in, at the hard machinery of life: money and mortgages; marriage and adultery and divorce; difficult pregnancies and difficult deliveries; work, work, more work. He thought that Sophia was right: at any point in history the human truth would be the same. Pick an era – pick a person – and you'd find someone worrying about all those things; trying, in the din of it, to remember love, the supposed point of it all.

When Kate had gone, leaving Oliver in a suddenly bleak silence, he thought again about his afternoon in the sun. It had the quality of a more distant memory, as if it had happened months ago. A few moments stood out: the soft-ness of the grass, bending and springing back against his palm; the sharp curl of the coffee steam; the miraculous blue sky. It was romantic only in a medieval sense, he thought, defensively: the hawk swooping to the wrist, the leather gauntlet. But almost immediately, as if to prove Kate right, his mind went to the touching bareness of Lena's delicate wrists, her dark, unexpectedly tranquil eyes.

To distract himself, Oliver went over the house, inspecting the work that had been done with the protectiveness of a parent. His rounds stopped abruptly in the back bedroom, arrested by the sight of all the radiators off the walls, revealing fragments of sea-green wallpaper, scattered leaves, lone flower petals – and the finely delineated head of a bird. All that was left of the room's former splendour. He moved his hand towards a petal; thought better of it; left his fingers to hover over the hand-painted strokes, like blind antennae, marvelling at their sense of colour. He peered into the glinting eye of the bird and thought he saw something melancholy there. Sympathy, perhaps, for Oliver himself; his efforts find some connection with the house; anything to hang meaning on to.

He thought he would leave instructions the next day for the wallpaper to be preserved. He didn't know what, ultimately, could be done with the few pieces that remained, but he didn't want them stripped away, either. He wondered what Sophia would have done with them. *Sophia, what happened to you?* he thought, not for the first time that day.

He realised that he had never been as interested in his own life as much as he was in the fate of a possibly fictional woman from the twenties, or even as much as this house. He still had the persistent sense that the two were somehow connected. Sophia had seen this bird, he knew it. He felt as if neither of their stories – woman or house – was over; that both had secrets to give up, though he couldn't rationally separate this conviction – so sharp and immediate – from his own desire to pursue a mystery, to live out his reawakening love of historical romance.

He went over the rest of the work uninterestedly, with no idea whether what he was looking at was right or wrong, then went back downstairs and opened a bottle of wine. He poured out a prim glassful, put the cork back in and put the bottle away as ostentatiously as if he had an audience. Today he had meant to make a start on clearing the sitting room, and he set himself at the task now, beginning with the piles of books, which he put into a box to take to the sarcastic bookseller in town. As he went, he took a few out, put them back in, then took them out again, deciding that there was no harm in keeping a couple.

Near the bottom of the pile he found *Labyrinths of the Ancient World*. A heavy cerulean book, published in 1915, its gold lettering faded and its spine peeling. He stared at it for a while before he understood exactly what it was he was holding. Then he opened it up to see the cut-away section, the folded pages, marvelling aloud, 'Sophia. You sneaky fucker.'

Labyrinths of the Modern World
S. L.

Dear reader! Welcome back!

Now, if you've no idea what on earth it is you're being welcomed back to, please return to your books. (A teacher wrote that once, on an essay of mine. 'Go back to your books, Sophia, and start again.') I've told you at the end of each chapter where I am to be found next. Must I also tell you where I've been? No, I'm afraid it might spoil you: you'd grow lazy, like a fat pasha being fed grapes. I'm doing this for your own good, my dearest darling reader. As Burke said: 'To read without reflecting is like eating without digesting.' By forcing you to do some of the work yourself, I shall make you quick; by teasing you, I'll make you strong.

There is – I confess – another, more practical reason for dividing this history into pieces. I simply haven't a book large enough to fit it all inside. Or not one that I care to eviscerate. At first I found it very difficult to take my scissors to the defenceless innards of any book, even one I didn't particularly care for. I didn't want to become another Arthur Evans, repainting throne rooms and building columns – or another Mrs Simmonds, for that matter. I liked to imagine myself in the past, but physically implanting myself there was quite another thing entirely.

But later I thought differently. These books are not history: they are somebody's idea of it. In this case, a man's idea – and a pompous, authoritative idea at that. In deciding who to disembowel, I picked the authors who irritated me most. Mr Geddes, who thought Elizabeth I a royal freak; a woman aping a man, an ageing virago with her breasts on show. And Mr Hart Wyndham, who said that the goddess of the labyrinth is female because the labyrinth, like the female mind, is circuitous and diffi-cult to navigate, yet leads only to a point within itself. It is true that history is written by the victors, and the victors are usually men. If one wants the woman's story, it is often necessary to read between the lines. I have taken it a step further: I am literally between their lines. I have broken in, uninvited, and I can't help but laugh at the image this calls to mind: of myself as a cuckoo, stealthily laying my egg in another bird's nest.

℮

While we're on the subject of pompous men, I shall open this part of my history with a scene at a GP's surgery. If you care to picture it, you need only think of a typical practice. The private patients arriving through the front door and being shown into a pleasant waiting room with a painted landscape of a Scottish glen and a vase of hothouse flowers. The poor – who comprise the greater part of the patients – coming and going through the back entrance, so as not to offend the sensibilities of their betters. (The poor to be envied in only one respect: that of not having to sit and look at the Scottish glen until its indeterminate greens and browns waver and merge and eventually cannot be viewed without provoking an associative upswing of nausea.)

In the consulting room, you will find that now-familiar woman in her dark coat and slightly outmoded hair. She is not looking quite so defiant this time. It isn't that she is no longer angry, but that she is sad, too, and anger and sadness rushing around together – colliding and crashing like waves – can often end in tears, and she is determined that she should not cry in front of Dr Harris. Dr Harris, for his part, resembles a silvered musk ox: the broad body, awkwardly clothed; the great, mournful head. The room is stuffy despite the cold of the day outside: the glass cabinets with their obscure bottles, the shelves of books, the sun-faded charts all crowd in so that the large body of the doctor seems to swell and fill the room, and the woman thinks she might faint, if she were the fainting type.

There: you have the scene. I personally don't care to picture it again, and now that I have written it down, I never shall.

I had made an appointment with Dr Harris – whom I had never much liked – out of desperation. I was ostensibly there to discuss my years of fertility: how many were used up, and how many I might reasonably have left. Despite everything, I had not quite given up hope that George and I might have children. I worried about George's state of mind – his moods, his looks, his secret thoughts – but I reasoned that I would be the one to spend the most time with our children, to raise them and love them. In my own secret thoughts I wondered if perhaps a child might help him; that through its very newness – its innocence, its complete difference to anything that had gone before – it might somehow bring him back to himself. And since the day I found him on the street with his shotgun, he had been more normal, more familiar, and I said hopefully to myself that he must have been shocked by his own oddness, and had worked to prevent its reappearance. I tried not to think that I simply hadn't been back to the library since then.

I had thought it better not to visit the Bodleian until my mistake could pass into not-too-recent history. I had written to Christopher (whose address, thank God, I now knew) to tell him I should not be able to meet him for a little while, and asked him to wait for me, if he could. I didn't explain; and his polite reply, when it came, was entirely incurious. He said he should be glad to accompany me again, when I was next disposed to visit. If he wondered about my personal life he never showed any sign of it.

I also hoped, that morning, to subtly fish for what else Dr Harris might know. A minor operation, extracting some small but important detail from the learned man's brain. At the forefront of my suspicions was a story I had been told by a friend of mine whose husband slept with a prostitute in Cairo. His doctor diagnosed the man and his wife with VD, but forbore to tell her what it was. She only found out what her mysterious illness had been years later, after a chance conversation with a nurse. So there I sat, steeling myself for news of this kind, only to be told – without hedging or stalling or softening of the blow – that I couldn't have children anyway.

'What?' I said. 'You must be mistaken.'

Dr Harris looked at me over his spectacles, his heavily fringed eyes blinking slowly. He was a man who evidently missed the Victorian age, back when he ran a strict practice and used not to tolerate female impertinence. It was with faint reproof that he asked, 'Did you not know this?'

'I'd no idea. None at all. Are you quite sure?'

He looked down; shifted through the papers that lay facing him. 'Oh, yes, I see. Well, it appears we didn't tell you. It was in the period following your miscarriage. This was caused by fibroids, as I believe you are aware. A fibroid was removed. It seems the damage was too great for there to be any possibility of another child.'

'Oh.'

I remembered that time. It wasn't long after George sailed: a day of startling red, of disbelief. Then several weeks of bed rest, floating in and out of strange morphine dreams, peopled by Chinese dragons and laughing fairy children, a fantastical haze through which pain occasionally made itself felt, like a falling icicle. The operation I remembered only as a part of these dreams; pale green tiles and a bird outside a closed window; masked faces, then, later, the endless crisp white of the bedclothes, a snowy landscape across which I roamed, lost and cold.

Later there were a few days of fever, during which I thought I could talk Russian, and that my hands and feet weren't attached to my body. Once I hovered above the bed, seeing myself lying below, my eyes vanished into blackness like a death's head, my face a luminous grey-white, phosphorescent. My wet hair, writhing on the pillow.

I had to wait until after his return and recuperation to give George two pieces of news: I was pregnant. I am no longer pregnant. When I told him, he wept. 'It's a punish-ment,' he said, which I thought odd. I wasn't sure which of us he thought was being punished, and for what. But he never said it again, and I put it down to his childhood as the son of a pastor: old words, not his own, jolted out of him by shock.

'Why did nobody tell me?' I asked Dr Harris now.

'You were naturally distressed at the miscarriage, and it was thought better for you not to know at that time. A woman only a few years before you had to be committed to an asylum under similar circumstances. The shock of the news had brought on a case of hysteria. When a woman is told that the entire reason for her existence, the central focus of her life, is gone – most cruelly and unfairly – it can upset the balance of her mind entirely. Hence Dr Dawlish – I believe it was he, yes, it was indeed – decided to tell you once your own mind was more settled and stable, rather than in the period of mourning that follows such an incident.'

I clenched my hands on the chair. 'It's been seven years.'

'Do try to keep calm, Mrs Louis. There has been a war, you know. Dr Dawlish's son died at Ypres. It is regrettable that you weren't told sooner, but we cannot expect your fertility to be at the forefront of everybody's minds, under the circumstances.'

George and I ate dinner together that night. It struck me with heavy irony that only a day before, I might have taken this for a good sign: that things had returned to normal, or at least what passed for normal in our peculiar household, hushed as a chapel – or a library. Sometimes it was strange to remember that there was a time when Boll and I had run up and down the stairs, shouting and waving swords, until Nanny hauled us off and told us to be little ladies. Or that the piano used never to go unplayed for more than a few days at a time, because my mother loved it so much; swaying faintly as she listened, as if physically stirred by the notes. The dining room itself, formerly so splendid under the chandelier that darted small points of light across the rich gold-papered walls, the glassy mahogany of the table, the Turkish carpet on which the small Sophia and Boll had seated themselves and shouted all the magic-sounding words they could think of, seemed an entirely different room these days. It was not simply that the chandelier was gone and we sat under the bold glare of the new electric light, but, I realised, George and I were fundamentally unable to provide the house with that enchanted sense of conviviality and ease, an atmosphere I used not to think twice about in times of surfeit.

I had always believed that the feeling of absence and desolation that hung about the house more and more frequently was a temporary state of affairs. Surely the house remembered its former joys; like myself, it was only biding its time, the drawing room waiting patiently to be filled with people in linen and silk in the summer, talking over the piano, cradling their delicate teacups like birds' eggs; the dining room anticipating the flurry of family at Christmas, a fug of mulled clove and orange and cigars. 'When we have children,' I often told myself – walking past the silent drawing room and feeling its chill run over my face and across my shoulders like a breath from the dark north – 'when we have children, everything will be all right.'

I couldn't summon the will, now, to eat my soup. My knowledge turned and turned ceaselessly in my stomach. Making conversation, as I usually tried to do, was impossible. George didn't appear to notice whether I was speaking or not; he spooned his own soup into his mouth with the efficiency of an automaton. He always ate like this: impassive, with a measured speed, his face set as if to say: *Let's get this over with.*

Eventually I couldn't bear it any longer and said, 'George, I saw Dr Harris today. He told me I'll never be able to have a family.'

George looked at me in surprise, his spoon arrested halfway to his mouth. 'Do you *want* that?' he asked.

'Why, I . . .' I stopped, and looked at him with dawning suspicion. 'My God, did you already know about this?'

He indicated with his spoon: yes.

'But . . . why didn't you tell me?'

215

He stared at me with equal incomprehension. 'Why ever would I . . . I didn't think it necessary. It's impossible . . . Why in heaven's name would we have children?'

I started to say, again, 'My God,' but somewhere partway through the words lost their cohesion, their consonant skeletons crumbling to fragments, and I found myself saying, 'God damn you' – or would have, if my voice hadn't queerly faded out, and I realised that my mouth had only gestured at speech, as if a great effort of will had been required to expel the sound and air, a power I did not have.

He barely noticed, continuing in a tone of growing horror. 'I don't understand what's wrong with you, Sophia.'

One word was all I could manage; a weak, sickly little 'What?'

'This isn't a world to bring children to. This filthy, tainted cesspool. Men killing each other, women killing their own babies, people turning on each other like animals. It's like Sodom and Gomorrah, without any God to strike it out. There's no beginning again. There's no hope. And you talk about throwing an innocent child into this hole, this pit? Crossing your fingers and hoping it stays afloat?' His voice had risen; he corrected it, and spoke with a cool, strange carefulness. 'Good God, I'd rather cut my own throat.'

Then, as if in conclusion, he placed his spoon precisely back into the bowl. His hands were trembling.

Watching him dabbing his mouth with the napkin, I gave up trying to answer. There was no point in arguing with him, accusing him of betrayal, of deceit, or neglect. I saw that he had passed beyond my comprehension. He

THE HOUSE OF BIRDS

lived in a place in which nothing was recognisable; in which kindness was a bad joke, reason was a trap, talk was meaningless, sex was a mocking call in the street, and duty and convention had been thrown on the fire, leaving only a heap of ash to blow in the scorching winds, through which he strode, the grim king of a grim land. My own eyes burned as I lowered them, stung rather than soothed by my rising tears, as if I had seen that place myself.

Before now, my thoughts on our marriage had always followed the same well-worn route. If I thought to myself that I deserved something of my own, the guilt called back, snappish and prompt, 'You are greedy, you expect too much'; if I went to the library, it warned, 'You are neglecting your duty to your marriage and your home: the things your mother devoted herself to, without a second thought.'

'Or any thanks,' I couldn't help but add, blackly. For *that* was the other side of it, and when I told myself: 'Sophia, you were never called up; asked to hand over your health and happiness in service to your country. The only thing asked of you is that you support the man who did, by devoting yourself to him,' something unknown would cry back, just as quickly:

'And so you did, for eight years, and what good has it done either of you?'

It was a route leading always back to its own beginning, like a snake endlessly biting its tail; a joined-up labyrinth. That night my thoughts veered off their usual track into the uncharted surrounding forests, but once there they quickly became lost, their energy flagged, and they came to a stop, exhausted. There was no promise in this break for freedom, no reward. I considered separation; divorce – bleakly, for I couldn't see George agreeing to either. Last year's Matrimonial Causes Act (which, according to Boll, had made it far easier for certain women of her acquaintance to extricate themselves from awfully dull marriages) was unlikely to help me, given that George hadn't committed adultery. Neither could I prove desertion, or cruelty. I imagined the impossibility of explaining George to a solicitor: his silences, his strangeness. Without George's own collusion, I had no chance of freeing myself. The courts were for men: a place where there was no rape within marriage, where a wife's murder was considered manslaughter, where the Sex Disqualification Removal Act failed to help the sixty-three female teachers in Wales, sacked because they were married.

I lay in bed and felt the night close around me, cool and impersonal. I put my head on the pillow with a sense of resignation, waiting for the tears I had held back over dinner to come at last, ready to give myself over. But no tears arrived, and no sleep either, though I lay there until the dawn came, waiting for one or the other. I was awake as the sun rose, watching the window fill with the weak, wet dawn, the light gradually blanching the room.

This had been my mother's room, once, but there was no suggestion of her presence in it. Under the eye of Mrs Simmonds, the elegant rosewood furniture that I remembered from my childhood had been moved to a guest bedroom and replaced by tawny burr-walnut monoliths. The lily-patterned wallpaper with its delicate pastels, white blooms floating like swans, had survived, only to be stripped later, after damp got in. I pictured my mother; the rare times we saw her in bed, with her hair in disarray, its wily grey curls running riot. I wondered what advice *she* might have given me, had she still been alive, but the truth was that she was never a woman to dispense advice, preferring to sit, and watch, and think her own thoughts.

Even when it was long past the time I'd usually get up, I hadn't the energy to turn myself, or propel my body out of bed. My arms and legs might have been made of lead, lying heavy and inert. I was thinking about the conversations I'd had yesterday with Dr Harris and with George; my grief faded now, replaced by a dull sense of the inevitable, a cold, enervating lethargy. I did not attempt to analyse or comprehend any of the words. The conversations simply revolved slowly through my memory, playing like records, and once they were over, I played them again.

Margaret knocked at the door, alarmed by the change in routine.

'Is everything all right, ma'am?'

'Quite all right, thank you.'

'Would you like anything brought up?'

'No, thank you.'

There was a short silence as she hovered at the door, before she gave up and I heard her footsteps move off towards the stairs.

For three days I hadn't the energy to leave my room, or even to wonder where that energy had gone. I told Margaret I had a cold and had food brought to my room, most of which I threw out of the window. Without enough will either to live or to kill myself, I floated in a strange, colourless stasis, seeing no point in either state. I slept intermittently, waking sometimes with the moon high in the night, or with the sun shooting the room full of glittering arrows. Noises came to me from outside the house: the cries of two small boys playing cowboys and Indians; the reverberations of the occasional car; the tap of wisteria at the window; the soft, low mourning of an owl. From inside the house I heard Margaret going to and fro, the ghostly creaking of the untrodden boards above me, the postman's knock, the clatter and chime of copper pans as Mrs Boxell prepared food she wasn't sure anybody would eat. Never a sound that I could attach to an idea of George, and at times I allowed myself a slide into fantasy: that he was not in the house at all, never had been, and if I were to open my bedroom door it would be the house of my childhood again, the sun wallowing on the patterned tiles of the hall like a golden cat, the sweet scent of the gardenias my mother favoured, the sounds of the piano rising through the banisters, as if to lure me downstairs.

I don't know, exactly, what brought me out of my stupor. Perhaps it was merely the act of catching my own eye. Margaret, on her way out of the room, must have been unable to resist passing her duster over the glass of the cheval mirror, and had left it tilted, reflecting the bed. I glanced up and saw myself half propped on a mass of pillows, my hair loose and – I noticed now – in need of a cut. Lack of sleep had stamped itself under my eyes: two dark crescents hung in the white, like inverted moons. Though I had spent most of my time pressed flat and still against the bed, I looked wrung out, dishevelled as a woman recovering from fever, or having recently given birth.

I thought of all the times people had told me that there was little point studying, or reading, or working, because soon enough I'd have to give it all up to take up the more important role of mother. I went back over the friends and family members who had said this to me, a long line of kind and well-meaning people, with a sudden longing to shake every one of them until their teeth rattled in their heads. My own teeth clenched. I hadn't felt so angry since my mother's funeral. The sensation was like the feeling returning to a numb arm, in intense pulses of pain. But it *was* feeling; it was an awakening. Even if it hurt, it was at least lucid, and I took a queer sort of pleasure in feeling it so sharply.

I looked at myself again, a fierce face in the mirror, and my own expression startled me. But the torpor was broken, as if the handsome prince had arrived at the bedside of Sleeping Beauty and given her not a kiss, but a ringing slap. I got out of bed, washed my face with cold water, brushed and pinned my hair, dressed, and wrote a note to Christopher suggesting we resume our afternoons at the Bodleian. Then I walked to the postbox and posted it myself. On the way back, the blood beat in my ears. *I am alive*, it repeated. *I am not dead yet.*

I had expected George to oppose the idea of my returning to the Bodleian, but when it came, the force of his resistance – the tenacity of its will, the new and strange forms it took – alarmed me, when I had thought myself fully prepared.

'But you're not well,' he said at first, startled.

'I'm fine now. As you can see.'

'You – you haven't rested enough. Going out so soon might be dangerous.'

'I tell you I'm quite all right.'

There was a short silence, in which invisible things struggled and shoved, and would not be subdued. Finally he looked up at me, his hands lifted to the sides of his face, as if to shield his eyes like blinders; it had the effect of funnelling his gaze on to me; a piercing, agonised stare.

'Don't go,' he said.

There was something childish in it – almost imploring – but within it too the shadow of the man; the authority to turn a plea into an order.

'George . . .'

'Why must you go there so often? Why must you go at all? When you know how I love you, and worry over you. God knows I've nothing in my life but you.' Even this he made grim-sounding, as if it were news of a death. 'You've been different lately, Sophia. I can't understand it. This new preoccupation with going out, this . . . I don't know what.'

This sudden accuracy unnerved me, but I thought it better to challenge him than stay silent, and seem guilty. I said, 'Why, it sounds rather as if you don't trust me.'

'No.' He ducked his head, as if to physically block the idea. 'No. I refuse to believe you have done anything wrong. You've an active mind, I know that. I don't say that you have done anything wrong . . . only promise me, Sophia. Promise me now you haven't changed – that you'd never think of anything . . . anybody else than our marriage.'

He stared at me again, and I was flustered now. Trying so hard to act naturally, I was beginning to forget what that entailed. I made my arms relax at my sides, instead of wrapping them – as I should have liked to do – protectively across myself, and gazed at him with as much hurt as I thought an innocent wife might feel.

'I should not have to promise – but I promise,' I said.

'I'm sorry, Sophia. You are right. Damn it, I know you are good. I simply can't stand being by myself, thinking of all the things that might happen to you out *there*' – he gestured to the street beyond the window, in which the sun lay peacefully on the pavement between the shadows of the trees, and some children called in the distance – 'and then not only that, but of all the things you might be doing.'

'George, I've done nothing wrong,' I said, but my voice was weak, and guilty-sounding.

He took my hands then, and gripped them hard until our bones drew painfully together, without letting his stare drop or soften.

'Do you believe me?' I asked, the sound thinner still.

'Of course,' he said. 'Of course.' But when he released my hands, he still did not seem satisfied, as if he had no answer, but rather had given up on finding one, and when he said, 'I trust you,' I had the distinct sense that he was not telling the truth. But I had never seen him lie, and so I couldn't be completely sure.

When I was a child, I had a poured wax doll named Cassandra, which I nursed as if she had been living; and indeed I steadfastly insisted she *was* alive, and I would gladly prove it, but unfortunately – obstinate doll that she was – she would only speak and move when she and I were alone. In this way, I had preserved a belief, against all evidence to the contrary, that the George I used to know before the war hid somewhere inside the George I knew now, waiting to come back to life. And in neither case – the doll or the man – was the division clear between my public untruths and genuine self-delusion. I really believed Cassandra would speak to me one day, just as I believed for a long time that George might really come downstairs one morning and say, 'Dear me, Sophia, I had the most ghastly dream. I thought I lost myself, but here I am, and won't you come over here and put your arms around me, and tell me what you'd like us to do today?'

I saw now that I did not know George at all; that his love, once so quiet and sweet, was unrecognisable, transfigured, like his face under the gas lights of the street, the coat gathered bulkily around the shotgun that I thought, sometimes, I heard him loading and reloading in the night. But perhaps *I* was going a little mad, and those metal clicks and clunks – or the times I strained to hear him come back up the stairs from one of his night patrols, yet heard nothing but the owls in the night, so that I lay in my bed picturing him sitting awake and erect in the drawing room, as if he were waiting for me to come home from the shops at 4 a.m. – were all in my imagination. But whether I was insane or not, the fact remained that the old George was gone, and in his place was a person who claimed to cherish me but didn't want to speak to me, sleep with me, have a child with me. The only time he thought of me was when I was heading for the front door.

The one thing we had in common was that both of us had been holding on to something imagined; something we were frightened to lose. George had his idea of me, a plaster saint on an unsteady shelf, beside which the real woman could be nothing but a disappointment. I had my hope of returning to the past, the land in which sunlight stretched endlessly across green lawns, and ice revolved in tall glass jugs, never melting; to go back and find the George I had loved there.

I imagine *you*, dear reader, should never do something so unaccountably silly as to let go of one illusion and fix immediately on another, equally unlikely dream. And so I can only ask you, very humbly, not to judge me too harshly for what I did next. For into the vacancy left by the hope that the George I loved might resurface had rushed another improbable romance: that of a woman and a library. Not the most typical of love stories, I grant you, but offering just as much opportunity for rejection and heartbreak.

Christopher wrote back promptly: a letter I was confident of being able to intercept while George was still in bed, avoiding the new day. I went to meet him a few days later, and then several more times after that, hurrying along to my reading as excited and impatient as a teenager. I gave the Bodleian all my love, and was content with its answering silence. I was accustomed, after all, to this kind of arrangement. Reciprocation would have startled me: to be tolerated was all I asked. Those few months of enlightenment between the dark shelves were some of the happiest times of my life, impossible and yet real, in which I held on to each day as if it were a great golden phoenix, dragging it back by its tail as it tried to fly away into the night.

I always knew my place at the Bodleian was on shaky ground; I was reminded of it whenever we had to avoid a lecturer Christopher recognised, or when an old man looked at me too severely, or when a young man hailed Christopher across the quad (with a rather mystifying cry of 'Philip! I say, Philip!'), stopping me in my tracks as I went towards him, and necessitating an absurd cloak-and-dagger performance of secret signals and doublings-back, ending in us having to lie low in the reading room in the Radcliffe Camera instead. Not that I minded this: the Camera was lighter and airier than the Bodleian, having the cerebral beauty of a Greek temple, with its Corinthian columns and busts of Hippocrates and Aristotle. The interior of the lofty lanterned dome was exceptionally delicate: ornate plasterwork of pale blue, gold and white, like a formalised firmament.

'If I were to pray, I should pray here,' I murmured to Christopher, who smiled and said nothing, as if he understood.

For though my claim on the Bodleian was a weak one – a small hand resting on a male arm, easily shaken off – I felt more and more confident of Christopher's goodwill. No, not only that: of Christopher's friendship. If he regretted bringing me there that first day, he never admitted it, and I detected no further evidence of unease on his part. I was becoming familiar with his presence beside me: his hand resting on the desk, its tiny golden hairs caught in the light as he turned the page; the steep angle of his jaw, folding into shadow; the darkening sand of his lowered eyelashes. I felt both more and less inclined to disturb his reading. I liked to talk to him – a little about our reading, a little about ourselves – but I hadn't the need for reassurance, the urgency of not feeling wanted. I could say to him, 'I thought it rude of you not to introduce your chum to your dear sister,' and know that he would laugh. I could ask, without worrying about asking too much, 'Tell me, why did he call you Philip?'

'Ah. Well you see, Philip is my name.'

'Christopher is an alias?'

'Of a sort. Christopher is my second name, but I prefer it. My family call me Philip. But their Philip is a man I don't much want to be.'

'How fascinating. Do explain.'

'Philip is an upright, rather prudish young man who firmly upholds the values of his society, whatever those values might be. He wouldn't dream of engaging in anything so effeminate as independent thought. He likes hunting (if war cannot be had), votes Conservative, says grace at dinner. He'll marry a simple-minded deb and spend the rest of his life at his club, avoiding her. Indeed, if she *were* ever to breach that male fortress, she might struggle to identify her own husband, being as he is utterly indistinguishable from all the other men there.'

'He sounds an awful bore.'

'Quite. Cross the street if you ever see *him* coming.'

'Then what luck that I ran into Christopher instead,' I said. He smiled, a moment of mutual amusement that went on for another moment, and then another; neither of us speaking, only smiling. It couldn't possibly last – yet it did, becoming something intimate, almost knowing. The sun was behind me, facing him, lighting his unflinching eyes an eerie blue. I expected him at any moment to look away, or frown, and the growing fear of this was what forced me, at last, to give a laugh as light and clattering as Bakelite, and demand, 'So tell me about *him*.'

He laughed. 'Well . . . it's not for me to say.'

'Who better?'

'Who worse? I'm hopelessly biased. Most of the time I agree with him, but then later, on reflection, I often think him an ass.'

'That's rather hard on him.'

'Very well, if you want my opinion: I think Christopher tries to be a decent enough fellow, and most of the time he does a decent enough job of it. His main fault is inexperience. His knowledge is academic. His opinions are untested, and he himself is untried. He talks about things he hasn't seen or touched. He wants to do things without knowing if he'll be able to do them. He longs to leave without knowing if he'll be satisfied when he arrives, or if he is simply a malcontent who will never be happy anywhere.'

'You plan to leave?'

'Of course. As soon as I'm able. I want to get earth between my fingers, and a sunburnt neck. My friend Pheugo – he and I share lodgings – has family in Athens and Crete. He's going back after he takes the bar, to join the family business. I visited once and they treated me like a son, so I hope to return and take further advantage of that generosity.' He smiled as he spoke, his eyes softening for a moment, as if on distant land.

'So you even have a nice new family waiting for you.'

'You ought to see them. They're utterly charming. If you asked them what they thought of Christopher, they'd tell you they think him good-humoured – unusually so – but a drunkard. And that he doesn't eat enough, of course, and that he needs a wife, and children . . . Sophia, you look strange.'

'Oh heavens, just a mild case of envy,' I said, waving a hand. 'I understand your situation. There really isn't anything to keep you here, is there?'

Presumably at this reminder that he was actually standing in Oxford, and not disembarking a boat at Heraklion, Christopher's smile faded. He looked at me and I wasn't sure what thoughts lay behind his expression, or what he might be looking for – because he was looking for something, I could tell, with all my practice in identifying the infinitesimal changes that curiosity makes to a gaze: lifting it, turning it, whetting it like a kitchen knife; a sudden glint, a keen edge.

'I have friends,' he said. 'You, for instance.'

I inclined my head in acknowledgement – a small smile of thanks – and looked away. I didn't want him to find out my disappointment, which had arrived suddenly, and had hurt more than I should have expected. If he guessed at that, he might also guess at the whole truth, that he was my only friend; the time we spent at the library my only pleasure. I said to myself, 'You got along very well for years without him,' but I knew this was not entirely correct. I *survived* perfectly well, it was true, but now I had a taste of real conversation – of unfeigned, unrehearsed laughter – and it was like the scent of whisky passing under the nose of a reformed drunk, the sound of hooves to an inveterate gambler. I couldn't bear for him to know that, and pity me.

I had told Christopher very little about myself. He knew that I was married, but that was all. He would solicit my opinions, demand I outline the structure of some reasoning or other, beg me to explain a laugh or a raised eyebrow at what he was saying. But he didn't ask about my marriage. He seemed to accept that my personal life should remain a mystery. I wasn't sure if this was delicacy on his part, or absolute indifference. Possibly he thought me so old, living a life so impossibly dull, that it was simply beyond his comprehension.

I never asked him about his own romantic life, and he offered no insights. Some mornings he would arrive looking tired, after a party or some other jaunt, and sometimes he mentioned girls' names, though none, I noticed, came up more than once or twice. The Miss Chandler of one anecdote would be replaced with a Miss Wainwright in the next, who in turn gave way to Miss Cross-Headingley.

I didn't ask about any of these girls, accepting them as they were presented to me: bit players in a one-off tableau, filing off afterwards into the darkness of the wings. Anything beyond the footlights I thought none of my concern.

I suspected that his true passion was his work; and I was glad of it. I didn't want him to change, to arrive preoccupied with secret joys or secret griefs – or, worse, not to arrive at all. There was something protective in the way I felt about this; as if my idea of his usual self was something sacred, which must remain untouched; and I was relieved when a girl's name passed out of currency, or when he brought up marriage only to laugh at the very concept.

'I say, Sophia. Josephus has it that when Herod's wife Mariamme disagreed with his idea of having her executed after his death to prevent her remarrying, he accused her of infidelity. They never did see each other's side. Eventually he ended the argument by having her killed first.'

'How queer! We're reading on the same theme. I've just finished Macrobius's account of Julia the Elder. When she was asked how she kept her infidelities from Tiberius, and how she managed to only bear children resembling her husband, she supposedly answered, "I only take on new passengers when the boat is already full."'

'Bravo, Julia.'

'Well. In the end it is thought he had her starved to death.'

'Christ, that just about sums it up,' Christopher said, with disgust. 'It's not so different now, either. I tell you, I don't know why a woman should ever want to marry,' and at that I had to turn away to hide my smile, which would have undoubtedly confused him.

e~

The day came – as such days tend to – when my luck ran out. Christopher was waiting in his usual spot, his hat low against the light rain, but below its brim he looked anxious, and when he saw me, he came to meet me, walking away from the library. I stopped, understanding immediately. I had been dreading this moment so long that when it came, it was almost without sensation: a flat thud, like someone dropping a shoe.

'Sophia, I'm dreadfully sorry,' was what he said.

Horrified at the prospect of his guilt, or his pity, I affected a lightness I did not feel, querying playfully, 'Have we been rumbled?'

'My family visited me. We ran into the don who so kindly helped my sister with her reading. Naturally, I introduced them. Naturally, he asked about my sister.'

'Naturally,' I echoed wanly. 'Christopher, I'm sorry.'

'*You're* sorry? For what?'

'For putting you in such a tight spot. Will you be in any sort of trouble?'

'Not really. I'm not an undergraduate, and there's no real precedent for this. It's rather more embarrassing for him. I think we'll both agree to maintain an absolute silence about the whole thing.'

'But your family . . .'

'Christ, don't worry about them. In fact, they think me quite the playboy. My parents said very little but I sensed quiet relief. I think they were concerned I was a sodomite. My brothers have been gruesomely familiar. Simon winked at me. Alec told me, quite against my will, about some chorus girl he had an arrangement with. Of course they don't quite understand why we would meet at the library, but . . . Oh God, I'm sorry. I've embarrassed you.'

'Not in the least,' I said, but it was apparent to us both that I was blushing.

'Anyway, it's all up with the Bodleian. I can't tell you how sorry I am.'

'Please . . . you've been far too kind already.'

'Look, I've given it some thought, and I believe I could get you some books. I'm able to borrow some – not all, but enough to keep you occupied for the time being. While we wait for the Equal Reading Rights Act to be passed.' He gave a smile, but his eyes were watchful and worried, and the smile soon slid away.

'It's really very kind of you, but . . .' Here I hesitated, before deciding that there was no reason not to be frank with Christopher. It wasn't as if it could make things any worse. I didn't believe I could see him again, and I owed him an explanation, at least. I was blushing again. For the second time that day our simple, honest friend-ship would have to be seen as others should see it: something illicit and grubby, if not a full-blown affair. 'Listen, my husband hasn't any idea that I've been meeting you. He knows I go to the library, but not who with.'

Christopher looked startled, then – as I had expected – deeply discomfited. He blinked and looked away, mouth narrowing. I hurried to explain. 'God knows, it isn't that there is anything that ought to bother him. He's just . . . rather jealous. Perhaps it was idiotic of me, but I decided not to tell him that my benefactor was young, and – well.'

The word I had omitted was *handsome*; it hung in the air between us, like a wink, or a spray of perfume, darkly knowing.

'You needn't tell me all this, if it's personal,' Christopher said, still looking stricken, holding himself stiffly, with what I took to be offended propriety.

'I should like to. I don't want you to misunderstand. I can't meet you openly to swap books; I can't invite you to the house. I'm really most desperately sorry to have involved you in this; I didn't want to explain before, because I didn't want you to know that you could ever be considered in that light, when you have done nothing more than be kind . . .'

My voice shook slightly here, and his expression changed, gentled.

'Please. You mustn't apologise. I'm sorry for . . .' He gestured vaguely. 'Are you . . . do you think he might . . . *do* something, if he found out?'

I couldn't answer this honestly, which was to say: I had no idea. I didn't know what moved through George's mind; his thoughts like drowning men in night water, thrashing, sinking, fleetingly pale, as they revolved downwards out of sight.

'He never has before,' I said. 'But he used not to be so . . . I don't know. He was quite different, before the war.'

There was a short, awkward silence, then I made an effort to smile, adding, 'But then, who wasn't?'

Christopher's answer was lost; we had to stand aside to make way for a small group of schoolchildren, shepherded by a teacher. It was a little while before their cries of laughter, high and piercing as gulls, retreated down the road, leaving us in silence once more. I fingered the fur of my coat, stirring it and smoothing it in a gesture that did nothing to comfort me.

'I should be very sad to think of you without your books,' Christopher said. 'Could I not . . . Could I meet you somewhere else, when I bring them? Somewhere public and above suspicion. Unless you're worried we might run into your husband . . .?'

'George never goes out.' An upswing of relief rose in me, dizzying, before I checked it. 'But I can't ask that of you.'

'You haven't asked. I offered. No – I'm insisting.'

'Thank you,' I said. We looked at each other for a moment, an open, simple gaze that in the next instant seemed too open; less simple.

'So who am I now?' he asked.

'What?'

'Who is the person who got you into the Bodleian, if not a young man?'

I laughed. 'Oh dear . . . this is too shaming.'

'Do tell me,' he entreated.

'You're an old don. A chivalrous dodderer. Couldn't bear to see a fair lady in distress, and so on.'

'I say, I much prefer him to Philip, and possibly even to Christopher. What's his name?'

'I kept it vague. Dr B something.'

'Dr Something. I shall add him to my list of aliases.'

The sun came out then, lighting his face white and his eyes the pale blue I always found so unearthly. I could still make out the small satellite of his iris. Then he raised his hand, and his eyes disappeared into its neat shadow.

'Will you write to me, then, and tell me when you'd like me to meet you, and what books I should bring?'

'Anything,' I said. 'You know my interests.'

'Yes.'

This confirmation of our familiarity had the effect of making both of us queerly shy: our goodbyes were slightly hurried, our eye contact missing its mark, so that I was smiling at him when he was looking away, and then only caught the end of his own quick nod. I went away down the dazzling street, a blaze of pale gold and trembling pools of rain left over from the morning, feeling embarrassed without knowing quite why (though God knows, the conversation had given me reason enough), and it was only later, once I was nearly home, that I was able to see the funny side again, and laugh to myself at the strangeness, the sheer absurdity of it all.

*

I didn't tell George that I would no longer be meeting Dr B something at the Bodleian: I thought it unwise to complicate the story, or in any way call attention to the insubstantiality of my beloved patron. (Poor Dr B: no friends, no face, only one daughter to keep him company in his dotage. A stiff wind might have blown him away; if he turned sideways, he would be as thin as a piece of paper.) And George had been acting so oddly lately. He did not argue with me any longer over my trips to the library; not pleading as I left but nodding at me, with a 'Goodbye, Sophia': this new acceptance – the coldness of his gesture, the familiar words so stony and strange – seeming to me somehow worse than his former agitation.

This was not the only change in him that I had noticed. He used not to look at me until I had spoken to him; I had to fish for his eyes with my own, to draw them, with an effort, up to my face. But these days he was more watchful. I often turned around to see him quickly look away. I could almost feel the sensation on my cheek or the back of my neck; a coolness on the skin, where his eyes had lately rested. I wondered if I was being paranoid, and so I tested him over dinner, gazing down into my glass then looking up suddenly, to catch his eyes switching away. I was never fast enough, however, to read their expression, and by the time they landed on the clock, or a picture, or the street beyond the window, they were almost comically blank, a parody of neutrality that was – again – more unsettling than the feelings they took such pains to hide. When he spoke, his tone guarded its meaning as closely as his face hid its feeling, until it sounded almost as if he were reciting lines, with the motionless, neutral expression of a somnambulist.

I caught a glimpse of his true feelings only once, after he startled me by noticing my dress, asking, 'What is that you're wearing? Is it new?'

I looked down at myself; my hands went to the accordion-pleated fabric, as if they weren't familiar with it either.

'Why, yes. I thought it rather pretty; not too modish. Do you like it?'

He stared at the dress for a while, apparently taking the question seriously. The flimsy silk couldn't withstand the weight of his consideration; I felt my body tense irrationally inside it, hairs raising.

'It's a strange colour. Neither one thing or another. Rather like' – there followed a hesitation, in which I wondered what on earth he was going to say – 'the sea,' he concluded, unexpectedly.

'Or your eyes,' I said. George looked baffled, and I explained: 'I can never tell what colour they are, either.'

Had he really forgotten that old joke? I wondered at him. When we were first married, we used to say that his eyes were brown when he was busy, greyish when he was bored, green at night. The implication was a sexual one, and referring to it now felt like a mistake. It was a wrong note to strike; a painful chord. That day his eyes were giving nothing away, colourless in the dim light of the rainy morning, as if his identity had got lost, suspended in between states.

He hadn't answered me, and I thought it a good moment to take my leave.

'I'll be back before luncheon,' I said.

'I expect I shall see you then,' he said, the casual words emerging precisely formed, and I looked at him closely, finally catching the expression I had been looking for – suspicion, hard and final – before it vanished away, and he turned back to his newspaper. Later that night I found the clothes in my wardrobe hanging in a different order, something I might not have noticed had I not put a few new things in there the previous day – but when I asked Margaret about it, she looked surprised, and said she hadn't moved a thing.

After that, a dark curiosity sprang up in me: to find out if I was under surveillance. Without any certainty that I really wanted to know the truth, or what I might do about it once I had it, I set my own traps. I waited for Margaret's day off to exhume an old trick of my teens, something I used to do when I suspected Boll of borrowing my clothes on the sly. I took one of my own hairs and glued it to the wardrobe, a taut span across both doors. Then I reconsidered, opened the wardrobe again, and – working with the utmost care – placed a tiny bead from an old evening cape on the furthermost shoulder of every dress that hung inside. I went through the rest of the room stringing hairs and balancing beads: on every drawer and everything within, between even the cold silk folds of the chemises and camiknickers, on each bottle of perfume on the washstand, every book on the pile of borrowed volumes beside the bed; finally placing – as if in a grotesque distortion of the tale of the princess and the pea – a bead under my own pillow, so that everything in the room was chained by spider threads and fairy weights, ready to sing out, 'Spy! Spy!' in thousands of tiny voices.

I told George I'd decided to go out for a walk that afternoon, news which was received with studied indifference. When I got home, he was in the sitting room, exactly as I had left him, down to the left leg crossed over the right at the ankle, the newspaper upright in his hands. But in my bedroom the hair on the wardrobe was snapped, and so were those on the vanity and the chest of drawers, and I began to realise as I examined the room that not one hair had escaped unbroken, nor one bead undisturbed; that even the pin I had placed between the bed frame and the mattress was gone, George apparently having thought it necessary to look underneath.

I sat on the bed, cowed, my hands in my lap like a chastened child. I had not been prepared to be proved so pitilessly right. The thoroughness of George's search frightened me – my own room frightened me. I heard that mother birds would never accept a lost chick once a stranger's hand had touched it; in the same way my own bedroom had become strange under a hostile hand. Even the house itself felt estranged from me in that moment. I had always felt that it was George who was the odd addition to my childhood home – the temporary occupant, the lodger – while the house and I were the constants; that even if we were sleeping under a blanket of dust and ivy, with all the music of the past run into silence, we were united in a shared dream of times gone by, a dream that might at any moment come true. I realised now that this was not the case. There was a spell, yes, but not the one I had thought. George had taken the house I loved and made it smaller somehow, in a nightmarish inversion of my fantasies about my paper gingerbread house. The child lying on her stomach gazing into the world of her book had looked back up and found that in her lapse of attention, several years had passed: the house around her had darkened and closed in, the walls tiptoeing forwards, the mirrors leaning in – though she would not look up at them, and meet her own eye.

℮

Picture a scene, dear reader. A man sits in a room. Though his face is not visible, he glances up at the door from time to time, and there is something furtive in the way he does it that draws one's interest. His hair is a subdued beige colour that hints it might be capable of better things – of gold, perhaps – given the right light. His hat rests on the wooden bench next to him, beside a plain leather bag. His hands are placed, deliberately nonchalantly, on his thighs. His back is very straight – perhaps alert, perhaps tense – and clothed in pale tweed.

This is a public place, through which various people pass, loiter, and pass on again, but this room seldom sees traffic – indeed, it has been forgotten even by the people who come to clean. A spider spins an elaborate Versailles in the corner, his ambition unchecked by feather dusters. The light falls in slowly, weakly, as if drugged, gleaming dully off the tall glass display cases. From the way its sole inhabitant is behaving, one might guess that this neglected room has been chosen for that very characteristic.

After a little while, there comes the sound of footsteps, clicking neatly, louder and louder, until another person enters the room. Peculiarly, the man now looks away from the doorway, as if determined not to acknowledge this new presence, though his back radiates awareness of the other. The second person sits on the bench, without saying a word, facing away from the first. The room falls once more into silence, in which the man looks again towards the empty doorway, as if to check nobody else might be approaching. Then, without a word or a glance, he pushes the bag over to the side of the bench occupied by his neighbour, who – again without a word or a glance – gathers it up. Then the woman – for it is a woman – laughs, and says, 'You'd make a rotten spy.'

'What?' Christopher exclaimed, sounding hurt.

'This' – I gestured at the half-finished display cases with their obscure contents, unclassifiable pieces of earthenware and bone – 'is far too quiet. You ought to hand over the contraband in a busier place. So nobody can tail us as we approach or leave.'

'I humbly apologise. I didn't realise it was you, Sidney Reilly. It's an honour. If I may say so, that's a disturbingly convincing get-up. What a delightful frock.'

'That's quite enough of that,' I said, laughing to shrug off the thought that had just sidled in: that while I was out on my rendezvous, my own room was in all likelihood being neatly turned over in search of intelligence.

'I must say, I hadn't expected the great man to be quite so merry.'

'Why, I shall take that as testament to the success of the various lies I have put out about myself. So, what have you brought me?'

Christopher opened the bag with a flourish. 'Something on the great explorers of the Renaissance: Columbus, Magellan and so on. I thought you might like it. I did, anyway. Taking to the seas in search of new lands and new people, and so on.'

I looked at him sharply, but his meaning was simple: he longed to set sail himself. The turning of the waves passed across his eyes; his expression was one of sudden yearning, before he recollected himself and brought out the next volume.

'This is something on the Myceneans that I recently finished. My choice here is quite selfish: I should like to have your thoughts on it.'

I leant over the pages of the first book so he should not see my smile. I liked it that he treated me as his academic equal, though he was a committed scholar and in terms of study I resembled nothing so much as one of those Victorian ladies who dabble in watercolours or flower pressing.

'You know, this history of the explorers reminds me of an American book I had when I was younger. It was called *A Book of Discovery*. It had chapters named "Baffin finds his bay" and "Bering finds his strait", as if they had them all along, but had simply misplaced them for a time.'

'And even if that were the case, Bering's strait was not even his own, but Dezhnev's. I don't know how that came about, though.'

'Dezhnev wasn't literate enough to record his discovery. This is why, if one wants to be understood, one should write everything down. Or else risk it being rewritten.'

'If one *wants* to be understood,' he repeated, thoughtfully.

'Some do. Or so I hear.'

'Did Baffin? I know very little about him, either.'

'His early life was certainly a mystery.'

'Then he must be a favourite of yours?'

'Oh, I think him quite marvellous.'

He glanced away and laughed, and shook his head. Then he said, simply, 'I think *you* marvellous.'

I was so taken aback by this that for a moment I couldn't speak. His words arrived like a threat; a high wind that rattled in my ears, made me blink.

Christopher, not noticing, went on: 'My God, the breadth of your knowledge is enviable. I expect you've been reading history your whole life.'

I coughed, embarrassed by my presumption. 'Why, yes, I suppose I have.'

'It's a crying shame you weren't given the opportunity to study,' he said, becoming vehement. 'When I think of the useless swine who used to sit around me in lectures, talking about cricket or women or drink – anything other than the subject at hand . . .'

'Well, I envy *your* depth of knowledge,' I said. 'I envy your field; your narrowing-down of history into one particular love.'

'People do that every day when they marry,' he said. 'I don't find it so very impressive. And in some cases it's quite ill-advised . . .' He noticed my expression. I should have liked to know what he saw there. Some unknown cocktail; mysterious in both ingredients and dilution. He said, 'Forgive me – I mean no offence. I was speaking generally.'

'Heavens, it didn't occur to me that you might be referring to me.'

I looked at him slyly then, in full consciousness of putting him in an uncomfortable spot. I hardly knew what

I was up to. One minute saw me shrinking from a misunderstood compliment; the next saw me sidling in, pressing and provoking, but to what end? I had the sensation of not knowing myself, akin to that of following one's self around in a dream, marvelling at its contrary and irrational behaviour.

Now he looked away, saying, 'I'm tired today,' by way of apology. I looked at him more closely: the soft skin under his eyes dark with loss of sleep, the eyes themselves seeming all the bluer for it, yet still sharp, still brilliant.

'Were you working late?' I asked.

'Shamefully – no. A dinner dance.'

'Oh,' I said. 'How I envy you!'

Dancing was something that still had the power to cause me pain. George had never loved to dance – even when we first met he had congratulated himself (mistakenly) on finding an unusual sort of deb, a thoughtful, quiet soul like himself, sceptical of the shimmy and the Missouri Walk – and since the war it was out of the question. It had been years since I had danced.

'Well. It was rather a simple affair,' Christopher said. 'A piano, no more than two violins. A few vases of flowers and a buffet with jellies and ices. That sums it up.'

'Was there a midnight supper?'

He inclined his head: yes.

'Ah,' I said. 'Much the best sort of dance.'

He looked at me uncertainly. 'You seldom dance?'

'Not now. I used to. I used to dance whenever I could. At a luncheon party; at a picnic, if anybody had brought a portable gramophone. Boll and I used to waltz together around the drawing room when somebody played the piano. My father taught us the steps when we were tall enough. It's one of the only things she and I have in common, actually.'

'I've been meaning to ask: why do you call her Boll?'

'Oh, it came from childhood. I used to embellish her name – come up with more and more elaborate variations. Anna-Bellina was one that stuck. My parents laughed; they said that was what the Spanish used to call Anne Boleyn. I think they regretted telling me that: when Boll and I played at Tudors, I would chase her and pretend to chop off her head.'

I remembered it vividly: hurtling around the apple tree in the garden, tripping on fallen fruit; Boll running from me, looking back over her shoulder, her white skin and red cheeks and fevered eyes: a paroxysm of delight and terror that could spill so easily – and often did – into tears.

'Who were you? Queen Katherine?'

'I think so. Though I wouldn't be her now. She was too proud, too stubborn. In adversity I would hope to be more like Anne of Cleves. She knew when to quit, and she was rewarded for it.'

'Tell me, does everybody you know have their counterpart in history?'

'Yes, and I shan't tell you yours.'

'One day, maybe,' he said, not quite smiling, and it was hard to interpret his tone. 'And is Boll really like Anne Boleyn?'

'No – really she's Katherine Howard. Living in the present moment, having fun, not thinking of the consequences. Anne Boleyn was more complicated, much more ambitious. She planned on a grand scale. It wasn't for lack of forethought that she died. I suppose the sex of her baby was the only thing she left to chance. She gambled, and she lost.'

'What a delicate thing to hang one's future on – a newborn baby,' Christopher observed. 'It's quite terrifying.'

'Indeed,' I said, but rather than sounding simple and dry, the words quivered and rippled, as if carried on water.

'Sophia – are you all right?'

I shook my head. On my way to the library, I had seen a young working-class couple outside the photographer's shop, dressed in their Sunday finest. The man's head, glossy in the sun, was bent over the lace-swathed, white-ruffled baby in its mother's arms. He held a flower in his fingers, dangling it and pulling it away, to make the child laugh. I had walked on, repressing the tears that rose into my eyes. But now they came, as if they had been something I owed, and the debt must be called in.

'I'm sorry,' I said. I patted my face with care, but one tear slipped maliciously past my fingers and landed on the pale silk of my skirt, a dark spot like a hole, painfully visible to us both.

He didn't draw back or stiffen, but surprised me by moving along the bench towards me. He took my hands and said, 'Tell me what's wrong,' and perhaps because of the surprise of it – the suddenness of the contact, neither of us wearing gloves, a queer shock of skin on skin, his warm and mine cold – I answered him truthfully. Of course, none of this was at all appropriate, I knew that, but the knowledge seemed to shrink away. That was the peculiar effect Christopher could have. Without explicitly declaring rebellion, he nevertheless gave off an air of disdain for the usual codes: the neat path between the clipped hedges. With him I found myself losing sight of what was and wasn't *comme il faut*. And so I said, 'I shan't ever have children, and sometimes it feels too hard to bear.'

He blinked, taken aback. Then he said, 'Christ. How absolutely bloody. Are you . . . quite sure?'

'Yes. Apparently the doctors knew about it years ago. I hadn't any idea.'

'Christ,' he said again. 'I can't begin to imagine what you must feel.'

'Sad, mostly. And angry, that nobody told me sooner. Though what difference that would have made, I don't know.'

I didn't tell him all my feelings. I forbore, for example, to tell him that children represented the entirety of the love I was to be allowed in life. My portion, my *share* – gold and shining, stolen while I floated in my leaden, opiated sleep. My parents were dead, my friends had slipped away. George and Boll were husband and sister in name only; yet I had to be loyal to those scant, fleshless names for ever. It seemed at that moment too much to bear.

'At least I have Daphne,' I said eventually, blowing my nose on Christopher's pocket handkerchief.

'Daphne? I haven't heard of a Daphne. You are always hailing me from beyond the limits of my knowledge.'

I laughed, rather damply. 'No, Daphne is my sister's child. But her personality is more like mine. She is interested, curious. She likes to take her time thinking everything over. She likes a historical tale or two at bedtime.'

'Not adultery and death, one hopes.'

'Never that. Though one day she will have to hear about it, I suppose.'

I handed him back his handkerchief, apologetically. 'I think I've finished blubbing now. I really am frightfully sorry.'

'You mustn't apologise to me,' he said. 'I . . .'

He broke off, and the many spectres of what he might have said hovered between us, transparent but pressing, clustering in. He appeared pained, though whether by my sadness or his own discomfort I couldn't tell. I didn't know exactly what I felt either. The silence seemed to gather in intensity. My tears had not brought any relief, or cleared any emotion away – rather, it was like a storm arriving in reverse: first the rain, and then the pressure, the black, heavy heat.

It was at this point that a middle-aged woman in a straw hat entered the room, and we both looked at each other with such startled faces that, seeing one another's expressions, we started to laugh. The woman frowned and – without looking in our direction – gave an emphatic little cough.

'Shall we visit some of the other displays?' I murmured.

'Good idea.'

We spent half an hour wandering around, past the beaded shawls of Red Indians, Egyptian faience, medieval cudgels, both of us suddenly in a mood of high hilarity, as if released from a particularly solemn church service. It was queer, I thought, how familiar my tears had made us. I wasn't at all used to confiding my secrets. I had learnt the art of keeping them close at school, where a secret could be used against one later. Even if it were not, I often felt uncomfortable giving up my innermost thoughts into less careful hands; I felt as if I had lost them; there was no getting them back. I even had the same sense when I played the role of confidante. If another girl gave too much away, I would feel pained by it, shivering in sympathy for her mistake. So it surprised me that I felt no sense of regret at handing my thoughts over to Christopher – just like that – without thinking twice. I felt again that disconcerting sense of not knowing my self, as if watching it running down a hill, about to disappear from sight.

When we parted, pausing at the gates of the Ashmolean, there followed a peculiar silence, as if the act of saying goodbye seemed to demand some sort of summation, a conclusion, but neither of us was exactly sure what had happened. Yet there was warmth there, and the last, quick smile he gave me, half turned away but somehow deeply meant, was something I bore off in triumph, walking down the street with it like a child with a balloon, and no doubt looking just as foolishly pleased with myself.

On impulse, I turned slightly out of my usual route home to walk along the banks of the Isis. The sun had come out; summer had arrived, quietly, while nobody was looking. I watched the boys in their white flannels punting along the river, droplets flung up, flashing in the sun. The voices across the water carried clearly one moment and were gone by the next, riding the rise and fall of the breeze. The long tendrils of the willows wove the sun into a gold tapestry; winking daisies studded the luscious green grass. My own road was all splotches of light and shade, like a leopard's coat, a shifting pelt under the branches of the trees. I forgot the children I wouldn't have and the husband I didn't know and felt almost light-hearted, at least until I got into the house and George said to me, conversationally, 'I waited for you today outside the Bodleian, but you didn't come out.'

I stared at him, feeling the impossibility of this. George, waiting on the street? That was what I said first: 'Outside?'

'Practically. I was in a tea shop not far from the entrance. I was taking a walk and I thought I might meet you when you came out, and accompany you home. As it was a pleasant afternoon.'

I knew that this claim – delivered as flatly as the pre-rehearsed statement of a suspect in some crime – was a lie, and a baffling one, but I was in no position to question him. I had to bail out my own scuttled boat.

'Oh, my pet don hadn't time to take me in today; he met me at the gate, then rushed off. A student was in a jam of some sort, apparently. I didn't like to ask. He loaned me a couple of books, and as it was such a pleasant day, I thought I might read for a little while by the river.'

George was silent for a moment, and I was able to quietly let my breath out.

'This don . . . what did you say his name was?'

'Dr Browne Colmsford.' (The name of this entirely innocent man had been given to me by Christopher, who had assured me that the old chap was thoroughly senile and 'in all likelihood *would* believe he had taken you to the Bodleian, if it came to it'.)

I could not interpret George's expression. He stared at me, but there was nothing personal in that stare;

nothing familiar or kind. I wondered – not for the first time – at this change in him after years of melancholia; at the speed of his transfiguration, the smallness of its cause. Such a modest bid for freedom on my part! A few trips to the library, and here we were, staring at each other like hostage and captor; prisoner and interrogator. I said, 'I'm sorry we couldn't have had the afternoon together. Is your leg better, now that it's warmer? We could walk together in Christchurch meadow. We could go out on the river.'

'Go out on the river,' George repeated, and I felt my put-on insouciance falter at his tone.

'George, you seem . . . Have I done something to offend you?'

'How am I to know?' he said. His eyes had sharpened; there was a new, true nastiness in his voice that I hadn't heard before. 'Why don't you tell me, Sophia? Have you done something wrong?'

In that moment I felt us both on a cusp; as if we could fall either one way or another. I knew I needed to talk – desperately – but I couldn't think of what to say. The pressure had emptied me of anything but a violent silence, a roaring vacuum. He seemed to be standing closer to me than I realised. I shook my head; I stepped back, and almost collided with Margaret, on her way into the room.

'Oh!' we both said.

George's look of brief savagery faded, and he turned away. Margaret did not notice; she was talking hurriedly;

'Ma'am, your sister Boll is here. I don't believe she was expected? But she said you'd be glad of the company.'

(She managed to fit a great deal of doubt into those last few words.)

'Dear me!' said the woman in question, sailing into the drawing room. 'No need for ceremony. We're not Victorians! Hullo, Sophia. How *are* you? Did you miss me?'

She embraced me, and for a moment I held on to her sharp, silk-draped shoulder with a sense of overpowering gratitude.

'Good afternoon, George,' Boll said coolly, catching sight of him over my shoulder as he hastily rose. 'I didn't see you there.'

'I'm afraid I was just going out,' George said. I looked at him with curiosity. 'An engagement in town.'

'How delightful,' Boll said, conveying an absolute lack of interest. 'I say, don't let me keep you.'

At this, George gave her an odd, awkward bow, and with a 'Good afternoon' to us both, was out of the door.

'He looks dreadful,' Boll observed. 'I didn't realise the war could continue to age one overnight, every night.'

'Hush, Boll. It's only that you look so horribly healthy.'

Boll smirked and extended her arms. Her dress was a deep, rather startling orange; it suited her tan. She had spent the last few weeks in the South of France, the apparent reason for her bohemian ebullience. She had, in fact, come to tell me all about her triumphs there. She and Piers had sailed to Le Touquet, where they had fallen in with a fashionable crowd, led by Bertie Bicester, and Nina Blount, Countess of Haverford. (These names were spoken expectantly, as if I ought to recognise them.) Boll and Piers had been pressed to stay on for an extra week at their villa.

'They said I was a scream,' she reported, her voice plump with victory. 'You should have been there, darling. But then I suppose George would never have let you out of the house.'

I thought of the way George had looked at me earlier. I must have imagined it: that cool, intense hatred. His eyes were a clear grey, like pale marble. I almost shivered, as if I felt them on me still.

'You look rather queasy,' Boll said. 'Envious?'

'Don't be ridiculous,' I said, dismissively. 'We simply couldn't afford it.'

Boll tossed her head at the unspoken question, which was: how had she and Piers afforded it? It suited us both just then to change the subject, and I listened as she returned to her theme, describing the champagne cocktails and coupé cars, the long, languid days on the beach, covered in oil, camps suitable for a sultan unrolling over the white sand: travel rugs and wine coolers and small dogs panting in the shade. Piers was awfully good at aquaplaning, until he stood on one leg – 'showing off' – and came a cropper. At night they danced until three or four in the morning to the revolutions of the over-worked gramophone. It was the gramophone more than any of the rest of it that caught my interest. I could almost hear it: the steel needle descending delicately on to the wax; the rise and fall of the record. The great coppery shell, from which emerged the fantastical leaps and drops of the jazz, playing over one's skin like tapping fingers, a delightful shiver.

'It was all very à la mode,' Boll sighed. 'So liberated; so refreshing. Parties were a perfect orgy. Some of the men made quite determined love to me.'

At this she gave me a quick sidelong look. Boll liked to talk to me as if I were something of a prude: quiet, bookish, easily startled. She would deliver stories she expected me to be shocked by, and sometimes I did pretend to be shocked, so as not to disappoint her.

'Dear me,' I murmured, and she smiled, satisfied. 'Did Piers mind?'

'Oh, half the time I never knew where Piers was. He fell asleep one night under the stars with Jacob Anstruther, and spent another in Bertie's bathtub.'

'He must have felt himself quite back at Cambridge.'

'I should say,' Boll laughed. 'Anyway, we're going to go to Murray's next weekend . . . You haven't heard of it? Oh, my dear! It's rather notorious. You can get hold of cocaine there quite easily.' She snapped her fingers, and the sidelong look returned.

'I'll remember that next time I'm looking for some cocaine.'

'Darling, you're too naïve. *Tout le monde* is doing it these days. Nina calls it dancing powder.'

'How witty of her.'

'*Isn't* it?'

Boll then embarked on an Iliad of an anecdote, involving Nina, an Afghan hound and an Algerian waiter, and I found myself tuning out; carried irrepressibly away on the seas of my own memory, as if floating on my back, further and further from the shore. One thing many diverse ancient peoples had in common was a belief in a flat earth, borne on a great body of water, an ocean circling their known land. It seemed to me that memory was the same: the solid present day cradled by the much wider waters of the past, to which, like Oceanus, the present owes its existence.

I allowed myself to be carried back to a time before the arrival of cocaine, before the rise of Nina and Bertie and Murray's, all the way back to Lady Rothwell's hospital: the first place in which I encountered drugs used not to fix the body but to absent the mind. I worked alongside Lady Rothwell's own daughter, Pamela. She had loved a childhood friend, and they were going to marry, until he was listed missing at the Battle of the Marne, and later, dead. I hadn't known Pamela before this happened, though I could guess at what she must have been like: a cheerful, stoical soul, whom the present-day Pamela made heroic efforts to reconstruct, though it was apparent that she was no longer able to remember exactly how that old cheerful self felt and acted, and sometimes her performance was almost frightening in its overdone normality, its guesses at gaiety. One day she dropped all pretence and took me into the room where the drugs were kept (neatly lined in alphabetical and size order, as decreed by her mother) and demonstrated to my shocked younger self how much morphine might keep one sane for the night. Her face was still then. It hung in the dim room like the moon; cold and white and far away.

Back then, I was shocked. Those days were the last in which I felt truly and deeply shocked by the world; a feeling that took a long time to pass. That was the thing about the shift from wartime to peace. When the war was on, I felt it might never end, and when it did end, I couldn't quite believe in it. It took a long time to wake up, blinking and staring around myself, trying to make sense of the sober dawn light. The war itself like a dream I hated to return to, but couldn't forget either: monotonous and feverish, a drawn-out nightmare in which horror repeated and repeated and turned, eventually, to tedium, a nonsensical flat emptiness.

When armistice came, England did not so much rejoice as pull its skirts up over its head and run around howling, like the woman the local papers gleefully reported on, who went up and down the Cornmarket waving a flag, with her skirts 'kilted up to her naked middle'. People kissed each other in the streets; went further in doorways, parks and alleys. Flags flew, horns blew. Most of us got drunk. But after the celebrations, it became apparent that the dream of war still hung in the air, humming like the reverberations of a giant clanging bell. I looked at England and thought I recognised that feeling. Like me, it did not know what to do with itself. Like me, it was still shocked.

England recovered, mostly. The music started again, the political squabbles over invalids and the General Strike and unemployment, the newspaper filling up again with complaints about women putting make-up on in public, and students getting tight and trampling flower beds. The people resolved back into two familiar halves: the rich with their centuries-old pleasures, and the poor with their centuries-old privations. Meanwhile I wandered in no-man's-land. I wondered if I should ever make sense of what had happened. The war felt too near, too close behind us. Yet after a few years it seemed as if only a few people could still hear the hum of that bell. And the men like George, of course, stricken from listening too close.

I wondered now how different my life should have been if George had never come back from the war. Then I pinched off the speculation, cutting its air. Did other people suffer this: these obscene or offensive detours of the imagination, coming out of nowhere, as if implanted by some sinister other? Perhaps everybody did, but nobody would admit to it. Perhaps it was only me. (Picture Sophia, talking with her sister, her husband, her acquaintances, feeling nothing but her own difference, her own aloneness.)

'I say, there's no need to look so queer,' Boll said. 'The waiter was fine. Didn't you hear me?'

'No. Sorry. Glad to hear it. Tell me, where is Daphne? I so seldom see her. You ought to have brought her with you.'

'Oh, Piers took her to London, to the zoo. He really does dote on that child. I must say I have no idea why. He's very impatient with stupidity, and children are nothing if not stupid small adults. Darling, would you ring for more tea? I've run quite dry.'

As we waited for Margaret, I leant back in my chair, looking at the fireplace, remembering Daphne's last visit.

'Is that Marengo?' she had asked, pointing at the rearing horse on the fireplace. She had been learning about the Napoleonic wars.

'Well, my father always said it was supposed to

be Bucephalus, but I see no reason why it couldn't be Marengo.'

'Who was Bucephalus?'

'A very heroic horse, who was afraid of his own shadow. He was untameable until Alexander the Great guessed what was distressing him, and turned him around so that he couldn't see the shadow any more.'

'But it was still there.'

'Perhaps later on he didn't mind it so much,' I said, and she nodded, as if she understood. 'But when I was younger, I used not to agree with my father. *I* thought the horse was Comanche.'

'Who was Comanche?'

'He was the only survivor – on the United States Army's side – of the Battle of Little Bighorn. Ah, you know it? How clever you are, darling. Well, Comanche was a wild horse originally. Perhaps that's how he survived. He was found severely wounded, but he recovered. He lived happily ever after, roaming the flower gardens at Fort Lincoln, excused from all duties.'

'How did he know what side he was on?'

'I think he was on his own side,' I said. 'My dear, I do like the questions you ask. I think it much the best way to learn history: asking the questions other people might not. Paying attention to everything, even if it seems small or silly or irrelevant. That goes for life, too, you know.'

Smiling to myself at the memory, I asked Boll, 'Did you ever have a name for that horse?'

She followed my pointing finger. 'Darling, I've not the faintest idea. Is this a trick?'

'Not at all.'

She looked at me warily. 'For a moment there I thought you were going to bring up that damned doll.'

I laughed. 'Ah well, I've given up on trying to get the truth out of you about *that*.'

Boll was referring to my Pierotti poured wax doll, Cassandra. How beautiful she had been, with her stiff white dress and distant blue eyes. There was always something vague about her; a misty beauty, as if she were a painted cherub. She was too delicate for little Boll, who hadn't been allowed anywhere within four paces of her. (Dear reader, by now I expect you see where this story is leading.) Needless to say, the day came when Cassandra was left unattended in the same room as Boll. Somehow she made her way from the chair to the hearth, where a fire was burning. When I got back, she was quite melted, her face spreading dolorously over the tiles. Boll loudly, wetly and redly denied having moved Cassandra, but later that night she cried secret, guilty tears, because she had only wanted to play with her, and hadn't known what the fire would do.

'I maintain the maid moved her,' Boll said now, sipping her tea primly.

'It doesn't matter now, darling.'

'Certainly not to you,' Boll said. Her tone, previously concealed behind the teacup held up as elegantly as a geisha's fan, was suddenly sharp. 'I got punished for it, in any case, because you were the favourite child.'

'Why, Boll,' I was taken aback. 'I'd no idea you thought that.'

'It's the simple truth.'

'Darling. They never had a favourite. You mustn't say that. They adored us both.' But as I reassured her, I wondered how much truth there was to her claim, and said nothing else, in case a trace of this uncertainty might be detectable in my voice, and while Boll was generally an unobservant woman, she was still my sibling, and I could never be entirely convinced (in much the same way as I couldn't talk myself out of saluting lone magpies) that she might possess some hitherto dormant sisterly telepathy.

'It's quite all right,' she said. 'When I was little I used not to understand why I never did anything right, and you never did anything wrong. But I do now; I've no illusions about it. It doesn't matter.'

'It sounds rather as if it does,' I observed gently.

'It's a lean living, not being the favourite, that's all.'

I decided not to answer this, sensing in her expression a darkness of mood that would not be flattered or distracted. We changed the subject and talked on a little more, but the conversation was awkward, and when Boll eventually took her leave, her lovely eyes glittering more than usual, the blue ice at the heart of the glacier, her kiss goodbye was a cold one.

I went back into the drawing room and stood for a moment by the fireplace, running my fingers absent-mindedly over the chilly flank of Comanche, remembering Daphne sitting on my knee as I told her about famous horses. She listened with her small head tilted like a squirrel's, her expressive eyes opened wide, as if she was determined to absorb everything that way, let the words sink into those reflective dark pools. Her face was the intense, soft white of a fawn's belly, or a cat's throat; not pallor but paleness both vivid and alive. I touched her cheek, brushing its warmth with my fingers, and she smiled, and said, 'Please, Aunt Sophia, may I hear another story?'

PART FOUR

OLIVER

In his previous encounters with Sophia, Oliver had read reverently, putting each page neatly aside, refolding them with great care. Now, he scanned her last pages in a hurry, his hands cold with excitement, and put them down so distractedly that they spilled over the edge of the chair. He got to his feet, staring at the marble fireplace; the horse rearing, its relief half submerged in black shadow. Not Incitatus but Comanche. Not his sitting room, piled with artefacts (though no grandfather clock and no piano) and papered in a shade of dirty rose, but Sophia's drawing room, blue-walled and serene. He went out hastily, tripping over the corner of a rug, and turned on the bare light bulbs in every room, examining the house under their stringent light. The purposeless magnolia room at the back of the house that collected the best of the late-afternoon sun had been the eau de Nil parlour in which Sophia's mother pretended to sew. Here was the kitchen doorway in which the lingering Sophia saw not a glum palette of seventies browns but a sanctuary, warily manned by Mrs Boxall. He went into the dining room next, but there was nothing left of the gold walls, let alone the mahogany table or Turkish rug, and the chandelier, of course, had been taken down by the time

Sophia came to write about it.

His disappointment increased upstairs, as he went from stripped room to stripped room, failing to work out which had belonged to who. He looked through Sophia's history again; found a reference to the wisteria at her bedroom window; ran back upstairs, only to find that the creeper had stretched up to the sills of both of the large bedrooms at the front of the house, and one at the back. To his disappointment, she did not mention the green wallpaper with its exquisite birds, now down to one, a lone jigsaw piece – but she *had* seen it. She had stood inside the room filled with colour and felt its full effect; the heat of the beauty that Oliver at the window had hungrily consumed cold.

Next he found the burr-walnut wardrobe – a minor triumph – but this could have been moved many times over the years, and Sophia hadn't been fond of it anyway. He opened its doors, knowing it was empty; reconfirmed the emptiness; closed them again. Finally he went to the kitchen window and stared out into the layered darkness of the garden in which – somewhere – stood the tree whose apples the small Boll had been picking at the moment her father died upstairs.

He noticed the sky lightening to a chilly grey over the roof-tops beyond, and checked his watch. It was past five in the morning. He couldn't feel tired, though his excitement had the hollow, jittery quality of a strong coffee on an empty stomach. There was an urgency to this high; it jabbed at him, demanding something, goading him forward. He went through the equipment the contractors had left and found some likely looking tools, which he used to rip up the corners of the hall carpet. Beneath he found a twilight world of silverfish and accumulated dust, overlying more 1970s brown in the form of a worn patterned lino. He excavated further, and there they were: the black-and-white tiles of the Mrs Simmonds regime. A savage joy burned within him, and he renewed his efforts, attacking the tiles with hammer and chisel, hardly noticing the dust and the noise, the stinging fragments that darted up into his face.

Half an hour and one black thumbnail later, Oliver had succeeded in levering up one white tile and most of the grout. Underneath he could make out the distinct lines of the geometric Georgian tiles Sophia had loved and lost. They seemed to shimmer, wavering in the ambiguous light of the dawn that was welling up from the horizon in a luminous fog. He ran his fingers over their worn surfaces: cream, red, blue. Then he laid his hand flat on them and felt a surge of tenderness, as if he was touching Sophia's own shoulder, offering some obscure kind of reassurance. He had no idea what he had to give her; only this inarticulate, blundering, protective instinct, still taking its first steps, but fixed on its direction. If he couldn't help her, he would save this house she had loved; preserve it somehow, against not only the minor physical damage of the Mrs Simmonds or Arthur Evans variety, but the greater spiritual threat posed by George, or anybody who would accidentally or on purpose turn the house back into something lost and desolate. In the short time he had spent here, he had felt a shift in its atmosphere, as if something benevolent was stirring after a long hibernation. It had warmed to him; it understood his intentions. Or at least that was how it felt.

Kneeling on the floor with his hand warming a small patch of terracotta, he could barely make sense of what his discovery would mean to Kate, or Lena, or even himself. Kate must have been wrong about the previous inhabitants of the house. That much was obvious. But he couldn't call her: she was out at some dinner; had sent a picture of champagne and a smiley face. He guessed – pained – that this meant good news for the New York job. It came like news from another time; a message he couldn't make sense of yet, just as he was struggling to comprehend the news that Sophia had lived here; that she had looked out of the same windows, run her hand down the same banister, trod the same floor as Oliver himself. If Kate was far in the future and Sophia was in the past, Oliver was sitting in same deserted rest stop between the two. He couldn't quite get his head around either woman's revelation, or what relationship they had to each other.

He went back to Sophia's last page, which – as expected – was marked with another coded note. 'Must read: *Heroic Explorers of the World.*'

He looked through the stacks of books in the sitting room, looked through them again, looked a final time and opened them all up just in case; then went into the other, empty rooms of the house, as if he might find more books had materialised there. His feet drummed fruitlessly over the naked floorboards, going forward and back until the sound made him aware of himself and he sent himself finally to bed, where he lay upturned, trying unsuccessfully to go to sleep. Sophia's identity, and the feud between the Calverts and the Castles, went remorselessly around his head until he gave up on the idea of sleeping, and when he did wake up, bathed in the nectarine light of the late morning, it was to the sight of the plumber and the electrician, temporarily united in their concern for him, or perhaps their mutual amusement, knocking on the window, calling, 'You all right, mate?'

Oliver felt every minute of the three hours he had to wait for the world to grind slowly on its axis, bringing Kate nearer to her own morning, which he was about to interrupt. In the event, she called him, high-pitched and excited, the hoarse yelp of her voice revealing that she'd just got home.

'Guess what!'

'What?' he asked, knowing already.

'I'm getting the promotion!'

Oliver rubbed his eyes; located his enthusiasm. 'Congratulations. That's amazing news. You deserve it, obviously.'

'I haven't had any sleep!'

'I can tell.'

She laughed; it sounded more like a cough. 'Maybe I should go to bed for a couple of hours. I can call back when I've sobered up. We should talk.'

'Definitely,' he said, fingers and toes curled with horror.

'Work's going to be *heavy*. Urgh.'

'Kate, sorry, I know you're tired and you need to go, but I've got some news about the house. I've realised that the book was *definitely* written by someone who lived here.'

'What? Sophia?'

'Sophia Louis – but I think maybe she's using a false name for some reason. Or perhaps you might have overlooked her when you were remembering it.'

'Oh God,' said Kate. Her voice expressed precisely the action of somebody putting their head in their hands. He thought he could hear the muffled impact. 'What is it you want to know? Everyone who lived there for the last hundred years?'

'Only up until 1920. Isn't the information in the emails from the solicitor? Maybe you could . . . look it up? Just quickly?'

'Jesus,' Kate said, but her voice was further off, and he

guessed she was looking at the emails on her phone. After a little while she said, 'Right. I've got it here. So it was last owned by Aunt Delia. Then before her, by my grandfather, William Castle. He got it from Tom Castle, who was his uncle. Tom Castle was married to Leonora Castle. Her parents, David and Elizabeth Calvert, owned it before then. There – that's a hundred years. Leonora's sister, Annabel Montgomery, started the whole stupid fuss over the house. She said it should have gone to the Calverts, not the Castles, when Leonora died.'

'Annabel! That's Sophia's sister. Sophia must be Leonora.'

'Right,' Kate said, shortly. He sensed her impatience, and hurried to get his last questions in, as if he could roll them like Indiana Jones under the closing door of her tolerance.

'Did Annabel have a daughter?'

'It doesn't say anything about it here. But she must have had children. That's why the Godwins are here today, bothering us. Because Annabel unfortunately reproduced.'

'And Leonora didn't.' He felt saddened, freshly disappointed, on Sophia's behalf. 'So Sophia's name was Leonora . . . Sounds like Lena. I wonder if she was named for her.'

'Who gives a shit?' Kate said, suddenly sharp.

'Kate, do you realise what this means? This history must have something to do with the case.'

'There *is* no case. They've given it up.'

'What do you mean?'

'I got an email this morning from Mr Hunt. The Calverts had to let it go because – as we all bloody well knew – their claim was based on nothing. We were right, and they were wrong, and now we can sell it, and if they're still pissed off they can just harass whoever buys it next.'

THE HOUSE OF BIRDS

'Oh.' Oliver thought Lena couldn't have known this when he saw her. Her parents must have decided it. He wondered what her reaction would be. 'What were the details of their claim?'

Kate gave a sigh, meant to be audible. 'You said this would be quick . . . Right, it says here that Leonora and Tom didn't have children. Leonora died first. The house went to Tom, obviously. Annabel didn't like that and claimed that Leonora wanted the house to go to the Calverts and that's what it said in her will, but Tom must have destroyed it. Conveniently! As I said, it's all bullshit.'

'Maybe he did. He seems pretty strange.'

'Except he's not called Tom but . . .?'

'George.'

'So it's fictional George that's strange. And what else – did fictional Sophia say anything about a will? Or leaving the house to her sister?'

'No. She doesn't get on with her sister either.'

'Okay, so even the fictional Calverts don't support the real Calverts' argument. Can we stop talking about it now?'

'Just one more question. Please. What did Leonora die of?'

'I have absolutely no idea. It doesn't really say here. It's a bit weird actually. It talks about her death in some places and her presumed death in others . . . Look, there are pages of this stuff. I don't have time to read it all and work it out. She's dead now, isn't she – does it matter how she died?' Her voice rose slightly, pained. 'Oliver, I don't get what this is all about. I've just told you that I'm getting a promotion – in New York – and all you can ask about is that diary. Is there something else going on that I should know about? Every time I try to talk about the future, you change the subject back to the house, or that book. At first I was worried that you were taking the Calverts' side or something. That you fancied Lena. Stupid stuff. But now I think maybe you just don't want to talk about our future. I don't know what's going on with you anymore. Big things are happening, but you don't seem interested. You hardly text me. Have you changed your mind about us? Or your life? What's going on with your job research, anyway? I tried not to question you, but I . . . I can't stand it anymore.'

The quality of these last words was so degraded that he could barely make them out. They were followed by a silence, during which he tried to work out if the almost inaudible sounds at the other end were her sniffing, or just the rustle and hiss of the Atlantic Ocean between their voices.

'Kate, I'm sorry. I know I've been . . . unhelpful. I can see why you're angry. I just – I don't know what I'm doing either. That's the truth of it.'

'Okay,' she said. Another long pause. Oliver, usually able to interpret Kate's telephonic silences – fill in a picture of her tapping her foot, or smiling, or biting her nails – couldn't make any sense of this one.

'And I'm so happy for you,' he continued.

There was another silence, this time so long that Oliver became concerned at its emptiness. 'Hello?'

'I'm here,' she said. Then she sighed. 'Look, we're both tired. There's no point talking now. I'll call tomorrow, once we've had some sleep. We'll talk tomorrow.'

e

Oliver spent the rest of the morning in a homeless state; sent scuttling from room to room by the arrival of plumbers, electricians, plasterers, window fitters and builders, all of whom were far more confident of their place in the house – and, in fact, the universe – than Oliver himself, who was hovering not only between rooms but between the past and the present, with no meaningful grasp on either. Once again at a loose end, he occupied himself by searching for Sophia's *Heroic Explorers of the World* online, at intervals giving up and lapsing into an ill-advised mulling of his own situation, which made him feel queasy.

He had an increasing feeling of disconnection from his life, which seemed at that moment little more than a mishmash of marketing slogans, rap lyrics, motivational quotations and New Age-ish materialism – work hard, play hard, 'C.R.E.A.M.', Vorsprung durch Technik, winners never quit, a diamond is forever – which were taken up and repeated by his friends, by himself, until they took on the quality of sacred tenets. Transport must be business class. Accommodation must be five star. Homes must be executive. Goods must be designer. Dining must be fine. Oliver must be the best Oliver that he can be.

He wondered what other Olivers he might have been. Versions of himself in alternate universes flitted by, radiant as soap bubbles; insubstantial as snowflakes. None of them stood up to close inspection. He thought of Lena and her birds of prey. He admired her (something he would never tell Kate) not only for her passion, but for her ability to identify it: for taking a flare of awareness and making a life out of it. He wondered if in his own life there had been similar moments, matches struck, but he just hadn't twigged, and they had burned down unnoticed.

As a child, Oliver was good at maths, which he didn't like,

and average at history, which he did. When it came to university applications his mother said, 'History? But what would you do with it?' while his form tutor said, 'Think of your strengths. Think of your prospects' (knocking on the table after each command, as if driving out a demon), and his father – always concise, if not elegant – said, 'Money's where the money is, son.' His mother didn't need to say, *Don't waste three years of your life on a dead end*; his form tutor didn't say, *With those predicted grades you'll be lucky to get into a poly*; his father didn't add, *Don't make the same mistakes as me.* None of them needed to. He might have legitimised a degree in history with a plan to write a best-selling book, or front a television series, but he felt nothing other than a vague, purposeless longing for the past that looked suspiciously like laziness. In the great debates over whether he ought to become an accountant or a stockbroker, he put history to one side (as his mother said, it wasn't like it was *going* anywhere) with the intention of studying it again one day. But then it was one day, and even though his father had been promoted in the end – something nobody had expected – and his parents had retired to Devon and no longer spoke so anxiously about money, it turned out that grown-up Oliver wasn't inclined to give up his City salary and apartment and future plans to become a student again. He thought he would just read history in the evenings instead, a piece of optimism that was, if anything, even more naïve.

He decided not to think about his life any more that day. He turned his attention instead to another puzzler: where was *Heroic Explorers of the World*? He couldn't understand why it wasn't with the other books. His thoughts see-sawed, each hopeful idea almost immediately tipped down again by its dour counterpart, going something like this:

Hopeful thought:

Surely, if someone had found the book's hidden contents, Kate's family would have heard about it. So it must be intact somewhere.

Answering thought:

If George had found it, he would probably have destroyed it. If anyone else had found it, they would have thrown it away.

Hopeful thought:

Perhaps the book had been sold, and might be bought back.

Answering thought:

What bookseller would buy or resell a book without leafing through it first? At which point its secret would be discovered, and the book would be thrown away.

This went on until the dreary to and fro was arrested by a slap of a realisation:

Kate had visited and thrown some junk into the skip

Followed by, about ten seconds later, the equally ringing realisation:

Lena had visited and salvaged some treasure from the skip.

He got up, drained his coffee (with the reasoning that he would need all its power when dealing with Lena), checked the bus schedule, cursed the council, called a taxi, glanced at himself, sighed, got changed into clothes that seemed less likely to provoke mockery, bade farewell to the contractors (who had taken to calling him Sleeping Beauty) and set off for Lena's place.

℮

Oliver sat in the back of the taxi in a miasma of artificial vanilla, his leg chattering up and down like a wound-up set of false teeth. He felt both dull and sharp; fighting a woolly headache on one side and a nervy tension on the other. He tried to clear his mind and focused on the wet countryside passing him by: fields softened with rain below a blanketing of cloud like a soggy eiderdown, thick and cold. The hedge-lined lanes all looked the same: greyish-green foliage rising to narrow his view to either side; the wet dark road curving to prevent him seeing too far ahead. Water smeared the windows, and he lost his sense of where the city was, and where Lena's house was, feeling again a strange sort of suspension, a hovering between two states.

'This it?' asked the taxi driver.

Oliver squinted through the window, his vision washed out with a sudden volley of rain.

'I . . . don't know.'

'It's the bird of prey place, right. This is it.'

'Thank you,' Oliver said, hearing the apology in his voice even as he wondered why the driver had bothered asking. He wondered if he would ever meet an Oxonian (he didn't count himself among their number) who wasn't several steps ahead of him. Looking at Lena's house from under his umbrella, feeling a gentle fibrillation of nervousness at the sight of the lights on within, he guessed the answer was: not today.

He slushed through the muddy gravel to the bird of prey centre first, which was – as he had suspected – closed. He stood for a moment in the parking lot before doubling back towards Lena's house. He realised as he went that this was exactly the sort of thing that wouldn't go down very well with Kate. If Lena didn't have the book, he thought, he would just leave quickly, and not mention that he'd ever visited. It wasn't as if the two women would be comparing notes.

He waited so long at Lena's door, the raindrops thudding off the eaves on to his umbrella like stones, that he began to wonder if she would answer at all. It was an odd reversal of their first meeting, except it seemed Oliver was somehow the anxious one again, doomed to his role whether he was standing on the doorstep or hiding inside. It occurred to him that her husband, Jim Lennox, might be off work, and would come to the door instead. He wasn't sure how he felt about that.

He was considering leaving when a small Lena shape appeared behind the glass, moving quickly, before the door flew open, as if kicked in.

'You?' Lena said. She appeared startled, then in the next instant, hostile. She looked as if she had been out in the rain herself: her hair was loose and wild and slightly damp, and she had scratches on her arms. She had the air of emerging from a recent tussle, still alight with confrontation and ready to take on the next challenger. *Who's next?* her black eyes demanded.

'Er . . . sorry to bother you,' Oliver began. He wasn't sure why she seemed so angry. Yesterday she had made him tea and invited him back to see the birds fly. Her last words, he recalled, were 'Take care.' Now he wondered if that had been a warning.

'Why are you here?' she asked, then added, before he could answer, 'How did you get here?'

'A taxi,' he said humbly.

She leant forward; he stepped quickly back, and she put her head out of the door. It was silently established that the taxi was gone.

'Fuck's sake,' she muttered. She held the door open, clearly undecided about what to do. He stood in silence, grateful now for the rain: despite her evident annoyance at seeing him, she was not the type to shut the door and leave him in it. 'Well,' she said at last. 'I'm busy. You'll have to call the taxi back here. You can wait inside.'

Oliver went in hurriedly before she could change her mind. At the last moment the ginger cat streaked in through the door along with him, its fur in spikes. It left a line of wet paw prints along the floorboards.

'Fucking open house day,' Lena said, and shut the door.

'Lena, have I done something wrong?' Oliver asked, now that he was safely past the threshold. 'I thought things were okay. Yesterday . . .'

'*Yesterday* my parents decided – were forced – to drop their claim on the house. Did you know that?'

He had known, but the knowledge had been swept off in the adrenalin of his subsequent discovery. 'Oh. Yes,' he said. 'I found out this morning. I'm sorry.'

She stared at him for a moment, looking baffled, before apparently deciding she wasn't curious enough to question him, turning away with the apparent intention of retreating to another room, and leaving him in the hall.

'Do you know anything about Leonora Calvert?' he asked, rushing the words out as if they could chase her down, like a pack of dogs. In the still air of the hall they sounded louder and more desperate than he intended.

She stopped. 'Do *you?*'

'Not what happened to her. Or why her sister thought that she'd left a will. Or how the will was lost.'

'Not lost. Destroyed.' Lena's apparent interest had dropped; she said this flatly.

'What did she die of?'

'Nothing natural. Look, what the fuck are you up to? You've already won, okay? The house is yours! You should be in Laura Ashley picking out fake period light fixtures. You don't have to come over here and Columbo me . . . What's so funny?'

'I hadn't heard Columbo as a verb. Sorry.'

'Glad it's so amusing to you,' she said sourly, but she dipped her head, and he wondered if she was subduing a smile. She'd do it ruthlessly, he thought – a quick cosh over the head, a bundling into the back of a van. When she looked back up, it was with unyielding dislike. The smile never stood a chance.

'Lena, I don't expect you to believe me, but it's not about the house as much as Soph . . . Leonora. I want to know what happened to her. I think your family might be right about Tom. Can we talk about it?'

Lena looked at him for a long moment. Time passed glacially. Oliver noticed that the pattering on the roof had stopped. The hall, narrow and white-painted and lined with coats, was chilly. Lena seemed to feel this at the same time as he did. She wrapped her arms around herself, still looking at him, but vaguely, as if he were only one part of her own internal debate. Whatever the outcome, it wasn't unanimously reached; and when she finally turned, with a slight shrug, and indicated that he should follow her into the house, she seemed almost uncertain.

'It's warmer in the kitchen,' was all she said by way of explanation.

Lena's kitchen was a relief, if only in the purest sensory terms. It was a larger, longer room than he had expected, with sage-green walls, a squat enamelled range as glossy as a cherry, wooden surfaces with the sheen of cooled caramel, worn into gentle curves. It was also a mess. The large Belfast sink was a white ship with a cargo of mugs and marmaladey plates; a small pile of teabags reposed next to the kettle. The far end of the room was clearly used as a study, walls lined with shelves surrounding a large oak table, pitted and ring-marked and covered in things Oliver looked at with interest: pens, letters, a handful of bay leaves, rubber bands, mints, books, torn-out pages from newspapers. Like the turned-out pockets of a schoolboy, he thought, except instead of a catapult there was an expensive make-up compact, glossy, black and gold. This evidence of . . . of what? . . . fascinated him.

In the next moment Lena, appearing behind him with a noise of annoyance (whether at the mess or Oliver, he couldn't tell), gathered it all up and carried it away, calling back to him to find himself a seat. He hovered by the table until he became aware of another point of consciousness in the room: the ginger cat, which had found itself a spot on the windowsill. He only saw it when he turned his head and found himself almost nose to nose with it. The cat didn't even blink its fiery golden eyes, which, after a while, defocused, returning to their own secret thoughts, as if Oliver was of no consequence at all, which he supposed was probably true.

Lena came back in and switched on some lamps, suspending soft amber spheres in the grey daylight seeping through from outside. She carried on tidying the kitchen, though it seemed weird to Oliver that she'd make an effort to make it warm and welcoming when she herself remained anything but. Or perhaps it had nothing to do with him: she was talking all the time she was going back and forth, raising a hot commotion of suds in the sink, switching on the noisy kettle, setting things at right angles, as if by imposing order on the kitchen she might somehow right the unfairness of the world.

'Everyone knows what happened to Leonora,' she said. 'But nobody could prove it. It's not like people really cared back then when it was only someone's *wife*. She vanished before she was even thirty. She had told Annabel that she'd made a will. The will vanished too, naturally. Turned out the solicitor was an old friend of Tom's. You see? After a while Leonora was declared dead, and Tom said she'd said something about killing herself and that was what she'd probably done. Thrown herself in the sea or something. And so he got the house. But their maid, Margaret, said she heard an argument between Leonora and Tom the night before Leonora disappeared. She said Leonora was crying, and frightened. She said everyone in that house was frightened of Tom but she was ignored. It was the nineteen twenties. The women were the only ones to speak out, and nobody was ever going to listen to them. Leonora didn't have a father or a brother to speak up for her, so she was fucked, basically.'

'Tom just carried on?'

'Yes. Living alone. He didn't remarry; but then who would have had him? He was a total cunt, according to everyone who knew him. Even the Castles wouldn't deny that. Not that they care, so long as they've got the fucking prime real estate.'

Oliver shook his head. He felt so grieved for Sophia – for Leonora – that he could hardly speak. He turned his head away, as if he were inspecting the bookshelves.

Lena misinterpreted his silence and said, defensively, 'We're not the same as them, if that's what you're thinking. We would never sell her house. It's *hers*. Someone who understands that ought to live there. But I wouldn't expect you to get what I mean by that. And I can't explain it to you, either.'

'I . . . ah . . . never mind.'

'Tea or coffee?' Lena continued, turning back to the mugs. 'Hey, Oliver. Tea or coffee? You listening to me?'

And there it was: *Heroic Explorers of the World*. Sitting in a row with some other books that had quite obviously been part of Sophia's collection, the leather softened and fading with use; worn gold lettering.

He stood up to take them down. 'These books – they came from the house, didn't they?'

'Hold on a second.' Lena moved quickly, going from a figure at the opposite end of the kitchen with a teabag in her hand to a fierce face at his shoulder. 'Those are my books now. I told you – they were in the skip. You people didn't want them. They were Leonora's, you know.'

'No – no, it's okay. I'm not trying to claim them. I'm glad you've got them. Look, let me finish making the tea. I've got something you need to read.'

He took Sophia's history, warm as an egg, out of his inside pocket. Lena took it, looking confused.

'I found it inside some of the books in the house. Leonora's books. It's her own story, written by her, under a fake name. I don't know why she didn't use her own name, but it's absolutely her. It's about her marriage, and how weirdly her husband is behaving, and how she's been going to the Bodleian with this guy who's her friend but I think she, er, might fancy him. And her sister Boll – Annabel, I mean – is in there too.'

Lena was looking at him blankly. He hurried on, 'Anyway, the next bit, I think, should be . . . here.'

He took down *Heroic Explorers* and opened it, holding it out towards her. They both looked at the pages folded inside.

'Good Lord,' Lena said, in a tiny voice, as if surprise had knocked all the swear words out of her.

'You saved it from being thrown away. I came over because I thought it might be here. I thought' – as he said it, he realised it was true – 'that you should know about her.'

Lena stared at him. She turned over the pages in her hand, examined the writing. Eventually she said, 'I can't believe this. It's all about her life? About her marriage?'

Her lips were slightly open; her eyes full of gathering energy, as if trying to understand everything at once. The fact of her beauty struck him like a palm in the face. A study he had once read about came back to him; it had found that people exposed to dangerous situations ended up more attracted to each other than they would otherwise. Something to do with adrenalin. He supposed that time with Lena was nothing if not an experiment in danger.

'Yes. I'll make the tea,' he said, giving her the book and moving away, worried that she might have noticed a change in his expression. But she was thinking of something else.

'Oliver – if this was really written by Leonora, it could mean that the truth comes out. Finally.'

'I guess so.'

'So why would you do this? You know what it means.'

Oliver didn't – and then he did. If they proved that Tom had killed Leonora, the house could go to the Calverts. Until now, all he had thought about was finding out what happened to Sophia. He hadn't connected her fate to current events.

He stared into his tea; reading his future. He saw Kate there. She wasn't happy with him.

Now Lena did notice his expression. 'Fuck the tea,' she said, suddenly. 'I need a whisky. You need a whisky. Then we'll read. Wait there.'

When she came back, she was carrying a bottle of whisky and two framed photographs. She held them out; an almost shy gesture. 'I didn't know if you'd . . . Have you seen her?'

He shook his head and took them, gratefully. The first was of Leonora and Annabel – he knew it before Lena named them – two dark-haired, white-skinned sisters. It must have been taken before Leonora had started her history: Boll's hair was not yet bobbed, and their dresses were similarly simple. Yet it seemed obvious also which girl was which. The outlines of their faces were the same, their slender noses and elvish jawlines, but Boll had a full, small mouth, an insolent kiss shape, and the lifted eyebrows to go with it. The rare blue of her eyes was not visible except by inference; she held them up as if they were something special, presenting them to the camera to be admired.

Leonora was something very different. He looked at her face for a long time. It was not that she wasn't beautiful too – she was – or that she was physically dissimilar to Boll – she wasn't – but there was a complexity to her that demanded a longer gaze. She looked as if her expression had changed very recently, and might change again. In the moment of the picture a world of possibility had been captured. At first glance she looked studiedly neutral, as if she had been warned not to smile. But her eyes seemed only temporarily serious, about to be amused, or sad. Her mouth was held in suspension as if she were about to speak, or had only just stopped talking. It was the quality of flux that distinguished a Rembrandt from a Renoir, a *National Geographic* portrait from a perfume advert.

He looked again at Lena, and said with surprise: 'You look like her. Leonora.'

'Really?' She inspected the picture. 'I don't see it.'

'You've got the same mouth. Look. Then you have the same large eyes, same jaw, same eyebrows.'

'Different nose. Different shading.'

'But the blueprint is the same. You can see the general plan. You . . .' He stopped, unable to keep converting thoughts into words. Though the production line had stalled, the thoughts kept on coming, piling up in his head. That there was also something exceptional about Lena, the same look of hidden thoughts, of secret possibilities; though she had no need to hide her thoughts, and often didn't. That as she examined the pictures, a half-smile settling over her mouth, her combative eyes thoughtful for the moment, he had the urge to put his hand on her arm, just to see what she felt like, whether her skin was warm or soft or cool or firm, and then there came other thoughts; shy, sly thoughts, best suited to their dim subterranean habitat, not to be brought out into the light of day.

'I what?' asked Lena.

'You look similar, that's all. Is this Daphne?' He held up the other picture.

'Yes. She died when she was quite young, too; before she was thirty. She'd just given birth to my mum. But there were complications, and she didn't make it.'

'I'm so sorry,' he said: meaning it not only for Lena and her mother, but for Sophia – and selfishly for himself, who might otherwise have met Daphne, had the chance to ask her, 'Do you remember your Aunt Leonora? What was she like? What were her gestures like? Her laugh? Her voice? Do you know any more of her stories? Do you remember the horse on the fireplace, at her house? Do you remember the birds?'

He studied the woman in the picture. She sat beside a pleasant-looking man, who seemed to have decided that a certain amount of dignity was required for a family photo and gazed through Oliver and beyond as if monitoring something of immense importance in the middle distance. Daphne herself looked slightly wistful, slightly amused. She had Leonora's reserves of irony, he thought. She was not as pretty as her mother or aunt; she had the same features as Leonora, the long mouth, the high eyebrows, but somehow in her they didn't join up so well. Her light hair could have been blond or brown.

'How sad – how ironic that she didn't survive giving birth.'

'Why ironic?'

'I mean because it was Annabel who had a fear of dying in pregnancy. She told Sophia she didn't want any more children.'

'Did she? She didn't have any more, that was true. How weird – you know more about my great-grandmother than I do.' He looked at her warily, but she was smiling. 'Right – I'm going to start reading from the beginning. And you can read this.'

She gave him the folded square of pages from *Heroic Explorers*, and Oliver was deeply moved. He was technically of no further use: Lena could have ordered him out and read the history alone, but she seemed to acknowledge his own connection to Leonora, whatever that was. They sat together in the clearing light of the window, side by side, both with their own books, and he thought, but couldn't say, 'It's just like *them*' – or not without explaining, which he didn't want to do. He thought of Sophia sitting next to Christopher as they read; her looking up, occasionally, at his lowered profile.

He didn't look at Lena, though all the time he could see her in the corner of his eye: a dark patch, complicated shapes of hair, arm, moving hand; a disturbance in his peripheral vision.

Modest Explorers of the World
S. L.

So . . . here we are again. Another chapter in my own history; another great work criminally vandalised. Perhaps one day I'll publish a book of my own, and someone else will come along and cut it up. Imagine that! You can purse your lips, dear reader, and say it served me right.

As I've told you before: if this is the first chapter you have found, you must go back to your books and look again. There you will find me, hiding within the histories of others, smuggling myself through customs like a heretical tract. By doing so I have taken a risk, and so it seems fair that you, dear reader, must also work a little, if only to show that you can be trusted. And on that note, I shan't be drawing you a picture – not today. We've known each other long enough now that I think it time for you to use your own understanding, your own vision.

Don't worry: there shall be no tutting, not even a raised eyebrow, if you get some of the details wrong – the wheres and whens – so long as you understand the whats, or the whys. It is of no importance what time the great church bells clanged, or the colour of Christopher's hat, or how many pieces of cake I ate at luncheon. Titles and names come and go. Remember the list of names and dates in my hospital diary? I threw it away, because to me it no longer represented the truth of the matter, or, at any rate, not the truth that mattered. The human truth is all we need concern ourselves with now.

So, without further ado, here I am at the Ashmolean, looking for Christopher, and glancing too at the other faces around me: a new habit I had picked up, just as I had learned to spin a story, presenting George with light creations as elaborate and fragile as icing. 'Just popping to the draper's, darling: I thought perhaps new curtains for the sitting room . . .' or 'It's such a ravishing day, I thought I might wander along the river to the botanical gardens. Can I tempt you to join me? Are you quite sure?' or, 'I'm meeting Professor B. again. He's found something on Macchu Picchu that he thought I might enjoy. I'll be lunching at Boll's afterwards.'

When I brought out these fibs, flashing them like twinkling paste jewels, a queer, slow understanding seemed to connect us. I would deliver my line, then George would politely decline his invitation, but wish me a pleasant day. All the while we were talking, our mouths making conventional noises, we would watch each other; eyes steady, flickering but never blinking. There would be a long stillness, during which I often held my breath, without realising I was doing it. Once outside the room, I would pant to get the air in, leaving the house with sweat girdling my stomach, crawling down the cleft of my shoulder blades. He was still spying on me, and I was still spying on his efforts, a meticulous investigation carried out every Thursday afternoon, when Margaret left early to visit her mother.

I wasn't certain if it was a comfort or another worry that Margaret herself had noticed the difference in George. That morning, before I left for the library, she had come to me quietly – solemnly – proceeding across the room in a slow, almost bridal step, holding out not a bouquet but the broken pieces of a framed photograph of George and myself, taken on our own wedding day.

'Dear me,' I said, wondering what had occasioned this sense of ceremony. 'But Margaret, you needn't worry over this. Accidents happen.'

'Oh, but . . . it wasn't me that broke it, ma'am. It was Mr Louis. I heard a smash and went to see what had happened.'

'Oh. Well then. He must have knocked it over. And by the looks of things, accidentally trodden on it. I'm sure the frame can be mended.' I spoke comfortingly, as Margaret still looked upset, though in truth the sight of my own face almost obliterated by the scar of a boot heel was rather unnerving. 'And I'm sure we have other photographs.'

Margaret did not seem comforted by this. She didn't turn to leave, but neither did she speak, standing mutely in front of me like a summoned spirit, waiting to be commanded.

'Is there anything else?' I enquired.

'I'm not sure it's my place to say, ma'am, but I was worried, and I thought perhaps . . . It's only that Mr Louis was so very angry with me, when I disturbed him.'

'He told you he was angry?'

'No, but he shouted at me to get the, um, get the hell out, ma'am, excusing my language.'

'Oh dear.' I thought for a moment. 'I'm awfully sorry he spoke to you that way. I've no idea what possessed him. I imagine he felt guilty at having broken the picture. He does take things rather hard.'

At this Margaret gave me an uncharacteristically searching look, apparently not at all convinced by my explanation – but not insulted by it, either, as well she might be. I saw pity in her look, and concern.

'That will be all, Margaret,' I said quickly, moving back and picking up a book. 'I do apologise again for Mr Louis' conduct. Perhaps, for now, it would be better not to offer him assistance, or interrupt him, unless he rings. Just until he's in a better mood.'

When Margaret had gone, I looked at the photograph again. The two of us stood stiffly, side by side, at the foot of a sinuous staircase, both snake and ladder. We looked as if we could not bear to touch each other, when, back then, the reverse had been true. George's face was shy; his eyes raised as if meeting the camera only painfully, trying not to wince in the light. From what I recalled, my own expression had been one of repressed hilarity: the photographer had sneezed and the jolt loosened a curl of his pressed and oiled hair, which sprang up like a question mark above his head. I tried to see the edges of that amusement in the remaining parts of my face – a slice of cheek, a portion of jaw – but it had left no trace.

I wondered at this new corner turned, the latest chapter in the story of George's journey towards . . . what? I didn't know. After a period of secrecy, his anger had at last broken cover, burst out from the bracken in a startling clap of wings. I put the picture down. I hadn't any idea how we'd ended up at this point, so quickly, after so long spent in our almost companionable suspension of life. It was as though my outings had tipped our fragile equilibrium like a trestle table, all the crockery smashing at once. He no longer patrolled the house at night (though I lay as staring and sleepless as if he did), and I wondered if this was because he had realised that the greatest danger to his marriage was not outside the perimeter of his house, but had been harboured within all along.

I didn't know if in his mind he had gone so far as to suspect me of an affair, or if he was simply resentful of the time I spent away from him. But George had never been stupid, or ignorant. He could tell I had given up trying to tease out his old self, and he could see how often I was out of the house, and even a stupid man must draw some obvious conclusions from the pairing of those things. Who could ever believe that I went out only to read, or – for that matter – that I had made a friend of a good-looking young man, in all innocence, and quite by accident? Perhaps it was not a matter of deduction and rational thought at all, but animal intuition: George sensing – with some primitive instinct, picking up a scent – that I was no longer hopeful or patient when I lingered over his chair; that I longed only to get away from him.

Dear reader: I hear your sigh. I feel the vibration of your tapping fingers. You are quite right to be irritated. I can't expect you to understand why I knew all of this yet didn't stop. Because I carried on exactly as I had before, except now I glanced around as I left our street, to check that George wasn't following me, moving stealthily between the chestnut trees; I watched passers-by, looking for faces I knew, so that if I saw them I could make a quick getaway. I told lie after lie. I spoke in a murmur and ducked into doorways and hid around corners – not, you understand, because I truly thought any of this a good idea, but because it was all I had, and I refused to give it up.

If by this point you have lost all patience with me, my dear, wise reader, I understand. If you simply can't bear to read on – as Christopher and I meet, week after week, growing bolder, moving out of the obscurest collections to loiter with the tourists around Guy Fawkes' Lantern and Powhatan's Mantle, as we sit on benches and talk, and laugh, and I become careless and forget to take note of who is passing us by, as we bump into Christopher's friend and fellow lodger, the law student Pheugo, and I stand and suppress a giggle as I am introduced as Mrs Louis – then stop now, do. Put this history down; there are plenty of others, in which the heroes will be strong and sensible; won't rail at ignorance one moment and behave like a perfect ass the next; won't close their eyes for fear of seeing their true selves, and put themselves in danger of tripping over.

. . . Are you still here, dear reader? I don't know if you are or not. But I should like to imagine you here with me, holding my arm as we take the winding path that leads us to the heart of the labyrinth. Nothing to keep us going but the hope that the stone walls will give way to grass, then a mountainside, up which we climb, passing under the pine trees, moving higher and higher into the dazzling light.

When Christopher arrived at the Ashmolean, he was looking worried: a paper of his was going to be published.

'But that's wonderful!' I exclaimed. 'Isn't it?'

'I'm making a few arguments against some very established theories. People won't like it.'

'People don't like new thoughts.'

'No, and why not? I think sometimes they resist them without even knowing quite what they're resisting. I expect it's natural to view the unfamiliar with suspicion.'

'Does this comfort you? When you think about your paper?'

'Not especially.'

'People are stupid,' I said.

He looked surprised by my vehemence, then laughed. 'That reminds me of Suetonius, saying that the Emperor Claudius didn't try to hide his stupidity, but rather claimed he had put it on so that he could survive the reign of Caligula. Nobody believed him. It wasn't long before a book called *The Elevation of Fools* appeared, arguing that nobody would pretend to be stupid.'

'Ha,' I said, thinly, but I was still irritated, and when our stroll took us past my least favourite exhibit, the scold's bridle, with its elegant and economical metalwork, carefully hammered bit, and chain attached to the nosepiece, I exclaimed, 'What hope have we, when ignorant people make no effort to understand more, and people that are clever make an effort to be ignorant? I tell you, it horrifies me. It seems sometimes as if real thought – not knowledge, but understanding – is an endangered creature. The males are hunted and put in zoos, and the females are shot.'

Christopher didn't laugh this time. He thought about it, then said, 'I suppose real thought is as inconvenient and frightening as bears and wolves.'

'I should like to give people a fright, if I could. I'd run wild in the libraries, and bite them.'

'I should like to see it,' he answered, with a slightly off-kilter smile, so close to his usual smile that it was almost impossible to detect the difference. But then he looked away, and I thought I had imagined it: a quirk of the dim and inconstant light.

My anger dissipating almost as quickly as it had arrived, Christopher and I passed an increasingly high-spirited hour under the disapproving eye of the museum attendants. We barely noticed the exhibits, except to enlist them into our jokes, and we were scarcely aware of the people around us, except that their frowns seemed to raise us to new heights of hilarity; knowing that we had transgressed. Tears came into my eyes when two matronly women fled ahead of us, noisy as panicked chickens, after overhearing Christopher commenting, 'Of course, this statue is incomplete. Ordinarily Min is depicted holding a flail in his right hand and his erect phallus in his left.'

'What a shame,' I said. 'Poor Min.'

Through my silliness I saw clearly to the underlying mechanisms of my self. When Boll and I were little, we used to play a game in which one sister would hold the other's arms down by their sides, as the trapped sister struggled to lift them. After a minute or so, the pinned arms were released, rising irrepressibly upward and outward as if buoyed by a cushion of air, magically floating. I felt like this now, as if I were ballooning upwards; a weightless pleasure. The sun came in through the window and caught Christopher in its light; his hair glowing like molten metal, his eyes suddenly luminous.

'I say, shall we go for a walk?' I said, on impulse. 'It's so dark and close in here, and so sunny outside. I'm thoroughly sick of being trapped indoors. We might go to the deer park, or the botanical gardens. Shall we?'

He laughed, a surprised sound. 'I should love to, but – er, you know, we did run into Pheugo, and . . .'

'Was that a problem?' I asked, dismayed. 'Did I say something foolish? I thought him tremendously nice – perhaps that made me too talkative.'

'Christ, no. He often asks after you. He's quite an admirer of yours.' Christopher hesitated, his mouth halfway between words, lips open as if in suspense. 'Ah, as . . . are we all. Naturally.' He looked slightly embarrassed: an awkwardness I had not seen since the early days of our friendship. 'Anyway, you spoke so eloquently about the Mycenaeans and Minoans that he thought you a fellow student and was immensely cheered. He adores educated women.'

'Oh yes, they're quite the thing. Like trained monkeys. Some of them even recite mathematical formulae.'

'Very funny. But it's not in the least like that. He doesn't share the attitudes of his elders. Or, for that matter, his countrymen. Or – for *that* matter – our countrymen . . . I say, rather a depressing lot of countrymen, all added up.'

'End to end, or stacked?'

He smiled, but spoke seriously. 'Pheugo has an enlightened heart. His instinct is towards freedom; egalitarianism. He'd call it absurd that a woman *not* be educated. It's almost a pity to see his nature confined by such an outmoded and unwieldy institution as the law.'

'Forgive me: I didn't mean to sound cynical. I did like him awfully. Does he think me an undergraduate still?'

'I let him think so: I didn't know whether to set him right.'

'I shouldn't like to be the reason for dishonesty between good friends. I don't see why you shouldn't explain the situation. Do you?'

'No, and I shall. But – what I said earlier: I wasn't talking about Pheugo. I meant to say: what if we bump into . . . somebody *you* know?'

'Oh. Then I shall adapt my museum story: "My darling! This is delightful Mr Konig. Mr Konig, please meet my dear friend Miss Nosy. Mr Konig has been a perfect angel. I dropped my handbag and he helped me gather everything up . . . I tell you, it was too shaming. Lipstick rolling across the gravel. All my secrets spilled out into the public gardens . . . I can hardly bear to think of it."'

He looked at me curiously. 'Is that how you sound when you talk to your friends?'

I was abashed. 'Well, yes. I don't have many. And they aren't the sort of friends I talk to with any real sincerity.'

'Ah. I didn't mean to embarrass you.'

'Please. You haven't in the least.'

'Then let's go outside,' he said. 'And talk with sincerity.'

We walked along the tidy gravel paths of the botanical gardens; past evenly spaced stone planters and clipped grass, the fountain throwing a thin silvery plume up towards the startling blue sky. The wind was restrained, stirring the leaves only mildly, stroking my hair back from my face, adjusting Christopher's scarf with a gentle hand. Summer had arrived in a quiet pastel blossoming, a fragile confetti of lilac, wisteria, daisies. Glasshouses confined the more extravagant flowers; stranger, brighter, like a zoo of exotic beasts. In the general orderliness I felt myself feral and unwanted. I had felt out of place at the library, then at the museum, and now here, as I sat on a bench below an oak tree, expecting at any moment a warden to appear and order us out. And yet there was a singular pleasure even in this thought: of having no safe place. I felt fear, but I also felt more authentic, and more awake, than I had in years.

It was easier, too, to talk to Christopher out here. It wasn't long before we had moved into new and unrevealed lands, slashing at creepers and undergrowth, standing at last before the forgotten cities of his childhood. I asked after his mother, and he said she had died a long time ago.

'I've no memory of her,' he continued. 'Sometimes I tell people I remember her voice, singing "Wiegenlied", because that seems to make them feel better. They leave off looking distressed and say, "Ah," as if that's all right, because I remembered the sweet, soft quality of her voice. Really I've no idea what her voice sounded like. She might have squawked and grunted for all I know.'

'Your father?'

'My father is a quiet tyrant. One of his sneers would chasten Genghis Khan. It's no surprise my brothers turned out to be such pompous asses: they spent their childhoods puffed up to impress him. I never bothered. He left me alone . . . didn't know what to make of me, I suppose. I didn't do anything wrong, exactly. I was an opening batsman, and a decent shot. Perhaps it was simply his failure to identify what was different about me that saved me.'

'What might he have done?'

'He was a drunk. He used not to be open about it, but on rare occasions he'd lose control of his temper. His subtlety would disappear and one could see that he was furious. He was boiling with it. He threw a decanter of whisky at my brother. Laid his eye quite open; he still has the scar. I never knew what could make somebody so angry. God knows they never did anything that wasn't meant to please him. They still don't.'

There was a silence. I longed to put my hand on his arm, though he spoke dispassionately enough.

'You loved your parents, didn't you?' he asked.

'More than anything. I sometimes wonder if I used up all my love luck early on. Do you not love your father? Your brothers?'

'Of course not.' He sounded confused that I should ask. 'Why should I?'

'I always thought it something one didn't have any control over. Like believing in God.'

'Do you believe in God, then?'

'Well, no. Not now. When I was young, I simply accepted that God existed, because my parents said so. Their version of God was like them – forgiving and gentle. I knew a few parables and the Nativity and I muddled those stories up with other nursery stories. For a long time I thought the dog in the manger had something to do with the birth of Christ. My parents didn't mention hell. Heaven was where my grandparents lived. That was it. I feel rather nostalgic about those days, actually. But I can't go back to them.'

'You and I are alike, then. When I was growing up I believed in God in much the same way as I believed in table manners. Dull but inescapable. Like a lot of things from my childhood, the first time I genuinely thought about it, I decided it didn't make any sense. That was the end of God for me.'

'How rational you are! That isn't quite what happened in my case. It was nowhere near so considered. I stopped believing after I started working at Lady Rothwell's hospital. I didn't mean to lose my faith; it just went away. I only noticed later, when I realised it had been gone for some time.'

'Is your husband a religious man?' he asked, simply – as if this were not a significant turn in our conversation, a departure from the usual rules.

'I don't know. I truly couldn't tell you. I'm not sure he knows.'

'What is it – shell shock?' he asked, in the same short, neutral tones, as if the brevity of the question might make it easier to answer. 'Do tell me if I'm asking too much.'

'Oh no, it's not that. I don't see any reason not to be honest. I suppose I'm not used to discussing it. Actually, I've never discussed it. I've never said shell shock out loud, can you believe that? Shell shock. How queer . . .'

'You've never seen a doctor about it, then?'

'No. He absolutely refused. He was quite adamant. I had read before about psychoanalysis, how it might help. Hospitals have opened now that specialise in nervous disorders. They *do* call them hospitals, you know, not asylums. And it's not as if he'd have been locked up for ever. I read that the men stay for a little while and then come back home, once their nerves have begun to recover. And when I read about psychoanalysis it sounded much the nicest way of treating people. I've heard of women who do it, just because they're unhappy, or neurotic, or . . . I don't know what else.'

'It's quite the thing in some fashionable circles.'

'I expect it is. I'd do it myself, if I'd the money.'

'You don't strike me as particularly inhibited, or repressed,' Christopher said musingly. 'Thwarted, maybe.'

I didn't meet his eye, for the first time in a good while. In previous conversations I had used not to match his gaze for long, ducking it like a prim schoolgirl, as if attempting to impose some sort of order on our eye meetings. At some point in our friendship, I had stopped bothering. But now, when he said *inhibited*, I looked away, though I couldn't have said why.

When we left the gardens, I walked with him. I felt not simple happiness, but almost an altered state of consciousness, a greater sense of connection with the world. The city seemed to shelter me, its buttery stone streets gathering intimately around me, worn smooth and warm. The cobbles arranged themselves under my feet so I shouldn't trip. The breeze whispered, the sun smiled. People around glanced at us and they seemed like us: happy in their own secret happiness. A group of students smoking pipes argued good-naturedly about Catullus outside a café, their voices crowding and barging each other just as one reached out and slung an affectionate arm over his friend's shoulder. All their brogues were the same, I noticed. I wondered if they knew this. The smell of coffee drifted out of the doorway behind them, bitterly delicious. An Indian student in a turban cycled by; I was struck by his finely shaped beard and eyebrows, like dark curls of ink. In that moment I felt myself woven into the city; its railings and hedges and arches and cupolas and tidy green squares of lawn; down to Christchurch meadows and the Isis, the willows endlessly combing the river, the deer flickering in and out of the private copses, the swans stark and white as lotuses, refusing to budge for anybody. I felt the city's griefs as well as its loves: the martyrs burned before Balliol College; the sweating sickness and the St Scholastica's Day riots; the day the devil visited Brasenose Street; the woman who lifted her skirt on Armistice Day and shouted, with tears in her eyes, 'No more war! No more death! No more suffering!'

A seagull cried out above us, as if in mockery of that remembered woman, and the dream I had the night before returned to my mind, complete and perfectly formed. I had dreamt that I was watching Christopher, who was sitting on a beach with his face turned up to the sun. The sky above him was a deep, perfect blue, like glazed china. One bird crossed it, high and dark. The Sophia of my dream stared unashamedly at him; his shoulders and back unexpectedly tanned, crystalline with sand. She hesitated, keeping back at the edge of the beach, standing in a cold shaft of shade. She waited, and she didn't move, and then the dream ended. When I woke, I had the feeling that my consciousness was pouring back into my body like water into a bottle, enclosed in its rigid glass walls. It took me a few moments to relax and unclench my muscles.

My fright faded as I remembered who I was, and where I was, and that in only a few hours I should be meeting Christopher at the museum. And now here we were, Christopher walking next to me, a person felt rather than seen; for I had no need to turn my head to fill in his detail: the biscuit-coloured suit and the cornflower tie, the golden hairs on the back of his hands, the clever blue eyes.

As if I really had turned to look at him, Christopher glanced at me and observed, 'You look positively seraphic. You ought to walk more often.' His tone of warm summation confused me, and only when he drew to a stop and I was forced to pull up abruptly beside him did I realise that we had reached the corner where I was to leave him. He looked at me with amusement and I forgot to be embarrassed, saying simply, 'It's not that. It's because this has been one of the nicest days of my life.'

Christopher was just out of sight when Piers hailed me from across the street. Any hope I might have had that Piers hadn't seen me wishing him goodbye was lost with his first words: 'Darling, who was that preposterously beautiful gentleman? I say, I didn't know you kept such good-looking company. Boll would have it that you only associate with scholars and dried-up old sticks.'

I waited a moment, unhurried, before I answered. 'I refuse to believe that, as a former journalist, you should consider Boll a reliable source.'

He held up his hands, laughing. I became aware that I was standing stiffly; as if at the sight of him my body had gathered itself together of its own accord, locking silently, muscles vibrating. I tried to unbend a little, before he should notice.

'Reports of my journalistic career are much exaggerated,' he said. He looked again towards the street down which Christopher had disappeared. 'Though I must say, I still have a nose for a good story.'

I found it hard to tell whether there was any serious intent behind his repartee. I had never known Piers very well – something Boll and I had in common – but I knew enough to be wary. His history during the war, as with the rest of his life, was incomplete: blank spaces across which stories flitted, and these only partial tales, of drinking exploits with his journalist friends in Malta or Cairo, waking up to find himself in bushes, unknown hotel rooms, motor cars, tanks heading for the front line. He portrayed himself as a simple dissolute; Boll had always liked to imply that he was a spy. I thought the truth might have been somewhere between the two. His habit of getting himself in disgrace made him an unlikely candidate for covert operations, but though he might be reckless and idle and self-sabotaging, he was not stupid – no, not in the least. Even his selection of a wife so apparently unlike him was a canny move; it would have been hard to find a girl more beautiful or incurious than Boll, and both of these things suited Piers very well.

It was evident that my family had always bored Piers; he used not to pay any attention to dinner conversations, betraying this in the incongruity of his reactions – laughing politely at bad news, murmuring a sympathetic 'dear me' at a joke. But when he was listening – as he was now – he was extremely perceptive. I had always thought that if he could have sustained his focus for any length of time, he might have been a politician, or a police detective. At present, this was not a comforting thought.

'I confess I can't claim close friendship with the chap in question,' I said. 'In fact, had I not been so frightfully clumsy, he should never have spoken to me at all.'

I relayed my little set piece concerning the spilled handbag, but the delivery was off; I was made nervous by the knowledge that to give away my nervousness would be a disastrous mistake. I didn't sound so light, or assured, as I had when laughing about it with Christopher. The part about my secrets rolling all over the ground did not sound quite so humorous now.

'Sounds rather a bore,' Piers said. 'I do marvel at how many things women manage to keep on their persons. I suppose maintaining such astonishing beauty must require a good deal of specialised equipment.'

'What an unsatisfactory compliment!'

He laughed. 'I do apologise. Really I'm thinking of Boll and her dressing room. It's like an alchemist's store cupboard and is held just as sacred. I tell you, she's in there for hours. I half expect explosions and demonic conjurings . . . frankly, it's almost a disappointment when she emerges in her usual red lipstick and a new scarf.'

'But *such* astonishing beauty,' I murmured.

'Well, quite.'

In the exchange of pleasantries that followed – dutiful

enquiries about George's health, insincere promises of cocktails and dinner parties – I watched Piers closely, but couldn't detect any signs of suspicion in his princely blue eyes, hooded around with their acquired folds and bagging, wincing in the painful light of the day. By the time he left me – 'A bientôt, dear Sophia' – I felt as exhausted as if I had run up a hill. My hands were cold in their gloves, and shaking. I understood how absolutely foolish I had been, putting myself in a position in which one word from Piers, dropped without any other purpose than bored, sly curiosity – could have consequences I could hardly bear to imagine. The thought of it was an upswell of nausea, turning and squeezing my stomach like dough.

One of my old acquaintances (another casualty of George's war, our friendship slain not on the battlefield but later, over glasses of port and idle chit-chat), a thwarted bachelor by the name of Archie, used to say that his life had been governed not so much by his efforts as his mistakes. But it wasn't at all fair, he had argued, how the two were weighted. 'I say, I should like to know how years of dedicated study can be written off in a single night getting tight and motoring down Piccadilly. Or how a chap might live alone and perfectly happily for years but find one foolhardy proposal near impossible to extricate himself from. Damn it, one might be a positively puritanical husband for *months*, but ruin it all with one drunken escapade.'

I heard his sensual, dry voice again now in my mind, saying: 'Or how a devoted wife of many years might, in one careless hour, come a frightful cropper.' The words arrived with all the black gaiety of that moment stripped from them, so that they seemed hard as hailstones, striking at me with their own particular menace.

'*Do* shut up, Archie,' I entreated, and the voice fell obligingly silent, but its accuracy lingered with me as I went home – hurrying, though I had no reason to hurry, and no longer paying any attention to the summertime beauty of the streets. I knew I had made a mistake, perhaps the life-changing sort, the full weight of which I had yet to discover. And yet Archie was wrong about one thing. A moment is never simply a moment. For me it was not the moment of getting caught by Piers, or the moment I first lied to George about a perfectly innocent friendship, or even the moment I crossed the square to meet Christopher. I had always carried this mistake in me: whether I made it or not, it was *there*, a tick-ticking in my brain, a heathen chant in my heart. I had grown up with it; it was myself – more Sophia than anything else about my ridiculous life, which had been so snipped at and trimmed over the years that it was as small now as a pocket handkerchief.

It was with defiance, then, that I went into the house; a defiance that quickly dissolved into surprise when I found myself face to face with George himself in the hallway, wearing his hat and coat, carrying a cane, his hand half outstretched to the door. It was the first time I had seen him since Margaret had brought me the broken picture, and I looked at him closely, trying to guess at his state of mind. But he didn't seem angry; rather, he looked as surprised as I must have at the unexpected meeting, a surprise running into discomfort and – more than that – a distinct caginess.

'George!' I said, because one of us had to speak. 'Were you coming to look for me? I'm not late home. Actually, I'm more than an hour early.'

I held out my watch, as if in evidence, but he shook his head at it and answered formally, 'Good afternoon. As it happens, I wasn't going out to search for you. As we've already established, you aren't easy to find. This afternoon I am actually visiting a friend.'

I gazed at him with what must have been utter incomprehension. 'You're . . . Which friend?'

He paused before answering, and I realised that this was Margaret and Mrs Boxall's day off, he had not intended anyone should know that he was going out, and he wasn't good enough at lying to come up with a serviceable cover story on the spot.

At length he replied, with all the reluctance of the truth-teller, 'I'm meeting with Francesco.'

'Francesco . . .' I said. George stood stiffly, reminding me suddenly of the wedding photograph of him poker straight with nerves. Now he was rigid with hostility. Perhaps it was the memory of his face in that photograph, so sweet and uncertain, hovering like a ghost over his own face; the sudden, ghastly, incongruity between the past and the present, that prompted me to ask, now, 'George – do you want a divorce?'

He took a step back, visibly shocked. Then he stepped forward. He was so quick that I didn't understand I had been struck until afterwards, or that he had said, 'You whore,' with such great force that I couldn't distinguish its ringing in my ears – nauseous ripples, spreading and collapsing – from that of the blow itself. I had fallen back against the banisters, I realised, my hand going to my cheek, just as hands always do, as if they are sceptics who cannot take what has happened on faith, and must feel the truth for themselves.

We both stared at each other, and I thought he must have looked as horrified as I did, before his expression changed, became crowded with various other things: anger, and defiance, and slyness, and a queer, almost pleading uncertainty, a pale face peering out from the throng, looking for all the world like a crying child, hoping for some comfort.

I addressed the child. 'My God, George,' I exclaimed. 'Are you mad?'

'You have a lover,' he accused, but he sounded shaken.

'Madness,' I said again, more emphatically, but he was recovering himself, gathering his rage back up.

'You deny it? You expect me to believe in this sudden interest in walks and shopping and the library? You're cuckolding me and you expect me to smile, and see about fixing up a divorce? I tell you, Sophia, marriage is sacred, until death, and I'll be damned if I see either of us out of it before then.'

I stood up straight and tried to ignore the pain in my cheek. 'To hell with you,' I said. 'I've never had a lover. Hit me again, if you like. Or are you thinking of killing me? Do it, then. God knows, if you won't believe me, you may as well. Better that than a miserable, lingering existence, knowing myself hated by my husband.'

I stared at him and saw tears come into his eyes. I didn't release him then; I stared on, finding myself quite unable to turn my eyes away, as if my outrage at all the barren years of dutiful silence had not gone anywhere – no – only wound around itself, tight as thread on a bobbin, and now must unspool, winding and winding until it was done. My eyes ached with their dry fury; my face sang out; my ears heard the world in a strange tide, roaring in and ebbing away, as if I were swinging between the present and the past. His head bowed under my terrible gaze; he muttered, confusedly, 'Forgive me,' and left, crashing the door closed in his haste.

As soon as George was outside, I leant against the banisters once more, trying to get myself back in order. But the black-and-white tiles shivered under my eyes, like water, and my thoughts flapped around like startled pigeons, fleeing in all directions.

I was supposed to be on my way to visit Boll. This had been part of my plan for the day; a deliberate tactic. I had told George that I should go straight from the library to my sister's house, but instead I came home earlier, with the intention of pretending that I had forgotten something, thus wrong-footing any attempts to waylay me along my expected route. But it was some time before I could find the will to tidy my hair, splash some water on my face, test the tender skin with my fingers, find the places where George's own fingers had left their invisible impressions, blot the sweat from the back of my neck, and go back out into the day as if nothing at all had happened.

As it turned out, I needn't have been concerned about

arriving late at Boll's house: the hostess herself was out, and the flustered-looking maid (young, new, as Boll's maids usually were) wasn't able to tell me when she might be home.

'It's quite all right,' I said. 'I'm perfectly familiar with Mrs Gaveston's memory lapses. Would you tell Mrs White – Miss Fanshawe, er . . . the nanny to bring Daphne down? We'll wait for her mother together.'

'Yes, ma'am. I'm sure Mrs Gaveston won't be long,' the girl said, hopefully. 'She's at a luncheon party, at Lady Cherbourne's house.'

'Splendid,' I said, allowing myself a little grimace once she had left the room. I had met Lady Cherbourne on a few occasions, a cool, cutting woman with a snakelike way of darting her head forward as she spoke. The sharpness of the delivery served to disguise the dullness of the things she said. Now, Boll had a peculiar ability to absorb something of the character of whichever person she had most recently happened to admire; the effect was temporary, but it meant that when she did get back, she would be at her most Cherbournishly acidic. I didn't relish the thought.

Boll didn't get back for an hour, in which time I sat with Daphne in the garden, the late-afternoon sunlight draping its long, slender shadows over the lawn, stretching from the beech trees almost to our spot on the terrace. I took Daphne's white shoes off and her bare feet shone in the light like cowrie shells. She asked for a story, so I told her about the island palace through which the Minotaur had supposedly roamed.

'Could the Minotaur come to England?' she asked.

'No, darling. The Minotaur was made up. It might have been a monstrous-looking man. Or it might have been nothing at all. It's just a story, not history.'

'What's the difference between stories and history?'

'Well, quite.' I laughed. 'Sometimes I think it hardly matters.'

'Then I think that too.'

'You needn't agree with your aunt on everything, my dear. Sometimes she can be very unwise indeed. I tell you what you ought to do: one day you must visit the ruins, and see for yourself.'

Daphne turned this over, her small fingers playing out the movement of it, mulling through the pebbles. Then she said, peering at me, 'Aunt Sophia – you look sad.'

'I do? Good heavens. I hadn't any idea. Sometimes my face simply falls into funny shapes.' I pulled a few, and made her laugh. 'Let's build a labyrinth.'

We piled pebbles and gravel, and made a devious path for a woodlouse, which rolled up and refused to play, and then a spider, which climbed over the walls and disappeared. Daphne, little by little, became quite silly. Her eyes were more colourful, skittish; a long piece of hair had sneaked out of place like a trailing ribbon. She squatted on her heels in her blue dress, which had a new mud stain on it, and shouted with excitement. I hardly heard Boll's return; the wheels of the motor car scoring long, careless lines in the gravel outside, ending with a high shriek of female laughter, but Daphne looked more sober at once, and stood up to brush herself off; another of her queerly adult gestures.

Boll came outside in high spirits. She was wearing a

beautiful violet silk dress, somewhat crushed from the car. I caught the sweet tang of cocktails on her breath; the dying throb of perfume at her neck. She smelt hot, and tired, like a little girl after a party. I looked from her to her daughter, and wondered at them both. A small melancholy fell over me, just as the sun finally bowed out behind the trees, and coolness descended.

'Darling Daphne!' she cried. 'Oh! What has Sophia done to you? Look at your feet! And your dress – I hope it isn't ruined. What a dreadful heathen you are, Sophia. Where is Nanny? I half expect to see her in the garden, roasting on a spit. Run along inside now, darling, and tell Nanny to tidy you up.'

It wasn't long, however, before Boll forgot any idea of grievance. It disappeared in a rush of alcohol and news – to be revived, perhaps, on another occasion. She wanted to complain about Piers and his friend Bertie, who had fallen out.

'Apparently it was all over thirty pounds. Piers borrowed it from Bertie to put on a horse. He was going to pay him back with the winnings, but the horse was lamed. How the devil could that be Piers's fault? *He* didn't lame the wretched creature. But Bertie was quite unsympathetic. He was rather a Jew about it. The whole thing is just too beastly. And now things are terribly awkward with all our lovely new friends, and I suppose we shan't be going to London next weekend now.'

'You'll have to content yourself with complaining about the Oxford set again,' I said.

'It's maddening, you know, that Piers and his friends can ruin *my* friendships too,' Boll said, taking up her tea so violently that a little slopped on to her dress, unnoticed. 'I don't understand men. They're like brothers – even sleeping in the same bed sometimes – and then the next minute they never want to speak again.'

'Strange creatures indeed.'

'Another reason I don't want more children. What if I have boys? Boy triplets! It would be too awful for words.'

At this I found I hadn't anything to say. Boll put down her tea and looked at me questioningly.

'I say, don't *you* want children?' she asked. 'You seem to love them, but you've none of your own. I said that to Piers the other day. I told him I thought it rather queer. He said that it was none of my business and we ought to be talking about Daphne's brothers and sisters, and where the hell *those* were. He always turns everything around on me somehow. It's so sly. We might be talking quite happily, and then the next moment he'll be laughing at me, or being bloody.'

I didn't see any reason, then, why I should keep the truth from my sister. Of course, once I had told her, a good deal of reasons suggested themselves almost immediately.

'Darling!' Boll exclaimed, surprised. 'But . . . you don't know how *lucky* you are. I know you love playing auntie, but actually raising children is too, too boring. You've much the best luck of the two of us. I envy you.' She lit a cigarette, distractedly, her thoughts hurrying along to their inevitable terminus: herself. 'But Sophia – what does this mean? What about our parents' house? If you have no children, it ought to go back to our side. The Calverts.'

I didn't say anything, but Boll read disagreement into the silence and pressed on, becoming more vehement. 'God knows it was never fair that *you* got the house. Piers and I are the ones who are broke. I've no idea what will be left to leave to poor Daphne. She might have to become a teacher! I suppose that ought to make you happy.'

I noticed that my own teacup was quivering; its surface roiling and tossing like a stormy sea. 'It's true I don't see that as such a shabby fate,' I said. 'But I will not discuss this with you now. You're tight.'

Boll drew back in almost comically dignified affront. 'I am decidedly *not*. I'm telling you the truth and you don't like it, that's all. You complain about being barren but you don't give two straws about a real child's future. You'd see Daphne turned out on to the street!'

Now it was my turn to put down the tea. I did it carefully. Then I lost my temper. 'So I suppose I ought to turn the house over to you as custodian? You'd fritter away any legacy long before it reached her! You don't give two straws about that house.'

'Spare me the history lecture, do,' Boll said cuttingly; her best Cherbourne impression yet. I was only sorry the lady herself wasn't around to witness it. 'Caring about a heap of bricks simply because they've been in that particular heap for a long time is absurd. You only care because you've nothing else in your life. Have you made a will, then, leaving it to the National Trust?'

'I *have* made a will. And, like everyone else, you'll find out what's in it when I die. But know this – I like that heap of bricks, and I'll make damn sure it isn't sold off.'

'Oh, oh, you're so very superior!' Boll cried. 'It's easy for you. You've so much money that you have the luxury of pontificating about history, and heritage. The poor don't care about that bosh – they can't afford to!'

I laughed incredulously. 'Christ! So now you care about the poor? Because you've decided you're one of them? I do hope Lady Cherbourne never finds out. She's a frightful snob, you know. I shouldn't like to think what might happen if she realised she'd been smoking imported cigarettes with a bona fide member of the great unwashed.' At this Boll went quite startlingly white with rage. She had never liked to be mocked, but I was angry too, at her greed and her heartlessness, and perhaps because I had been struck that morning, and the bitter spirit of war was still in me, not distinguishing between victory or defeat but pressing only for a fight; a hoarse rallying cry in my ears, and I continued, 'And I suppose this will be the end of your days lounging on the beach in the South of France. You'll have Bolshevik meetings to attend, and protest marches.'

'Shut up,' Boll said, in a low, furious voice. 'I tell you – stop laughing at me.'

'I can see it now,' I carried on. 'Walking home at the end of the day in your – what was it? – cheap nylons. Irritating more refined ears with your coarse lower-class hilarity. Hanging out the washing, making tea ready for Piers when he gets back, boiling fresh water for him to scrub the oil off his hands.'

Before Boll even spoke I understood that I had gone too far. Her face was transfigured. Without a glance at the ashtray, she stubbed her half-finished cigarette down

THE HOUSE OF BIRDS

violently on the cover of *La Vie Parisienne*. Her eyes were large and wild, a livid blue. 'Damn you. You're so fucking clever. You know everything, don't you? Did you know that Daphne is George's child?'

'What?'

'Oh? You didn't! Christ in heaven: something Sophia doesn't know! Daphne has more claim to that damned house than you do. It ought to go to her. George and I spent a night together – when you were working at that wretched hospital. We drank brandy to console ourselves, and then we went to bed together.' She said this last with a flourish, almost as if she expected applause. In its absence, in the silence, she carried on. 'God knows, nobody suspected, or cared. You were away at the hospital every day, neglecting George and your own family, and all Mother could do was talk about what a saint you were! I had that every day like church service. Nobody ever paid any attention to me. I dare say nobody would have noticed if I'd been hit by a Zeppelin. You were the favourite daughter because you were clever, and sensible, and everybody thought me a little idiot. That damned story about me playing under the apple tree while Father died . . . how many times did I hear that? And you'd all laugh at me, and say that explained it all; the reason I was such a fool. Then they gave you the house because I was too much of a fool to be trusted with it. Perhaps if people had thought better of me, and trusted me, I should have been better with money.'

I hardly heard her, beyond her tone; a fury passing into a scolding hurt, finally becoming plaintive. I was no longer in the room. I was standing before George, that

317

night in 1917, when I came home to find him in such unaccountable distress. I didn't know he was drunk; I hadn't got that close. He kept me back with his outstretched hand, prevented me from comforting him. His face had been strange in the darkness; his lips held gripped and twisted, his eyes pinched closed. It seemed like I had stood for a very long time watching him cry. Perhaps it hadn't been long at all. Time expands and contracts in the memory, moments are stretched into a dark age, years are compressed into a bright, fading flash, like a firework. My afternoon with Christopher seemed like a blink of an eye, a thousand years ago.

What had happened after that night? I had given up my work at the hospital. Boll had acted strangely for a while, then married Piers that summer, and cheered up. George had kept his silence.

'Listen, Sophia, she's *his* child,' Boll said again. She was crying.

I got up, and went out of the house.

I walked until dusk. I didn't know where I was going, my course only directed by the places I could not go. I could not go back to Boll's house. I could not go to my own. I could not go to the Bodleian, or the Ashmolean. The coffee shops and cafés were closing their doors; it felt as if the city, formerly so sympathetic, was turning its face away.

I was shocked, I knew that. But the shock had given me a strange, insane lucidity, a piercing kind of madness. My vision was so clear and bright it felt supernatural, as if I were an eagle hovering far above myself, seeing with absolute accuracy: a bird's-eye view; a god's view.

In this fashion I considered the facts. It seemed unlikely that George had realised Daphne was his child. Even if he had understood and calculated the dates, the thought might have been too horrifying to gain admittance. I had spoken about her often, but he had never reacted as guiltily or awkwardly as he had when confronted with her mother. I doubted that Piers knew the truth: he was a complex man, but his adoration of Daphne was something simple. I thought it likely that Boll had been sleeping with Piers before they married, and so he would have had no reason to question the timing of the birth.

I saw that George was not sane, or good, but I saw too that there was nothing I could do about it. I should never be free of him. If I told anyone what he had done, Piers and Daphne's lives would be devastated along with Boll's. I'd never see Daphne again. I understood that so long as George believed I was innocent, he would never divorce me, but if he believed I had done something wrong, I should be lucky if divorce was his only thought. I felt sick to think of what he might do to me, or himself, or to Christopher. Even if George only tried to draw Christopher into a divorce case, it would ruin his career, which was just beginning. And over nothing – nothing at all. In all the time I had known him, he had done nothing more than look at me, and I couldn't ever identify what was in those looks.

For me it hadn't been nothing. Hovering over myself like a stone in the sky, with my cold eagle eye, I saw that too.

Picture it: a woman walking quickly along a street,

through the decaying lavender light. Flowers close up, doors shut. The birds chatter, quieting as she passes under their eaves and trees. Her hands are by her sides and her face is stricken, but rigid. Yet sympathy for such a woman, who has methodically excluded herself from every possible comfort of her community, would strike the woman herself as odd – inappropriate, even. She has no parents, no siblings, no confidantes, no committees, no elderly relatives to read the papers to. She doesn't care about society; she doesn't believe in God. She is not allowed to vote, and the government could go hang as far as she is concerned. She has no alma mater, no mentors. As of today, she doesn't believe in the sanctity of marriage.

What she understands is that though she owes allegiance to nobody, she cannot do what she likes. And she has been unforgivably selfish in trying. She has held on to someone she cannot possibly have, and endangered him by pretending that this refusal to loosen her grip was innocent. She has realised that if she breaks off the friendship now, hurting only herself, the least amount of damage might be done. She hopes it mightn't be too late for that. *Just one little heart, in exchange for his safety*, she thinks. *Please. Please.* She finds her thoughts keep running this way, taking the form of an entreaty, though she doesn't know to whom or what it is addressed.

e

I stood finally in the doorway of Christopher's house, a place I had never been, though I knew where it was, a light on somewhere far off at night, a glowing spot in the city, just beyond the reach of my bedroom window, felt rather than seen. The light was on now, in an upstairs window.

I will not write at length.

When he saw me there he gave me a look I understood perfectly – both gentle and piercing, and as suddenly close as if he had put his hand on me. I went inside, but in the hall I turned away rather than face him, though I forced myself not to look around, either, to see what his home was like. I could smell him there: a fragrant, almost sweet scent, lemon and cologne and mint and brandy. Neither of us spoke; he seemed to know that things had changed. It was a silence not of too little, but of too much: the impossible thing was naming it. He didn't try; he waited – as always – for me to explain myself. I hesitated, put my hands to my forehead – ashamed – then forced them down again, conscious of my cowardice.

I explained myself. I said that Boll's revelation had made me understand that I was the same as them – as Boll and George. He must understand. Did he? He nodded – he made no pretence otherwise. I told him what my feelings were; I berated myself for not putting a stop to them. He shook his head, and tried to interrupt me, but I talked on. I told him that my foolish infatuation had endangered him, unforgivably. I said it was unforgivable in one breath and begged his forgiveness in the next. When he gave it, I wept, and said I didn't deserve it. Time escapes me: I don't know how long I went on for. Too long, certainly, for two adults who understood the situation perfectly; both realistic, both miserably lucid. As I talked, all I allowed myself to see was a cut-out, a shadowy man standing in the hallway; his shoulders, his gestures indicating his distress. There was one moment when I let myself meet his eyes again. How perfectly blue they were, with that one floating mote, something lost and stray; not a flaw but a mark of intent, a bird in the sky, a boat on a wide sea. I saw then, before he covered them with his hand, that he loved me.

Enough.

I have tried to be a faithful historian, but I can't transcribe that conversation. I can't revisit that meeting. Suffice to say, the friendship is over, and I will never write what I feel.

℮

There isn't much to say, dear, patient reader, about the months that followed. Summer disappeared in showers and fog. It had replied to the RSVP, it had been expected to come, but it didn't, and then it was too late, and everybody afterwards talked about it resentfully. My life narrowed yet further; something I might not previously have thought possible. Boll and I did not speak, and I did not see Daphne. I knew that seeing her again might be painful in small, sly ways – a glimpse of George in her eyes, perhaps, or her profile – but I should have liked to see her, all the same. I don't really believe she is a product of history. How could I? Her way of turning her pale face up; the small movements of her fingers, stacking stones on top of stones, are hers alone. I want to see her again if only to see her Daphne-ness, and take heart from it, a new shoot in the prevailing darkness.

I have, of course, abandoned my library trips. I told George that Dr B. Something was away, on an Italian tour. Soon I shall have to think of a more permanent lie. George, in any case, seems incurious. Neither has he asked why I haven't seen my sister. I can't tell whether he has decided not to look either of these gift horses in the mouth or whether he is ashamed of his behaviour, and prefers not to question me. Though he seems subdued, I don't believe it is the latter. His paranoia, no longer attached to a simple object, now hangs dark and diffuse over us both, becoming claustrophobic whenever we have to speak to each other, which we seldom do.

I suppose I ought to feel angry with him for holding me to such a high standard; a standard he always knew he himself had not met. But I can't. Perhaps it was that all my anger really did unwind itself that day, and I lost hold of the end of the thread. Or perhaps it is simply that I can't see him as somebody subject to normal standards. He stands apart like a grave, mad angel, weighing his sword in his hands. At times when I am reading or writing he appears in the door of my room and watches me. I pretend to be absorbed in my work, so that I might not have to notice him there. After a while he leaves, as silently as he arrived. At night, after Margaret and Mrs Boxall go home, I lock my door before I go to bed, disturbed by the idea that he might watch me then, too.

My own existence is monkish; I have taken holy orders of my own devising. I spend my time now in quietness and solitude, confining myself to reading the books I can afford or borrow, writing letters, or finishing my history. As I write, I think back, taking a grim sort of pleasure in forcing myself to reread my own story, the words standing out wet blue or black on white, like soldiers shivering in the snow. I am not sure, ultimately, if this does me any good.

This is a very ordinary history – as you have no doubt noticed, dear reader – and because of this, I wonder if it will last. The people we remember from the past lived at the highest points, escaping the flood of time that swept everybody else away. If someone were to climb high enough, they might live for ever – but not, perhaps, in the form they might choose. I don't much care about any of that. All I ask is that this history survives long enough to serve its purpose.

I find that small things come back to me as I write – irrelevant, silly thoughts. For example, I forgot to explain the difference between mazes and labyrinths to Daphne, when we were building our own from rocks. I like to imagine that we are back in the garden with time to talk, that Boll's car has a flat tyre, or some other mysterious ailment. As her mother leans out of the car and laughs at the men gathered around its wheel, shading her enchanting eyes from the glare of metal, I sit in the late sun with Daphne, and stroke her hair.

'Darling Daphne,' I tell her. 'I need you to understand this. In very ancient times there used not to be any difference between mazes and labyrinths. Now, the original labyrinth of the Minotaur – that made-up creature – was undoubtedly a maze, because Theseus needed a ball of string to find his way out. But since then mazes and labyrinths are known as very different things. A labyrinth is a single path. Though it may be as complicated as a cat's cradle, when one follows it there is only one beginning and one end. But a maze is full of wrong turns and dead ends, and one might get lost in there for ever, going round and round. Do you follow?'

Here Daphne nods, because she always follows, no matter how difficult the conversation.

'One might think of historians as rather like Theseus, with his ball of string. Their job is to turn the maze into a labyrinth. When a historian writes a history, the same rules apply as when an author tells a story. They impose an order – a path. They take a maze in all its nonsensical, meaningless wanderings and turn it into a journey that can only end up in one place. It helps to know the ending, of course.'

'Are you a historian?' Daphne asks. She has put down her pebbles, and gazes at me. Her eyes are almost blue under the vivid sky; so brightly new, seeing clearly.

'Dear, clever Daphne! That's an awfully good question. You know, it's a sad fact that only men are usually allowed to be historians. Perhaps because one has to have a certain amount of power to impose a path on events; to choose a beginning and an end. If a woman should try it, they may have to be a little more covert, or cunning. And much, much less dictatorial.'

'What does that mean?'

'Well, let's say you read a history written by a woman. By your aunt Sophia, even. Firstly it might tell you what is felt, or what is experienced, rather than what is official and recorded and important. Secondly it may not tell you outright where things end up. Remember, your aunt the lady historian may not have the power to decide those things. And if there *were* a destination, the female history may have to follow its path secretly, making hardly a sound. If you want to follow, you must be quiet too, and listen hard. Listen until you hear it tiptoeing, just a little ahead of you, through the queer and winding maze, and then you shall follow it, right to the end.'

'I understand,' Daphne says.

I take her hand. 'Darling, I knew you would. Now, enough of this . . . do you hear that? I believe your mother is home.'

Autumn came on slowly. Yesterday I looked out of my bedroom window on to the road, a silent highway across which the fallen leaves, previously idle, started and scurried under the whip of the wind. The houses beyond were cloaked by their evergreens, or revealed through branches pared back to skin and bone; the pale bright green of summer all gone from the world and only the darker green surviving: needles and glossy, leathery leaves, heavy as venous blood, with their poisonous-looking berries in yellow, white, red.

It was early in the morning – a Sunday – and George was asleep. I stood for a little while at the window, weighing a book in my hands as if weighing up a decision, heavy and sombre. The book was one that I had borrowed from Christopher – or rather, from the Bodleian. When I saw him last I had given his books back, but one of my own volumes, a maroon leather doppelgänger, had got into the pile, and now here, hiding within my bookshelves, was the original.

I might have taken it to the post office the next day, but I thought this errand might require more explanation than if I were to simply slip out now, go to Christopher's house, leave the book and a note with his maid, and be home by the time George rose. If George were to wake up before I got back, I should just tell him I'd been for a walk. I knew that Christopher himself escorted his neighbour – a shaky-fingered spinster named Miss Aliquis – to church on Sunday mornings, where he managed a passable pretence at piety.

I dressed hurriedly, suddenly grateful for the clothes I had often felt so hemmed in by: the narrow gloves, the stiff twill coat with its swathed scarf, the hat cleaving so low to my head that I sometimes felt like a hermit crab peering from its shell. If I tilted my face down, as if guarding it from the autumn wind, nobody should know me if they passed. I paused in the hall before I left, and listened, but there was a deep, snowed-in silence in the house. Margaret and Mrs Boxall were at church, and George would still be off on his own melancholy pilgrimages, through the dark and smoke-lit plains of his dreams.

The streets were queerly abandoned, emptied of gowns, bowler hats, shopping bags. The shops were all shut up; the sky above shuttered too, as if God had gone out, with no sign hung up to say he would be back shortly. The strange, pewter light felt like a cunning replacement of the real thing. It lay heavy on my eyes, and I squinted to see the few people who moved in the distance, failing to make out their small shapes. All the colour had leached from the spires above, leaving them pale husks against the dark sky.

I passed the botanical gardens for the first time since the early summer. They were closed; the river quiescent in the absence of the punts with their cargo of young men. I looked over the bridge and heard only the faint clopping noise of the water striking the bricked banks, a lethargic rippling to and fro. I remembered the last time I was here, with Christopher; all the noises of the exuberant city hushed to a tiny choir in my ears; the whole city lazing in the heat, basking, bathing in the sun as if it were a great golden lake.

I shivered, and went on. There was a strange feeling of dread in my stomach; a knot drawing tighter the further I went from home, pulling on the cord that connected me to George. I looked behind me but there was nobody there. Yet I felt as if someone were following me, and every now and again I heard their footsteps, and stopped, but the sound would vanish, and I thought I must have been imagining it. I thought how ironic it would be if I were now, finally, to go insane, and this idea lingered unpleasantly with me right up until I left Christopher's house, and saw George waiting for me outside.

Last night as I lay in bed, I thought about the last book I had read, and one story in particular, that of the Japanese warrior poet Ōta Dōkan. He was a samurai and a Buddhist priest, and the architect of Edo Castle. Unfortunately for Ōta Dōkan, his fame as a tactician did not guarantee him those twilight years of contemplation in which he might have composed his greatest poetic works. By 1486, he had been falsely accused of disloyalty to the Uesugi family, whom he served, and he was murdered in the home of Uesugi Sadamasa, while bathing.

It was his final words – some of the only surviving fragments of his famous artistry – that I remembered now: a poem composed before his death, according to the ancient Japanese tradition. It turned over and over in my mind, until it seemed to do so quite without my own participation.

> Had I not known
> that I was dead already
> I would have mourned
> my loss of life.

Such grace seemed utterly beyond my own reach. Perhaps I might have had a fraction of a sense of it – a tiny glimpse of enlightenment – had I thought I might be able to leave something so perfect behind me. But I hadn't the time. It had got away from me somehow. My fingers were loosening – soon, I knew, I should have to let go.

When I crossed the boundary between consciousness and sleep, I found Ōta Dōkan had accompanied me. He moved with a deliberate grace, an almost sad elegance. I tried to look at him, but each time I turned my head he became vague, and eventually I gave up and simply walked, and he walked silently by my side. In this way we came to understand one another. He moved ahead, and I followed. When I looked back, I saw that we had crossed an arched wooden bridge over a moat. We came to Bairin-zaka, the slope of plum trees; a delicate haze of pink and white blossom. A beautiful silence descended. We stood under the branches and I looked up at the sky, which was a brilliant, familiar blue, in which one dark moon circled. I could hear the sea behind me.

'I know where I am,' I said.

'Not yet,' Ōta Dōkan replied. His eyes were a constant black, soft and ineffable.

'Will it hurt?' I asked.

He didn't answer, and I thought he hadn't understood me. Abruptly he turned, and began to walk away. I followed him again, and we came to a shrine. He stood aside, indicating that I should go inside.

'Will it hurt?' I asked again.

The doorway to the shrine trembled. I looked at it harder. It resembled nothing so much as my own bedroom door, and the noise that came from it was the familiar metal groan of the handle as it turned. It stopped, arrested by the lock. I was sitting up by the time I realised that I was not in Japan, and Ōta Dōkan was not beside me. I could not be sure if the handle had really been tried – or if the feet behind the door, two shadows in the faint light of the hall, were planted in my dream or in reality, for by the time I was fully awake, they were gone.

Look up: *Cretan Law under Mamalakis*,
by O. N. Koroneou.

PART FIVE

OLIVER

Oliver held the last page as if he were still reading, so that he could stare over the top of it at Lena. His eyes were aching from their own labyrinthine movement; following the writing curling around and across, towards an ending that was still unknown. Lena slid and blurred in his vision. He pressed his fingers to his eyes; took them away again. Through lightning spots and flashes she came back into focus; reading with a slight frown, her elbows leaning on the table and head down, as if physically attuning herself to the words. She had finished most of her part of the history, the pages she had read stacked in a neat pile next to her untouched drink. She was a much faster reader than Oliver. Perhaps the result of a breakfast room (a term Lena would probably scorn) lined with books, instead of a large television and a black-and-white picture of the city skyline, as if the city skyline weren't already visible from their window. He had never liked that picture.

Sophia's – Leonora's – last words had disturbed him intensely. He did not quite understand them, but this increased rather than diluted their peculiar, close menace. He sensed rather than knew her meaning: that her dream was a death vision, ending in the outlines of George's shoes beyond the bedroom door. It upset him to think of her sitting up in bed in a twilight state, a momentary mingling of dream and reality, as one slid away and the other rose in its place. That intense brightness – the white heights of the sea, the sun collecting in the branches of the plum trees, lighting up the blossom – fading away, leaving her faced with the hostile dark. The figure of Ōta Dōkan melting away, replaced by a silhouette, the meaning of which she grasped completely. She hadn't written it down, but Oliver understood what she felt then – he felt it move in his own heart – the arrival of fright, sluggish and cold. She would have been alone at the end, too, and completely aware. She had made sure of it; had spared herself no pain. The thought was unbearable.

Trying not to disturb Lena, he quietly picked up his glass and knocked back the contents. Throat stinging, smothering a small cough, he remembered he had always hated whisky. Lena, absorbed, didn't notice this minor slapstick occurring across the table. He slid the rest of the history over to her; she acknowledged it only with a nod, not looking up. He was grateful for this. He felt uncomfortable having more information about her ancestry than Lena herself; the unwanted knowledge that in a short time her idea of herself and her family was about to take a significant hit.

For a little while, then, he would be alone with his own sadness. He realised that this might be the only time that it did feel like his own: that soon Lena, her family – even Kate – would have more claim on it than he did, that in a short time he would have to hand it over to them, his only remaining function that of offering comfort, or just keeping out of the way. It was an odd kind of sadness, this; the sadness for a tragedy that was over and half forgotten. A new light had been shed on an old pain, a fresh grief for the long-dead. It was a sadness that arrived as if already exhausted, in embers; a tired, resigned desolation.

He got up, stood for a moment and looked out of the window. The cat glanced up at him, then closed its eyes again. He felt as if he had come out of the cinema in the late afternoon, expecting the evening to have dropped down, hushed and dreamlike, but being confronted instead with the noisy, sober day. Outside the trees were dripping greenly and the roofs of the birds' aviaries were reflective with rain. A volunteer in wellingtons passed by, swinging a leather bag of dead baby birds and whistling a pop song.

Oliver, for once, felt the need to reoccupy the usual world. He wanted to move around, feel surfaces against his skin, hear his own voice.

'Coffee?' he said to Lena, positioning himself so she couldn't meet his eye, though as he had suspected, she didn't even look up.

'Thanks.'

He put the kettle on and tried to clear his mind of everything but its jaunty racket; washed and dried two mugs, hunted out the jar of coffee. He didn't think it was fair, somehow, to be pondering over the most recent chapter before Lena had had the chance to look at it, but he couldn't help but wonder what purpose Leonora had meant her history to serve. All the time he was making the drinks the question beat at him: *Where is the next book? Where is it?*

He gave Lena her coffee and inspected the bookshelf. *Cretan Law Under Mamalakis* wasn't there. Impatient, he took the older books out one by one and went through them all, finding nothing. Then he sat down and thought about Sophia, until Lena looked up and said, 'What the *fuck*?'

She was staring at him, but it was apparent that she was not really expecting an answer. Her gaze moved on, to the bookshelves, the window, the cat, without taking any of it in. Hardly looking at the glass, she downed her whisky.

'I'm sorry,' Oliver said, awkwardly.

'I'm related to a fucking *murderer*? I'm more related to him than to Leonora! And – oh God – I've got to tell my mum.'

She cast about, picked up the whisky glass again, seemed to realise that it was empty, put it back down, then, unexpectedly, burst into tears.

Oliver stood for a moment, not knowing what to do. He was very acutely aware that he was a stranger here; that Lena had just received the sort of shock that should only be witnessed by a parent or a husband. He wondered where Jim Lennox was, without really wanting Jim Lennox to come home. He went over and put his hand out before knowing exactly where it ought to end up. It landed on her shoulder, so lightly and tentatively that the contact could only have been felt as an irritation.

Lena didn't seem to notice what he did. She cried softly, with her face in her hands – becoming all hair, dark curls twitching like a strange, disturbed creature – and he didn't know if it was an attempt to protect her privacy, or something self-conscious, or just an old habit. He realised with relief that he could make himself useful by getting her a tissue, and he went off as narrow and solemn in his task as a medieval knight. There turned out to be no lavatory downstairs, and when he looked in the sitting room (messy, rug-strewn, cinnamon-scented) and the dining room (pristinely tidy, evidently never used), he couldn't find any boxes of tissues. Finally, his certainty wavering, he went upstairs. The feeling that he was entering forbidden territory intensified as he ascended, peaking as he passed one and then two bedroom doors both open on to the sight of a recently slept-in bed. He found the bathroom at the end of the corridor, took a handful of loo roll, and scarpered.

When he went back into the kitchen, Lena was already wiping her eyes with a tissue.

'It was in my pocket,' she explained. 'But thanks . . . It just seems ironic, you know. All the time I spend going on about history and heritage. It's like a fucking bad joke.'

'What you said earlier – you *are* like Leonora,' Oliver said, staunchly. 'More than Boll or George.'

'Ha – thank you,' she said, with a short laugh. 'No, I do mean that. It does make me feel better. Really. Right – more whisky.'

She said it as if it were a command, and Oliver found himself drinking with her, not wanting to disobey, until she stopped and said, just as suddenly, 'Okay, that's enough. We can't sit around getting drunk. We have to find that Ancient Crete book, for a start. And we have to go and see my mother.'

Oliver was surprised, delighted and frightened to hear that he was included in all of this, then dismayed at how little help he was likely to be. 'I don't have the book,' he said. 'I can't remember the titles, but I've opened all the books in the house. And it isn't on your shelf, either. I just looked. Did you save any others?'

'Shit. No. That's all of them. Where *is* it?'

They stared at each other, then Lena said slowly, 'Either someone has taken it. Or it got lost. Or she didn't get to finish it.'

Oliver thought again of Leonora sitting up, peering into the shadows compressed all around her. It was an image he couldn't get rid of. He heard her thoughts, even, the lines repeating slowly, like someone following the last orders of an anaesthetist, counting to ten. *Had I not known that I was dead already.* He wondered if she had managed to believe it, by the end.

'Look, we need to go and tell my mother about all this. Can you wait here while I get changed? Maybe, I don't know, google the book or something. I wonder if there are any local book dealers . . .'

Oliver imagined himself explaining the situation to the sarcastic bookseller. Then he imagined Lena talking to the man. He almost smiled.

'No, that wouldn't work,' she continued, on her way out. 'They'd have found it already, or thrown it out. Maybe Mum will know what might have happened to it.' Her voice came back, climbing the stairs into near-inaudibility. Then she shouted from the landing, 'Hey, Oliver! Now's the time to get that taxi of yours back here.'

Oliver had only just finished talking to the taxi company when she called him again. He went to the foot of the stairs and hesitated there for a moment, not sure whether she had meant him to go up.

'. . . Yes?'

'Oliver, I just thought! This proves that there was a will, and that Tom *must* have got rid of it. His visits to the solicitor, remember? Up until now, it's only been Annabel's word that there was one. But Sophia said it herself!' Her voice was slightly out of breath, and he tried not to think of her undressing just above him. After a little pause, she went on, 'I just can't work out why she wrote it. And hid it. She said she had a purpose. So who was meant to find it and read it? Who is the dear reader?'

Oliver realised with embarrassment that up until now he had believed it was him.

'I don't know. Maybe she wanted whoever it was to know the truth.'

There was a short silence, then Lena said, 'If she died.'

'Yes.'

'So why did she disguise the names?'

'I don't know. I thought maybe it was in case Tom found it before it was finished. But if he'd read it properly, he would have known who the people were. Then I thought she was just joking; playing with the reader.'

'But you know what – it does protect Christopher. Did you notice? She's pretty fucking cagey about him. If that's not *his* real name, you'd have no chance of googling him.'

'I know. I tried.'

He heard her laugh, dimly, as if through fabric. 'What were the search terms? Man. History. Two brothers. Nasty dad.'

'Pretty much. It wasn't a huge success.'

'Clearly not everybody would be able to get her into the library. But she doesn't say how he did it, or who helped him.'

'She knew she might put him at risk. She said as much.'

Lena appeared now at the top of the stairs. She was wearing a red wool dress and dark tights, in which her legs were narrow and graceful. He turned away from them politely as they descended towards him. As she passed, he caught a sly curl of her perfume, newly applied, rich and amberish. Her proximity was, as always, an unpredictable thing. When he thought she might be angry, she could be surprisingly calm; when he thought she was pensive and quiet, and that it might be a good moment to take in her profile, surreptitiously breathe in her scent, she might turn around suddenly and demand – as she did now – 'God, where the fuck is the rest of it?'

'I wish I knew.'

'We're just speculating without it, aren't we? It's pointless.'

A memory came back to him. 'Lena – do you remember earlier, when you told me those books were Leonora's? How did you know?'

Her eyes sharpened. She stepped towards him, coming in quite close. 'Yes! That's it. When I told my mum I'd taken the books, she said, good, because they were Leonora's, and they were supposed to be ours. I don't know how she knew that.'

They looked at each other. She grinned. Her eyes were black and glittering. They were almost nose to nose. Then she spun away, hurrying down the hall with an impatient cry: 'Christ! Where is that fucking taxi!'

'We need to get to the Ashmolean, please,' Lena said to the taxi driver.

Oliver was confused. 'Why are we going there?'

She looked puzzled too, then smiled. 'You don't know . . . No, of course you don't. That's where my mum works. Weird, right? She does tours and tells kids not to be rowdy.'

'Okay,' Oliver said. 'But – "Get us to the Ashmolean"?'

They both started to laugh.

'I've got to get to a library . . . fast!'

'Shut up.'

When they arrived, Oliver, hurrying to keep up with Lena, tried to take in as much of the building as he could without tripping over. He hadn't actually seen it before; it looked like a cathedral to him, many-pillared, beige, immensely dignified. The still air that hung in the paved forecourt was cold and unyielding against his face, like a sheet of ice. He was reminded of Sophia's final visit to Christopher's house. Odd to think that it was the same time of year now; that she must have moved through the same streets under the same strange failure of illumination; the approaching dim of winter, all the clouds stony overhead.

Lena left him in the atrium while she went in search of her mother. It was brighter inside than outside; the daylight falling through the glassy heights of the remodelled space, trapped and endlessly reflecting against the tall white walls. He felt like a spider in the bottom of a jar.

'She's just finishing up,' Lena reported when she came back. 'Look . . .'

'You need to talk to her first,' Oliver said quickly. 'I can wait for you. I've actually got to make a call myself, so . . .'

Lena smiled at him, evidently relieved. 'Perfect. Meet you back here? Under the statue with the tiny cock.'

'Great!' he said, trying not to sound insincere but misjudging it slightly, so that he came across as rather too enthusiastic, and Lena gave him an odd look as she left.

Not wanting his conversation to echo up through every floor of the museum, Oliver went outside to call Kate, though he had no idea what to tell her. As the phone rang, he tried to think of a good way of putting things. The purring ringtone may as well have been a klaxon. Panic emptied him out. By the time Kate picked up, he was none the wiser and more than a little flustered.

'Oliver?' she said, with the slightly strained politeness of having been interrupted at work. 'I can't talk for long. If this is about the last time we spoke, can it wait?'

Oliver, still preoccupied with the need to explain himself, didn't understand her at first, then remembered that the two of them were technically on hiatus before returning to their earlier argument.

'I'm really sorry, but Kate, quite a lot's happened.'

'What? With the house?'

'Yes, sort of. Look, I found the final part of Leonora's diary. I know you're not going to like this. But it turns out she did have a will. Annabel was right. And it sounds like George probably did . . . uh, I think he killed her. I'm so sorry to have to tell you over the phone. She doesn't say it, obviously, but the diary is unfinished, and by the end she's clearly frightened of him. He found out . . . well, he was wrong, but he thought he found out that she had a lover. Well, she did like this guy but nothing was happening. But George is – was – clearly a very disturbed man. He thought he'd caught her out being unfaithful – even though he was unfaithful, and Annabel's daughter Daphne was his child, though he didn't know that – and anyway, what I mean to say is that he was very angry. Murderous angry. That's how it ends.'

There was a short pause, and then the sound of a door closing behind her. A thick silence preceded her next words. 'What did you say – there's a *will?*'

'Not a physical will, no. She said she had made one, but it's obviously gone missing. And she says she doesn't like their solicitor – George's friend, so I guess he helped destroy it.'

'Did she say what was in the will?'

'No.'

'Okay. So . . . Daphne was his kid, but she wasn't in his will. And there's no body. You didn't find *that* in a book?' There was a pause, filled with the activity of Kate's thoughts. When she resumed, her tone was conclusive. 'Right. I think this is okay. I don't think there's anything to worry about.'

'I don't understand,' he said.

'What don't you understand?'

'It's a murder, Kate! That's something to worry about.'

'Hold on, you don't know she was murdered. She probably ran off with that guy she was hanging out with.'

'She gave him up.'

'Well, more fool her.'

'So . . . what? You think this is okay? I don't understand.'

Now she was angry. 'Oliver, *I* don't understand *you*. What is it you want? Do you want the Calverts to get the house?'

'No. I just want justice to be done. For Leonora's sake.'

'Leonora! You never met her! And you think Leonora wants the Calverts to get the house?'

'I don't know!' he said, exasperated, knowing at the same time that this was true. 'But you don't need the house. You didn't know anything about it until a few months ago.'

'Jesus! Have you gone totally mad? Who *needs* that house? We've all got houses. You think the Calverts will turn it into a shrine for bloody Leonora? No – they'll sell it. It's the only way to pay the inheritance tax, for a start. You're the only one being sentimental about justice for someone who died before any of us were born.' She paused for breath – a half-second in which Oliver decided not to explain that he was with Lena and her mother, both of whom seemed likely to be sentimental – and continued. 'And there's no evidence that George did anything. It's hearsay. Put about by the Calverts, who just can't accept that they didn't get the bloody house. Anyone could have killed her.'

'So you *do* think she was killed?'

At this Kate became evasive. 'What? No. I think she probably just left him.'

'And she got rid of her own will, and left the diary behind out of spite to frame him? Really?'

'There's no need to be sarcastic. Something like that actually happened in a thing I saw recently.'

'Oh yeah, that new documentary. With those people who looked like famous actors. Oh no – wait – that was a *film*.'

'Oliver, I . . .' Kate said, before she broke off, then said, sounding suddenly upset, 'You've never spoken to me like this.'

The pained note in her voice sobered him. He made an effort to sound calm. 'I just don't see how you can deny it. It's frustrating.'

'But nobody *knows*! Maybe Tom did something. It's not exactly a secret that he was a weirdo. My dad said it. But maybe he didn't. And it's all over now. They're all dead! What does it matter, really, how Leonora died? Look, the diary doesn't prove anything. It's just going to be a legal nightmare – for your beloved Calverts as well as for me. The best thing to do would be to just . . . get rid of it.'

Shock made Oliver ask, 'The diary?' though he knew very well that was what she meant.

There was a short silence.

'Look,' Kate said, and now she sounded slightly abashed, 'I don't know. This is a massive mess, Oliver. I'm not greedy, for God's sake. You sound horrified. If she *actually* left a will, I wouldn't contest it. I don't want a legal fight and solicitors' fees and all that shit. I don't care about this stupid bloody family history. I don't know anything about it and I wish I never had to. But I don't see that the Calverts deserve the house more than me. They're chancers, and they've got no proof. The diary isn't enough proof. You know that! All it's going to do is bankrupt all of us fighting over it. It's better if it just . . . gets lost.'

'You're not thinking properly,' Oliver said.

'*I'm* not thinking properly? Look, Oliver, I have to go. I've got four people waiting for me outside a glass door and they can see my side of the conversation and they must be wondering what the hell is going on.' She sounded as if she too was trying to speak calmly. They had always agreed they didn't believe in arguing. Now it was happening more and more often, and he got the feeling that they were both frightened by it: two unskilled combatants who had lost control of their weapons.

'We should talk . . .'

'No, Oliver! I can't talk about this now. I'll call later and maybe you can explain what the hell is happening, because I have no idea. I mean . . . whose side are you on, exactly?' Her voice was gathering momentum. 'You said, what, I don't *need* the house? It's worth over a million pounds, but you think I don't need it, so you're going to award it to the Calverts? That's pretty bloody high-handed of you. Tell me again about the part in the diary where Leonora said, "Oliver, I want the house to go to the Calverts, so can you please sort that out for me?" She didn't say anything, did she? And please, remind me again what any of this has to do with you. You got a few plumbers in and read a diary and now you're in charge of *justice*?'

'Kate, don't go. We need to talk about this.'

'No – we don't. You need to get rid of that diary. You need to not screw me over. That's it.'

She hung up. He tried calling back, but her phone was off, and after the third or fourth time of being shunted straight to a pre-recorded Kate – a carefully enunciated apology, in the voice she used for strangers – he began to have the odd sense of his own future shadowing the present, until, disturbed, he gave up his attempts.

'Oliver? You all right?'

Oliver looked up, startled. He had been standing, preoccupied, before the Perspex case holding the Alfred Jewel; a bright column of light in the surrounding darkness, a small point of enamelled colour. Now Lena was by his side, saying, 'Only you look like someone died.' She waited, expectant. 'That's a joke. Cause . . . Oh, never mind.'

'Sorry. I get it. Very funny.'

She examined him now, head cocked. '*Are* you all right?'

He nodded.

'Okay,' she said, unconvinced, then continued, in a tone of determined (and uncharacteristic) cheerfulness, like a teacher unsure what to do with a strangely silent pupil, 'Well, anyway, this isn't where we were supposed to meet. I've been looking for you everywhere. Though, look, here's another statue with a tiny cock. Did you get muddled? There *are* a lot of them about.'

This might not have been convincing as a burst of jollity, but it did have the result of catching Oliver's thoughts, turning him away from the end of his conversation with

Kate, setting him down roughly back in the Ashmolean, where he found himself once again at a loss, no stranger to smut but somehow embarrassed now, hearing Lena say *cock* with such gusto.

'Sorry,' he said. 'I lost track of time. I, er, just hadn't seen this before.'

'The Alfred Jewel? It's cool, isn't it?'

They read the description together, side by side. Again he was reminded, unsettlingly, of Sophia and Christopher.

'I wonder if Leonora saw this. I think she would have liked it,' he said.

'In what way?'

'Well, according to this, nobody really knows what the jewel was for. People think it might have been an aestel. The word hasn't been translated, but it probably means a pointer for reading. I was thinking she would have appreciated that. You know – that the jewel itself is mysterious, the word for it is unknown, the actual pointing bit is missing, and even the words it would have pointed at are missing.'

'*Your* point being . . .?'

'Well, it was supposed to help people understand, but now it just confuses them instead. Its meaning has sort of been lost in history. I thought Leonora would have approved.'

Lena didn't say anything to this. She looked at him with an unfamiliar expression, made up of various elements, none of which he understood, and yet he couldn't see scorn among their number.

'Come on,' she said finally. 'My mum's waiting.'

e⌐

From a distance, as they crossed the atrium, Lena's mother seemed a simple proposition: a small, rounded woman enveloped in draped fabric – miscellaneous flutterings and tassels (scarf or cardigan or shawl, he had no idea) – a recognisable type with pinned-up, disorderly striped hair; the sort of mother who tucks a pen into her bun and forgets about it. Up close she was more disconcerting. He immediately made out the resemblance to Lena, and to Boll. She had the latter's pale skin, the same little mouth and dark-lined eyes. He guessed she too had always been a beauty. Her expression, as they were introduced, hovered somewhere between unconsciously winsome and sharply curious.

Oliver was grateful to realise that Lena must have already explained his presence: Charlotte Godwin held out her hand without questioning what the hell Oliver had to do with anything. 'How lovely to meet you,' she said, smiling, becoming even more like her grandmother, and far more deliberately feminine than her daughter, standing next to her with her arms folded and a gathering frown.

'It's lovely to meet you too, Mrs Godwin,' he said politely.

'Call me Charlotte. Please. So you're Kate Castle's . . . boyfriend? Fiancé?'

'I just told you that,' Lena said impatiently. 'So there's no need to pry.' She turned to Oliver. 'Mum, as I've just found out, doesn't seem to give two shits who her grandfather was.'

'*Language*,' Charlotte said, rolling her eyes in Oliver's direction, as if they had both long despaired of Lena. 'I just don't see what there is to make a fuss over. *I'm* not suddenly going to turn into a murderer. And I already knew that Grannabel was a dreadful old so-and-so.'

THE HOUSE OF BIRDS

'Granny Annabel,' Oliver said, amused. He couldn't imagine Boll, siren of the Isis, liking that name much.

'You know,' Charlotte continued, 'I'm more enchanted by the idea that Leonora used to come here for secret meetings with the object of her desire. I had no idea!'

'She said they used to meet in the quietest rooms, where nobody went,' Oliver explained earnestly. 'At least at first.'

'Well I never. We *do* still get schoolchildren going astray. Teenagers. You know what they're like. Heavy petting behind the mummy cases. Et cetera.'

'Eurgh,' Lena said.

'I suppose it could be called a grand tradition.'

'You ought to do an alternative tour,' Oliver suggested. 'A history of romance at the Ashmolean.'

'Only if you would be my assistant,' Charlotte said. 'A handsome young man like you ought to revive visitor numbers.'

Oliver, abruptly out of his depth, didn't have anything to say to this. Lena, holding her hands up like a policeman in the middle of a fracas, saved him the trouble of coming up with a response.

'No,' she said. 'No, no, no. You two are not fucking flirting. That's an end to it.'

'Strictly business, is it?' Charlotte said, in stagy disappointment. There was a professionalism to her coquetry that he admired, guessing it to be a routine that had been perfected over the years, taking on a high shine, a flawless polish. Then, in the next instant, it was gone. 'Well then. Leonora's diary. What was this you were saying about the names being changed? I knew about Boll, of course. That became a family nickname. But who were the others?'

'She and Tom became Sophia and George Louis. Then her friend was Christopher Konig.'

'Philip Christopher Konig, actually,' Oliver added.

Charlotte laughed, disbelieving. 'Honestly! These names mean nothing to you?' They shook their heads. 'Don't they teach your generation anything these days? We had to learn the kings and queens of England off by heart. George Louis? Sophia and Philip Christopher? No? Dear me. She's making a joke. Well, George Louis was George I of England. The first of the Hanoverians.'

'She *did* title her first chapter "A Revised History of the House of Hanover",' Oliver put in eagerly, hoping to make up some lost ground. In his peripheral vision he saw Lena give him a look he didn't need to meet to identify: the eternal contempt of the school rebel for the teacher's pet.

'There you go. So, George was married to this beautiful young girl, Sophia Dorothea of Celle, before he took the English throne. They weren't happily married. It was a very sad story, actually. He treated her cruelly and had a mistress. But he was outraged when he discovered that *she* was in love with Philip Christoph von Konigsmarck, a Swedish count. Nobody knows, really, if anything actually happened there – there were love letters, but they may have been forged. Philip Christoph disappeared, presumed murdered, and George had Sophia imprisoned for the rest of her life. She never saw her children again.'

'Oh,' Oliver said.

'I think Leonora's point was clear, don't you?' Lena remarked.

'The poor woman,' Charlotte said. 'Were there any other names?'

'Piers Gaveston? Annabel's husband.'

'Oh, Eddie! I'm not sure about that one . . . No, wait.' She laughed. 'I remember. Piers Gaveston was one of Edward II's "favourites". Quite a lot of historians think they were probably lovers.'

'Well, nobody could accuse Leonora of not having a sense of humour.'

'Funny, really, because Boll saw herself as such a woman of the world. But she clearly had no idea about that.'

'Eddie and Grannabel certainly led almost separate lives in their later years,' Charlotte told Oliver. 'He spent his retirement in Italy.'

'At least he got to retire,' Lena said. 'What's sad is that Leonora said she'd be Anne of Cleves if she could. But she knew she wasn't. She wasn't allowed to retire to safety.'

'Like Comanche,' Oliver said. They looked at him, not understanding. 'The horse on the fireplace. At Leonora's house.'

'Well, you'd know more about that than we do, dear,' Charlotte said mildly.

Embarrassed, Oliver was silenced. Lena, not noticing, tugged at her mother's arm; an unexpectedly childlike gesture of impatience. 'So, can we go back to yours and look through the letters?'

'Yes, yes. I told them I was leaving early. It's all rather exciting, isn't it? The prospect of things finally being brought to light. Wrongdoers identified . . . justice being done.' She headed away across the atrium before turning back to cry, 'The truth, at last, prevailing!' and exiting, triumphantly, through a door marked Staff Only. The echo hummed in the air. A small group of schoolchildren turned to watch her go.

There was something contagious in Charlotte's enthusiasm – Oliver felt it; Lena felt it, or at least he thought she did, detecting a small, secret pleasure in her shrug – but these last words reminded him uncomfortably of Leonora's own discourses on the truth, and he wondered if it would really be as simple as that, given that they were all relying on whatever information Leonora – the sworn enemy of historical accuracy, of cold, hard *fact* – chose to give them.

℮

Charlotte reappeared a short while later, having added a flowing wool coat to her already impressive collection of drapery, and Oliver found himself folded economically into the back of her hatchback as the two women talked in the front. Though they were heading at speed towards Charlotte's house – in which there was a box containing Boll's old letters and keepsakes – real life continued, and Lena wanted to know if her dad, Benedict Godwin, was enjoying his visit to family in the West Indies.

'I didn't speak to him last night, my darling. He rang me to tell me I was the love of his life. He'd been out with his cousins. He hasn't seen them for years. Of course they got straight into the rum. I couldn't get any sense out of him so I told him to call me today. I think he's having a splendid time.'

'He texted me randomly to ask if I'd send him some aspirin. Then when I asked if he was okay, he didn't reply. I was worried he was getting a bit senile.'

Charlotte made a noise of outrage. 'We're not *that* old, you rotten girl. He was just drunk. So stop worrying about us.'

Oliver said nothing, not only because he had nothing to contribute on the subject of Mr Godwin, but because his mind was fifteen minutes behind, having stopped at Charlotte's earlier explanation of why she was late meeting them in the car park.

'I forgot to take my name tag off, and got waylaid. Tourists looking for the dodo. Honestly, about half the enquiries we get are about that wretched bird. I always say we should put up a poster at the entrance: "For all dodo enquiries, go to the Museum of Natural History." I'm not even sure it's a real one. Humans, eh! First they wiped them out, then they couldn't even preserve a stuffed one.'

He remembered his first visit to Lena at her house when he had compared himself without much thought to a dodo. At the time it seemed appropriate: bumbling along, failing to plan, oblivious to his own impending downfall. He had said it later to Kate, in one of their lighter conversations, and – though the joke took them on to shaky ground – she had laughed.

He didn't think Kate would find the comparison funny any more. Ironically enough, it was Oliver, the dodo, who had turned out to be the nasty surprise. It was innocent and unsuspecting Kate who was facing the fact that her high-flyer was in fact a ground dwelling creature; that he was unlikely to be able to join her in New York; that in quiet moments he longed, secretly, to touch her cousin's hair, to brush it back when it got (as it frequently did) into her eyes; that he had betrayed her by handing Leonora's diary over to the hated Calverts; that he was sitting even now in between two of them as they argued about whether or not Lena's younger brother had a look of George about him.

'What a fucking terrible thing to say!' Lena said.

'Oh, love. It doesn't mean a thing. If ancestry worked that way, the Queen would be a homicidal maniac. But she's just a dear, dull old lady, isn't she, Oliver?'

Here Charlotte gave Oliver a frankly seductive wink via the rear-view mirror.

'I wish *you* were a dear, dull old lady,' Lena said.

'You seem edgy. Worrying about that temper of yours?' Charlotte said slyly. 'Listen to this, Oliver: when Lena was seven, I got a call from her teachers asking me to come and pick her up from school. She'd been fighting over—'

'God, Mum!' Lena said, sounding much younger. 'Oliver doesn't want to hear this.'

'I most certainly do,' corrected Oliver.

'"She's only seven," I said to the teachers. "She's not a wild beast, for goodness' sake. You've got it wrong." But they showed me the boy's arm and I knew it was her, because she had one wonky tooth. One little indent out of place, in those two perfect crescents. If it had been today, of course, the mother would probably have sued.'

'For fuck's sake,' Lena said, through her teeth, as if reluctant to display them.

'Murderer's blood,' Charlotte said cheerfully. 'That explains it all.'

℮

In the Godwins' sitting room, a draughty, loosely art nouveau space, its mismatched marquetry and stacked newspapers reminding Oliver slightly of his own temporary home, Charlotte brought out an inlaid Indian box with a theatrical flourish.

'What the hell is that?' Lena asked. 'You said that when you had the solicitors over you went through your files. This isn't a file. You said you were *organised*.'

'They didn't mind in the slightest,' Charlotte said. 'We had a few glasses of wine; it was all rather jolly. *Would* anybody like some wine? You two aren't driving, are you? Red or white?'

'And you wonder why your claim never got anywhere,' Lena said, unheard. She was going through the box. 'Hey, look at this.'

She held up a flat silver box. 'A. M. . . . Annabel Montgomery.'

'So she did get her monogrammed cigarette case.'

'And here's a letter from Eddie. Hotel writing paper . . . Cannes. Ha. Listen to this: "Darling, darling Annetta. Patience! I think of you always. What's a few more weeks to a love as eternal as ours? Eddie. PS Hughie knows someone who's selling a leopard cub. Would you like a leopard, darling? Say the word and it's yours."' She laughed, then divided up the papers and handed some to Oliver – 'Annabel's letters from her solicitor. You may as well look through these' – in a gesture of trust he found touching.

'That's all pretty depressing reading,' Charlotte warned, returning with a bottle and three glasses. '*So* misogynistic. Domestic violence was given short shrift back then. Murdering one's wife was basically manslaughter.'

But it wasn't all depressing, and the three of them became pretty merry as they went through the letters and the wine, reading out the occasional line.

'Here's Grannabel accusing Daphne of being pig-headed about choosing her own wedding dress. Annabel thinks it's ghastly: "Queen Victoria would have thought it frumpy."'

'Postcard from Eddie – "Getting a tattoo."'

'Um,' Oliver said, eventually. 'This might be relevant. It's a letter from Miles Wilcox, their solicitor. Also known as Francesco Salviati, the treacherous Archbishop of Pisa. He denies all knowledge of a will and even claims he hadn't seen Tom in the months leading up to the disappearance.'

'A total lie!'

'Surely that strengthens the case?' Lena asked.

Charlotte inspected the letter. 'I should think so.'

'But we need the *will*. It's not enough yet. Leonora doesn't say what's in it. And they could argue that she said she'd made the will just to piss Annabel off. They'll argue that Tom didn't do anything to her – they can't claim that he wasn't a total lunatic, but they can still say she killed herself, or that she ran away.'

There was a pause, and then both women looked at Oliver. Presumably they were wondering how he was taking this. Oliver wasn't sure himself. Whenever he tried to look into his own thoughts – a wincing, hesitant exploration – he saw not Calverts or Castles, not even Kate or Lena, but Leonora. She had asked him to picture her, and he had, and now he couldn't get the picture out of his head, of a woman sitting up in bed, understanding that the only thing she had left was the shadow cast by her husband in the light below the door.

He pretended not to notice their scrutiny, leaning forward to continue going through the papers. Under a heap of old newspaper clippings he saw a letter edge, Leonora's blue handwriting, his hand darting like a greedy chicken to pluck it out. After reading it, he held it out to Charlotte. 'I'm confused . . . How do you have this? It's a letter from Leonora to George – while he was away. But she never sent it.'

'Oh yes. I know that one. It was inside a pocket book of Leonora's that Boll borrowed: the two of them were living together at that time. Then she forgot to give it back. We found it much later. The letter was tucked into the back pages. I don't think she ever spotted it, or she'd probably have thrown it out.'

'Unsurprisingly. It's pretty dismissive . . . Boll's complaining, and her "raffish suitor".'

He smiled as he read it again, as affectionately as if he had been reunited with his own long-lost sister. A letter more notable for what it omitted than what it mentioned. And yet it did make one incomplete thing whole. From the lone head of a bird volant on a field vert he now had a whole childhood bedroom, and the identity of its owner. The room filled with birds that he had peered into had been Leonora's room when she was the same age. It was a strange and lovely thought. Birds of paradise. He turned the words over in his mind, liking the sound of them.

He offered the letter to Lena, but she shook her head. 'I know it off by heart,' she said. '"A lovely face with a slightly broken nose and a gap in the teeth, and if those things were fixed it shouldn't be so beautiful, or at least not so queerly bewitching."'

'That's exactly it.'

Moved, he tried to catch her eye, but she was looking through papers again. 'Here!' she said, holding up more of Leonora's handwriting; a short note, written on the same paper she had used for her history.

Dearest Boll,

When we last saw each other we quarrelled. I should like to forget that, if you can? I should like us to think kindly of each other. Please know that I am not angry with you.

You asked me about Daphne's legacy: well, this is a gift for her. They are important to me and I hope she might find something of use in them. Please give them to her when she is of age, and tell her that her aunt Leonora loves her always.

Your sister,

L

'Ah, there. That's what I was looking for,' Charlotte said. 'And just there is the letter from Margaret. I put them together. See, Lena, I *was* organised. Read that letter, Oliver. Nobody paid it any attention before; it may as well have its day now. Margaret wrote her account before *she* died. She gave it to my father. My mother had died by then.' She put her hand on Oliver's arm and looked at him earnestly. 'You see, when Margaret was alive, justice was owned by men. Not by wives or working women. But she didn't give up hope that some day, a little of it might pass into their hands.'

'That's a direct quote from your Women and Witches tour,' Lena said.

'Yes, I think it's rather a good one,' Charlotte said, unabashed. 'You wouldn't believe how apposite it is in all sorts of situations. There, Oliver, on the second page. Read from there. Read it out to us.'

. . . *All I ever saw of that marriage,* Oliver read, *was Mrs Castle putting her husband before her. She never raised her voice, or questioned his treatment of her, which was cruel in my opinion. She never gave him any reason to get angry but he was always cold towards her. It was shameful what women tolerated in those days, when I was young, and she was one of the kindest women. My old colleague Mrs Boxall used to say the same thing. She said it up until the day she passed away, nearly ten years ago. Now I suppose I'll be doing the same thing.*

I said in court that I believed he killed her, and I believe it to this day. I was told that none of what I saw or heard counted for anything. I should like to know how the judges and solicitors can look themselves in the eye after what they did, letting that man go free. It felt to me almost as if she'd been murdered all over again. I lost my faith in the law that day, Mr Stack. They said I had a grudge against Mr Castle because he gave me my notice with no reference, and no pay. Who wouldn't bear a grudge for that? They were wrong, though, because I was hardly thinking about that, I was grieving her loss. I heard he died recently, and I was sorry to hear it, because he got away with it, but I hope there is really a heaven and a hell because I know which one he would be in.

Here is my statement, for what it's worth. These are the things I witnessed with my own eyes and ears, in the days before Mrs Castle disappeared.

1) *On the afternoon of September 17th, I heard an argument between them. I couldn't hear all the words but I heard Mr Castle shouting. He called her a d—d liar and other names I can't write down, he said she had tricked him, that everything he thought about her was a lie. I don't know what this argument was about, but only a few days before, I had seen him stamp on their wedding photograph, and smash it. I didn't hear much of what Mrs Castle said, because she was crying, mostly. She didn't say a lot. But I heard her tone when she spoke and it was frightened.*

2) *Later that day I went into Mr Castle's room. I had thought he was downstairs. He used to be so quiet that you wouldn't know where he was in the house half the time. When I went into the room he was sitting facing away from me with his gun on his knees. It made me jump. I knew he kept a gun in his room but I hadn't seen him with it before. I went out again, and I'm not sure he even heard me come in, because he didn't look around. I didn't see Mrs Castle. She stayed in her room all day*

and didn't eat anything, though she drank the tea I took in to her and I could see she had been crying again.

3) The next day, September 18th, Mr Castle went out. He said he was going to see Mr Wilcox – for the second time in a week. That was odd, as he never went out usually. Almost as soon as he left, Mrs Castle came to me with a box. She said it was very important that it go to Daphne. It was all her books. I now believe that she must have suspected she was in danger, and she wanted her books to go to Daphne because she loved her niece and her books more than anything else. She was in a hurry, and told me to go right away.

4) When I got home, I went to Mrs Castle and told her secretly that I'd done what she wanted. She thanked me and leaned forward, as if she wanted to whisper something. She looked white, and tired. I thought she was scared, too. Before she could say anything, she looked up and Mr Castle was there in the doorway. He was just watching us. I can't forget the look on his face. He hated her, I could see that right away. Mrs Castle said, 'That'll be all, Margaret,' and I had to go away then. I didn't like to leave them alone that night, but what else could I do?

5) When I went back to the house on September 19th, I went straight up to Mrs Castle's room, but she wasn't there. I looked around her bedroom and I remember very clearly that all her clothes were still there. The wardrobe door was open, and so were her drawers. I thought that was odd. Her jewellery was there. Her hairbrush was on her wash-stand, her cold cream and hairpins – everything. I ask you, what woman would run away and leave everything behind, even her undergarments and her hairbrush?

6) *When I went downstairs again to see where everybody was,
Mr Castle was there. He gave me my notice on the spot and
stood waiting until I left the house. By the time the case
went to court, all the clothes and everything had been got
rid of. Mr Castle said he threw them out, or gave them away,
but I believe he did that so it couldn't ever be proved that
she hadn't taken any of it.*

*Mr Stack, this is all I know. Everything I saw is honest and
accurate, and I swear it on the Bible, and hope one day this
will help prove that there was most definitely foul play, and Mrs
Castle's soul will have justice at last.*

Oliver put down the letter. Lena looked as if she might cry.
Her hands were clenched on her knees. She drank the rest of
her wine with a look of concentration, like a child ordered to
finish her milk.

'Thank you, Oliver,' Charlotte said. 'What a lovely reading
voice you have.'

'I don't understand,' he said. 'Leonora sent the books to
Daphne? How come they ended up at Tom's again?'

'Well, that's the awful thing. Grannabel said that one day
all Leonora's books just arrived, with this note. It was a time
that she and Leonora weren't speaking. They had been
arguing over inheritance – Annabel was rather coy about the
details of that, now that I think about it – and she took it as
an insult. A taunt. So she sent them back, with an angry note.
By the time they arrived back at the house, Leonora was
dead.'

'Oh no.'

'Yes, I'm afraid so.'

'So Daphne was the dear reader,' Lena said. 'The whole thing was meant for her. Leonora must have wanted her to read it when she was old enough. But . . . not just that! She said it was her legacy, didn't she? And there's a book missing.'

'What do you mean?'

'Leonora thought Annabel and Eddie didn't deserve the house, right? They would have sold it and spent the money. But she knew Daphne wasn't like them. She said somewhere that whoever understood the history of the house should live in it. Something like that. And Daphne listened to her and asked her questions. They talked about labyrinths and the horse on the fireplace and stuff like that.'

'I have no idea what this horse is you two keep going on about,' Charlotte murmured.

'It meant something to them, that's all,' Lena said impatiently. 'She didn't only want Daphne to know who her father was and what had happened to her – Leonora. She wanted her to have the *house*. There was another book with the rest, right? She wouldn't have shipped them off without it. It had the will in it. It must have! It's not like she had time to write any more of her memoir. It ends almost the day before she died.'

'That does all make sense,' Charlotte said. She looked reflective, then satisfied. 'I knew I'd have a clever daughter.'

'So where did the last book *go*?' Lena asked, ignoring her.

'Did Daphne try to get the books back, once she realised?' Oliver asked Charlotte.

'No. It was a pity, but they all thought they were just . . . books. I mean, she had her own books by then. Newer histories. Sounds odd, doesn't it? Updated histories. Plus, Grannabel wouldn't have let her go anywhere near Tom, certainly not to ask him for the books back. And the way

THE HOUSE OF BIRDS

things turned out, Daphne didn't end up with much opportunity to read. There was no money by the time she was eighteen. She probably would have liked university, but they couldn't afford that. Annabel had a silly idea that my mother would marry money and they'd all live happily ever after, but Daphne was too shy and too intelligent for that sort of scam. She became a teacher, and then she married my father, who didn't have any money either. Then she died. She was twenty-seven.'

'A teacher . . .' said Lena, with a look at Oliver, then, 'Oh, Mum.' She got up and put her arms around Charlotte, who was patting at her eyes with the corner of her scarf.

'I'm just so sorry that she isn't here now. Reading what was meant for her.'

Oliver got up himself and went to the window; not simply out of delicacy, but to have the excuse of turning his own face away. *Missed connections*, he thought. Leonora lost Christopher, and then she lost Daphne too, though she would never have known about that. He shied away from imagining what she must have felt as she parcelled up her books to send away. He wasn't sure if it was better or worse – more or less painful – that she didn't live to see the books sent back and the death of her niece; her house passing down from Castle to Castle, its own enchantment stripped away: a house magically transformed by Leonora's antecedents from a heap of bricks into a treasury of living memory, falling after her death back into a heap of bricks, to all but a few people – the faithful Calverts, and one nosy schoolboy at a window.

He put his hand up to the thin film of mist on the window, as if he could wipe it away to reveal the many-coloured room again, this time with a dark-haired girl lying on the bed inside, reading a book. Her eyes moved over the page intently, oblivious to the birds of paradise singing all around her, the alien touch of his stare. The glass under his fingers was shockingly cold, bringing his defocused thoughts smartly back into the world. His hand had left behind a print, beyond which could be seen the abstract stars of the holly just outside the window, stirred by the rain. Beyond this he made out a long garden, the shivering tops of the trees against the navy clouds.

He turned back to the room and looked at Lena and Charlotte. Neither of them noticed his movements, standing as he did beyond the rim of lamplight. As the daylight had sunk away, Charlotte, distracted, had only switched on the lamp closest to her, and she and her daughter were spotlit now in the darkness. Lena had left her mother's side and was cross-legged on the rug, piling papers according to their date and nature, with a fixed, narrow look, as if determinedly busying herself. Charlotte was turning her scarf in her hands, running it through her fingers. She had also retreated, in her own way, and seemed almost wilfully vague. Two bottles of wine had been and gone, he noticed. He felt muddied with alcohol himself, destabilised by its slow, red circling; realised he hadn't eaten since the morning, which seemed like a very long time ago.

'I don't know anything about inheritance law, but won't being Tom's descendants give you more of a claim on the house?' he asked Lena and Charlotte.

'No, love,' Charlotte said. 'It doesn't matter whose kid was whose. Tom had Leonora declared dead, and because she supposedly died intestate, he inherited the house and the right to do whatever he wanted with it. Which was to bequeath it to his nephew.'

'I'm glad,' Lena said, suddenly fierce. 'I wouldn't want it that way. If that was the only reason we got it – our connection to that horrible fucker – then I don't want the stupid house. I'm not a Castle.'

'Language, Lena,' Charlotte said, tiredly. 'I really don't know where you got that from. Your father only said the F word once in his life, and he was very ashamed of himself indeed.'

'He's not dead,' Lena snapped. 'He may yet say it again.'

Oliver realised he was looking at Lena with a foolish, drowsy affection, strangely grateful to see her anger again. She had been sadder and quieter since hearing Margaret's letter; without realising it, he had missed her enlivening outrage. Its resurfacing now was like the return of an old friend.

'I do agree with you, though,' Charlotte said, as Oliver, unnoticed, cast about for a more appropriate expression. 'I'd rather not think of it that way either. We're Calverts, not Castles. Not, of course, that there's anything wrong with the present-day Castles,' she added, glancing at Oliver. 'I'm sure they're all lovely.'

'The most important thing now isn't the house. It's justice,' Lena said, though with the low, furious emphasis she gave to this last word, it could well have been exchanged for others – war, vengeance, bloodshed – with no loss of meaning.

'Quite right, darling,' Charlotte said, more cheerfully. She blew her nose. (Oliver glanced up curiously, but she had procured a tissue from somewhere, and hadn't used the scarf.) 'Now, I hate to give you the bum's rush, but I need to get ready for this evening. I'm hosting my reading group here. I need to tidy these empty bottles away, for a start. The girls will start to worry about me!'

Lena stopped sifting papers. 'What? You're going to host a what?'

'I can't cancel. That would be very rude, at such short notice. I chose the book, too. I feel guilty enough about that already.' She leant forward confidingly. 'You know, it really is *dreadful*.'

'I can't believe you,' Lena said. 'What about working this out? We need to find out where the will is!'

'Well it's not here,' said Charlotte. 'So I may as well just carry on and host my reading group.'

Lena stared at her, appalled.

'Now, Lena, don't give me that look. There's nothing we can do tonight. You always get yourself so wound up. Remember how we used to make you count to ten when you were small? In fact, both of you look quite haggard. Why don't you go home, have a cup of cocoa, and try to get some sleep. We'll deal with all this tomorrow. We've got a decent enough case without the will.'

'But Leonora—'

'Leonora's waited ninety years; she can wait another night.'

'But don't you want to read the history?' Oliver could hear in Lena's voice that this was a token protest, without real force. He had an insight into the family workings; the usual outcome of Lena's anger. It simply vanished into her mother's infinite cosiness, like a hot coal dropped into a sea of milk.

'No, love, I'll read it tomorrow morning,' Charlotte said. 'It's too much to take in today.'

'Fine. I'll take it home with me. I want to read it again.'

'Don't tire yourself out,' Charlotte said, as Lena began putting on her coat. 'You really ought to wear more layers, Lena. I read something about thin people losing heat faster. It's a real worry. Either that, or eat more.' At the door, she took off her glasses and said, 'It was truly lovely to meet you, Oliver,' with a hint of her former flirtatiousness. 'You're rather an old-school type, aren't you? Like an honourable knight. I hope you don't get in any trouble for all this.'

'Er,' said Oliver, but Charlotte didn't seem to require a reply. She kissed him (her perfume arriving as she did so, a tropical confusion of different flowers) and embraced Lena at length. Then she shut the door and they were left in the darkness of the porch, as deep and clenchingly cold as Arctic water. They looked at each other in silence, Oliver without anything to say; Lena, it was apparent, with too much.

'The absolute *fucking*—' she started furiously.

Oliver interrupted her. He had no plan. But as soon as he started talking, the right thing came to him. 'Look, why don't we go back to Leonora's house? We could look for the book again. I went through them all to check for cut-out sections, but if it's just a will, it could be tucked in between the pages or something. I didn't check the titles either, because I didn't know what I was looking for back then.'

She looked at him, considering this.

'And we could pick up some food on the way back. We both need to eat. It's not far to walk to the house from here, and there are some places on the way.'

'Actually,' she said, slowly, 'now I think about it, I am absolutely bloody *starving*.'

e⌒

At the house, Oliver went into the kitchen to look for plates and cutlery for their fish and chips, while Lena lingered in the hall with her phone. 'Better explain where I am,' she said. 'I don't want people to worry.' (*People*, noted Oliver. Not *My husband*. Not *Jim*.)

He washed up the ornamental plate and the cake forks he had been using for his takeaways, but found nothing else in the kitchen, its contents having presumably fallen victim to Kate's eccentric purge.

He didn't want to think about Kate.

'What are you doing?' Lena said, in the doorway. 'We don't need plates and forks, do we? I don't, anyway. You can go back to the city and tell all your friends about this yokel you knew who ate chips with her fingers.'

'They wouldn't believe me,' Oliver said, handing her the packet.

She looked curiously around the kitchen, which had managed to take on an air of utter abandonment in a very short space of time. Forgotten graduations of brown and dirty cream, one cupboard door hanging slightly off its hinges, every surface covered with dust. It looked like a deserted room in Chernobyl.

'I like what you've done with the place,' she said.

'This will be the last room to be done, probably. I haven't chosen anything for it yet, and . . .' He stopped, wary of causing offence.

'Let's have a look around,' she said, giving him a sudden and clandestine smile. 'You know, I haven't seen the house properly. I've never even been here except to shout at you.'

They went from room to room as they ate their chips. Lena was interested in everything: opening up Elizabeth Calvert's burr-walnut wardrobe, with one catlike sniff of the wooden interior; squinting into the black expanse of the garden as if she might – if she focused hard enough – see the apple tree standing in the distance; knocking experimentally on the darkened oak doors that had been covered until now by glossy plywood. In the bedroom at the back of the house he showed her the fragment of Leonora's bird of paradise wallpaper.

'Remember? From her letter.'

'God . . . look at the feathers. The detail of it.'

'I looked in here once, when I was a kid. I came with Kate. Back then the wallpaper was still up, and it was spectacular. I didn't know it was Leonora's bedroom. I knew she had her mother's old room later on, at the front of the house, but this must have been where she slept as a child. It was something I'd always wanted to know. I used to think of it as the house of birds,' he said; then, struck by a new thought, 'But I guess your house has more claim to that title.'

'Maybe it does now,' she said. She put her fingers up to the wallpaper, then hesitated, lowered them; the same way he had when he found it. When she added, reflectively, 'I wish I'd seen it back then,' it was without resentment; only a slight, vague smile at whatever it was she was imagining.

They went back downstairs to look again at the hall floor, which had been finished that day in his absence: all the layers that intervened between Sophia's time and his own stripped back to expose the Georgian tiles, a radiating design of blue and white and rust colours.

'It's lovely.' Lena knelt down and ran her hand over them. 'They're all worn. Like the tide's been over them. Like sea glass.' She looked up at him with a delight that was not exactly childlike, but not adult either, having a purity that was of no time, no fixed abode. As if some switch had been effected – a key turned – by that smile of hers, he had the odd sense of time lifting up and away within the house, so that in the sitting room he felt himself moving through Leonora's life as well as his own: the ghost of flames in the fireplace, the barely visible outline of the sofas, the grandfather clock. The tiles of the hearth were a molten shimmer; a doll lay, for a moment, in the flickering light.

'Comanche,' he said, pointing. Lena laughed. Her fingers moved over the horse's nose and mane, gently, as if it were alive.

He said, 'You know, when I got here, this house felt so strange and uncared for. But it didn't seem to take any time for it to go back to how it must once have been. I don't know . . . I might be imagining it. But I do feel it's like – how did Leonora say it? In her letter? Like a lion stretching out in the sun. Ah . . . I don't know. I'm getting carried away, aren't I?' She was looking at him sharply, and he felt embarrassed.

Lena paused; looked back down at Comanche, as if to consult him. When she spoke, it was slowly and with notice-able care, as if her eloquence needed anger to fuel itself, and didn't run well on sympathy. 'Oliver, I did you a disservice before. When I said you couldn't expect to understand what the house meant to us. But you understand it completely – that it's not just a heap of bricks. Because it wasn't to her. It *is* her, to us. And they were both wronged, weren't they . . . but this is all that's left.'

'All that we can put right.'

She smiled at him, quick and unexpectedly watery, before putting her hands up to her face, exasperated.

'No. Fuck's sake. I'm *not* crying again. Let's talk about some-thing else. What else? Does the fireplace work?'

'I haven't tried it. It's just been cleaned. But I, er, don't really know what I'm doing. With fires.'

She didn't, as he had expected, scoff at this. She picked up her chips again, propelling the last one thoughtfully around the oily paper, gathering up each grain of salt. 'That reminds me of a recurring nightmare I used to have when I was a kid. I'd be running away from fires, and get backed into a corner. I really felt the heat. It was unbearable. Then I'd wake up.'

'Do you still get them? I never remembered my dreams when I was young, but now I get nightmares. You'd think it would be the other way around.'

'Oh, I still have nightmares,' she said. 'Not about fire any more, though. Now it's adult stuff, grown-up fears, like negative equity, abandonment, fucked-up sex.'

He wasn't sure if she was joking or not, and then she shrugged, crumpled up the paper, and said, 'Let's make a fire. I'll show you.'

'There's no coal.'

'You've got plenty of timber in that skip. And junk mail. I'd suggest burning those kitchen units but I think it might be dangerous. Formaldehyde fumes or something.'

Oliver went through the rest of Leonora's books while Lena lit the fire. Page after page and nothing so much as a note on a flyleaf. No sign of *Cretan Law under Mamalakis*. He looked for the title online and came up with a list of nonsense search results: social media profiles, videos, pages in Greek. Mamalakis seemed to be a popular surname. He found no ancient kings; only a priest, a professor, a twenty-something self-confessed handbag addict, a law firm and an estate agency in Athens. Furthermore, there was no such author as O. N. Koroneou in existence.

'I don't get it,' he said to Lena.

She sat back on her heels, watching the fire stretch up into the chimney, snakes' tongues of red and gold. When she turned, the light of it glowed through her hair, quivering over the smooth surfaces of her face and arms. The red dress looked almost living in the reflected heat.

'I don't either. It must be long out of print. Maybe tomorrow we could try some specialists. I don't know. Or see if we can find out if any of the Castles who lived here might have taken stuff away, or given it to people.'

Oliver hesitated to say it, but had to ask. 'What if Tom happened to open that book?'

'I'd thought that too,' she said. She spread her hands, philosophical. 'I think that probably *is* what's happened. Even if he didn't, I've pretty much accepted that we're not going to find the will. But I think we still have a chance without it.'

Now it was Oliver who was dissatisfied. 'It just doesn't seem fair.'

'No. Hey – you have wine.'

She indicated two bottles, next to the sofa. 'Oh yes. I'd forgotten about that. I've got into some bad habits living alone.'

'I can help you with that,' Lena said, and for a moment he was taken aback, then realised she meant the wine.

He gave her his brandy snifter, found a teacup for himself, and they raised their glasses to each other with a grim smirk. 'To murderer's blood,' said Lena.

After that, they talked, sitting on Oliver's ersatz divan in front of the fire, which Lena would occasionally toss wood to, as if it were an animal waiting to snap it up. Oliver realised, somewhere around the third glass of wine, that he was no longer intimidated by her, even though she was still unpredictable to him: the unexpected turns of her conversation, the changing weather of her eyes, from rain to fog to sudden lightning. He found he was enjoying it. When she got quickly and wholeheartedly angry at the price he had been charged by the plumbers ('You got screwed. Who are they? Are they local?'), he admired the purposefulness of her reaction. Where he was depressed by unfairness or wrongdoing, she was galvanised. She seemed more alive than he.

'What *have* you done in here?' she asked now, looking around at the room. 'I know I've already commented on this, but seriously – what's the rationale? I want to understand. It's like an antiques shop.'

'Or the contents of a skip,' he said, before he realised this could be taken as a criticism of Kate, and went red.

This did not escape Lena. 'Sure, after your girlfriend's been tidying up.'

'Well, you know – Kate has a good eye for design, usually. She just prefers new things to old, I guess. But she has other interests. She's very smart, her general knowledge is really quite phenomenal . . .'

He realised he was making it worse; that Lena had started to laugh. 'Oliver – nobody questioned Kate's intelligence. Why should she know about antiques? Hardly anyone does. If everyone was an expert on antiques and not computers or farming or the financial markets, we'd all be dead. You're the one who seems most bothered that she couldn't pick a Ming vase out of an identity parade.'

He acknowledged this, lifting his hands in surrender. 'I suppose . . . it's not antiques really. I don't care much about *stuff* either. It's more . . . I don't know.'

Without naming Kate, or being even more disloyal than he had been already, he tried to communicate something of his recent feeling to Lena. At the Ashmolean he had realised that he hadn't been to a museum since he was a child. He and his friends had lifestyles but not culture, news but not history. They liked shopping, sunbathing, skiing. Ruins and castles were something that might be pointed out from a car window, or co-opted as a backdrop for a selfie. They would watch a film in which a steroidal Hollywood star would play Henry VIII, and Oliver would be laughed at for looking up the actual events on his phone, later, at the bar. They lived their lives as if on the tip of an iceberg; the immense accumulation of the past below them as they walked oblivious over its surface, discussing the relative merits of the Maldives versus the Bahamas, arguing over whether fusion food was dead.

'Obviously, this isn't a relationship thing,' he added, worrying that he had got carried away. 'It's just life in general.'

'Fuck's sake, Oliver,' Lena said, gently enough. 'Are you really telling me you're sad because none of your yuppie friends want to go to Stonehenge with you? Go yourself! Or – better yet – give up your job and study history. Then maybe you'll be able to enjoy a few cocktails on the beach without feeling you should be thinking about the Aztecs instead.'

'*You* don't study history,' he said, defensive, 'but you enjoy it. It's part of your life but it's not your job.'

'Yeah, so, I'm a well-rounded individual who doesn't know that George Louis was the King of England. I'm okay with that. But is that what you want to be? Look, I don't even bloody know you and I don't think you'd be satisfied with that.'

He said, 'It's ironic, really. Leonora knew exactly what she wanted, but she couldn't have any of it. I've had the opportunity to do whatever I want to do, and it seems like in almost thirty years I've only just managed to work out what that might be.'

'You never had an idea?'

'Well, maybe once, when I was young. But I tried to make practical decisions. That's how I ended up in the City. My parents had some lean years, and they always told me to work hard and be financially secure, and I did, but somewhere along the line that kind of . . . mutated. Into this *lifestyle*. I seem to have ended up with all these ambitions and I don't really . . .'

The prospect of disloyalty stopped him again.

'You don't like your job, either?' Lena asked.

'Not really. I always felt like other people were motivated by passion and ambition. Whereas I worked more out of – I don't know. Fear and obedience. But nobody ever noticed the difference and it didn't seem to matter. I know I'm using the past tense . . . I actually quit my job a couple of weeks ago. I'm meant to be thinking about what I want to do next. We were planning to move to New York. And I feel this panic like I'm fucking everything up, my career and all my plans, even though I never really liked any of it in the first place.' He stopped again, too late this time. 'Nobody knows any of that.'

Lena looked at him in silence.

'But yes, basically I don't know what to do,' he said.

'Don't look for another job. Start again, and study history.'

'What?'

'I'm serious! You don't like your work. You like history. So stop worrying about your work and study history. Do it in New York – if that's where you actually want to be.'

Oliver couldn't immediately think of a reply to this. He looked into the fire. It made his eyes sting, but it was easier than facing the unsparing vivisection that was Lena trying to be helpful.

She took in his expression and laughed. 'Oh . . . sorry. I was meant to murmur cryptically and let you work it out yourself in your own time. That's how it's done, isn't it? I just don't have enough patience. Let's pretend I didn't say anything.'

'You think I'm an idiot, don't you?'

'No! Why would I think that? Don't be so hard on yourself,' she said.

'Why – because you're here?' He started to laugh. 'I suppose we can't both be hard on me. It would be like bullying.'

Her hand darted out: a mock swipe, but he made a show of dodging, raising his hands to protect himself. 'Count to ten! Count to ten! Don't bite me!'

'Fucker. I should have known *that* would come up. But I've had braces since then, look.' She bared her teeth, a glossy, neatly stacked display. 'Nobody could prove it was me. So watch out.'

There was something provocative in this – or so he thought, anyway; a signal originating and ending in the mind of Oliver alone. A tree falling in the woods with only himself as witness. Nevertheless, he was stirred, and had to look away.

'I admire Leonora, too,' Lena said musingly, not having noticed his reaction. 'She wanted an education, a job, Christopher, and children. If she didn't get any of it, it wasn't for lack of clear-sightedness.'

'But you have what you want.' Oliver was confused. 'Don't you have what you want?'

'Not exactly. I've always said I don't want children, but it turns out my husband does. A few months ago I got pregnant by mistake, and that's when it all came out. He thought I'd change my mind, apparently. I had an abortion. Since then it's been a little . . . strained.'

Oliver remembered the separate bedrooms. 'Do you think it'll be okay?'

'Fuck knows. I'm not sure. At the moment, I'm just sort of holding out. I don't know what for, though.'

'Hoping he'll change *his* mind?'

She laughed blackly. 'Yeah. I guess so.'

Oliver contemplated parenthood; something he didn't often do. He had assumed he would end up having children, just not yet. Each year of his twenties the 'not yet' was pushed ahead of him, a little further off into the future. Kate wanted them. She had had her own abortion, when she was seventeen, after a one-night stand. She didn't regret it but she was grieved by it. Tears came into her eyes when she told him, and when he saw them he took her hands, overwhelmingly moved, and told her they'd raise their own family and it would make up for that lost opportunity; they'd have two children, or three or four, anything it took to make her feel an excess of love, rather than an absence.

'But even if you don't have what you want, at least you still know your own mind,' he said. 'Um, I'm not sure if that's comforting or not. Sorry.'

'No, it kind of is. I'm still lucky compared to Leonora in terms of what I've got. I'm still quicker on the uptake than you in terms of what I want. That makes me feel better.'

'Very funny.'

'There's just a lot I want to do, you know. I haven't finished travelling. I want to go to Central America and see some Mayan ruins, for a start. I thought of that the other day . . . I'd like to do it for Leonora, almost. I still like parties. I still like spending all day reading a book if I want to. The birds take up a lot of time, even with the volunteers, and Jim helping.

Basically I don't have time for children, and if my life turns out the way I want it to, I never will. There'll always be too much else to do . . . What?'

'Now *you're* explaining when you don't need to.'

'I am, aren't I?' She turned the glass slowly in her hands, reflective, as if watching it take shape. 'I think it's because I feel ambushed. I really didn't see this coming. I'm thirty five – blame the media, but I genuinely thought it was all over. Ovaries had retired, or whatever. I thought it was all settled. I was happy with that.'

Oliver felt a tiny flinch of dismay, at this being the extent of Lena's marital problems. Without conscious judgement he somehow had got the impression that her husband was a bit of a prick, realising his assumption only now that he was disappointed to hear that this wasn't in fact the case.

'You have a brother, right?' he said, quickly. 'Does he have children? I'm thinking about who the house might pass down to.'

'Yeah, it'd be them. They're a nice family. You'd like them. My brother's doing a PhD, something to do with mindfulness. He's a very calming presence.' She caught his eye. 'Yeah, I know. Sort of the opposite of me. My dad's very relaxed too. When I was a child, I used to have to create my own arguments at Christmas.'

'I think I'd rather have an owl than a child,' Oliver said. He hadn't really meant to say it out loud. He realised he was drunk.

Kate's claim came back to him: *She's fucked mostly everybody.* The words revolved slowly in his body like tentacles underwater, flexing mermaid tails in the half-seen depths, a pewterish glimmer, movements deliberate and unsettling. He wished she hadn't said it. It wasn't that he really believed it; it had just been her idea of an insult, revealing more about Kate herself – the remnants of a suburban prissiness that she'd tried and failed to escape – than Lena. But he knew he half hoped it was true, because then – what? – there would be the possibility that she might fuck *him*.

She was gazing into the fire. He was grateful for it: as long as it was alight, keeping the night back, they could talk. He had no idea what the time was; he didn't want to ask or look at his watch and break the enchantment – because it *was* an enchantment, a spell over the house, the past and the present reunited for this one night, a suspension of usual time.

Lena said now, 'Funny you should say that. One of my tawny owls does think he's my child. I raised him from a chick and he imprinted on me. He sits and watches films with me, in the crook of my arm, like this' – she cradled one arm, with a tender expression – 'and I stroke his head. You can't really pet the other birds; they've got this oily waterproofing. But owls are different; their feathers are soft, so they can fly sneakily through the night. Surprising the mice. You know, despite their public image, they're not gentle birds. They're assassins.'

Oliver didn't doubt it. He couldn't see himself attempting to pet any of the birds; offering the eagle, say, a tickle under the chin. They had a way of looking at him that reminded him of the first time he met Lena. He said as much to her.

She looked offended. 'What do you mean, the first time you met me?'

'"Fucking yuppie", I think that was the accusation . . .'

'Oh. All right, sorry about that.'

'And "mad". You said that a few times. Also my "weird piles

of bric-a-brac" came in for some flak. "Yuppie" was the one that really hurt, though.'

'Okay, I've said sorry!' she cried. 'Stop! Or maybe I will bite you.'

He didn't reply, only held out his arm. As soon as he did it – offering it up, wrist exposed – he realised that the gesture was unmistakable. There was no explaining it away. She stopped laughing, and looked at him. Her pupils were large in the low light; they seemed to merge with her black irises, unreadable. The moment was a long one; he could feel it stretching, like a drawn-out spool of honey; the tension in the thread an instant before the drop. Neither of them spoke. He felt, later, like she had waited for several minutes before she leant in – looking so serious, almost sombre – and, disregarding his outstretched arm, kissed him; but it must have only been seconds, or not even that.

Time tumbled from that moment, like something falling downhill, picking up pace. Her hands were in his hair and his shirt half stripped away without him understanding how she had managed it. His own hands moved across her legs, which were so exactly as he had imagined them to be, building them from his glances that day when she wasn't looking, that he felt almost as if he had touched them already, run his fingers up her thighs many times before. She gave a pleased sigh in response, as if she too knew and welcomed this move.

In conversation with Lena he had always felt he had to watch what he said, not just for fear of giving offence, but because she had a habit of wrong-footing him, so that one minute he might feel on safe ground and the next know, miserably, that he had just said something completely stupid. Kissing her was different; unexpectedly harmonious. Nothing he did seemed to annoy her. He unzipped her dress, leaving his hand at the base of the zip, and she arched against it. When he pushed her back on to the mattress, she pulled him down with her; when he bit her neck – light and questioning – she laughed softly. He considered telling her this; the thought falling out of his head almost as soon as it wandered in, chased by other thoughts, only briefly haunting, of other women – Leonora, Boll, Charlotte (disturbingly), Kate, with a sudden whipcrack of guilt – and then, finally, only Lena.

Afterwards they lay together in the cooling light of the fire. The sheets radiated outward from the bed like blown flower petals; the aftermath of some bomb blast. His arm was over her; her leg over his. She smiled and closed her eyes. He stroked her side, the long concavity of her body, trying to collect his thoughts – which, like the bedsheets, were all over the place.

The only word he could think of to adequately describe sex with Lena was revelatory. The problem with revelatory was that it forced him to think of what had gone before; every night with a previous lover falling under its shadow. Comparisons, unwanted, flooded in. Lena's abandonment had surprised him, used as he was to Kate's routines, which he had learned not to vary. If he tried something different, she would be accepting but quizzical, with a quick look, a little laugh of bemusement ('What *are* you doing?' or 'You are funny') that killed the impulse almost immediately. Then, after the pristinely smooth surfaces of Kate, he had been fascinated by Lena's variety: had touched the dry skin of her elbows with delight, her unevenly curling hair, the startling crispness of her pubic hair. Where Kate had become ticklish and self-conscious, Lena encouraged him closer, then closer still, until he felt as if he were roaming a landscape of scents, at first tentatively, then in the wild spirit of exploration. Her hands smelled of the lavender bathroom soap, of chip salt and smoke, her mouth of alcohol, the crooks of her arms like warm hay, her armpits sweet and powdery from her deodorant; her hair rustled up a waft of almond shampoo. Between her legs: warm bread; her back had the faint trace of his own aftershave, from where he had gripped her. Her neck smelled of the remnants of her perfume and the hot night, a heavy scent, musk and honey and dark, dense woods.

In bed her style had not been classifiable – he could not have said whether she was rough or gentle, dominant or passive. She hovered between signifiers, undefinable. It was intimate – that was what struck him most. He felt closer to her in bed than he had felt with anyone. He understood, now, what people meant when they talked about sex feeling right. He was stunned by the ease of it: their sudden and complete accord, her large pupils opening up like velvety black flowers, luxuriating in the sun.

He lay there, smiling, until a thought struck him.

'You know,' he said. 'Leonora didn't change Daphne's name. Do you think maybe she meant that Daphne didn't have to be another example of history repeating itself? She could be whatever she wanted to be.'

But Lena didn't answer, and he realised she had fallen asleep.

Oliver once saw a slow-motion video of somebody dropping a Slinky. The spiral extended fully before the hand in the video let go. It seemed that the top dropped while the bottom hovered for a moment in mid-air, before it apparently remembered the existence of gravity and the whole thing hit the floor. There was a scientific explanation for the phenomenon that he didn't understand, but someone had helpfully simplified it, writing: 'The bottom doesn't know it's falling until it's told by the coil above.'

That was what he experienced the next morning, when he woke up and opened his eyes and saw Lena sitting on the chair beside him, almost dressed and pulling on her boots. He sat up and smiled at her. He didn't get it. It was already over, of course it was, but Oliver – still hovering for a languorous moment in the air – didn't understand that yet. Then he saw that she wasn't smiling back. She was a faded kind of pale in the morning light, her mouth tired. She looked at him with a dreadful solemnity, and he wanted to put his hands over his eyes and cry, *No, no, no!* as if he were back in school. *No fair! No take-backs!*

'Oliver, I'm so sorry,' she said.

'Why are you sorry? Please don't say sorry.'

'That's what people usually say when they do something wrong, isn't it? We did something wrong.'

'Then don't apologise to me.'

'You're right, it's the others we should be apologising to. Oh God. God. Look, Oliver, I know this sounds cold, but can we . . . keep this to ourselves? I don't think either of our relationships needs this, on top of everything else. And it's not like it's something we're going to repeat. It was exceptional circumstances, right? We were so drunk. This whole weird situation with Leonora's diary . . . I don't really know what

happened to me. I've felt so emotional and . . . I don't know
– strange. I feel a bit mad. I can't explain. I'm not saying any
of this is an excuse . . .'

'You just felt *mad*? That's all it was?'

She looked at him, eyes large, a broken light on them like
cracked glass.

'That's not what I meant.'

He argued; partly out of hurt, partly because he had no
other way of keeping her in the room. 'It sounds like it didn't
mean that much to you.'

That made her angry. She stood up abruptly, pulled her coat
straight, its buttons punctuating a strict descending line. 'Sure,
Oliver, I don't have any human emotions. We'd got to the end
of the diary and I was bored and it was just something to do.'

He started to speak but she interrupted him, becoming more
incensed. 'What good would it do if I told you I'm hurt too,
that I care – all right, that I'm fucking devastated. Don't act
like I'm the unfeeling one because I'm pointing out that there's
really only one thing we can do now. You think that's easy for
me? *You've* got the easy job, looking sad and protesting the
decision. But where would we be if we both did that? I mean,
are you really telling me you'd leave Kate?'

She said it scornfully, reminding him of their first meeting,
a fortnight ago, when she stood in the same spot and didn't
hold back, lavishing him with her plentiful contempt. He had
watched her in dismay, but even then with a subterranean
understanding, a flicker of recognition.

'My relationship is over,' he said.

It was not so much an offering to Lena as his own, private
realisation; one that felt oddly the same as the moment he
understood what had happened to Leonora. It might have been

a new insight, but it wasn't news. It was sad, but a strangely familiar sadness, one that had collected in him over the months, half-known, steadily ignored; a sorrow pooling still and low like a flooded basement, fed by a slow but constant leak.

Lena, in contrast, had not seen it coming. She sat down as if suddenly compressed by guilt, a comprehensive weight of it. The effect was almost surreal to watch: all the anger rushing away, her mouth opening slightly, her face stricken.

'Christ, Oliver, I'm sorry. I didn't realise. I thought you were just . . . I don't know.'

'Playing it up to get laid?' he said, without rancour.

She looked down, and he said, 'Please don't apologise. I don't blame you. It's not like we knew each other's feelings.'

Lena put her face in her hands. 'I've just fucked up massively, haven't I?' she said, her voice filtering through the gaps in her fingers, pressed almost into meaninglessness. He felt like he should either touch her or move back – but marooned in the bed in the middle of the room, uncomfortably naked under the sheets, he could do neither. He felt as if he were in a specific type of bad dream; the one of paralysing inertia. Trying to run but only being able to struggle slowly forward, pushing against the unyielding air; a miniature of his life so far, condensed into a few unbearable seconds.

'Lena,' he said, urgently, 'Lena, listen. You have to stay. You *can't* be happy with your husband. Would you have done this if you were happy? You told me to quit my job, but don't you see that you're doing the same thing in your marriage? You're not doing it properly. You're sleeping in separate rooms, you're sleeping with me. Slept with me. How is that different? I know what love should be, and—'

'Oliver.'

387

She looked up, and they stared at each other for a little while. There was a long, weighted silence, full of the understanding that they wouldn't see each other again.

'I'm sorry,' she said.

'Don't apologise.' He tried to smile. 'Aside from anything else, it's just weird. I'm the one who usually apologises.'

She smiled effortfully, skewing the tears running to the side of her nose, sending them over her cheeks and into her hair. She wiped her eyes with the backs of her hands.

'You did so much for me, Oliver.'

'No.' He shook his head.

'I know you could have stopped all this – Leonora's diary. God knows it would have been easier for you not to help us.'

'I hope it's enough to prove the truth.'

'Who knows, without the will. Maybe it is. Thank you. I . . .' She hesitated over the words, and it was both unusual and horrible to see her like this, not assured or impassioned, but picking her way through the necessary summings-up with tense care, like a cat balancing along a high wall. 'I hope you find something that makes you happy.'

You're not happy, he wanted to insist, but what was the use of that? He had to give up: sit there in the bed she had vacated; watch in horror as she put an end to it; keep silent and not interrupt, as she went through the rest of her big goodbye. He only really heard bits of it, phrases he knew were sincere, but were too well-used to mean anything. She wished nothing but the best for him. She hoped that whatever was right for him and Kate would come to pass. She'd always think of him. She was sorry, sorry, sorry.

He nodded as she got up and left, not able to do anything else; trapped on the floor with all the bedclothes drawn up tightly around him. It struck him bleakly how preposterous he must look, but it was better than following her to the door under the duvet like a giant bare-legged hermit crab. He used to go around the house like that when he was a child, he remembered. It was comforting, especially to the young Oliver who had stayed up and watched *Poltergeist* without permission. Comforting, but not fully effective. Even wrapped in a duvet, he couldn't forget the ghost, and twenty years on, a different duvet was failing to protect him from real life. Misery crawled into his tightly wrapped world. He thought of Leonora, unable to write about her parting from Christopher. He wished he could do that: leave a blank space in the text of his own life. An ellipsis before picking up again, years in the future, by which time it might not hurt quite so much.

Oliver spent the rest of the morning in a daze of labour, talking to contractors, postponing and cancelling, getting the house into a state to hand over to Castles or Calverts without confusing either side. He didn't think as he worked; rather, he turned over events in his mind ceaselessly, a churning process without synthesis, all the elements remaining exactly as they were. Only the empty bottles of wine, the crumpled oily paper, and the embers of the fire he had to sweep disturbed the strange, disconnected state he had achieved; like sudden poking fingers. When he went outside to carry the rubbish of the night before to the bin, he was startled to step into a fog; the curdled sky flatly white, the street beyond drowned in mist.

By the afternoon, he was almost finished. As he washed his hands under the temperamental bursts of the bathroom taps, he looked at himself in the mirror and felt a disappointment – not an unexpected one, but a sense of previous suspicions being finally confirmed. In the glassy blue-grey light that made its way through the narrow window his face looked unhealthy; softer, as if it had lost structural integrity, beginning to dissolve in the fog he had breathed in. His sadness itself was diffuse, melancholic, accumulating as he went from room to room, as if sorrowing over its half-done state, its past only partly restored, future as uncertain as his own.

He stopped in the hall, running out of energy, and sat on the bottom step staring out over the complex patterning of the tiles. He didn't know how long he sat there; long enough to feel something invisible gathering around him, as if he had walked into a forest, silencing the many-coloured birds, then sat so still and quiet for so long that they were coming back, resuming their usual activies. It was a strange kind of life that thrummed around him now: a swell of history, of various human truths. He heard a brief, experimental glissando of piano keys; Elizabeth Calvert's mouse-like rustlings; the exquisite piccolo of Boll laughing upstairs, then the low slam of her door. From where he sat he could see Leonora in the drawing room, her pale dress bluish in the light that dipped and billowed as the white curtains blew slowly in and out. She was standing by the fireplace, looking away. He willed her to turn around, but here his imagination failed him. As if he had tried to push a lucid dream too far, he found himself unwillingly awake again, hearing only distant cars, a broom sweeping somewhere further down the street.

He didn't want to leave, he didn't want to stay. He couldn't picture himself living here – not now – but neither could he see himself in London, or anywhere. As if refusing any further labour, his imagination stalled at considering not only the past, but any possible future beyond the next ten minutes. He went into the drawing room, in which everything was sad: the books and china and pictures arranged in boxes along one wall, the window bare without the balding velvet curtain, rigged up and fallen down and rigged up again and finally taken down and thrown away. He had left the bed until last, delaying the moment in which he would fold up the sheets, with whatever was left of Lena's perfume, and heave the mattress into the skip outside. He wrestled it up and out of the door now, catching as he did the ambiguous gaze of Comanche.

He didn't know how much of his sadness was for the loss of Lena and how much for the loss of Leonora. The previous night seemed like just now and like years ago. As with Leonora's history, it was both an an intimate presence and an unsurmountable absence. He wondered if, when he got back to London, time would straighten out again, resolve itself into a rational linear form. Oxford might as well have been the Bermuda Triangle, in which time was a drawn-out tide, leaving only pieces of itself behind, and history had its own mind; cornering him one moment, evading him the next.

He checked that the doors and windows were locked, and put the keys in a kitchen drawer. He glanced out of the window at the garden, in which the apple tree was nearly hidden by mist. The heating was off and the house was starkly, preposterously cold. His rucksack, holding all of his things, waited for him in the hall. The message seemed clear: *holiday's over*.

He closed and locked the front door in the full consciousness of his outsidership. As he walked, he eyed the fog hanging poetically over the spires of the city and thought bitterly: typical pretentious Oxford, unable to resist a simile. In this instance, his own life, once so clear and rhythmic and predictable; all of it turned now to mist.

At the station, he remembered the day of his arrival, stepping out into the hallucinogenic sunlight: that last encore of summer, its air of general intoxication, ice creams and bare legs, bottles of champagne discarded by the river. Now he stood on the platform, staring at the frosted metal fence across the tracks with the other passengers, their breath rising in vanishing plum-blossom bursts. He found it hard to believe that he was going back to the apartment; that nothing there had changed since he left. Perhaps time wasn't quite right in London either: it had just stopped. In a couple of days, when Kate got back, it would set off again, with a heave and a slow groan, carting him into the darkening light of the not-too-distant future.

e~

Back at their apartment, Oliver put his bag down by the door and closed it softly behind him, as if trying not to disturb some invisible occupant. The rooms smelt of nothing much. Ironically, this place too felt like a holiday let, marked as his only by a few signs of mess; evidence of human life. A toothpaste mark in the sink, peeled-back bedsheets, a cup with the coffee dried into a dark ring like a scorch mark, a balled sock – a missed shot – lying next to the laundry basket. He tidied up and watched some television, hardly hearing it or seeing it, the images rebounding off his corneas as if repelled by their glaze. That night he fell asleep on the sofa, waking with a shocked spasm early the next morning, focusing with surprise on the familiar: the sight of his usual life.

Later, he began to pack his possessions into bags and boxes, partly to fill the time before Kate got back, and partly in an attempt to clear himself away as considerately as possible, leaving behind no unsightly reminders of his presence. It seemed like the decent thing to do. Halfway through, he realised he didn't know where any of these bags and boxes – or Oliver himself – were meant to end up. He called his parents, who were delighted to hear from him, which made him feel guilty for not calling sooner, and asked if he could stay with them for a few weeks. After having discussed taxis (his suggestion) and lifts (theirs), his mother put his father on for what she delicately called a 'man-to-man chat', the nature of which hadn't become fully clear to Oliver's father, who immediately asked, 'So when's Kate coming down?'

There was some muttering, beyond the receiver.

'Oh, right. Well how was I to know? Why don't you talk to him, then, if I'm doing such a bad job of . . . okay. Never mind. You still there, son? Good, good. Right you are. Just give us a ring when you're on your way.' There was a silence, in which Oliver imagined he could hear murmured urgings, after which his father added, sounding unconvinced, 'It'll be great fun.'

Oliver checked his phone again before bed, but, as expected, there were no calls from Kate. He hadn't questioned her silence; he realised he had been so busy preparing to be dumped that he had almost forgotten that it hadn't happened yet. He had tried so often over the last fortnight not to think about her, it had almost become second nature. Now, as if embarking on a meditation, he sat on the edge of the bed and looked for her, hunting through the scenes of their life together, which seemed to pass like photographs; as if he were viewing his own social media profile. Kate with her face propped on her hands, bare shoulders over the edge of a hot tub. Oliver raising a glass self-consciously; holding friends' babies with a determined, helpless expression. Kate waving on a snowy slope, ski jacket brilliant against the sky, scarlet and cobalt. When he tried to think of her face, he saw her picture instead, the one that showed on his phone screen when she called. Turned slightly to the side, one curving sheet of hair undulating over her raised eyebrow. Low-key tan, neat white teeth.

With a medieval urge for mortification, he went over their happiest, brightest times, whetting them until they were sharp. There was the night when they came home to find a pigeon watching television. It had got in through a window that had been left open, and was sitting as if mesmerised on the back of the sofa. They never established whether Oliver had left the television on or whether the pigeon was responsible: it had been one thing that reliably made them laugh. There was the surprise Valentine's meal Kate planned when she first moved into the flat, before she realised she hated cooking, so that Oliver came home and found her crying in frustration over the smoking rim of a pan. One astonishing night on acid. The occasional Sundays when she would consent to linger in bed, drinking coffee carefully and giving an animated run-down of the events of the night before, until he could tell she was getting more and more impatient, and would finally spring out of bed and into the shower.

It hurt, but not enough – not yet. He went back to the night they met as adults – though that did not seem strictly accurate, suffused as she had been by a haze like a wash of colour, the light of the past shining through her. What had he seen that night? The garden; the birds; the shadows of trees striping the pavements under their bicycle wheels; the distinct tang of death. Her beauty; ironically the one thing that had endured. Finally he imagined her standing in the doorway of the flat; the sight of her face, the minute sigh as she put down her case, pushed back her hair and looked up for him. That did it. The real pain came, and he shut his eyes, keeping himself focused on her as if holding his hand against a hot stove, steadfastly watching her face, her changing, collapsing expressions, as he told her the truth.

Then, on Saturday afternoon, there she was, standing in the doorway, looking almost exactly as he had imagined her. Her sleek surfaces slightly ruffled from the flight; a shine on her nose and a bit of hair sticking out at a different angle. She looked tired, and wary. He felt a new rush of sorrow, not covered in rehearsals. He found he could hardly speak.

'Hi, Oliver,' she said. She closed the door but didn't move very far into the room. 'So, what happened?'

'I gave Leonora's diary to the Calverts. I thought it belonged to them. She'd sent it to Daphne.'

'Right.' She looked so still, almost like a paused television image, if it were not for the tension in her body: a condensed, humming stasis, extending up from her legs, her compressed arms, her thin, rigid shoulders, all the way into her eyes and mouth. She was waiting; listening so intently it was impossible to guess at her own thoughts.

'Nobody found a will. The only new evidence they have is the diary. There was a book missing, but we couldn't find it.'

'We?'

'I met the Calverts,' he said, knowing how cowardly and inadequate that was, but unable to explain it any other way. He couldn't give Lena away, so that was one lie that would have to go with him, riding on his shoulders like a child, holding on to his neck, intermittently kicking his chest with its heels.

'Right,' she said again. She still hadn't moved.

'I'm sorry, Kate. I thought it was the only thing to do. It's what Leonora wanted. I didn't have the right to get rid of it. And I don't know if it would prove anything anyway. It could be argued, like you said, that she ran away, that she wasn't telling her sister the truth and there wasn't ever a will.'

'I don't need your legal opinion,' Kate said. A flicker of strain in her voice. 'I'll talk about it with the solicitors.'

'You're going to fight it?'

She hesitated a moment, looking again as if she was trying to control her anger. 'I'm not going to let them have it when they've got no better claim on it than me. You want to know the truth? I almost wish a will *would* show up. I wouldn't fight it. I hate that house. Since it ended up on my hands, everything has gone to shit. Look at what it did to Aunt Delia. Look at *us*. It's like a curse, like Tutankhamun or something. It would probably serve the Calverts right if they did get it.'

'I understand,' he said, humbly. 'Kate, I do believe I did the right thing, but I know that I betrayed you by doing it. I don't expect you to forgive me.'

'Okay,' she said, looking down. It was hard to work out her tone.

'You can have the flat, for as long as you want.'

'What?'

'Or if you don't want it, that's fine too,' he said hurriedly. She was staring at him. 'I could just put it straight on the market. I don't want to live here anymore, and I guess you won't be in London for long. I'll do whatever you want, Kate. I know I owe you that.'

By the time he had finished talking, he was hardly aware of what he was saying; only how it had transformed her. She had put her hands up and pushed her hair away from her face; the effect was of barely restrained rage, fingers quivering just short of tearing. Her eyes were wide; her tan seemed wrong, as if beneath its colour the blood had retracted from the surface of her skin.

'You're *finishing* with me?' she said.

Oliver was startled. 'I . . . uh, well, I thought you didn't want to be with me. After everything I've done. Don't you want to break up?'

'No, Oliver,' she was high and loud now, 'I didn't want to break up. Jesus! I came in hoping things were going to be okay. I was angry, obviously, but I thought we could sort things out. I knew you wouldn't be able to get a job in New York immediately, or maybe you'd want to study or something, but we've got plenty of savings, and we could have made it work.'

'Oh.'

'And then I get back and you've already come to terms with the fact that it's over?'

There was a silence. Her eyes slowly narrowed as she followed her thoughts all the way along their most logical route. Then she said, 'I get it.'

Oliver waited in fearful expectancy.

'You don't like our relationship. You don't like our life. I don't think you really like *me*, but you'd never end it yourself. You just ruined everything and then you waited for me to kick you out. Now you look shocked that I'm not going to oblige. But I won't. Take some responsibility, Oliver! You don't want me. I'm not going to dump you and let you off the hook. Just bloody admit it. *Say* it.'

Even at first impact her accusations had the terrible ring of truth. He stood mutely, absorbing the force of it, as Kate, having apparently run out of energy, turned, laid her forehead against the wall, and sobbed.

'Kate, I'm sorry,'

He could hardly hear what she said, but he made out, again, 'Admit it.'

'You're right, I don't want us to be together. It's not that I don't like you. I think you're perfect. But I just don't . . . I don't think we're suited. I can't explain it. There's something wrong with me. Obviously. Not you.' He stopped, aware that he was descending into cliché. She was crying so painfully that he wanted to put his arms around her, but she must have sensed the beginnings of his move towards her, because she looked up with sudden hostility, and said, *'Don't.'*

He stopped, hands lifted like a criminal. 'I just wanted to . . . I don't know. I'm sorry.'

'Lena was wrong, you know,' she said, almost conversationally. 'You are a cunt.'

Then she cried again.

Oliver watched her helplessly. He went over his own words and found unexpected sense in them. He didn't want her, it was true; their relationship wasn't enough, though he wasn't sure why. When they first met, he had been so shocked at first that she would be interested in him, it would have seemed ungrateful to question their suitability. Later, as he got to know her, pursuing her like a unicorn across the coffee shops and cocktail bars of London, the romance of her neglected house and family feud and dead parents and – yes – her long blonde hair had given way to a woman, but one who was hardly less mythological. The real Kate might as well have been created by an upmarket women's magazine. She was kind, healthy, intelligent and beautiful. As was often the case, she only ever doubted the last of these. She exercised, she networked, she shopped savvily, styled herself and her home, asserted her needs and identified her goals and went to yoga twice a week. She wanted a career, a white wedding, and two children, in that order. Was it Oliver's fault that he hadn't quite believed in this Kate either; that on some level he had been waiting for something else to reveal itself? Yes, he answered himself. He had said to her once, on their second or third date, that she wasn't like other women. He thought this was a compliment, but she was dismayed. 'I'm not different,' she had said. 'I don't *want* to be different. I'm just a normal person.'

She was more than that. She *was* perfect: in the same way that a perfect computer-generated face is absolutely average. She was the platonic form, the flawless archetype of a normal person. She had been clear with him, but he hadn't listened. Perhaps it was his childhood love of secrets, his eagerness to believe in hidden histories, secret codes, buried treasure, but he had ignored what she told him – not just that day but in the months after, never quite accepting that what he saw was what he'd got – and now she really was suffering, in the way that he had only ever imagined her suffering, for being simply what she had always said she was.

PART SIX

CRETAN LAW UNDER MAMALAKIS

e∽

Oliver lay in an unfamiliar bed in the blue-and-white-painted guest room that used to be his childhood bedroom, staring at the brilliant white ceiling. His parents – ever pragmatic – had not left the room as a shrine to young Oliver, and he was trying to fill in its former details from memory: the rubbery line-up of dinosaurs, the row of books (treasure islands and lost pyramids, naturally), the trophies gathered on windy English beaches: fossils, shells, stones with squiggles or indentures that could, if he squinted hard enough, be some form of ancient script. Later this had all been cleared out; the dinosaurs taken to the charity shop, the stones thrown away, the poster of a monster peering over a jungle temple replaced by one of a girl as naked as his parents would allow her to be, which was not very. He saw his bedroom – his life – in layers of time; he examined the strata of his childhood, trying to work out at which point he had gone wrong. Perhaps the moment the dinosaurs left, in the back of his mother's car.

He shut his eyes and went back to the house in Oxford, the night of Lena's second visit. Darkness outside the windows, the inside of the glass all fire. The nymphs and the rearing horse almost moving in the rushing shadows. That moment had ceased to exist; its enchantment blinked out like a blown light bulb, yet the room still had a significance; a darkened reverse face. Something intimate had occurred, and now that it was over and its protagonists had fled the scene, the place could only stand as a reminder of the moment that could never be returned to. The thought that the house would come to mean other things to other people he found disturbing, like the idea of a stranger sleeping in his bed. He wondered, briefly, what Leonora would have thought if she could have looked in on her drawing room that night.

He didn't have any such feelings about the London flat. Not simply because its considered surfaces – its slick, impersonal air of a lobby in a luxury hotel – had never appealed to his own tastes, or that his presence had made so little impression on it that even when all his possessions were taken away it showed no sign of his erasure. It was more that it hadn't been the scene of any of his suddenly discovered passions, or the arrival of the new Oliver – wounded, dumbstruck, but awake – whom he now considered to be his essential self. He wondered if Kate felt the same about the place. She had only been there for three months, but it was so much hers that he hoped she would not identify it with the ending of their relationship; maybe, eventually, she would even see that transition as something fitting, restoring both the flat and Kate herself to their natural state. But then he supposed she would probably be in New York before that process could get under way.

His main feeling about their break-up, now that the initial pain had ebbed lower, and the recurring memory of her so upset was taking longer and longer to come round (hourly intervals, at the last count), was one of shame. As she had correctly identified, his own loss hadn't seemed to come into it. Over the last weeks, his love for Kate had been covered over by other things: guilt, evasion, worry, the unpleasant certainty that she was going to end the relationship. He had assumed that underneath those things he had still loved her; that if the clouds were all to clear away, the sun would still be in the sky, as simple and bright as it had always been. Then that happened and he found himself staring at a flat, vacated blue. He felt disbelief at this absence of love at the same time as recognising his own stupidity, not to have understood it sooner. The way he had started to unquestioningly think of her in the past tense, for example, as if she had already dumped him. He had assumed the decision would be devastating, but his numb acceptance of that supposed future devastation was suspicious in itself.

'Just go,' she had said to him, that day. He couldn't see her face. 'Or I'll go. I don't care which.'

'I'll go. I already got my stuff ready.'

'Of course,' she said, with a thin bitterness, too tired to gather itself into outrage. 'Of course you did.'

What were their last words? He couldn't remember. He knew that he had apologised again; that she brushed it off, which was the only possible response. There was no sense of understanding between them; just a long silence, in which the gathered emotional pressure cooled and dispersed. He went out of the door, wanting but knowing not to touch her, almost skulking by. The thought of his own exit, that hunched scuttle along the wall, made him wince with self-hatred. It was this shame that curled him, bringing his head into his chest and his hands up when he thought of her. He would have rolled into a ball if he could, like a woodlouse.

He supposed he had some self-knowledge at last: deep, precise, but not quite as rewarding as he had hoped. Ironic that his first real insight into himself came at a time when the view was the worst: familiar landmarks uprooted, dust rising from new tranches, scored earth and heaped brick. A yellow paper promised further development, but this was a long way off. He was dismayed to think of how he had spent his adult years so far. Flying under the radar; phoning it in. Kate had been right: he didn't like his life but he had gone along with it anyway; propping it up like a cinema standee, for the first strong wind to take away. He hadn't been unhappy with her, exactly: she had suffered only from a sudden and crashing comparison. He ought to have worked it out sooner, for her sake. Kate had been authentic; Oliver was the fraud, pretending to be the same as her. He had wasted her time, something she hadn't accused him of, but that would no doubt have occurred to her by now.

It had occurred to *him* that the best thing he could do – to in some way justify the clumsy trampling of his previous commitments – was to get on with something different. An idea of his new life hung in the distance, far off still, and hard to see, but giving off its own distinct light.

Picture an eccentric history professor, said Leonora. Picture a man with hair growing over his collar more by accident than design, a study walled with books, and a tweed coat; cherishing secret suspicions about Atlantis that he might confide in a few, favoured students; writing a book about Caligula, or Queen Zenobia. He is prone to gazing out of windows, and occasionally he loses his thread in a lecture, but the students don't mind. He's fond of red wine, which doesn't help. Sometimes he tells his students he used to have a good job in the City, earning a fortune, but he chucked it all in, stayed at his parents' place and worked in a bar; studied history as an undergrad. Nobody believes him.

He wanted, suddenly, to tell Lena that she had been right: to thank her for the Occam's razor with which she had pared down his future. Without knowing if he would actually call her, he got out of bed and looked for his phone. He found it in the bottom of one of his bags, blank-screened after a week of chirping hopelessly under a weight of socks. He plugged it in and went back through the accumulated voicemails and messages of the last few days, none of which were from her. This realisation sobered him, and he put the phone down. Without ever having expected her to call, he still felt disappointed. Unfair how that worked. Hope sneaks up and crouches behind you, then disappointment gives you a shove backwards.

He was reminded of his last day at work. He had known from his extensive experience of movies that he ought to feel an exhilarating, whooping triumph at his final victory over his tyrannical boss, but as he stood with head down and hands clenched in the long glass tube through which the lift made its slow descent, he felt a silence close over him instead; a horizonless moor, a windswept and desolate thing. He had felt the rightness of his decision, in the same way that he felt it was right for his relationship with Kate to end, but neither thing had brought him immediate joy or relief. He wondered if this was common to all people who found themselves without one single thing they didn't want, but not one single thing they did.

He *knew* what he wanted now, at least – at last – but the knowledge was painful to him. He wanted not just to study history but to do it at Oxford, to live in Leonora's house, to make a fire – he remembered how – and invite Lena over to scoff at it. The shadow of the flames would ripple over the blue walls like the warm currents under the sea. For the first time he had a dream; his vision of the future absolutely clear even if it was laughably impossible, if it had ended before it began. He wondered if by reading Leonora's history some black magic had occurred, a bargain or an exchange, and now he would have to share her fate. It was like a curse in a legend – to know one's greatest wish, then be forced to see it taken away.

Picture a middle-aged history professor. Every other Saturday morning he goes to the Ashmolean; has a coffee with his good friend Charlotte; speculates about the state of history today, and – sometimes – about their old friend Leonora. He never asks Charlotte about her daughter, though he thinks he saw her once, walking down the Broad, with two small boys in football socks.

Since the night he left the apartment he had not cried about the end of his relationship. But when he thought of Lena sitting beside him on the grass, holding her arms out to the sun, tears came into his eyes. Every single time.

In one of Oliver's dreams, he and Leonora were sitting in a bar at sunset, ordering drinks. The man who brought them was Ōta Dōkan. Oliver had never seen him before, and as a consequence, the Ōta Dōkan of his dream looked a lot like an old geography teacher he used to be fond of. Before he could drink, he found himself shuffled out of this scene, pushed past the frame, until he was watching Leonora alone on the screen, with a rising feeling of dread. In another dream he was running from a fiery house, knowing as he ran that this was not his dream, but Lena's, which – even in his dream – struck him as pretty unfair.

It was after one of these dreams that he went downstairs and stood in the kitchen with a glass of water, looking out at the orderly rows of houses, large gardens filled with bird tables and greenhouses and trampolines, a civilised veneration of the outdoors. It was too early to be up and too late to bother going back to sleep. The too-soft bed had made him ache; he rolled his shoulders, tried to stretch out his back. He thought it was fitting: waking up at last, but paying the price of having slept too long in the same position.

He wished he'd had a chance to read Leonora's history again. There were things that bothered him about it, and not only because it had been painful to give it up, feeling a flinch of loss as it passed to the Calverts. He was still confused by Leonora's apparent decision to hide her will in a book, leaving it exposed to chance – loss and damage and discovery – when she had constructed every other element of her story so carefully, even to the extent of disguising her identity to the casual reader. The apparent non-existence of the book itself also troubled him. Not one search result. That seemed unlikely. If she hadn't left the books to Daphne, he might have suspected her of playing some kind of joke; making a point about the nature of historical research, or something. But he knew she wanted Daphne to have the house. Nothing made sense otherwise.

He typed Mamalakis into his phone and waited in the kitchen as the pages loaded. The white light from the screen stretched over the dim, angular shapes of the room. A wheel spun. The same search results as before came up: people and companies. But even if the book couldn't be found, surely he ought to be able to find some evidence of the king that ancient Crete had supposedly been under. He felt strongly that he was missing something. He wished he could have the history now. What had Leonora said to Daphne? Something about everything in a history being relevant. Asking different questions.

He looked through the results again, and again, staring at them until, like a Magic Eye picture, one entry slowly took form, standing out from the others. Mamalakis. A Greek law firm. Established in the late 1800s. From the translated page – its sense broken up and rearranged like a Rubik's Cube – he saw that there were branches in Athens, Thessaloniki and Crete. He clicked on the last one, waiting for his phone to take him helpfully to a map of the location. The little pin dropped neatly down, about halfway along Koroneou Street.

He almost laughed; it seemed so obvious now. It had been the only book with an author. O. N. Koroneou: on Koroneou. Not an author, but a joke, just as *Cretan Law Under Mamalakis* wasn't a book but the location of the will; the endpoint of the game Leonora was playing with her niece, leading her to her inheritance. She had sent the will to a place that meant something to her, presumably so that Daphne would go there; that one of them, at least, would see it. She had talked Daphne through a labyrinth, all around the complex path, towards the only possible ending.

He sat down at the kitchen table, unable to do anything but wait for the dawn to hurry up and dawn. Previously he had enjoyed being alone with Leonora's writing, being the only reader. Now he could only think of calling Lena. He knew she got up early to look after the birds, but he wasn't sure how early. The cat-shaped kitchen clock's tail swung back and forth.

He watched it feverishly. At half past six, the light a pale grey over the fences beyond the window, he rang her. She didn't answer. After half an hour he tried again. The third time the call rang out, he realised she was ignoring him. The fourth time, her phone was switched off.

He sat and clattered his hands against the table in a faulty tribal rhythm. The sun was up now – a frosty white disc in the battleship-coloured clouds – and he could hear his parents getting up too; a mysterious process he had never heard as a teenager. The boards creaked; a loo flushed. His father sneezed. In Greece, it was half past nine.

As he had expected, the woman who answered the telephone at the Cretan branch of Mamalakis spoke in Greek.

'*Kalispera*,' he said. 'Do you speak English?'

Somehow he had not expected the answer to this to be no. The woman continued in Greek. She seemed to be trying to make something clear to him.

'No Greek,' Oliver said. '*Signomi*. English?'

'English, yes,' the woman said, and explained something in Greek.

'*Signomi*,' said Oliver. 'I don't understand. *Signomi*.'

'Sorry!' said the woman, and hung up.

Oliver got up and poured himself a bowl of cereal. He ate a few mouthfuls then fell to stirring it meditatively. He was still doing this when his parents came down.

'I'm going to go to Heraklion for a long weekend,' he told them. 'I thought I could do with a break.'

His mother was alarmed. 'Oliver . . . really? When did you decide this? Why there? Do you know people there? Where would you be staying? Isn't it very short notice? I mean, it's nice to get away, and you've been very stressed, but why such a rush? Are you all right? You don't seem yourself. When did you get up? Did you sleep?'

His father, not hearing him properly, or thinking that Heraklion was a local attraction, nodded. 'Good, good,' he said, saluting Oliver with his spoon. 'Great fun.'

'What about your job?' Oliver's mother continued.

Oliver hadn't actually told his parents about his quitting, having decided to deliver one shock at a time in as gentle a drip-feed as possible. But he was out of time and simply said, 'I quit that.'

Oliver's father put his spoon down. It dinked loudly in the silence.

'I know this is going to worry you,' Oliver carried on, hurriedly, 'but I haven't been happy there. I want to study history instead. You remember how I wanted to do that before? Well, I should have done it. I want to be a historian. I got a good job but I hated it and I was exhausted and I nearly got sacked because I was tired and wasn't paying attention and fucked up, excuse the language. It's nothing to do with how it ended with Kate, I'm not having a breakdown, and it's not a phase. And you mustn't worry about how I'm going to fund my study; I've got savings. And the money from the sale of the flat. So I won't starve. That's not to say I'll ever be rich, obviously. But that's okay with me.'

Having thus answered all the things he thought his parents might ask, he sat back and eyed them both warily.

There was a short, painful silence, in which his mother's eyes filled with tears. Then she cried, 'Oh, Oliver! This is my fault.'

'What? How?'

'I feel terrible. I pushed you into doing something you didn't want to do. It was only that I worried . . . you being an only child and everything . . . still, I worried too much.'

'I always said that, didn't I?' his father said. 'That you worried too much.'

'Thank you, Bernard,' his mother snapped. 'You were the one who said he was a daydreamer and ought to do a decent day's work.'

'I don't think we need to go into all this now,' Oliver said. 'It's not a matter of blame. The important thing is that I know what I want to do. At last. First I'm going to make myself another bowl of cereal. Then I'm going to get on with it.'

Two days later, no call from Lena, and Oliver was stepping out of a plane on to the tarmac, looking up at the sky in unison with all the other tourists, as if arriving at the end of a devotional pilgrimage to pay their respects to the sun. Heat rose stickily from the asphalt, glowering in the cloudless sky. It was only a short drive from there to Heraklion itself, a scrappy, dusty settlement strung all over with telephone wires and bougainvillea, facing the magnificent sea. The city drew in closer and closer towards the centre, as if gathering itself inward. Tourists collected at the Morosini fountain, cars bunched in the roads, narrow shops were crammed down narrow streets, edged with bright lines of mopeds.

Oliver had rented a small apartment in the Old Town, a functional space with a tiled white cupboard for a bathroom, a foldaway bed and an afterthought of a kitchen in one corner, dominated by a humming, leaking fridge. Voile was pinned over the windows but a few flies frequented the old plaster ceiling, dodging in and out of the unmoving wings of the fan. He opened the shutters and looked out on to a small oleander-planted courtyard. A stray cat was asleep between two large urns. Palms flickered in tatters in the faint breeze off the sea. Just beyond, in the street, a man was selling watermelons from the back of a pick-up. Oliver went out and bought one, sawed it up with a small dinner knife and ate it sitting by the window. He felt inexplicably happy. Then he changed out of his clothes, which were covered in watermelon seeds, and walked through the noisy streets to the offices of Mamalakis Law.

His conversation with the receptionist, a middle-aged blonde woman with newly drawn eyebrows, was so similar to his phone call that they both gave each other an odd look. This time, however, she was heading for the door as she said, 'Sorry.' When she got to it, she put her head around it and called, 'Prokopis! Prokopis!'

'Sorry!' she said again, turning back to him. Oliver smiled at her, bemused. She smiled back and went through the door, leaving him alone.

Oliver was beginning to feel slightly stupid. He had flown over here in a surge of rightness, an armoured certainty, because he was sure he had worked out Leonora's secret message – and still with the irrational sense that she was somehow thinking of *him* – but now that he was standing in this small office, with a rubber plant and a water cooler with a sign on it in Greek that he already knew translated to 'PLEASE be considerate to others and throw used cups into the BIN' and the receptionist's coffee steaming gently on the desk, he wasn't so sure.

He was trying to get an internet signal to find out whether

Prokopis was a name or if it meant something quite specific, like 'Security', when an older man came in, followed by the secretary.

'Hello,' he said. 'I apologise: Renata does not speak English. I am Prokopis Vassis. May I help you with something?' His voice came as if from a distance, grainy as an old radio. He had an extraordinarily lavish amount of white hair, standing up from his forehead, gathered in clusters above his eyes, a bristling in his ears and nose.

Renata sat back down and smiled at him again.

'This is quite strange,' Oliver said, after introducing himself. 'But I'm looking for a will. I think it might have been, er, held in trust here. Or something. It's an old will from the 1920s. Under the name of Leonora Castle. I think the circumstances might be a bit unusual . . . I was hoping it might be on file somewhere.'

'Are you a relative of this person?'

'No. I suppose I represent her descendants.'

'You are a lawyer?'

'No. Just a family friend.'

'We do not represent a big amount of English clients here, Mr Mittell. And so I can tell you that there is nobody of that name with our practice.'

'Leonora Calvert, perhaps.'

Mr Vassis shook his head, but he was looking so blank, almost deliberately neutral, that Oliver had the distinct impression that Mr Vassis knew what he was talking about. There was a silence as Oliver stared at him, puzzled.

Eventually Mr Vassis prompted: 'May this person you wish to locate go by another name?'

'Not . . . Sophia Louis?'

At this Renata looked up, her calligraphic eyebrows arched beyond all plausibility.

'Ah,' Mr Vassis said. 'You will please follow me?' He indicated the doorway.

They sat in a small office with the air conditioning turned up so high that waves of chilled air broke across the back of Oliver's neck. The hair on his arms lifted, though whether this was the cold or the strangeness of the situation he couldn't say.

'Do you have any identification?' Mr Vassis asked.

'Er, I have my driver's licence. My passport is back at my flat.'

'I ask you please to excuse me, but may I take a copy of this? For our records.'

Oliver wondered what on earth was going on, and yet there was something so innocently earnest about Mr Vassis, and even his office, with its carpet in swirls of blue and red, and dark fake-wood cabinetry, that he nodded, and handed the licence over. Mr Vassis thanked him and went out with it. He was gone for what seemed like a little while. Oliver tried and failed again to get a signal on his phone, finally resorting to waving it around his head in figures of eight, like a child with a toy aeroplane.

There was a flurry of Greek in the corridor outside, and then a young man came in. He looked at Oliver with unconcealed curiosity, before offering him a drink.

'No thank you,' Oliver said, and the young man nodded and left. Oliver, facing the window and not the corridor behind, was acutely aware that people seemed to be passing the office frequently – too frequently for a five-person law firm on a Thursday afternoon. He had a strong suspicion that they were looking in at him as they went by, and wished he could turn his chair around; lessen in a small way his evident disadvantage.

Eventually Mr Vassis came back, with the driver's licence and a beige file.

'Here is the will,' he said.

Oliver, staring at it stupidly, didn't reply. He was too shocked at the suddenness of it. He wasn't sure what he had expected to have to go through to get hold of it: lengthy arguments, running up and down flights of stairs, banging on doors, the acquisition and recital of secret codes, professors dragged out of retirement, initiation into various esoteric cults. But this all just seemed too simple. Even when Mr Vassis removed the papers from the file and pushed them encouragingly across the desk towards him, he didn't immediately reach out to take them, in case it was a trick.

'This is Leonora's will?' he asked. 'Sophia's will?'

'Yes,' Mr Vassis said. He sat back and smiled at Oliver expectantly. 'I am sorry for the delay. I do not know the usual procedures for dealing with a case of this sort.'

'That makes two of us,' Oliver said. Mr Vassis looked confused. 'Can I . . .?'

'Of course.'

Oliver picked up the will. It was a long document, and he realised he had no idea what he was reading. A pressure was building behind his eyes. He could hardly focus. He turned blindly to the last page, and gazed at Leonora's circuitous signature. She had signed as Leonora Castle.

'Would you like me to summarise?' Mr Vassis said.

Oliver nodded.

'You will inherit the Oxford house, and all contents belonging to Leonora Castle. None of the Greek assets are to be included in this bequest. None of Dr Strickland's assets are included.'

'What?'

Mr Vassis seemed equally mystified. 'Do you not know the details of this? You came to get the will. You did not know the will?'

'I have absolutely no idea what's going on. Who is Dr Strickland? Why did you call her Sophia Louis? What do you mean, *I'll* inherit the house?' Through the odd physical reactions he was undergoing – a collision of the air conditioning with the rising pressure that seemed to be slowly cooking him from the inside out, his skin a narrow boundary between two warring states, coated in a film of sweat that instantly cooled to freezing – he realised he sounded uncannily like his mother.

'Are you well, Mr Mittell?'

'I'm fine. I just don't understand.'

'Mrs Strickland left very specific instructions with this practice. Very complicated to put on to paper, but we did it.' (A hint, here, of professional pride.) 'She said that the first person who asked for her here, under the name of Sophia Louis, would be the beneficiary of the will. This person is you.'

'Mrs Strickland is Leonora? How did she manage to organise all of this? What about Daphne? Is this a joke?'

He had spoken too quickly, and Mr Vassis, whose English was ponderous, blinked and answered his final question.

'It is not a joke.'

'Please – what is going on? Why did you say Mrs Strickland? Why isn't Daphne in the will?'

'I apologise: I called her Mrs Strickland out of habit. Daphne is . . . her niece, yes? Mrs . . . Leonora's original will did leave

her estate to Daphne. It was some years later that she changed
it. Many years later. She also added a letter, intended for her
heir, which is to say, you.' He indicated an envelope that Oliver
had not noticed until now.

A silence.

'Are you well?' Mr Vassis asked again. 'Were you offered a
drink?'

Oliver had never been concussed, and so couldn't make a
comparison, but he imagined it would feel like he did at that
moment. The carpet reeled in and out; the air conditioning
sang in his ears, gaily battering him. He heard Mr Vassis's softly
textured voice asking if he wanted a glass of water, and he
nodded.

By the time Mr Vassis came back in, Oliver had collected
himself enough to speak, if not to understand.

'I'm sorry,' he said. 'But please can you explain everything
to me. Everything about Leonora.'

'Of course,' Mr Vassis said, and now he looked pleased;
almost eager. 'I can tell you, this will has been quite a legend
at our practice. For years we have not thought anybody would
claim it. It is very strange now that you are here. I found this
story very interesting when I came to work here for Mr
Demetrios Mamalakis, who is now sadly with God.' Here his
eyes went respectfully towards the ceiling; Oliver – whose
comprehension was labouring under a slight time delay –
almost glanced up too. 'Mr Mamalakis came to us from Oxford
University. His parents owned the company at that time. A
very important family, and they all lived in Athens, of course.
But Demetrios Mamalakis was not so interested in working in
Athens, which was a bigger business – more successful. He
liked the sea here, and the peace. And his dear friend Dr

Anthony Strickland was also coming to Crete with Leonora, and they were all good friends who did not want to be parted.'

Anthony Strickland must have been Christopher Konig. Mamalakis must have been Christopher's Greek housemate. Oliver couldn't remember what he had been called in Sophia's history. Probably another made-up name, another joke of hers.

'But Leo . . . Soph . . . Leonora? How did she come here?'

'She arrived with Dr Strickland at that time, as his wife. Though they were not in fact husband and wife, but nobody knew this information. I only heard of it myself when she changed her will. Previous to that, Mr Mamalakis handled their affairs. I do not know those details; I do not know why the name Sophia Louis. Perhaps this will be explained in her letter. I took over her business when Mr Mamalakis died, and a short time after that she asked for her will to be rewritten. She was an old woman then. At that time she asked for Daphne to be removed, and we drew up the will you find here. I tried to ask, in a polite way, about Daphne, and if she understood that nobody in England would be notified of her death, but she was sad then. She didn't want to talk about that. She said it was not important that anybody be told. She just explained very precisely that we were to give the Oxford estate to the first person who asked after Sophia Louis, and I trust this is exactly what we have done, in the way she wanted.'

'You met her,' Oliver said. 'You knew her. What was she like?'

Mr Vassis smiled. His eyes moved off and upwards, as if the past were displayed high in a corner, like a hotel room television. 'After we had drawn up the will, Mrs Strickland joined me to drink a glass of retsina. She was not sad by then. I remember she told me, "I would like to see into the future, Prokopis. I would like to see who might come." She was a very graceful and happy woman. Even when she was old. I didn't think of it as so special when I was young, but now I am old I would like to know how to be like her. Mamalakis said that she had the art of happiness. She was like a ballet dancer or a composer at the top of their power. She did it so beautifully that it was always a pleasure to see. Mamalakis said that true happiness was true wisdom, and there is not one without the other. I liked that because Sophia – as you may know – means wisdom, in Greek.'

Oliver was still a little way back, paddling desperately. 'So, Leonora and Anthony lived here their whole lives?'

'Not in Heraklion. They had a villa near the sea. It was a beautiful house. It is a hotel now. Dr and Mrs Strickland wanted their property here sold and all their money to go to a charity for children of poor families. They did a lot of work for this charity. They did not adopt children and I believe this was only because of the difficulty of the two not being married. They looked after many children though, particularly in the war, and in the hard years after. They gave them a lot. They never cared about money themselves.'

'What did they do, the Stricklands? While they were here?'

'They did many things. Many great things for this island,' Mr Vassis said proudly. 'Even in their retirement time they had a company that took the tourists to Knossos. Dr Strickland did a little work, early in his arrival, with Dr Arthur Evans at Knossos. That was before the war came. After that, all work such as this stopped, and Dr Strickland helped his friend John Pendlebury in the preparations for the defence of Crete. John Pendlebury died in the invasion – a hero – and

Dr Strickland survived and continued to work with the resistance. Mrs Strickland left their house and the Germans occupied it. She and Athena Mamalakis spent the war years also working for the resistance. Mrs Strickland had to pretend to be Greek in that time. When the German rule ended, the two women joined the Red Cross. They were very well known in Heraklion and the villages. Many people had stories about them and Dr Strickland. After the war, Dr Strickland published several books. He told everybody that his wife was his editor and had written parts of the books too. But she said her name should not be on the covers, because she was not a doctor. They both went to Santorini, when the Akrotiri ruins were discovered there – they wrote about that place too. I have been told the books are very well respected. But this' – he slid the letter over to Oliver – 'will surely contain more information.'

'She went to Santorini,' Oliver said. He took the letter and gazed at it. He was deeply moved. Perhaps because of his difficulty in comprehending what Mr Vassis was telling him, this final news struck him hardest. His eyes filled with tears and he laughed, a surprised laugh that kept reeling out of him, as if he was being gradually unwound but couldn't stop it, and after a moment Mr Vassis laughed, though he watched Oliver too, peering surreptitiously out over the top of his own broad smile, looking confused, and uncertain, but wanting to be part of the fun, to master the art of happiness – as if Oliver, as Sophia's pupil and heir, represented an unexpected opportunity, his last chance of doing so.

Oliver spent the next day trying to do what he thought Leonora would have wanted him to do, which, given the startling new Leonora he had so recently been confronted with, hadn't been a simple task. By the late afternoon he was in a hire car on the way to the last stop on his hastily decided, randomly ordered to-do list; on which even the last stop did not – now that he was on his way there – feel quite as much like the natural last stop as it had early that morning.

He had opened all the windows to allow the air to whip and billow through the car; the sea on one side, the mountains on the other, each growing and shrinking in turn as the car wound through the island roads. The land seemed starkly unclothed; the bald mountainsides speckled with small, stubby trees, rocky outcrops and olive groves. In the distance they merged into a perspectiveless pointillist layering of gritty ochres. He passed goats grazing desultorily by the side of the road, white-painted roadside shrines, unfinished houses with their steel rods jutting jarringly into the glossy blue sky. Whenever the car slowed, the sound of cicadas rose up, along with the waft of petrol fumes, the salt wind carried off the surface of the sea.

He was tired. He hadn't slept last night, though his memories of those restless hours were as if he had dreamt them; surreal and fragmentary. Late at night he heard a woman in an apartment not far away singing something unidentifiable. The sound ended in a smatter of laughter, a closed door. After that the usual noise of the city seemed to well up again; a continual traffic, a distant chorus of human voices, none of it ever seeming to pass close enough to be distinguishable. The fridge in the corner chattered and squealed above it all, making a range of noises so extraordinary that he eventually got up and opened the door to check that there wasn't a

Siamese cat trapped inside. This morning he had felt sleepless but clear-headed, brimming with an unearthly lucid energy that he knew would – at some point in the day – abruptly run out. He was aware that his reserves were empty, but he couldn't feel it. He recognised the feeling from the brief coke phase he'd gone through after university, which in turn always reminded him of a cartoon character running off a cliff edge into thin air, grinning and buoyant, legs powering along, until its momentum inevitably ran out, and it plummeted towards the rocks.

He still didn't have a clear sense of how he felt. Only shock, so far. There was a queue of strange and impossible things that he had yet to get his head around; the first being understanding what on earth Leonora had done – the spell she had worked, the unwritten history she had escaped into, like Alice passing through the looking glass. He hadn't yet been able to think about everything as a whole; instead he had tried to divide up the revelations; consider them piece by piece. He had spent most of the night doing this, rereading Leonora's letter, reading it again and again, until he could almost see the lines – typed this time, with her signature at the end – scrolling upwards whenever he closed his eyes.

My dear reader! she had begun, and Oliver, first reading in Mr Vassis's office, had felt her return as if it was something physical. Mr Vassis seemed to understand his expression, and left the office on the pretext of hunting out some old photos to show him.

My dear reader!
So here you are, at long last. I'm really, truly sorry that I am not able to meet you in person – face to face, like I once

promised – but I do at least have a genuine excuse, that of death, which has most inconveniently prevented many other interesting tête-à-têtes (Catherine the Great and Voltaire; Gandhi and Tolstoy – Hitler and Stalin, even) and has made no exception for us. This is all the more vexing given that our meeting was to be my only opportunity to discover your identity. I wrote my history in the belief that I knew my reader, but as it turned out, I was wrong. So now we are in the strange position of you knowing me – rather intimately, in fact – while I have absolutely no clue about you.

And yet . . . I do know one or two things. I know that you are the kind of person who would read my history to the end, and so I know that you are curious, and sympathetic – by which I mean you possess a genuine understanding of the inexplicable and irrational goings-on of the human heart. Otherwise you should have read no more than a few pages before you swore and chucked the whole thing into the bin. I know, too, that you worked out where to find me, which means you are observant, and thoughtful. Finally I know that you are the sort of person who would come to find me, and so I know that you are decisive, and enterprising. So in a way I have got to know you, and you mustn't think it at all premature when I say I'm very glad to meet you.

It is a shame that you will never meet Anthony, whose acquaintance you have already made, in a roundabout way. Neither will you meet our noble Pheugo – or Mamalakis, as he is known in these parts. Perhaps . . . perhaps you knew Daphne. If so, I envy you. Some relatives of Mamalakis's living in England were so kind as to keep an eye on her over the years that we were apart. I didn't trust everything to fate, you know. If she had not found my history and read it; got to know her aunt; picked up the clues that had been laid for her; forgiven me for playing games; recognised the need for caution; and finally come to me quietly, secretly, I should have found another way of sending a message. I was patient: I thought I would have plenty of time to find her. But the Second World War cut off my means of correspondence, and by the time it ended and the dust had begun to settle, she had been dead for two years. After that, I didn't ask for news of my family, or the Oxford house, or my home country. Daphne died, and Tom did not, and that was the end of England for me.

And yet. The house has found its way into my thoughts, often at the oddest times. I have walked in a pine forest with the light sliced into neat lines, combed by the needles, a deep, dark green scent rising all around me and a softly crackling carpet under my feet, and remembered the light stealing through the leaves of the apple tree, and the creak of the wisteria like a woman sighing. On the deck of a boat crossing the Aegean I thought of the white curtains of the drawing room flying against the blue, stiff as sails. In the dark basement of a house, the disrupted rhythm of German boots passing back and forth above us, I heard – uncannily clear – the notes of the old piano, my mother's distinct hand on the keys. Have you an idea of that feeling? I believe you must. It isn't only a house, to me, or to you. In fact, you might be the only person in the world who understands its innermost thoughts; the queer pull of it, now that I am gone.

It occurs to me that I ought to write some handover notes to you: the new custodian of the house. Have you seen the Georgian wallpaper in my old bedroom? Perhaps the birds of paradise are gone by now. If not, it might interest you to know that the traders of the sixteenth century first brought specimens of these birds into Europe from the south-west Pacific without their wings or feet; these having been removed by the native traders. As a consequence, it was widely thought that the birds could neither fly nor land, instead floating on currents of air, carried by their plumes. (I suppose native traders must amuse themselves somehow.) In all the confusion about their true nature, the birds were even briefly mistaken for the legendary phoenix itself. Sometimes I wonder if it was during those childhood mornings lying in bed, half dozing, contemplating those mysterious birds that populated my room, that my long-held opinions about the unknowability of history and the uncertainty of evidence were formed.

Anyway, I digress. I ought to let you come up with your own thoughts about the birds, particularly as they are yours now. Back to the notes. If you haven't done so already, you really ought to pull up the black-and-white floor in the hall to uncover the original tiles, which are still underneath. You might also consider coming up with your own name and history for the horse on the fireplace, which has been too long without an owner. And – now I think of it – if you find yourself in front of the fireplace, you might as well go to the side nearest the window, where there is a gap between the stone and the wall (about half a centimetre at its widest point), into which you can slide a hook or a wire of some sort and with it fish around, until you are able to pull out a copy of my will. This was the copy Tom and I kept at home (the other being retained by the delightful Miles Wilcox). I thought it prudent to stash it in a safe location when Tom began acting so unpredictably. That way if something should, by chance, happen to Miles's copy, my original intentions should still be preserved. You might well find it useful.

What else, my dear reader? I close my eyes and strain to catch your voice, which is far off as yet, and indistinct. I try to anticipate your questions. Perhaps you are wondering about things that were not spoken, or written. Perhaps you suspect me of withholding them on principle. But I have changed a little since we last met. I've softened, like an old apple, and am inclined to fill in a few gaps. More than this, I find I need to justify myself; I find – curiouser and curiouser – that I'd like my reader's good opinion.

I worry that you think me awfully callous, leaving so many people behind without a second thought. The truth is that I deliberated about it for a long time, in those last months of isolation; reading, writing my letters, writing my history. I was not so determined or single-minded as you might think. Even up until the final days of buying tickets and choosing a meeting place, I felt guiltily divided between obligation and longing. Then Tom caught me out, and I had to jump, and not look back. Have you ever tried skydiving? (If not, you really must: it is utterly exhilarating.) I did it once in the sport's early days (not my early days: I was an old crone by then), when almost anyone could get chatting to a pilot one night over a couple of retsinas, and throw themselves out of a plane the next morning. My friend Athena went before me but stopped at the last moment, paralysed with fear. The fellow she was attached to made the decision for them. He went forward, giving her a little push, and she was carried with him. She liked it in the end.

I didn't need a push: I was done with dithering.

To get back to the point, that last visit to Anthony was the first time we had risked meeting in person since we had made the decision to shuck off our friendship, which had got rather confining, and become lovers. Funny sort of lovers, you might think, but we had to be patient. That day I had not trusted the post and taken him my last set of instructions inside a book. When I saw Tom outside, with the expression that still disturbs me now when I think of it – like a thorough chill that takes a long time to leave, lingering in the vital organs – all my indecision left me. He might as well have been a burning bush, or a pillar of cloud. I knew that if I stayed he would end up killing me, or Anthony, or himself, or some horrifying combination of the three.

I don't expect that he has come to see it the same way I do, but really my leaving was a blessing to him. I waved a wand and made the object of all his fear and jealousy disappear, and in doing so I really believe I saved him from doing something terrible. As I walked up the Harwich ferry's gangway (if never the aisle) with Anthony, the choppy English water snapping below us, absurd images came to mind of what Tom might do with his new lease of life. I saw him doing calisthenics, joining a kite-flying society, practising the tuba. I put my hand to my mouth, and Anthony misinterpreted the gesture and squeezed my other hand comfortingly. I have no idea whether Tom ever really took up any of these things, or anything else, but I like to imagine he did.

Did you ever know Annabel? I wonder. My own Anna-Bellina, Anna Bolena. Boll, poor Boll. I don't feel so very bad about leaving her in ignorance. In my own private accountings I have marked us down as quits. Nothing paid, nothing owed. She is a remarkably resilient woman, and her ability to tell a story and make it true, even to herself, always surpassed mine. I was confident she would come up with something to excuse herself. Really I had forgiven her even before I left. I wondered, uncom-

fortably, how much of her bad behaviour was simply an effort to secure her own recognition: the position of good girl already having been filled. I had always thought her a shallow hedonist; my mother liked to say that her sense had got lost under the apple tree; even the love of her life neglected her. No wonder, really, that she turned out the way she did.

I do feel badly about Mrs Boxall and Margaret – especially Margaret – but I simply couldn't risk telling them. A year or so after I left, I sent them both some money anonymously, which must be a source of ongoing bemusement. That is something you could do for me, dear reader, if you don't mind. If they are still alive, please do tell them I'm not dead – by which I mean not dead right now, though I will be by the time you read this – and I'm awfully sorry for all the trouble.

My dear, curious reader, by now you are probably wondering what sort of life I escaped to. You might demand – slightly impatiently, and quite understandably – 'Well, Sophia, are you happy now?'

It is with relief that I can answer you honestly. I recall I was rather given to bemoaning my lot when we first met. I once complained, I think, about not having my share of love. Now I have a surfeit. I do not have Daphne, of course. She is my deepest regret: the single dark spot in a blue sky. But it is always a blue sky, wide and cornerless, depthless; a ceiling that can never be reached. One might fly in it with one's eyes closed and arms out, the wind stirring one's skin, the sun gentle on one's eyelids, knowing oneself in no danger, no possibility of harm.

As for the detail . . . I confess I've little patience for appendices, or lengthy biographical notes. Human truth is the thing: remember, dear reader? Mr Vassis can tell you the rest. Anthony fulfilled his ambition to work with Arthur Evans, a promising alliance that stopped being promising after a few months, and stopped being an alliance a few months after that. The situation wasn't helped by Anthony writing a paper arguing that Evans should not have gone so far with his reconstruction of Knossos. At that time Evans was busy reconstituting the palace according to what he insisted was its original design, but which Anthony called 'self-indulgent fantasy'. Evans was short-tempered but just as quickly forgiving; even so, the friendship between the two men did not survive the paper's publication, and things became rather awkward for a time among our small group of English expats.

Anthony's and my friendship with Evans's new assistant, John Pendlebury, and his wife, Hilda, fared better, based as it was on a shared love of Crete, hiking, and bitching about Evans. Pendlebury was a good mimic: we created a character named Mrs Arthur Simmonds, stumping preposterously about whichever room she was in, waving a cane, ordering frescoes and singing obscene mantinades. Hard to believe that decades separate me from that time. How time slips and slides. The Pendlebury I remember, raising a glass of whisky with a rueful tip of the head, as if to deny responsibility, his good eye lit by the candles that drew the moths in a dizzying orbit, as if dancing with us, seems like a moment ago. In reality he died in the summer of 1941. He was recuperating from injuries in a cottage in the countryside when the Germans found him, took him outside and shot him.

I never thought we would see another war like the Great War, much less be a part of it. We lost many friends. Those years were our darkest, and I prefer not to dwell on them. They have been described well enough by others, the facts laid down *for future generations to guess at the feeling. I prefer to remember other times: the first time I swam in the Aegean, my first visit to Knossos, the first time I woke up with Anthony beside me – the first time in years that I had shared a bed with anyone else – and jumped out of my skin. The first time I looked out over the dig at Santorini, crying foolishly over the prescient Minoans, who packed up and evacuated before the lava reached them.*

My dear reader, before you hurry back to your Oxford house, you really must visit Santorini. And see the rest of the island. The Minotaur's labyrinth at Knossos; the bottomless lake Voulismeni at Agios Nikolaos, in which Athena bathed; the Psychro Cave, site of Zeus's birth. (You may notice that nobody here is very good at separating myth from history, fact from feeling.)

That is all I'd really have to tell you, if we had been able to meet in person. Picture my bony hand setting down its coffee, earnestly clutching your arm; picture yourself humouring an old woman. 'See Crete. Visit Santorini,' she commands. 'And be happy.' Then she releases you, having no better advice, and nothing else left to say.

After Oliver had read the letter for the last time that day, he went to the nearest post office, at which he mailed copies of Leonora's will and her letter to Charlotte's house. He had wanted to call Lena, or to write to her personally, but he understood the meaning of her silence. She didn't want to be contacted by him.

After he'd posted the letter – with an odd sense of giving up his ending, sending it out into the world, in which it would go on to live its own life without him – he thought of the last time he had seen her. Crying; still beautiful; though not as beautiful as she'd looked leaning back with one elbow on the grass, glancing at him with a slow, unwilling amusement.

He felt as if rather than the two of them reaching a natural conclusion, something wrong had happened instead, leaving a fault line, a tear in the landscape behind him, so that when he tried to look back across it to the other side – where he knew there was sunshine greenly vivid on the grass, a bird wheeling in the spotless sky above them – he couldn't see across the wide black line of her silence. She seemed very far away now; it was her and not Leonora who felt like years ago. He considered his feelings with the melancholy objectivity of distance, and thought that if he couldn't have love, he might have got – perhaps – a better understanding of what love ought to be. He supposed that he had learned a lot from the experience, a concept he found annoying, because he had wanted Lena, not a fucking lesson about life.

In his letter he tried to explain to the Calverts as simply as he could (which was not very) what had happened in Crete. He told them he would give them the Oxford house. He had, at a late hour of the night, felt more than a small inkling of possessiveness; the distinct temptation to just keep it, but he knew he couldn't have done that, any more then he could have given it to Kate. He had an increasingly clear vision of what Leonora would want to happen. He believed she would have liked Lena, and Charlotte, and the Godwins he hadn't met (and wouldn't meet): the father off on his holiday, the meditative brother. It wasn't just that they were the only ones who seemed to care that Leonora's supposed death had been ignored, its perpetrator in the clear. It was an idea he had of them all gathered together: their easy, faintly combative closeness. Amid the eye-rollings and the casual give and take of offence, a simple enthusiasm for each other. Leonora had run away from everything to have a chance at that everyday sort of happiness. Now it could be reintroduced to her house, like a family of wolves airlifted into a denuded Scottish forest.

Oliver hadn't reported everything that Mr Vassis had said to him that day. He told the Godwins, briefly, that the new will ought to be legally binding, because Tom and Miles Wilcox had committed fraud by destroying the original one and having Leonora declared dead, and that the existence of the hidden will would prove this. If he ever saw them again, he would tell them the rest of what Mr Vassis had explained: about the limitation period for taking legal action after the discovery of a fraud, a ruling that would not be applicable in this instance, because Leonora's letter clearly showed that she had no idea that her will had been destroyed or that she had been declared dead.

'That's pretty lucky,' Oliver had said. 'That she didn't realise.'

'Perhaps. Speaking off the record, a woman as resourceful as Leonora might take care not to give that knowledge away, if she had it. With information on the legality of her position, she might even take steps to demonstrate her ignorance. You understand me?'

'Oh. Yes. Perfectly.'

In his letter, Oliver had simply reiterated his own opinion that now the will had been found, its wishes wouldn't be contested. He had said as much to Mr Vassis, who raised his eyebrows.

'Are you sure of that? When large sums of money are involved, people can behave unexpectedly.'

'No . . . I know this person isn't like that. Though she might seem that way, if you didn't know her well. She'd always do what was right. And the other side of the family – they weren't after the money either. Everyone was just arguing over what was right.'

'Then that is very unusual,' Mr Vassis said.

'Yeah – in an otherwise perfectly normal inheritance dispute,' Oliver said, and after a little pause, the slow progress of meaning from one language to another, Mr Vassis laughed.

In the letter he had enclosed a copy of a photograph. He had another in his breast pocket, occupying the sheltered spot once reserved for Leonora's history. A black-and-white image, taken in the early thirties: Leonora and Anthony on the beach. Leonora's hair was short by then; she wore a blouse and a skirt that she had tucked up under her bare legs. She was smiling widely. Next to her was Anthony, in a bold feline sprawl on the sand, bare-chested, wearing sunglasses. His hand was raised in a wave. The sunlight had stripped away much of the detail of the picture, leaving the raw human elements. Their friend Demetrios had been right: their happiness *was* beautiful, an art that was original, not imitative; two virtuosos performing without an audience, delighting in their own talent.

⁓

After Oliver left the post office, his second stop of the day had been a visit to the Stricklands' former villa, which was not white but an unexpected sand-coloured stone that reminded him of the house in Oxford; a thought that must also have occurred to Leonora herself, even if she hadn't intended it as homage. He didn't go inside the hotel: he knew when to stop, pulling up short at the line where history ended. He didn't need to see the reception desk and the bar, the family in swimming trunks crossing the lobby to the pool. He wandered the gardens instead, a palm-dotted slope of soft green lawns with the not-quite-right Mediterranean grass that sprang back into shape once his feet had lifted away. Improbable flower beds were tended by revolving sprinklers; trees that looked like pineapples, flowers that looked like parrots. He thought of Comanche, wandering through the gardens of his retirement, looking back philosophically – as a horse surely would – at his old life.

He had lunch at a restaurant in the small harbour nearby, where he ate squid and drank a strong coffee at a taverna under a gently undulating canopy, surrounded by other English people. Above the old cash register was a poster of the snake goddess figurine at Knossos. He thought that he would probably go there tomorrow. Then on to Santorini, maybe, once he'd delayed his flight.

But first he had to do this last thing that felt less and less like a last thing the closer he got to it: parking his car at a silent roadside; walking up the hill towards a white church; shading his eyes because he had forgotten to pack his sunglasses, only half able to see the simple domed church and its gathering of pines, the sea twinkling in the corner of his eye as he ascended the dusty steps set into the slope. Mr Vassis hadn't been able to tell him Leonora's precise burial spot, something he was intensely apologetic about. 'Don't worry,' Oliver had said. 'I like browsing graveyards.

It's interesting.' As he wandered up and down the rows, trying to make out the remnants of eroded names, the sun dwelling lovingly on the back of his neck, he wondered if this was exactly true.

There was nobody in sight. Everything here seemed as if it had been abandoned a long time ago, hundreds and hundreds of years. Even the grey bark of the few stray olive trees looked like rock, as if they had petrified into their twists and knots. A little lizard may as well have been chipped out of stone. The hushed chatter of the cicadas, swelling and dropping as he passed, was the only sign of life. Optimistically, he tried the door of the church, and found it was locked. He stood for a while in the shade of the pines to cool off, breathing in their herbaceous dark green scent; set off again in a different direction, and found the Stricklands within a few steps, the first grave he came to.

The headstone was tall, white and dirty. Grey discoloration inched up its once glittering face. The design was simple: an engraving of a labyrinth, above two names. Dr James Anthony Strickland. Mrs Leonora Charlotte Strickland. They had died within a year of each other, he saw. There was nothing else on the grave besides some writing, in Japanese. Oliver already knew what it said. He had found those lines so horrifying when he first read them. Now he understood: it was a joke.

After a while, he started to laugh.

True to form, Leonora hadn't told all of her story. The details of her relationship with Anthony were hardly touched on, a hand hovering then taken away, leaving the fragments of history undisturbed. For example, the day she went to Anthony's house to end their friendship. In her original account of this she had declared her silence: a sudden (and now he thought conspicuous) lacuna, a yawning canyon between the lines, in an account that had so unsparingly visited every other moment of intimate pain; the marital bed, the deathbed, the doctor's office. Even in her final letter she had eschewed further description.

She had always urged her reader: *picture it.*

A woman and a man, standing in a hallway. The door has been closed and the dim daylight has faded even further, until they almost appear to rise from the shadows of the floor, floating above it like apparitions. The woman is so keenly beautiful that the reader puts his book down and stares at her, knowing the general outlines of her face but never having seen it in the flesh: the fineness of detail; the immediacy of feeling that flares in her like the candle in a paper lantern, ready to be released. He sees, properly, the blue Calvert eyes, formerly black and white and evasive, now in full colour, open like pulled curtains, revealing a stinging blue sky. The man looks at her, too, with a held-in longing so sternly repressed it almost vibrates. As has previously been observed, he is a handsome devil: blue-eyed, broad-shouldered, visible health shining off him. But not a simple-looking man – no, not with his intent gaze, that narrow, sombre mouth.

The two of them talk for a few moments. It is apparent they are both crying, the woman more openly than the man. After a little while they stop talking and stare at each other. A few moments after that they kiss, with the force of two well-bred people who have spent the last few months sitting neatly beside each other in public places, gripping each other now as if they can't believe their luck: her hands white with tension, his carefully gentle, but moving reflexively over her back, and at this the reader – abashed, and moved, and obscurely pained – finally has to look away.